ACKNOWLEDGMENTS

My thanks for their invaluable advice and research to:

Simon Bainbridge, Sir Rodric Braithwaite,
William Browder, Maria Teresa Burgoni, Jonathan Caplan QC,
Captain Rod Fullerton, Moonpal Grewal, Vicki Mellor,
Sir Christopher and Lady Meyer, Andrey Palchevski, Melissa
Pimentel, Alison Prince, Catherine Richards, and Susan Watt.

Praise for Jeffrey Archer

"Cunning plots, silken style . . . Archer plays a cat-and-mouse game with the reader."
—*The New York Times*

"One of the top ten storytellers in the world." —*Los Angeles Times*

"Archer is a master entertainer." —*Time*

"There isn't a better storyteller alive." —Larry King

"Archer plots with skill, and keeps you turning the pages."
—*The Boston Globe*

"A master at mixing power, politics, and profit into fiction."
—*Entertainment Weekly*

"I'm possibly not the first person to say this, but Jeffrey Archer really can spin a cracking yarn." —*Reader's Digest*

"The economy and precision of Archer's prose never fails to delight."
—*Publishers Weekly*

HEADS YOU WIN

"Archer, no stranger to sprawling epics, covers three decades in the life of Alex/Sasha, working his way to a stunning conclusion that packs a wallop. Typical for an Archer novel, the writing and characterizations are superb, and the book features several plot twists that send the story lines off in surprising new directions. There are a couple of moments, late in the novel, that should make readers' jaws drop—moments so unexpected and surreal that they require a second reading, just to make sure we really just read what we think we did. A splendid novel, featuring one of Archer's most elegantly told stories." —*Booklist* (starred review)

"In Archer's clever novel, a *Sliding Doors*–ish bildungsroman, fate hinges on the toss of a coin. . . . A fun, fast-paced novel." —*Publishers Weekly*

"A twist so big your mouth will drop. You never see it coming. . . . A masterful job by Jeffrey Archer to write such a compelling novel with great characters and story that I haven't seen much in years. Just a really well-done job."
—*Red Carpet Crash*

"It's a classic Archer page-turner with a memorable final twist that made me shout out loud."
—*Daily Mail* (UK)

"This deftly balanced, edgy novel—with its dual story lines of immigration, achievement, backroom dealing, cutthroat politics, high society, and patriotism—will keep Jeffrey Archer in his top position as one of the best storytellers of our time."
—*Bookreporter*

Praise for The Clifton Chronicles

"The Clifton Chronicles saga . . . has all the ingredients of compelling novels—rogue aristocrats, low-life scoundrels, wars, and excellently drawn characters. . . . It, siren-like, lures its readers deeper into the lives of its characters."
—*Business Day* (South Africa)

THIS WAS A MAN

"All of the trademark Archer storytelling elements are here in abundance. . . . A satisfying conclusion to the saga."
—*Booklist*

COMETH THE HOUR

"Archer continues his storytelling magic to create characters of spellbinding substance, and readers can count on his surprising twists and shocking conclusion. Here, just when the end seems too tidy, Archer provides a killer cliff-hanger."
—*Publishers Weekly*

"Archer spins out dialogue that's spot-on . . . and his settings will inspire thoughts about the cost of tickets to London."
—*Kirkus Reviews*

MIGHTIER THAN THE SWORD

"Archer packs a plot with thrills and chills enough for readers to keep turning the pages, saying, 'What's gonna happen next?' . . . Expect once more unto the breach: the conclusion's a turbo-charged cliff-hanger that'll have fans screaming, 'Arrrcherr!'" —*Kirkus Reviews*

BE CAREFUL WHAT YOU WISH FOR

"Archer's . . . tight plotting makes for a page-turning rich man's soap opera. . . . Entertaining." —*Kirkus Reviews*

BEST KEPT SECRET

"No family saga would be complete without a villain, and this book has a good one, a well-drawn and believable character whose motivations are understandable. This thoroughly engaging old-school, multigenerational saga harks back to the work of Malcolm Macdonald, Belva Plain, and Irwin Shaw." —*Booklist*

"What-will-happen-next reading." —*Kirkus Reviews*

THE SINS OF THE FATHER

"Archer can plot a story. . . . An amusement suitable for airplane or beach reading." —*Kirkus Reviews*

ONLY TIME WILL TELL

"Archer knows how to dole out tiny crumbs of suspense right up to the last page, which ends with . . . a really excellent cliff-hanger." —*The Washington Post*

"What appears at the outset to be a straightforward coming-of-age tale becomes, by the end, a saga of power, betrayal, and bitter hatred. . . . An outstanding effort from a reliable veteran." —*Booklist* (starred review)

"Archer delivers another page-turning, heart-stopping saga, with delightful twists, and a surprise ending." —*Publishers Weekly*

ALSO BY JEFFREY ARCHER

THE CLIFTON CHRONICLES

Only Time Will Tell
The Sins of the Father
Best Kept Secret
Be Careful What You Wish For
Mightier Than the Sword
Cometh the Hour
This Was a Man

NOVELS

Not a Penny More, Not a Penny Less
Shall We Tell the President?
Kane & Abel
The Prodigal Daughter
First Among Equals
A Matter of Honor
As the Crow Flies
Honor Among Thieves
The Fourth Estate
The Eleventh Commandment
Sons of Fortune
False Impression
The Gospel According to Judas
(with the assistance of Professor Francis J. Moloney)
A Prisoner of Birth
Paths of Glory

SHORT STORIES

A Quiver Full of Arrows
A Twist in the Tale
Twelve Red Herrings
The Collected Short Stories
To Cut a Long Story Short
Cat O' Nine Tales
And Thereby Hangs a Tale
Tell Tale

PLAYS

Beyond Reasonable Doubt
Exclusive
The Accused

PRISON DIARIES

Volume One—Belmarsh: Hell
Volume Two—Wayland: Purgatory
Volume Three—North Sea Camp: Heaven

SCREENPLAYS

Mallory: Walking Off the Map
False Impression

JEFFREY ARCHER

HEADS YOU WIN

St. Martin's Griffin
New York

Published in the United States by St. Martin's Griffin, an imprint of St. Martin's Publishing Group

www.stmartins.com

The Library of Congress has cataloged the hardcover edition as follows:

Names: Archer, Jeffrey, 1940– author.
Title: Heads you win / Jeffrey Archer.
Description: First edition. | New York : St. Martin's Press, 2018.
Identifiers: LCCN 2018036308 | ISBN 9781250172501 (hardcover) | ISBN 9781250172518 (ebook)
Classification: LCC PR6051.R285 H43 2018 | DDC 823/.914—dc23
LC record available at https://lccn.loc.gov/2018036308

ISBN 978-1-250-23672-2 (trade paperback)

First St. Martin's Griffin Edition: September 2019

10 9 8 7 6 5 4 3 2 1

TO BORIS NEMTSOV

I wish I had his courage

BOOK ONE

1
ALEXANDER
Leningrad, 1968

"What are you going to do when you leave school?" asked Alexander.

"I'm hoping to join the KGB," Vladimir replied, "but they won't even consider me if I don't get a place at the state university. How about you?"

"I intend to be the first democratically elected president of Russia," said Alexander, laughing.

"And if you make it," said Vladimir, who didn't laugh, "you can appoint me as head of the KGB."

"I don't approve of nepotism," said Alexander, as they strolled across the schoolyard and out onto the street.

"Nepotism?" said Vladimir, as they began to walk home.

"It derives from the Italian word for 'nephew,' and dates back to the popes of the seventeenth century, who often handed out patronage to their relations and close friends."

"What's wrong with that?" said Vladimir. "You just exchange the popes for the KGB."

"Are you going to the match on Saturday?" asked Alexander, wanting to change the subject.

"No. Once Zenit F.C. reached the semifinals, there was never any chance of someone like me getting a ticket. But surely as your father's the docks' supervisor, you'll automatically be allocated a couple of seats in the reserved stand for party members?"

"Not while he still refuses to join the Communist Party," said Alexander. "And when I last asked him, he didn't sound at all optimistic about getting a ticket, so Uncle Kolya is now my only hope."

As they continued walking, Alexander realized they were both avoiding the one subject that was never far from their minds.

"When do you think we'll find out?"

"I've no idea," said Alexander. "I suspect our teachers enjoy watching us suffering, well aware it will be the last time they have any power over us."

"You have nothing to worry about," said Vladimir. "The only discussion in your case is whether you'll win the Lenin Scholarship to the foreign language school in Moscow, or be offered a place at the state university to study mathematics. Whereas I can't even be sure of getting into university, and if I don't, my chances of joining the KGB are kaput." He sighed. "I'll probably end up working on the docks for the rest of my life, with your father as my boss."

Alexander didn't offer an opinion as the two of them entered the tenement block where they lived, and began to climb the worn stone steps to their flats.

"I wish I lived on the first floor, and not the ninth."

"As you well know, Vladimir, only party members live on the first three floors. But I'm sure that once you've joined the KGB, you'll come down in the world."

"See you in the morning," said Vladimir, ignoring his friend's jibe as he began to climb the remaining four flights.

As Alexander opened the door to his family's tiny flat on the fifth floor, he recalled an article he'd recently read in a state magazine reporting that America was so overrun with criminals that everyone had at least two locks on their front door. Perhaps the only reason they didn't in the Soviet Union, he thought, was because no one had anything worth stealing.

He went straight to his bedroom, aware that his mother wouldn't be back until she'd finished her shift at the docks. He took several sheets of lined paper, a pencil and a well-thumbed book out of his satchel, and placed them on the tiny table in the corner of his room, before opening *War and Peace* at page 179 and continuing to translate Tolstoy's words into English. *When the Rostov family sat down for supper that night, Nikolai appeared distracted, and not just because . . .*

Alexander was double-checking each line for spelling mistakes, and to see if he could think of a more appropriate English word, when he heard the front door open. His tummy began to rumble, and he wondered if his mother had been able to smuggle any tidbits out of the officers' club, where she was the cook. He closed his book and went to join her in the kitchen.

Elena gave him a warm smile as he sat down on a wooden bench at the table.

"Anything special tonight, Mama?" Alexander asked hopefully.

She smiled again, and began to empty her pockets, producing a large potato, two parsnips, half a loaf of bread, and this evening's prize, a steak that had probably been left on an officer's plate after lunch. *A veritable feast,* thought Alexander, compared to what his friend Vladimir would be eating tonight. There's always someone worse off than you, his mother often reminded him.

"Any news?" Elena asked as she began to peel the potato.

"You ask me the same question every night, Mama, and I keep telling you that I don't expect to hear anything for at least another month, possibly longer."

"It's just that your father would be so proud if you won the Lenin Scholarship." She put down the potato and placed the peel to one side. Nothing would be wasted. "You know, if it hadn't been for the war, your father would have gone to university."

Alexander was very aware, but always happy to be reminded how Papa had been stationed on the eastern front as a young corporal during the siege of Leningrad, and although a crack Panzer division had attacked his section continuously for ninety-three days, he'd never left his post until the Germans had given up and retreated to their own country.

"For which he was awarded the Defence of Leningrad medal," said Alexander on cue.

His mother must have told him the story a hundred times, but Alexander didn't tire of it, although his father never raised the subject. And now, almost twenty-five years later, after returning to the docks he'd risen to Comrade Chief Supervisor, with three thousand workers under his command. Although he wasn't a party member, even the KGB acknowledged that he was the only man for the job.

The front door opened and closed with a bang, announcing that his father was home. Alexander smiled as he strode into the kitchen. Tall and heavily built, Konstantin Karpenko was a handsome man who could still make a young woman turn and take a second look. His weather-beaten face was dominated by a luxuriantly bushy mustache that Alexander remembered stroking as a child, something he hadn't dared to do for several years. Konstantin slumped down onto the bench opposite his son.

"Supper won't be ready for another half hour," said Elena as she diced the potato.

"We must only speak English whenever we are alone," said Konstantin.

"Why?" asked Elena in her native tongue. "I've never met an Englishman in my life, and I don't suppose I ever will."

"Because if Alexander is to win that scholarship and go to Moscow, he will have to be fluent in the language of our enemies."

"But the British and Americans fought on the same side as us during the war, Papa."

"On the same side, yes," said his father, "but only because they considered us the lesser of two evils." Alexander gave this some thought as his father stood up. "Shall we have a game of chess while we're waiting?" he asked. Alexander nodded. His favorite part of the day. "You set up the board while I go and wash my hands."

Once Konstantin had left the room, Elena whispered, "Why not let him win for a change?"

"Never," said Alexander. "In any case, he'd know if I wasn't trying, and leather me." He pulled open the drawer below the kitchen table and took out an old wooden board and a box containing a set of chess pieces, one of which was missing, so each night a plastic salt cellar had to substitute for a bishop.

Alexander moved his king's pawn two squares forward, before his father returned. Konstantin responded immediately, moving his queen's pawn one square forward.

"How did you do in the match?" he asked.

"We won three nil," said Alexander, moving his queen's knight.

"Another clean sheet, well done," said Konstantin. "Although you're the best goalkeeper the school's had in years, it's still more important to win that scholarship. I assume you still haven't heard anything?"

"Nothing," said Alexander, as he made his next move. It was a few moments before his father countered. "Papa, can I ask if you've managed to get a ticket for the match on Saturday?"

"No," admitted his father, his eyes never leaving the board. "They're rarer than a virgin on Nevsky Prospect."

"Konstantin!" said Elena. "You can behave like a docker when you're at work, but not at home."

Konstantin grinned at his son. "But your uncle Kolya has been promised a couple of tickets on the terraces, and as I have no interest in going . . ." Alexander leaped in the air as his father made his next move, pleased to have distracted his son.

"You could have had as many tickets as you wanted," said Elena, "if only you'd agree to become a party member."

"That's not something I'm willing to do, as you well know. Quid pro quo. An expression you taught me," said Konstantin, looking across the table at his son. "Never forget, that lot will always expect something in return, and I'm not willing to sell my friends down the river for a couple of tickets to a football match."

"But we haven't reached the semifinal of the cup for years," said Alexander.

"And probably won't again in my lifetime. But it will take far more than that to get me to join the Communist Party."

"Vladimir's already a pioneer and signed up for the Komsomol," said Alexander, after he'd made his next move.

"Hardly surprising," said Konstantin. "Otherwise he'd have no chance of joining the KGB, which is the natural habitat for that particular piece of pond life."

Once again, Alexander was distracted. "Why are you always so hard on him, Papa?"

"Because he's a shifty little bastard, just like his father. Be sure you never trust him with a secret, because it will have been passed on to the KGB before you've reached home."

"He's not that bright," said Alexander. "Frankly, he'll be lucky to be offered a place at the state university."

"He may not be bright, but he's cunning and ruthless, a dangerous combination. Believe me, he'd shop his mother for a ticket to the cup final, probably even the semifinal."

"Supper's ready," said Elena.

"Shall we call it a draw?" said Konstantin.

"Certainly not, Papa. I'm six moves away from checkmate, and you know it."

"Stop squabbling, you two," said Elena, "and lay the table."

"When did I last manage to beat you?" asked Konstantin as he placed his king on its side.

"November the nineteenth, 1967," said Alexander, as the two of them stood up and shook hands.

Alexander put the salt cellar back on the table and returned the chess pieces to the box while his father took down three plates from the shelf above the sink. Alexander opened the kitchen drawer and took out three knives and three forks of different vintages. He recalled a paragraph in *War and Peace* that he'd just translated. The Rostovs regularly enjoyed a five-course dinner (better word than "supper"—he would change it when he returned to his room), and a different set of silver cutlery accompanied each dish. The family also had a dozen liveried servants who stood behind each chair to serve the meals that had been prepared by three cooks, who never seemed to leave the kitchen. But Alexander was sure that the Rostovs couldn't have had a better cook than his mother, otherwise she wouldn't be working in the officers' club.

One day . . . he told himself, as he finished laying the table and sat back down on the bench opposite his father. Elena joined them with the evening's offering, which she divided between the three of them, but not equally. The thick steak that along with the parsnips and the potatoes, had been "repatriated"—a word Alexander had taught her, had been cut into two pieces. "Waste not, want not," she could manage in both languages.

"I've got a church meeting this evening," said Konstantin as he picked up his fork. "But I shouldn't be back too late."

Alexander cut his steak into several pieces, chewing each morsel slowly, between mouthfuls of bread and sips of water. He saved the parsnip till last. Its bland taste lingered in his mouth. He wasn't sure if he even liked it. In *War and Peace* parsnips were only eaten by the servants. They continued to talk in English while they enjoyed the meal.

Konstantin emptied his glass of water, wiped his mouth on the sleeve of his jacket, stood up, and left the room without another word.

"You can go back to your books, Alexander. This shouldn't take me too long," his mother said with a wave of her hand.

Alexander happily obeyed her. Back in his room, he replaced the word "supper" with "dinner," before turning to the next page and continuing with his translation of Tolstoy's masterpiece. *The French were advancing on Moscow . . .*

As Konstantin left the apartment block and walked out onto the street, he was unaware of a pair of eyes staring down at him.

Vladimir had been gazing aimlessly out of the window, unable to concentrate on his schoolwork, when he spotted Comrade Karpenko leaving the building. It was the third time that week. Where was he going at this time of night? Perhaps he should find out. He quickly left his room and tiptoed down the corridor. He could hear loud snoring coming from the front room, and peeped in to see his father slumped in his ancient horsehair chair, an empty bottle of vodka lying on the floor by his side. He opened and closed the front door quietly, then bolted down the stone steps and out onto the street. Glancing to his left he spotted Mr. Karpenko turning the corner and ran after him, slowing down only when he reached the end of the road.

He peered around the corner, and watched as Comrade Karpenko went into the Church of the Apostle Andrew. *What a complete waste of time,* thought Vladimir. The Orthodox Church may have been frowned on by the KGB, but it wasn't actually banned. He was about to turn back and go home when another man appeared out of the shadows, whom he'd never seen at church on Sundays.

Vladimir was careful to remain out of sight as he edged his way slowly toward the church. He watched as two more men came from the other direction and quickly made their way inside, then froze when he heard footsteps behind him. He slipped over the wall and lay on the ground, waiting until the man had passed before he crept between the gravestones to the back of the church and an entrance that only the choristers ever used. He turned the heavy door handle and cursed when it didn't open.

Looking around, he spotted a half-open window above him. He couldn't quite reach it, so using a rough stone slab as a step, pushed himself up off the ground. On his third attempt, he managed to grab the window ledge, and with a supreme effort pulled himself up and squeezed his slim body through the window before dropping to the floor on the other side.

Vladimir tiptoed silently through the back of the church until he reached the sanctuary, where he hid behind the altar. Once his heartbeat had returned to almost normal, he peered around the side of the altar to see a dozen men seated in the choir stalls, deep in conversation.

"So when will you share your idea with the rest of the workforce?" one of them was asking.

"Next Saturday, Stepan," said Konstantin, "when all our comrades come together for the monthly works meeting. I'll never have a better opportunity to convince them to join us."

"Not even a hint to some of the older hands about what you have in mind?" asked another.

"No. Our only chance of success is surprise. We don't need to alert the KGB to what we're up to."

"But they're certain to have spies in the room, listening to your every word."

"I'm aware of that, Mikhail. But by then the only thing they'll be able to report back to their masters will be the strength of our support for forming an independent trade union."

"Although I have no doubt the men will back you," said a fourth voice, "no amount of rousing oratory can stop a bullet in its tracks." Several of the men nodded gravely.

"Once I've delivered my speech on Saturday," said Konstantin, "the KGB will be wary of doing anything quite that stupid, because if they did, the men would rise as one, and they'd never be able to squeeze the genie back into the bottle. But Yuri is right," he continued. "You're all taking a considerable risk for a cause I've long believed in, so if anyone wants to change his mind and leave the group, now is the time to do so."

"You won't find a Judas among us," said another voice, as Vladimir stifled a cough. The men all stood as one to acknowledge Karpenko as their leader.

"Then we'll meet again on Saturday morning. Until then we must remain silent, and keep our counsel."

Vladimir's heart was thumping as the men shook hands with each other, one by one, before leaving the church. He didn't move until he finally heard the great west door slam shut, and a key turn in the lock. He then scurried back to the vestry, and with the help of a stool, wriggled out of the window, clinging to the ledge before dropping to the ground like a seasoned wrestler. The one discipline where Alexander wasn't in his class.

Aware that he didn't have a moment to lose, Vladimir ran in the opposite direction to Mr. Karpenko, toward a street that didn't need a NO

ENTRY sign, as only party officials ever considered entering Tereshkova Prospect. He knew exactly where Major Polyakov lived, but wondered if he had the nerve to knock on his door at that time of night. At any time of the day or night, for that matter.

When he reached the street with its leafy trees and neat cobblestone pavement, Vladimir stood and stared at the house, losing his nerve with every second that passed. He finally summoned up enough courage to approach the front door, and was about to knock when it was flung open by a man who didn't like to be taken by surprise.

"What do you want, boy?" the major demanded, grabbing his unwelcome visitor by the ear.

"I have information," said Vladimir, "and you told us when you visited our school last year looking for recruits, that information was golden."

"This had better be good," said Polyakov, who didn't let go of the boy's ear as he dragged him inside. He slammed the door behind him. "Start talking."

Vladimir faithfully reported everything he'd overheard in the church. By the time he'd come to the end, the pressure on his ear had been replaced by an arm around his shoulder.

"Did you recognize anyone other than Karpenko?" Polyakov asked.

"No, sir, but he mentioned the names Yuri, Mikhail, and Stepan."

Polyakov wrote down each name before saying, "Are you going to the match on Saturday?"

"No, sir, it's sold out, and my father wasn't able to—"

Like a conjurer, the KGB chief produced a ticket from an inside pocket and handed it to his latest recruit.

⊸o⊷

Konstantin closed the bedroom door quietly, not wanting to wake his wife. He took off his heavy boots, undressed, and climbed into bed. If he left early enough in the morning, he wouldn't have to explain to Elena what he and his disciples had been up to, and even more important, what he had planned for Saturday's meeting. Better she thought he'd been out drinking, even that there was another woman, than burden her with the truth. He knew she would only try to convince him not to go ahead with the prepared speech.

After all, they didn't have too bad a life, he could hear her reminding him. They lived in an apartment block that had electricity and running water. She had her job as a cook at the officers' club, and Alexander was waiting to hear if he'd won a scholarship to the prestigious foreign language school in Moscow. What more could they ask for?

That one day everyone could take such privileges for granted, Konstantin would have told her.

He lay awake, composing a speech in his mind that he couldn't risk committing to paper. He rose at five thirty, and once again took care not to wake his wife. He doused his face in freezing water, but didn't shave, then dressed in overalls and a rough, open-neck shirt before finally pulling on his well-worn hobnailed boots. He crept out of the bedroom and collected his lunch box from the kitchen: a sausage, a hard-boiled egg, an onion, and two slices of bread and cheese. Only members of the KGB would eat better.

He closed the front door quietly behind him and made his way down the stone stairs before stepping out onto the empty street. He always walked the six kilometers to work, avoiding the overloaded bus that ferried the workers to and from the docks. If he hoped to survive beyond Saturday, he needed to be fit, like a highly trained soldier in the field.

Whenever he passed a fellow worker in the street, Konstantin always acknowledged him with a mock salute. Some returned his salutation, others nodded, while a few, like bad Samaritans, looked the other way. They may as well have had their party numbers tattooed on their foreheads.

Konstantin arrived outside the dock gates an hour later, and clocked on. As works supervisor, he liked to be the first to arrive and the last to leave. He walked along the dockside while he considered his first assignment of the day. A submarine destined for Odessa on the Black Sea had just berthed at dock 11 to refuel and pick up provisions, before continuing on its way, but that wouldn't be for at least another hour. Only the most trusted men would be allowed anywhere near dock 11 that morning.

Konstantin's mind drifted back to the previous night's meeting. Something hadn't felt quite right, but he couldn't put a finger on it. Was it someone and not something, he wondered, as a vast crane at the far end of the dock began to lift its heavy load and swing slowly toward the waiting submarine on dock 11.

The operator seated in the crane's cab had been chosen carefully. He could unload a tank into a ship's hold with only inches to spare on either side. But not today. Today he was transferring barrels of oil to a submarine that needed to remain submerged for days at a time, but the task also demanded pinpoint accuracy. One piece of luck—no wind that morning.

Konstantin tried to concentrate as he went over his speech once again. As long as none of his colleagues opened their mouths, he was confident everything would fall neatly into place. He smiled to himself.

The crane operator was satisfied that he had judged it to an inch. The load was perfectly balanced and still. He waited just one more moment before he eased a long heavy lever gently forward. The large clamp sprang open and three barrels of oil were released. They crashed down onto the dockside. Inch perfect. Konstantin Karpenko had looked up, but it was too late. He was killed instantly. A dreadful accident, for which no one was to blame. The man in the cab knew he had to disappear before the early shift clocked on. He swung the crane's arm back into place, turned off the engine, climbed out of the cab, and began to make his way down the ladder to the ground.

Three fellow workers were waiting for him as he stepped onto the dockside. He smiled at his comrades, not spotting the six-inch serrated blade until it was thrust deep into his stomach and then twisted several times. The other two men held him down until he finally stopped whimpering. They bound his arms and legs together before pushing him over the side of the dock and into the water. He reappeared three times, before finally disappearing below the surface. He hadn't officially signed on that morning, so it would be some time before anyone noticed he was missing.

⊸o⊷

Konstantin Karpenko's funeral was held at the Church of the Apostle Andrew. The turnout was so large that the congregation spilled out onto the street, long before the choir had entered the nave.

The bishop who delivered the eulogy described Konstantin's death as a tragic accident. But then, he was probably one of the few people who believed the official communiqué issued by the dock commandant, and only then after it had been sanctioned by Moscow.

Standing near the front were twelve men who knew it wasn't an accident. They had lost their leader, and the promise of a thorough investigation by the KGB wouldn't help their cause, because state inquiries usually took at least a couple of years to report their findings, by which time their moment would have passed.

Only family and close friends stood beside the grave to pay their last respects. Elena sprinkled some earth onto the coffin as the body of her husband was lowered slowly into the ground. Alexander forced himself to hold back the tears. She wept but stepped back and held her son's hand, something she hadn't done for years. He was suddenly aware that, despite his youth, he was now the head of the family.

He looked up to see Vladimir, whom he hadn't spoken to since his father's death, half hidden at the back of the gathering. When their eyes met, his best friend quickly looked away. His father's words reverberated in Alexander's mind. *He's cunning and ruthless. Believe me, he'd shop his mother for a ticket to the cup final, probably even the semifinal.* Vladimir hadn't been able to resist telling Alexander that he'd got a stand seat for the match on Saturday, although he wouldn't say who had given it to him, or what he'd had to do to get it.

Alexander could only wonder just how far Vladimir would go to make sure he was recruited by the KGB. He realized in that instant they were no longer friends. After a few minutes Vladimir scurried away, like Judas in the night. He'd done everything except kiss Alexander's father on the cheek.

Elena and Alexander remained kneeling by the graveside long after everyone else had departed. When she finally rose, Elena couldn't help wondering what her husband had done to cause such wrath. Only the most brainwashed party member could have accepted the official line that after the tragic accident the crane operator had committed suicide. Even Leonid Brezhnev, the party's General Secretary, had joined in the deception, with a Kremlin spokesman announcing that Comrade Konstantin Karpenko had been made a Hero of the Soviet Union, and his widow would receive a full state pension.

Elena had already turned her attention to the other man in her life. She had decided she would move to Moscow, find a job, and do everything in her power to advance her son's career. But after a long discussion with her brother, Kolya, she reluctantly accepted that she would have to remain in Leningrad, and try to carry on as if nothing had happened. She would be lucky even to hold on to her present job, because the KGB had tentacles that stretched far beyond her irrelevant existence.

On Saturday, in the semifinal of the Soviet Cup, Zenit F.C. beat Odessa 2–1, and qualified to play Torpedo Moscow in the final.

Vladimir was already trying to work out what he needed to do to get a ticket.

2
ALEXANDER

Elena woke early, still not used to sleeping alone. Once she'd given Alexander his breakfast and packed him off to school, she tidied the flat, put on her coat, and left for work. Like Konstantin, she preferred to walk to the docks, and not have to repeat a thousand times, *How kind of you*.

She thought about the death of the only man she'd ever loved. What were they hiding from her? Why wouldn't anyone tell her the truth? She would have to pick the right moment and ask her brother, who she was sure knew far more than he was willing to admit. And then she thought about her son, whose exam results were due any day now.

She finally thought about her job, which she couldn't afford to lose while Alexander was still at school. Was the state pension a hint that they no longer wanted her around? Did her presence continually remind everyone how her husband had died? But she was good at her job, which was why she worked in the officers' club, and not in the docks' canteen.

"Welcome back, Mrs. Karpenko," said the guard on the gate when she clocked in.

"Thank you," said Elena.

As she walked through the docks several workers doffed their caps and greeted her with a "Good morning," reminding her just how popular Konstantin had been.

Once she had entered the back door of the officers' club, Elena hung up her coat, put on an apron, and went through to the kitchen. She checked the lunch menu, the first thing she did every morning. Vegetable soup and veal pie. It must be Friday. She began to inspect the meat and then there were vegetables to be sliced and potatoes to be peeled.

A gentle hand rested on her shoulder. Elena turned to see Comrade Akimov, a sympathetic smile on his face.

"It was a wonderful service," her supervisor said. "But no more than Konstantin deserved." Someone else who obviously knew the truth, but wasn't willing to voice it. Elena thanked him, but didn't stop working until the siren sounded to announce the mid-morning break. She hung up her apron and joined Olga in the yard. Her friend was enjoying the other half of yesterday's cigarette, and passed the stub to Elena.

"It's been one hell of a week," said Olga, "but we all played our part in making sure you didn't lose your job. I was personally responsible for yesterday's lunch being a disaster," she added after inhaling deeply. "The soup was cold, the meat was overcooked, the vegetables were soggy, and guess who forgot to make any gravy. The officers were all asking when you'd be back."

"Thank you," said Elena, wanting to hug her friend, but the siren sounded again.

⊸o⊷

Alexander hadn't cried at his father's funeral. So when Elena arrived home after work that night and found him sitting in the kitchen sobbing, she realized it could only be one thing.

She sat down on the bench beside him and put an arm around his shoulder.

"Winning the scholarship was never that important," she said. "Just being offered a place at the foreign language school is a great honor in itself."

"But I haven't been offered a place anywhere," said Alexander.

"Not even to study mathematics at the state university?"

Alexander shook his head. "I've been ordered to report to the docks on Monday morning, when I'll be allocated to a gang."

"Never!" said Elena. "I'll protest."

"It will fall on deaf ears, Mama. They've made it clear that I don't have any choice."

"What about your friend Vladimir? Will he also be joining you on the docks?"

"No. He's been offered a place at the state university. He starts in September."

"But you beat him in every subject."

"Except treachery," said Alexander.

⊸o⊷

When Major Polyakov strolled into the kitchen just before lunch the following Monday, he leered at Elena as if she were on the menu. The major was no taller than she, but must have been twice her weight, which was, Olga joked, a tribute to her cooking. Polyakov held the title of Head of Security, but everyone knew he was KGB and reported directly to the dock commandant, so even his fellow officers were wary of him.

It wasn't long before the leer turned into a close inspection of Elena's latest dish. While other officers would occasionally come into the kitchen to sample a tidbit, Polyakov's hands ran down her back, coming to rest on her bottom. He pressed himself up against her. "See you after lunch," he whispered before leaving to join his fellow officers in the dining room. Elena was relieved to see him rushing out of the building an hour later. He didn't return before she clocked off, but she feared it could only be a matter of time.

⊸o⊷

Kolya dropped into the kitchen to see his sister at the end of the day. Elena turned on the water in the sink before she gave him a blow-by-blow account of what she'd had to endure that afternoon.

"There's nothing any of us can do about Polyakov," said Kolya. "Not if we want to keep our jobs. While Konstantin was alive he wouldn't have dared lay a hand on you, but now . . . there's nothing to stop him adding you to a long list of conquests who'll never complain. You only have to ask your friend Olga."

"I don't need to. But something Olga let slip today made me realize she must know why Konstantin was killed, and who was responsible. She's obviously too frightened to say a word, so perhaps it's time you told me the truth. Were you at that meeting?"

"It was a tragic accident," said Kolya.

Elena leaned forward and whispered, "Is your life also in danger?" Her brother nodded, and left the kitchen without another word.

Elena lay in bed that night thinking about her husband. Part of her was still unwilling to accept he wasn't alive. It didn't help that Alexander had worshiped his father, and had always tried so hard to live up to his impossible standards. Standards that must have been the reason Konstantin had sacrificed his life, and at the same time condemned his son to spend the rest of his days as a dock laborer.

Elena had hoped their son would join the Ministry of Foreign Affairs, and that she would live long enough to see him become an ambassador. But it was not to be. *If brave men aren't willing to take risks for what they believe in*, Konstantin had once told her, *nothing will ever change.* Elena only wished her husband had been more of a coward. But then, if he had been, perhaps she wouldn't have fallen so helplessly in love with him.

Elena's brother, Kolya, had been his third in command at the docks, but Polyakov clearly didn't consider him a threat, because he kept his job as chief loader after Konstantin's "tragic accident." What Polyakov couldn't know was that Kolya hated the KGB even more than his brother-in-law had, and although he appeared to have fallen into line, he was already planning his revenge, which wouldn't involve making impassioned speeches, although it would take every bit as much courage.

Elena was surprised to see her brother waiting for her outside the dock gates when she clocked off the following afternoon.

"This is a pleasant surprise," she said, as they began to walk home.

"You may not think so when you hear what I've got to say."

"Does it concern Alexander?" asked Elena anxiously.

"I'm afraid it does. He's begun badly. Refuses to take orders, and is openly contemptuous of the KGB. Today he told a junior officer to fuck off." Elena shuddered. "You must tell him to knuckle down, because I won't be able to cover for him much longer."

"I'm afraid he's inherited his father's fierce independent streak," said Elena, "without any of his discretion or wisdom."

"And it doesn't help that he's brighter than everyone else around him, including the KGB officers," said Kolya. "And they all know it."

"But what can I do, when he doesn't listen to me any longer?"

They walked in silence for some time before Kolya spoke again, and then not until he was certain no one could overhear them. "I may have come up with a solution. But I can't pull it off without your full cooperation." He paused. "And Alexander's."

⊸o⊷

As if Elena's problems at home weren't bad enough, things were becoming worse at work, as the major's advances became less and less subtle. She had considered pouring boiling water over his wandering hands, but the consequences didn't bear thinking about.

It must have been about a week later, as she was tidying up the kitchen before returning home, that Polyakov staggered in, clearly drunk, and began to unbutton his trousers as he advanced toward her. Just as he was about to place a sweaty hand on her breast, a junior officer rushed in, and said that the commandant needed to see him urgently. Polyakov couldn't hide his frustration, and as he left, hissed at Elena, "Don't go anywhere. I'll be back later." Elena was so terrified, she didn't leave the kitchen for over an hour. But the moment the siren finally sounded, she pulled on her coat and was among the first to clock off.

When her brother joined her for supper that evening, she begged him to tell her the details of his plan.

"I thought you said it was far too great a risk."

"I did, but that was before I realized I can't avoid Polyakov's advances any longer."

"You told me you could even bear that, as long as Alexander never found out."

"But if he did," said Elena quietly, "can you imagine what he might do? So tell me what you have in mind, because I'll consider anything."

Kolya leaned forward and poured himself a shot of vodka before he began to take her slowly through his plan. "As you know, several foreign vessels unload their cargo at the docks every week, and we have to turn them around as quickly as possible, so any waiting ships can take their place. That's my responsibility."

"But how does that help us?" asked Elena.

"Once a ship has been unloaded, the loading process begins. Because not everyone wants bags of salt or cases of vodka, some vessels leave the port empty." Elena remained silent while her brother continued.

"There are two ships due in on Friday, which after they've discharged their cargo will leave on the Saturday afternoon tide with empty holds. You and Alexander could be hidden on one of them."

"But if we're caught we could end up on a cattle train to Siberia."

"That's why it's important to take our chance this Saturday, because for once the odds will be stacked in our favor."

"Why?" asked Elena.

"Zenit F.C. are playing Torpedo Moscow in the final of the Soviet Cup, and almost all of the officers will be sitting in a box at the stadium supporting Moscow, while most of the workers will be cheering on the home side from the terraces. So there'll be a three-hour window we could take advantage of, and by the time the final whistle blows, you and Alexander could be on your way to a new life in London or New York."

"Or Siberia?"

3
ALEXANDER

Kolya and Elena never left for the docks in the morning at the same time, and they didn't return home together at night. When they were at work, there was no reason for their paths to cross, and they were careful to make sure they never did. Kolya came down from his flat on the sixth floor every evening, but they didn't discuss what they were planning until after Alexander had gone to bed, when they talked of little else.

By Friday evening, they'd gone over everything they imagined could go wrong again and again, although Elena remained convinced something would trip them up at the last moment. She didn't sleep that night, but then she hadn't slept for more than a couple of hours a night for the past month.

Kolya told her that because of the cup final, almost all the dockers had opted for the early shift on Saturday morning—six until midday—so once the noon siren blasted, the docks would only be manned by a skeleton crew.

"And I've already told Alexander I wasn't able to get him a ticket, so he's reluctantly signed up for the afternoon shift."

"When will you tell him?" asked Elena.

"Not until the last moment. Think like the KGB. They don't even tell themselves."

Comrade Akimov had already told Elena that she could take Saturday off, because he doubted if any of the officers would bother to come in for lunch, as they wouldn't want to miss the kickoff.

"I'll pop in during the morning," she told him. "It's just possible they might not all be football fans. But I'll leave around midday if no one turns up."

Uncle Kolya had managed to pick up a couple of spare tickets on the terraces, but he didn't tell Alexander that he'd sacrificed them to make sure his deputy loader and the chief crane operator wouldn't be around on Saturday afternoon.

⤙o⤚

When Alexander came into the kitchen for breakfast the following morning, he was surprised to find his uncle had joined them, and wondered if he'd managed to get hold of a spare ticket at the last moment. When he asked him, Alexander was puzzled by his reply.

"You could be playing in a far more important match this afternoon," said Kolya. "It's also against Moscow, and one you can't afford to lose."

The young man sat in silence as his uncle took him through what he and his mother had been planning for the past week. Elena had already told her brother that if Alexander didn't want to be involved, for whatever reason, the whole enterprise would have to be called off. She needed to be certain that her son wasn't in any doubt about the risks they were taking. Kolya even offered him a bribe to make sure he was fully committed.

"I did manage to get a ticket for the match," he said, waving it in the air, "so if you'd rather—"

He and Elena watched the young man carefully to see how he would react. "To hell with the match," was his immediate reaction.

"But it will mean your having to leave Russia, perhaps never to return," said Kolya.

"That won't stop me being a Russian. And we may never get a better chance to escape from those bastards who killed my father."

"Then that's settled," said Kolya. "But you have to understand I won't be coming with you."

"Then we won't be going," said Alexander, jumping up from his father's old chair. "I'm not leaving you behind to face the music."

"I'm afraid you'll have to. If you and your mother are to have any chance of getting away, I'll have to stay behind and cover your tracks. It's no more than your father would have expected."

"But—" began Alexander.

"No buts. Now I must get going and join the morning shift so I can supervise the loading of both ships and everyone will assume that, like them, I'll be at the football match this afternoon."

"But won't they become suspicious when no one remembers seeing you at the match?" asked Elena.

"Not if I get my timing right," said Kolya. "The second half should begin around four o'clock, by which time I'll be watching the match with the rest of the lads, and with a bit of luck, by the time the final whistle blows, you'll be outside territorial waters. Just make sure you report for the afternoon shift on time, and for a change, do whatever your supervisor tells you." Alexander grinned as his uncle stood up and gave him a bear hug. "Make your father proud of you," he said before leaving.

As Kolya stepped out of the flat he met Alexander's friend coming down the stairs.

"Have you got a ticket for the match, Mr. Obolsky?" he asked.

"I have," said Kolya. "In the north end terrace with the rest of the lads. So I'll see you there."

"Afraid not," said Vladimir. "I'll be sitting in the west stand."

"Lucky boy," said Kolya as they walked down the steps together, and although he was tempted, he didn't ask what he'd had to do in return for his ticket.

"What about Alexander, will he be with you?"

"Sadly not. He's having to work the afternoon shift, and I can tell you, he's pretty pissed off."

"Tell him I'll drop by this evening and give him a blow-by-blow account."

"That's good of you, Vladimir. I'm sure he'll appreciate it. Enjoy the game," he added as they went their separate ways.

Once Kolya had left for the docks, Alexander still had a dozen more questions for his mother, some of which she couldn't answer, including which country they would be going to.

"Two ships will be sailing on the afternoon tide around three o'clock," said Elena, "but we won't know which one Uncle Kolya has chosen until the last moment."

It was clear to Elena that Alexander had already forgotten about the football match, as he paced excitedly around the room, preoccupied by the thought of escaping. She looked on anxiously. "This isn't a game, Alexander," she said firmly. "If we are caught, your uncle will be shot, and we'll be transported to a labor camp, where you'll spend the rest of your life wishing you'd gone to the match. It's not too late for you to change your mind."

"I know what my father would have done," said Alexander.

"Then you'd better go and get ready," said his mother.

Alexander returned to his room while his mother packed the lunch box he took to work every morning. On this occasion it wasn't filled with food, but with all the notes and coins she and Konstantin had scraped together over the years, a few pieces of jewelry of little value, other than her mother's engagement ring, which she slipped on next to her wedding ring, and finally a Russian–English dictionary. How Elena now wished she'd spent more time concentrating when Konstantin and Alexander had spoken English every evening. She then packed her own small suitcase, hoping it wouldn't attract attention when she turned up for work later that morning. The problem was deciding what to include and what to leave behind. Her photos of Konstantin and the family were her first priority, followed by one change of clothes and a bar of soap. She also managed to squeeze in a hairbrush and a comb before forcing the lid closed. Alexander had wanted to take his copy of *War and Peace*, but she had assured him he'd be able to get another copy wherever they landed.

Alexander was desperate to get going, but his mother wasn't willing to leave before the agreed time. Kolya had warned her they couldn't afford to draw attention to themselves by arriving at the dock gates before the siren sounded at twelve. They finally left the flat just after eleven, taking a circuitous route to the dockyard where it was unlikely they would run into anyone they knew. They arrived outside the entrance just before twelve, to face a stampede of workers heading in the opposite direction.

Alexander battled his way through the advancing army, while his mother, head bowed, followed in his wake. Once they'd clocked in, Elena reminded him: "The siren will go at two for the mid-afternoon break, then we'll have twenty minutes, no more, so make sure you join me at the officers' club as quickly as possible."

Alexander nodded, and headed for dock number 6 to begin his shift, his mother going in the opposite direction. Once Elena reached the back door of the club, she opened it cautiously, poked her head inside, and listened intently. Not a sound.

She hung up her coat and made her way through to the kitchen. She was surprised to find Olga sitting at the table smoking, something she would never have done if an officer had been on the premises. Olga told her that even Comrade Akimov had left moments after the siren had sounded at midday. She blew out a cloud of smoke, her idea of rebellion.

"Why don't I cook us both a meal?" said Elena, putting on her apron. "Then we can eat our lunch sitting down for a change, as if we were officers."

"And there's half a bottle of that Bulgarian red left over from yesterday's lunch," said Olga, "so we can even drink to the bastards' health."

Elena laughed for the first time that day, and then set about preparing what she hoped would be her last meal in Leningrad.

At one o'clock, Olga and Elena went into the dining room and laid the table, putting out the best cutlery and linen napkins. Olga poured two glasses of red wine, and was about to take a sip from her glass when the door burst open and Major Polyakov strode in.

"Your lunch is prepared, Comrade Major," she said, not missing a beat. He looked at the two wine glasses suspiciously. "Will anyone be joining you?" she added quickly.

"No, they're all at the match so I will be dining alone," said Polyakov before turning to Elena. "Be sure you don't leave before I've finished my lunch, Comrade Karpenkova."

"Of course not, Comrade Major," Elena replied.

The two women scurried back into the kitchen. "That can only mean one thing," said Olga as Elena filled a bowl with hot fish soup.

Olga took the first course through to Polyakov and placed it on the table. As she turned to leave, he said, "Once you've served the main course, you can take the rest of the day off."

"Thank you, Comrade Major, but one of my duties after you've left is to clear up—"

"Immediately after you've served the main course," he repeated. "Do I make myself clear?"

"Yes, Comrade Major." Olga returned to the kitchen, and once the door was closed she told Elena what Polyakov had demanded. "I'd do anything I can to help," she added, "but I daren't cross the bastard." Elena said nothing as she filled a plate with veal stew, turnips, and mashed potato. "You could always go home now," said Olga. "I'll tell him you weren't feeling well."

"I can't," said Elena, noticing that Olga was undoing the top two buttons of her blouse. "Thank you," she said. "You're a good friend, but I fear he wants to sample a new dish." She handed the plate to Olga.

"I'd happily kill him," said Olga, before returning to the dining room.

The major pushed his empty soup bowl to one side, as Olga placed the plate of hot stew in front of him.

"If you're still on the premises by the time I've finished," he said, "you'll be back serving those scum in the works canteen on Monday."

Olga picked up the soup bowl and returned to the kitchen, surprised by how calm her friend appeared to be, even though she couldn't have been in any doubt what was about to happen. But then, Elena couldn't tell her why she was willing to endure even Polyakov's advances if it meant that she and her son would finally escape the KGB's clutches.

"I'm so sorry," said Olga, as she slipped on her coat, "but I can't afford to lose my job. See you on Monday," she added, before giving Elena a longer than usual hug.

"Let's hope not," whispered Elena as Olga closed the door behind her. She was just about to turn off the stove when she heard the dining room door open. She swung around to see Polyakov walking slowly toward her, still chewing a last mouthful of stew. He wiped his mouth on his sleeve before unbuttoning a jacket covered in medals that hadn't been won on a battlefield. He unbuckled his belt and placed it on the table beside his pistol, then kicked off his boots before starting to unzip his trousers, which fell to the floor. He stood there, no longer able to hide the rolls of surplus flesh that were usually hidden beneath a well-tailored uniform.

"There are two ways we can do this," said the KGB chief as he continued walking toward her until their bodies were almost touching. "I'll leave the choice to you."

Elena forced a smile, wanting to get the whole thing over with as quickly as possible. She took off her apron and began to unbutton her blouse.

Polyakov smirked as he clumsily fondled her breasts. "You're just like the rest of them," he said, pushing her toward the table while trying to kiss her at the same time. Elena could smell his stinking breath, and turned her head so their lips didn't touch. She felt his stubby fingers fumbling under her skirt, but this time she didn't resist, just stared blankly over his shoulder as a sweaty hand moved up the inside of her thigh.

He shoved her up against the table, lifted her skirt, and thrust her legs apart. Elena closed her eyes and clenched her teeth. She could feel him panting as he lurched forward, praying it would be over quickly.

The two o'clock siren sounded.

Elena looked up when she heard the door on the far side of the room open, and stared in horror as Alexander came charging toward them. Polyakov turned around, quickly pushed Elena to one side, and reached for his gun, but the young man was now only a yard away. Alexander lifted the pot from the stove, and hurled the remains of the hot stew in Polyakov's face. The major staggered back and fell to the floor, delivering a stream of invective that Elena feared would be heard on the far side of the yard.

"You'll hang for this!" Polyakov yelled as he grabbed the edge of the table and tried to pull himself up. But before he could utter another word, Alexander swung the heavy iron pot into his face. Polyakov collapsed to the floor like a puppet whose strings have been cut, blood pouring from his nose and mouth. Mother and son didn't move as they stared at their fallen adversary.

Alexander was the first to recover. He picked up Polyakov's tie from the floor and quickly bound his hands behind his back, then grabbed a napkin from the table and stuffed it in his mouth. Elena hadn't moved. She just stared blankly ahead, as if paralyzed.

"Be ready to leave the moment I get back," said Alexander, grabbing Polyakov by the ankles. He dragged him out of the kitchen and down the corridor, not stopping until he reached the lavatories, where he crammed the major into the end cubicle. It took all his strength to lift him onto the toilet, and then tie him to the pipe. He locked the door from the inside, and climbing up onto the major's legs, pulled himself over the top and lowered himself to the floor. He ran back to the kitchen to find his mother on her knees, sobbing.

He knelt down beside her. "No time for tears, Mama," he said gently. "We have to get going before the bastard has the chance to come after us." He helped her slowly to her feet, and while she put on her coat and collected her small suitcase from the larder, he gathered up Polyakov's uniform, belt, and gun and dumped them in the nearest waste bin.

Taking Elena firmly by the hand, he led her out of the kitchen to the back door. He opened it tentatively, stepped outside, and checked in every direction before standing aside to allow her to join him.

"Where did you agree to meet Uncle Kolya?" he asked, responsibility once again changing hands.

"Head toward those two cranes," said Elena, pointing to the far end of the dock. "Whatever you do, Alexander, don't mention what just happened to your uncle. It's better that he doesn't know, because as long as everyone thinks he was at the match, there will be no way of connecting him with us."

As Alexander led his mother toward dock 3, her legs felt so weak she could hardly place one foot in front of the other. Even if she had considered changing her mind at the last moment, she now realized they had no choice but to try and escape. The alternative didn't bear thinking about. She kept her eyes on the two idle cranes that Kolya had said would be their signpost, and as they drew nearer, they saw a lone figure step out from behind two large wooden crates by the entrance of a deserted warehouse.

"What kept you?" Kolya demanded anxiously, his eyes darting in every direction like a cornered animal.

"We came as quickly as we could," said Elena, without explanation.

Alexander stared down into the crates to see half a dozen cases of vodka neatly stacked in each one. The agreed tariff for a one-way trip to . . .

"All you have to do now," said Kolya, "is decide whether you want to go to America or England."

"Why don't we let fate decide?" said Alexander. He took a five-kopek coin from his pocket, and balanced it on the end of a thumb. "Heads America, tails England," he said, and flipped it high into the air. The coin bounced on the dockside before coming to rest at his feet. Alexander bent down and looked at the image for a moment, then picked up his mother's suitcase and his lunch box and put them in the bottom of the chosen crate. Elena then climbed inside, and waited for her son to join her.

They crouched down and clung to each other as Kolya placed the lid firmly back on top of the crate. Although it took him only a few moments to hammer a dozen nails into the lid, Elena was already listening for another sound. The sound of heavy boots heading toward them, the lid of the crate being ripped off, and the two of them being dragged out to face a triumphant Major Polyakov.

Kolya tapped the side of the crate with the palm of his hand, and suddenly they felt themselves being yanked off the ground. The crate swung gently from side to side as they were lifted higher and higher into the air, before it began its slow descent toward the hold of one of the ships. Then, without warning, the crate landed with a thud.

Elena could only wonder if they would spend the rest of their lives regretting not climbing into the other crate.

BOOK TWO

4

SASHA

En route to Southampton

Sasha heard a firm rap on the side of the crate.

"Anyone in there?" asked a gruff voice.

"Yes," they both said, in two different languages.

"I'll be back when we're outside territorial waters," said the voice.

"Thank you," replied Sasha. They heard the sound of heavy boots fading away, followed a few moments later by a loud bang.

"I wonder—"

"Don't talk," whispered Elena, "we need to conserve our energy." Sasha nodded, although he could hardly see her in the darkness.

The next noise they heard was the rumbling of a vast piston turning over somewhere below them. This was followed by a feeling of movement as the ship eased away from the dock and began its slow progress out of the harbor. Sasha had no idea how long it would take before they crossed the invisible line that maritime law recognizes as international waters.

"Twelve nautical miles until we're safe," said Elena, answering his unasked question. "Uncle Kolya told me it should take just over an hour."

What's the difference between a land mile and a nautical mile, Sasha wanted to ask, but he remained silent. He thought about his uncle Kolya, and could only hope he would be safe. Had anyone found Polyakov yet? Was he already wreaking revenge? Sasha had told his uncle to start a rumor that his friend Vladimir had masterminded the escape, which he hoped would derail Vladimir's chances of joining the KGB. He thought about his homeland, and what he would miss most, and even wondered if Zenit F.C. had beaten Torpedo Moscow and lifted the Soviet Cup.

It felt like far longer than an hour before they heard the heavy footsteps returning. Another tap on the side of the crate.

"We'll have you out in no time," said the same gruff voice.

Sasha gripped his mother by the arms as they listened to the sound of nails being extracted one by one. Finally the lid was raised. They both took a deep breath, and looked up to see a short, scruffy man dressed in grubby overalls grinning down at them.

"Welcome aboard," he said after checking to make sure the six cases of vodka were in place. "My name's Matthews," he added, before offering Elena his arm. She stretched stiffly for a moment before grabbing his arm and climbing unsteadily out of the crate. Sasha took the small suitcase and his lunch box, and handed them to Matthews before joining his mother.

"I've been told to take you both up to the bridge so you can meet Captain Peterson," said Matthews, before leading them to a rusty ladder attached to the side of the hold.

Sasha picked up his mother's case, and was the last to climb the ladder. With each rung, the sun shone brighter, until he was looking up at a cloudless blue sky. When he finally stepped out on deck, he paused for a moment to look back at the city of his birth for what he both hoped and feared would be the last time.

"Follow me," said Matthews, as two of his crew mates began climbing down into the hold intent on claiming their bounty.

Elena and Sasha followed Matthews toward a spiral staircase that he began to climb without looking back. They quickly followed like obedient spaniels, and moments later stepped out onto the bridge, feeling slightly giddy.

The helmsman standing behind the wheel didn't give them a second look, but an older man dressed in a dark blue uniform, with four gold stripes on the arm of his double-breasted jacket, turned around to face the stowaways.

"Welcome aboard, Mrs. Karpenko," he said. "What's the lad's name?"

"Sasha, sir," he replied.

"Don't call me 'sir.' Mr. Peterson, or skipper, will be fine. Now, Mrs. Karpenko, your brother told me you're a fine cook, so let's find out if he was exaggerating."

"She's the finest cook in Leningrad," said Sasha.

"Is she indeed? And what do you have to offer, young man, because this isn't a pleasure cruise. Everyone on board has to pull their weight."

"He can serve at table," said Elena before Sasha had a chance to reply.

"That will be a first," said the captain.

It certainly will, thought Sasha, who'd never been inside a restaurant in his life, and apart from clearing the table and washing up after supper, was rarely to be found in the kitchen.

"Is the cabin next to Fergal's free, Matthews?" asked the captain.

"Yes, skipper, but it's hardly big enough for two."

"Then put the boy in with Fergal. He can sleep on the top bunk, and his mother can have the spare cabin. Once they've unpacked," he added, glancing down at the small suitcase, "take them to the galley and introduce them to the cook."

Sasha noticed that this statement brought a smile to the lips of the helmsman, although his eyes remained fixed on the ocean ahead.

"Aye, aye, captain," said Matthews. Without another word he led his charges back down the spiral staircase and onto the main deck. Once again Sasha stared toward the distant horizon, but there was no longer any sign of Leningrad.

They followed Matthews back across the deck, and descended an even narrower staircase to the bowels of the ship. Their guide led them down a dimly lit corridor, coming to a halt outside two adjoining cabins.

"This is where you'll be sleeping during the voyage."

Elena opened the door of her cabin and looked up at a swinging bulb that threw a small arc of light onto a narrow bunk. The rhythmic thumping of the ship's engine guaranteed that even if she hadn't slept for the past week, she certainly wasn't going to for the next one.

Matthews opened the next-door cabin. Sasha stepped inside to find a double bunk that took up almost the whole space.

"You'll be on top," said Matthews. "I'll be back in half an hour, when I'll take you up to the galley."

"Thank you," said Sasha, who immediately climbed onto the top bunk. It wasn't any better than his bed in Leningrad. He couldn't help wondering if he'd chosen the right crate.

"Now listen up," someone shouted, "because I'm only going to say this once."

Everyone stopped what they were doing and turned to face the chef, who was standing in the center of the galley, hands on hips.

"We have a lady on board, and she'll be working with us. Mrs. Karpenko is a trained cook, who has a great deal of experience, so you will treat her with the respect she deserves. If any one of you puts a foot out of line, I'll chop it off and feed it to the seagulls. Do I make myself clear?" The nervous laughter that followed suggested that he did.

"Her son, Sasha," continued the chef, "who is also traveling with us, will be assisting Fergal in the dining room. Right, let's all get back to work. We have dinner to serve in a couple of hours."

A thin, pale young man with a shock of red hair strolled across the galley and stopped in front of Sasha.

"I'm Fergal," he said. Sasha nodded, but didn't speak. "Now listen up," he added firmly, placing his hands on his hips, "because I'm only going to say this once. I'm the chief steward, and you can call me 'sir.' "

"Yes, sir," said Sasha meekly.

Fergal burst out laughing, shook his new recruit by the hand, and said, "Follow me, Sasha."

Sasha followed him out of the galley and up the nearest staircase. "So what am I expected to do?" he asked once he'd caught up.

"As you're told," said Fergal when he reached the top step. "Our job is to serve the passengers in the dining room."

"This ship has passengers?"

"Only a dozen. We're a cargo vessel, but if you have more than twelve passengers, you're registered as a cruise ship. The company does own a couple of ocean liners, but we're part of their cargo fleet," he added as he pushed open a door and entered a room containing three large circular tables, each with six chairs.

"But there are eighteen places," said Sasha. "You said—"

"I can see you're sharp," said Fergal with a grin. "As well as the twelve passengers, there are six officers who also eat in the dining room but sit at their own table. Now, our first job," he added, pulling open a drawer in a large sideboard and extracting three tablecloths, "is to lay up for dinner."

Sasha had never seen a tablecloth before, and watched as Fergal skillfully cast one over each of the three tables. He then returned to the sideboard, took out matching cutlery, and began to set each place.

"Don't just stand there gawping. You're my assistant, not one of the passengers."

Sasha grabbed some knives, forks, and spoons and began to copy his mentor, who double-checked each setting, making sure everything was lined up and in its correct place.

"Now, the most important job you'll be responsible for," Fergal said once he'd added two glasses to each place setting, and a salt and pepper pot in the center of the table, "will be to organize the dumbwaiter."

"What's a dumbwaiter?"

"You. But we luckily have a more useful example over here." Fergal walked across to the far side of the room and opened a small hatch in the wall to reveal a square box with two shelves and a thick rope on one side. "This goes down to the kitchen," he said as he pulled the rope, and the box disappeared. "When chef is good and ready, it will be sent back up with the first course, which you'll place on the sideboard before I serve it. You don't speak to anyone unless they speak to you, and then only if they ask you a question. At all times, address the guests as sir or madam." Sasha kept nodding. "Now, the next thing we have to do is find you a white jacket and a pair of trousers that fit. We can't have you looking like some sea urchin that's been washed up on the beach, can we?"

"Can I ask a question?" said Sasha.

"If you must."

"Where do you come from?"

"The Emerald Isle, to be sure," said Fergal. But Sasha was none the wiser.

⊸o⊷

The cook glanced across at Elena, who was making a sauce from some leftovers. "You've done that before," he said. "When you've finished, would you prepare the vegetables, while I concentrate on the main course?" He looked up at a menu pinned to the wall. "Lamb chops."

"Of course, sir," said Elena.

"Call me Eddie," he added, before making his way across to the fridge and removing a rack of lamb.

Once Elena had prepared the vegetables and arranged them in separate dishes, Eddie inspected them. "Good thing you're leaving us when we dock in Southampton," he said, "otherwise I might be looking for a job."

I will be looking for a job, Elena wanted to tell him, but satisfied herself with, "What would you like me to do next?"

"Take the smoked salmon out of the fridge and prepare eighteen portions. Once you've done that, put them in the dumbwaiter, ring the bell, and send them up to Fergal."

"The dumbwaiter?" said Elena, looking puzzled.

"Ah, at last something you don't know about." He smiled as he headed toward a large square hole in the wall.

⟜○⟝

A buzzer sounded.

"First course on its way up," said Fergal, and a few moments later, six plates of smoked salmon appeared. Sasha placed them on the sideboard before sending the dumbwaiter back down. He was unloading the last three plates of salmon when the door opened and two smartly dressed officers walked in.

"Mr. Reynolds, the chief engineer," whispered Fergal, "and the purser, Mr. Hallett."

"And who's this?" Mr. Reynolds asked.

"Sasha, my new assistant," said Fergal.

"Good evening, Sasha. I believe we have you to thank for half a dozen cases of vodka, which I can assure you the ratings will appreciate."

"Yes, sir," said Sasha.

The door opened again, and the passengers began to trickle in one by one and take their places.

Sasha never stopped pulling the rope up and down, before placing the contents of the box on the sideboard. Fergal served the fifteen men and three women with a relaxed charm that the chef assured Elena came from regularly kissing the Blarney Stone. Something else he had to explain to his new assistant.

An hour later, after the last diner had departed, Sasha collapsed into the nearest chair and said, "I'm exhausted."

"Not yet, you aren't," said Fergal, laughing. "Now we have to clear up before re-laying the tables for breakfast. You can start by hoovering the carpet."

"Hoovering?"

Fergal gave him a short demonstration on the strange machine before returning to lay the tables. Sasha was fascinated by the vacuum cleaner, but didn't want to admit he'd never seen one before, although it couldn't have been more obvious as he bumped into chairs and table legs. Fergal let him become familiar with it, while he laid eighteen places for breakfast.

"That's it for today," said Fergal, "so you can shove off now."

Sasha made his way back to the sleeping quarters and knocked on his mother's door. He didn't enter until he heard her say, "Come in." The first thing he noticed when he walked into her cabin was that she had unpacked both her suitcase and his lunch box. He also thought the room looked far tidier than he remembered.

"What's it like being a waiter?" was her first question.

"You never stop moving," said Sasha, "but it's great fun. Fergal seems to have them all under control, even the captain."

Elena laughed. "Yes, chef told me he's broken several hearts over the years, and only gets away with it because the passengers are rarely on board for more than a fortnight."

"What's the chef like?"

"An old pro, and so good at his job that I can't understand what he's doing on a small ship like this. I would have thought the Barrington Line could have put him to far better use on one of their cruise liners. There has to be some reason why they haven't."

"If there is," said Sasha, "Fergal will be sure to know, so I'll find out long before we reach Southampton."

5

ALEX

En route to New York

When Alex heard the cargo hold close and the boat ease away from its moorings he began to hammer on the side of the crate with a clenched fist.

"We're in here!" he shouted.

"They can't hear you," said Elena. "Uncle Kolya told me the hold won't be opened again until we're well outside Soviet territorial waters."

"But—" Alex began, then simply nodded, although he was beginning to understand what it must be like to be buried alive. His thoughts were interrupted by the unsteady rumbling of an engine somewhere below them, followed by movement. He assumed they must at last be making their way out of the harbor, but he had no idea how long it would be before they were released from their self-imposed prison.

Alex had hoped to be going to a football match with his uncle that afternoon, and ended up in a crate with his mother. He prayed to whatever gods there were that his uncle would be safe. He assumed that Polyakov had been found by now. Was he even trying to have the ship turned around? He'd told his uncle to start a rumor that his friend Vladimir had helped him to escape, which he hoped would end Vladimir's chances of joining the KGB. He began to think about what he'd left behind. Not a lot, he concluded. But he would have liked to know the result of the match between Zenit F.C. and Torpedo Moscow, and wondered if he ever would.

He eventually drifted into a half sleep, but was woken by the sound of the hold door crashing open, followed by what sounded like someone tapping on the side of a nearby crate. He clenched his fist again and thumped the side of his prison cell, shouting, "We're in here!" This time his mother didn't try to stop him.

Moments later he could hear two, or was it three, voices, grateful they were speaking a language he recognized. He waited impatiently, and when the lid of the crate was finally torn off, he saw three men towering over him.

"You can get out now," said one of them in Russian.

Alex stood up, and helped his mother as she slowly unwound her stiff body. He took her hand as she stepped gingerly out of the crate. He then grabbed her small suitcase and his lunch box before climbing out to join her.

The three deckhands, dressed in navy blue, oil-stained overalls, were peering into the crate to make sure their promised reward was in place.

"You both come with me," said one of them, while the other two began to remove the cases of vodka. Alex and Elena obediently followed the man who'd given the order, as he dodged in between several other crates until they reached a ladder attached to the side of the hold. Alex looked up to see the open sky beckoning him, and began to believe for the first time that they just might be safe. He followed the deckhand slowly up the ladder, the suitcase in one hand, while his mother tucked his lunch box under her arm.

Alex stepped out onto the deck, and took a deep breath of fresh sea air. He stared back in the direction of Leningrad, which looked like a tiny village melting in the early evening sun.

"Don't hang about," barked the sailor, as his two mates hurried past, each carrying a case of vodka. "Cook doesn't like to be kept waiting." He led them across the deck and down a spiral staircase into the bowels of the ship. Alex and Elena were quite giddy by the time they reached the lower deck, where their guide stood in front of a door displaying the faded words MR. STRELNIKOV, HEAD CHEF.

The sailor pulled open the heavy door, revealing the smallest kitchen Elena had ever seen. They stepped inside, to be greeted by a giant of a man dressed in a grubby white jacket that had several buttons missing, and blue-striped trousers that looked as if they'd recently been slept in. He was already unscrewing the top off a bottle of vodka. He took a swig before saying in a gruff voice, "Your brother told me you're a good cook. You'd better be, or you'll both be thrown overboard and then you'll have to swim home, where I expect you'll find quite a few people waiting on the dockside to welcome you back."

Elena would have laughed, but she wasn't sure the cook didn't mean it. After taking another swig, he turned his attention to Alex. "And what's the point of you?" he demanded.

"He's a trained waiter," said Elena, before Alex could reply.

"We don't need one of them," said the chef. "He can wash the dishes and peel the potatoes. As long as he doesn't open his mouth, I might even let him have one or two scraps at the end of the day." Alex was about to protest when the cook added, "Of course, if that doesn't suit you, your worship, you can always work in the engine room and spend the rest of your life hurling coal into a blazing furnace. I'll leave the choice to you." The words "the rest of your life" had a haunting conviction about them. "Show them where they'll be sleeping, Karl. Just make sure they're back in time to help me prepare dinner."

The sailor nodded, and led them out of the galley, back up the narrow staircase, and onto the deck. He didn't stop walking until he reached a lone lifeboat swinging in the breeze.

"This is the royal suite," he said, with no suggestion of irony. "If you don't like it, you can always sleep on deck."

Elena looked back in the direction of her homeland, which had almost disappeared from sight. She found herself already missing the meager comforts of their tiny flat in the Khrushchyovka. Her thoughts were interrupted by Karl barking, "Don't keep cook waiting, or we'll all live to regret it."

⊸o⊷

Most chefs occasionally taste their food, while others sample each dish, but it soon became clear to Elena that the ship's cook preferred to devour whole portions between swigs of vodka. She was surprised that the officers, let alone the rest of the crew, were ever fed.

The kitchen, which Elena would quickly learn to refer to as the galley, was so small that it was almost impossible not to bump into someone or something if you moved in any direction, and so hot that she was soaked in sweat within moments of putting on a not very white jacket that didn't fit.

Strelnikov was a man of few words, and those he uttered were usually prefaced by a single adjective. He looked fifty, but Elena suspected he was only about forty. He must have weighed over three hundred pounds, and had clearly spent a considerable portion of his wages on tattoos. Elena watched as he stood over a vast stove inspecting his handiwork while his assistant, a tiny Chinese man of indeterminate age, squatted, head bowed, in the far corner, endlessly peeling potatoes.

"You," barked the chef, having already forgotten Alex's name, "will assist Mr. Ling, while you," he said, pointing at Elena, "will prepare the soup. We'll soon find out if you're as good as your brother claims."

Elena began checking the ingredients. Some of the scraps had clearly been scraped off the plates of previous meals. There was also the odd bone of an animal that she couldn't immediately identify floating in a greasy pan, but she did her best to salvage what little meat was left on them. She dropped what remained into the bin, which only brought a frown to Strelnikov's face, as he wasn't in the habit of throwing anything away.

"Some of the deckhands consider bones a luxury," he said.

"Only dogs consider bones a luxury," mumbled Elena.

"And sea dogs," snapped Strelnikov.

Strelnikov focused on preparing the dish of the day, which Elena later discovered was the dish of every day: fish and chips. Three fish at a time were being fried in a vast, round, burned pan, while Mr. Ling expertly sliced each potato the moment Alex had finished peeling it. Elena noticed that only three soup bowls and three dinner plates of different sizes had been laid out on the countertop, although there had to be at least twenty crew on board. Strelnikov interrupted his frying to sample the soup, and as he didn't comment, Elena assumed she had passed her first test. He then ladled a large portion into each of the three soup bowls, which Mr. Ling placed on a tray, before taking them off to the officers' mess. As he opened the door, Elena saw a long queue of morose-looking figures, billycans in hand, waiting to be served.

"Only one ladle each," grunted Strelnikov, as the first deckhand held up his billycan.

Elena carried out his orders, and tried not to show that she was appalled when Strelnikov dropped a fried fish into the same billycans as the soup. Only one member of the crew greeted her with a warm smile, and even said "thank you," in her native tongue.

Once she'd completed the task, twenty-three men in all, the cook returned to the stove and began to fry the largest three pieces of fish, one by one, before tipping them onto the officers' plates. Mr. Ling selected only the thinnest chips to accompany them, then placed the plates on his tray before leaving the galley once again.

"Start clearing up!" Strelnikov barked, as he sank into the only chair in the room while nursing a half-empty bottle of vodka.

After Mr. Ling had returned with the empty soup plates, he immediately began to scour the large pots and the two frying pans. When he heard Strelnikov begin to snore, he grinned at Alex and pointed to a pan of untouched chips. Alex devoured every last one of them, while Elena continued scrubbing the pots. Once she'd finished, she glanced across at Strelnikov. He was fast asleep, so she and Alex slipped out of the galley and made their way back up the spiral staircase and onto the deck.

Elena began to unpack her little suitcase and place each item neatly on the deck, when she heard heavy footsteps behind her. She quickly turned around to see a tall, heavily built man approaching them. Alex put down his dictionary, leaped up, and stepped between his mother and the advancing giant. Although he knew it would be an unequal contest, he didn't intend to give up without a fight. But the man's next move took them both by surprise. He sat down cross-legged on the deck, and smiled up at them.

"My name is Dimitri Balanchuk," he said, "and, like you, I'm a Russian exile."

Elena looked more carefully at Dimitri, and then remembered he was the man who'd thanked her at supper. She returned his smile, and sat down opposite him. Alex folded his arms and remained standing.

"We should arrive in New York in about ten days," said Dimitri in a soft, gentle voice.

"Have you been to New York before?" Elena asked.

"I live there, but I still consider Leningrad to be my home. I was on deck when I saw you climbing into the crate. I tried to warn you to get into the other one."

"Why?" said Alex. "I've read a lot about New York, and even though it's full of gangsters, it sounds exciting."

"It's exciting enough," said Dimitri, "although there are just as many gangsters in Moscow as there are in New York," he added, with a wry smile. "But I'm not convinced you'll ever get off this ship without my help."

"Are they going to send us back to Leningrad?" asked Elena, trembling at the thought.

"No. The Yanks would welcome you with open arms, especially as you're refugees fleeing from Communism."

"But we don't know anyone in America," said Alex.

"You do now," said Dimitri, "because I'd do anything to help a fellow countryman escape from that repressive regime. No, it's not the Americans who will be your problem, it's Strelnikov. You've cut his workload in half, so he'll do anything to prevent you getting off the ship."

"But how can he stop us?"

"The same way he does Mr. Ling, who joined the crew in the Philippines over six years ago. Whenever we approach a port, Strelnikov locks him in the galley and doesn't let him out until we're back at sea. And I suspect that's exactly what he has planned for you."

"Then we must tell one of the officers," said Elena.

"They don't even know you're on board," said Dimitri. "Even if they did, it's more than their life is worth to cross Strelnikov. But don't panic, because I have an idea which I hope will see the cook ending up locked in his own galley."

⊸o⊷

Although she was exhausted, it was some time before Elena fell asleep, as she couldn't get used to the pitching and swaying of the lifeboat. After she had finally managed an hour, perhaps two, she opened her eyes to find Mr. Ling standing by her side. She clambered out of the boat and shook Alex, who was fast asleep on the deck. They accompanied Mr. Ling back down to the galley with only the moon to guide them. It was clear that they weren't going to see the sun for the next ten days.

Breakfast consisted of two fried eggs and beans on toast for the officers, served on the same three plates as their meal the evening before, with cups of black coffee to accompany them, while the crew were handed two slices of bread and dripping, and a mug of tea, with no suggestion of sugar. No sooner had Elena, Alex, and Mr. Ling cleared up after breakfast than they had to begin preparing for lunch, while Strelnikov took his morning siesta. More sleep than Elena had managed the previous night.

Elena and Alex were given a short break after lunch, but were not allowed to go back on deck, as Strelnikov didn't want the officers to find out they were on board. They sat alone in the corridor, hunched up against the wall, wondering how different things might have been if they had climbed into the other crate.

6

SASHA

En route to Southampton

By the end of their first week on board, Sasha had mastered the dumb-waiter so well that he even found time to help Fergal serve the passengers, although he wasn't allowed anywhere near the captain's table. Once they'd laid up for breakfast each night, Sasha would return to his mother's cabin and regale her with what he'd overheard the passengers talking about, and what he'd said to them.

"But I thought you weren't allowed to speak to the passengers."

"I'm not, unless they ask a question. So now they all know you're working in the kitchen and looking for a job in England, and if you haven't got one by the time we dock at Southampton, we won't be allowed past immigration, and will have to remain on board. And here's the bad news. Once they've reloaded, and the new passengers have come on board, they're going straight back to Leningrad."

"We certainly can't risk that. Have any of the passengers shown the slightest interest in our plight?"

"Not a dicky bird."

"What does that mean?"

"It's cockney rhyming slang for 'word.'"

"What's a cockney?"

"Someone who's born within the sound of Bow bells."

"Where are these Bow bells?"

"No idea. But Fergal will know."

"Are there any English passengers on board?" asked Elena.

"Only four, and they rarely speak to each other, let alone anyone as lowly as a waiter. They're standoffish."

"I've never heard that word before."

"Fergal uses it a lot, particularly when he's talking about the English. I looked it up in the dictionary. It means distant and cold in manner, unfriendly."

"Perhaps they're just shy," suggested Elena.

⊸o⊷

With only three days to go before the ship was due to dock in Southampton, the chef informed Elena that Mr. Hallett, the purser, wished to see her when she came off duty.

"What have I done wrong?" she asked anxiously.

"Nothing. In fact I suspect the exact opposite."

Once the cook had released the kitchen staff for the afternoon, Elena went straight to the purser's office. She knocked on the door, and when she heard a voice say, "Come," she walked in to find two men seated on either side of a large desk. They both rose, and the purser, dressed in a smart white uniform with two gold stripes on the sleeves, waited for her to be seated before he introduced Mr. Moretti, and explained that he was a passenger who had asked to meet her.

Elena took a closer look at the elderly gentleman dressed in a three-piece suit. He addressed her in English with a slight accent that she couldn't place. He asked her about her work in Leningrad, and how she had ended up on board the ship. She told him almost everything that had happened during the past month, including how her husband had died, but didn't mention why her son had nearly killed the local head of the KGB. By the time Mr. Moretti came to the end of his questions, Elena had no idea what sort of impression she'd made, although he did give her a warm smile.

"Thank you, Mrs. Karpenko," said Mr. Hallett, "that will be all for now." Both men rose again as she left the office.

She returned to her cabin in a daze, to find Sasha waiting for her. Once she had told him about her interview with Mr. Moretti, he said, "That must be the Italian gentleman who owns a restaurant in somewhere called Fulham. I know he's also asked to see the chef and Fergal, so keep your fingers crossed, Mama."

"Why Fergal?"

"He wants to know how I'm getting on in the dining room. I think he's hoping to get two for the price of one. So Fergal's going to tell him I'm the best assistant steward he's ever had."

"You're the only assistant he's ever had."

"A minor detail that Fergal will not be mentioning."

⟜o⟝

The meetings with the chef and Fergal must have gone well, because Mr. Moretti asked to see Elena a second time, and offered her a job at his restaurant in Fulham.

"Ten pounds a week, with accommodation above the premises," he said.

Elena had no idea where Fulham was, or if it was a good wage, but she happily accepted the only offer she was likely to get, if they didn't want to go straight back to Leningrad.

The purser then proceeded to ask her several more questions about why she was seeking asylum, while he filled out a long official Home Office form. Once he'd double-checked each entry, he and Mr. Moretti signed on the bottom line, having agreed to act as her sponsors.

"Good luck, Mrs. Karpenko," said the purser as he handed the completed form to Mr. Moretti. "We will all miss you, and if things don't work out, you can always get a job with the Barrington Line."

"That's kind of you," responded Elena.

"But for your sake, let's hope not, Mrs. Karpenko. Before you leave, don't forget to collect your wages."

"You're going to pay me as well?" said Elena in disbelief.

"Of course." The purser handed her two brown envelopes. He then walked to the door of his office, opened it, and said, "Let's hope we never see you again, Mrs. Karpenko."

"Thank you, Mr. Hallett," said Elena, who stood on her toes and kissed him on both cheeks, which left the purser speechless.

She went straight to her cabin, keen to let Sasha know about the offer. When she opened the door, she was both surprised and delighted. Delighted to find her son waiting for her, but surprised to see a large parcel on the bed.

"What's that?" she asked, taking a closer look at the bulging package wrapped in brown paper and tied up with string.

"I have no idea," said Sasha, "but it was there when I came off work."

Elena undid the string and slowly removed the wrapping paper. She gasped when she saw all the clothes that spilled out onto the bed, along with a card that read, *Thank you both, and good luck.* It was signed by every member of the crew, including the captain. Elena burst into tears. "How can we ever pay them back?"

"By being model citizens, if I remember the captain's exact words," said Sasha.

"But we're not even citizens yet, and will remain stateless until the immigration authorities are convinced that we're genuine political refugees, and have real jobs to go to."

"Then let's hope that they're a bit more friendly than the English passengers on board, because if they aren't, we're about to find out the true meaning of the word 'standoffish.'"

"The chef's also English," said Elena, "and he couldn't have been kinder. He even apologized for not being able to act as one of my sponsors."

"He daren't risk it," said Sasha. "There's a warrant out for his arrest. Whenever the ship docks in Southampton, he has to remain on board. Fergal tells me he locks himself in the kitchen and doesn't reappear until they've left the harbor."

"Poor man," said Elena.

Sasha decided not to tell his mother the reason the British police wanted to arrest Eddie.

⊸o⊷

Elena and Sasha joined Mr. Moretti on the passenger deck the following morning, but not before Sasha had vacuumed the dining room, and Elena had left the kitchen spotless.

"*Magnifico,*" said Moretti, when he saw Elena in her new dress. "When did you find time to go shopping?" he teased.

"The crew have been so generous," said Elena. "But don't say anything about Sasha's jeans," she whispered. "Fergal isn't quite as tall as him, and he's still growing."

Mr. Moretti smiled as Sasha leaned over the railings and watched two dockers winding one of the ship's heavy ropes around a bollard and tying it fast.

"Let's hope the immigration authorities are equally understanding," said Moretti, as he picked up his bags and headed for the gangway with Elena and Sasha in his wake. "But you have one thing going for you—the British hate the communists every bit as much as you do."

"Do you think they'll let us in?" asked Elena anxiously as they stepped onto the dockside.

"Thanks to the purser, we can be confident that all the necessary forms have been correctly filled in, so we'll just have to cross our fingers."

"Cross our fingers?" repeated Sasha.

"Hope we get lucky," said Moretti. "Now remember, Sasha, don't speak unless you're spoken to, and if the immigration officer asks you a question, just say 'yes, sir,' 'no, sir,' 'three bags full, sir.'"

Elena burst out laughing. Sasha couldn't stop looking around him as they walked along the dockside. Some buildings looked as if they'd been built quite recently, while others had just about survived the war. The locals appeared to be relaxed, and no one had their head bowed, while the women were dressed in colorful clothes and chatted to the men as if they were equals. Sasha had already decided he wanted to live in this country.

Mr. Moretti headed toward a large brick building with the single word ALIENS chiseled in stone above the door.

When they entered, they were greeted by two signs: BRITISH and NON UK CITIZENS. Elena crossed her fingers as they joined the longer queue, and couldn't help wondering if they would be back on the ship bound for Leningrad long before the sun set on what was left of the British Empire.

Sasha watched as those holding British passports received a cursory inspection, followed by a smile. Even tourists were not kept waiting more than a few moments. The Karpenkos were about to find out how the British treated those people who didn't have a passport.

"Next!" said a voice.

Mr. Moretti stepped forward and gave his passport to the immigration officer, who checked it carefully before passing it back. Moretti then handed over several sheets of paper along with two photographs, before turning to acknowledge his wards. The official didn't smile as he slowly turned each page, and finally checked that the photographs matched the two applicants standing in front of him. Moretti felt confident that everything was in, to quote the purser, "apple pie" order, but couldn't help wondering if that would be enough.

Elena became more nervous by the minute, while Sasha just seemed impatient to find out what lay beyond the barrier. Eventually the officer looked up and beckoned the two would-be immigrants to step forward. Elena was only thankful that they weren't dressed in their old clothes.

"Do you speak English?" the officer asked Elena.

"A little, sir," she replied nervously.

"And are you in possession of a passport, Mrs. Karpenko?"

"No, sir. The communists don't allow anyone to travel outside the country, even to visit relatives, so my son and I escaped without any papers."

"I'm sorry to say," began the officer—Elena's heart sank—"that given the circumstances I can only authorize a temporary visa, while you apply to the Home Office for refugee status, and I can't guarantee that will be granted." Elena bowed her head. "And," the officer continued, "you will be subject to several conditions while your application for citizenship is being processed. Should you fail to comply with any of them, you will be deported back to"—he looked down at the form—"Leningrad."

"Where they would be locked up for the rest of their lives," said Moretti. "Or worse."

"Be assured," said the officer, "that will be taken into consideration when their applications come before the Home Office." He smiled at Elena and Sasha for the first time, and said, "Welcome to Britain."

"Thank you," said Mr. Moretti before Elena could respond. "But may we know what those conditions are?"

"Mrs. Karpenko and her son will have to report to the nearest police station once a week for the next six months. Should they fail to do so, an arrest warrant will be issued, and when they are apprehended they will be placed in a detention center. They can then expect their applications for citizenship to be refused. I should add, Mr. Moretti, that as their sponsor, you will be responsible for them at all times, and if either of them should attempt to abscond, you would not only have to pay a heavy fine, but would also face the possibility of a term of imprisonment of not less than six months."

"I fully understand," said Moretti.

"And if anything claimed on their application form should prove to be bogus . . ."

"Bogus?" said Elena.

"Inaccurate. If that should be the case, your application will automatically be declined."

"But I have only told the truth," protested Elena.

"Then you have nothing to fear, Mrs. Karpenko." He handed Moretti a small booklet. "You'll find everything you need to know in there."

Elena shuddered, and couldn't help wondering if they had climbed into the right crate.

"I can assure you, officer," said Moretti, "Mrs. Karpenko and her son will be model citizens."

"Will the young man also be working in your restaurant, Mr. Moretti?" asked the officer, not even looking at Sasha.

"No, sir," said Elena firmly. "I want him to continue with his education."

"Then you will have to register the boy at the nearest local authority school." Elena nodded, even though she had no idea what he was talking about. The officer turned his attention to Sasha for the first time, looking down at his ankles. "I see you're growing fast," he said. Sasha remembered Mr. Moretti's advice, and remained silent. "You'll have to work hard when you go to your new school if you hope to succeed in this country," said the officer, giving the young immigrant a warm smile.

Sasha returned the smile and said, "Yes, sir; no, sir; three bags full, sir."

7

ALEX

En route to New York

Alex stared out at endless miles of flat, uninterrupted sea, and could only wonder if he'd ever see land again, while his mother just continued to get on with her job. The menu didn't vary from one day to the next, so Elena quickly mastered the simple routine, and began to take on more and more responsibility while Strelnikov's siestas became longer and longer.

She and Alex looked forward to being released each evening, when Dimitri would join them on deck and tell them more about life in "the Big Apple," and his small flat in Brighton Beach, Brooklyn.

Elena told Dimitri about her husband and her brother, Kolya, and why Major Polyakov had been the reason they'd had to escape. Alex watched Dimitri carefully, and couldn't help feeling that the friendly Russian knew exactly who Polyakov was, and even wondered if they'd put his uncle in danger. But the subject that continued to occupy them was how Elena and Alex would get off the ship once they'd docked in New York. Alex reluctantly accepted that without Dimitri's help they were never going to make it.

"What will we do if Strelnikov locks us in the galley while the ship's cargo is being unloaded?" asked Elena.

"There are still a couple of bottles of vodka left over that he doesn't know about," said Dimitri, "and they might just mysteriously appear in the galley the day before we're due to arrive in New York. With a bit of luck, by the time he wakes up you'll be on your way to Brooklyn."

-o-

For the next week, Elena and Alex worked endless hours, never once complaining, even though the chef rarely left his chair.

With only a couple of days to go, Strelnikov ran out of vodka, which meant he didn't fall asleep quite as easily, and they both had to suffer his wrath.

As Dimitri had promised, another couple of bottles appeared while Strelnikov was taking his siesta on the afternoon before they were due to arrive in New York. Elena had to take over cooking lunch, because the moment Strelnikov woke and saw the bottles by his side, he opened one of them immediately and had taken several gulps before he demanded, "Where did these come from?"

Mr. Ling shrugged his shoulders and continued to slice the potatoes, while Elena checked the soup. Strelnikov showed more interest in finishing off the first bottle than in preparing lunch. Elena could only marvel at how much the man could consume without collapsing, and it wasn't until after dinner that he finally slumped in his chair and fell into a deep sleep.

Elena and Alex crept out of the galley and made their way up onto the deck, but couldn't sleep as they gazed out across the open sea, willing Manhattan to appear on the skyline, becoming more confident by the minute that Dimitri's plan would work. But just as the sun peeped over the horizon, a voice behind them bellowed, "Thought you'd get away with it, did you?"

They turned to see Strelnikov standing over them brandishing a meat cleaver. Alex leaped up and glared at him defiantly.

"Be my guest," said the cook. "You wouldn't be the first, and after the gulls have picked your bones I can assure you no one will miss you, other than your mother."

Alex didn't budge. Behind them, the skyscrapers of New York were appearing on the horizon. Strelnikov was distracted when he spotted Alex's lunch box. He bent down, opened it, and pocketed their life savings. He then picked up Elena's suitcase, and after a cursory inspection hurled the contents overboard. "You won't be needing those any longer," he snarled.

Still Alex refused to move, until Strelnikov grabbed Elena by the arm, placed the blade of the meat cleaver to her throat, and began to drag her downstairs, leaving Alex with no choice but to follow.

Once they reached the lower deck Strelnikov stood aside and ordered Alex to open the door of the galley, before pushing him and Elena inside, and slamming the door behind them. Elena burst into tears when she heard the key turning in the lock.

Mr. Ling was lounging in the cook's chair, clutching on to the remaining bottle of vodka. He didn't even glance in their direction as he drained the last drop, and quickly fell asleep.

The sound of the ship's foghorns as they entered New York harbor reverberated in the galley but Elena and Alex were powerless to do anything about it. They could feel the ship slowing down, until it finally came to a shuddering halt. Ling continued to snore peacefully as Elena and Alex sat helplessly on the floor, aware that when the ship returned to Leningrad, Strelnikov wouldn't even have to lock them in.

It must have been an hour, possibly two, before Mr. Ling finally stirred. He stretched, rose slowly from the cook's chair, and made his way over to his workbench. But instead of starting to peel another bucket of potatoes, he knelt down, lifted one of the floorboards, and rummaged around. A few moments later a large grin appeared on his face. He made his way unhurriedly across the galley, placed a key in the lock, turned it, and pushed the door open.

Elena and Alex stood and stared at him. Finally Alex said, "You must come with us."

Mr. Ling bowed low. "No, not possible. This my home." The first words they'd ever heard him speak. He closed the door behind them, and again they heard the key turning in the lock.

Alex cautiously climbed the staircase. Once he'd reached the top step he looked out, as if he was a submariner peering through a periscope searching for the enemy. He waited for some time before he was convinced that Strelnikov and the rest of the ship's company had gone ashore, leaving only a skeleton crew on board.

He bent down and whispered to his mother, "I can see the gangway leading to the dock. When I say 'Now,' follow me, and whatever you do, don't stop."

Alex waited for a few more seconds, and when no one appeared he climbed out onto the deck and began walking quickly, not running, toward the gangway, only glancing back to make sure Elena was a pace behind. Just as he reached the top of the gangway, he heard someone holler.

"Stop those two!"

His mother ran past him.

He looked up at the bridge to see an officer signaling frantically at two deckhands who were unloading a crate from the hold. They immediately stopped what they were doing, but Alex was already halfway down the gangway. When he reached the dockside he looked back to see the two crew members running toward him, while Elena stood frozen by his side. He then heard footsteps coming from behind him and clenched his fists, although he knew he now had no chance.

"They won't be any trouble," said Dimitri quietly, as he took his place by Alex's side. The two deckhands came to an abrupt halt the moment they saw Dimitri. They hesitated for a few seconds before retreating and climbing back up the gangway. "Two good lads," said Dimitri. "Truth is, they'd rather lose a couple of days' pay than a couple of teeth."

"What now?" said Alex.

"Follow me," said Dimitri, and immediately marched off, clearly knowing exactly where he was going. Elena gripped Alex's hand. Her son couldn't hide his excitement at the prospect of living in America.

Alex noticed that a number of passengers from other ships were heading in the opposite direction. Some of them were carrying leather bags while others were pushing laden trolleys, and one or two even had porters to assist them. Elena and Alex had no luggage. Everything they possessed had been either stolen or thrown overboard by Strelnikov.

They followed in Dimitri's wake as he headed toward an imposing stone building that announced above its entrance in bold white letters, ALIENS.

When Elena entered the building she froze on the spot, staring in disbelief at the long queues of stateless people babbling away in so many different tongues, while all hoping for one thing—to be allowed to pass beyond the barrier and enter a new world.

Dimitri joined the shortest queue, and beckoned Alex and Elena to join him. Alex didn't hesitate, but Elena remained rooted to the spot, immovable as a statue.

"Keep our place," said Dimitri, "while I go and fetch your mother."

"Elena," he said as he reached her side, "do you want to go back to Russia?"

"No, but—"

"Then get in line," said Dimitri, raising his voice for the first time. Elena still looked unconvinced, as if weighing up the lesser of two evils. Finally Dimitri said, "If you don't, you'll never see your son again, because he certainly won't be going back to Leningrad." She reluctantly joined Alex at the back of the queue.

Alex couldn't wait to get moving, but had to watch a large black minute hand circle a massive clock three times before they finally reached the front of the queue.

He filled the time by peppering Dimitri with questions about what they might expect once they had crossed the white line. Dimitri was more interested in making sure they had their story straight before they were questioned by an immigration officer who'd heard everything. Elena was convinced that when they heard her unlikely tale she would be marched straight back to the ship, and handed over to Strelnikov, before making the one-way journey to Leningrad, where she would find Major Polyakov standing on the dockside.

"Make sure you both stick to the story we agreed on," whispered Dimitri.

"Next!" shouted a voice.

Elena tentatively stepped forward, her eyes never leaving the man seated on a high stool behind a wooden desk, wearing a dark blue uniform with three stars on his lapels. Uniforms only meant one thing to Elena—trouble. And the more stars, the more trouble. As she approached the desk Alex pushed past her and gave the officer a huge grin, which was met with a frown. Dimitri pulled him back.

"Are you one family?" the officer asked.

"No, sir," replied Dimitri. "But I am an American citizen," he said, handing over his passport.

The officer turned the pages slowly, checking dates and entry stamps before handing it back. He then opened a drawer in his desk, extracted a long form, placed it on the counter, and picked up a pen. He turned his attention to the woman in front of him, who appeared to be shaking.

"What is your full name?"

"Alexander Konstantinovitch Karpenko."

"Not you," he said firmly. He pointed his pen at Elena.

"Elena Ivanova Karpenko."

"Do you speak English?"

"A little, sir."

"Where do you come from?"

"Leningrad, in the Soviet Union."

The officer filled in a couple of boxes before he continued. "Are you this lady's husband?" he asked Dimitri.

"No, sir. Mrs. Karpenko is my cousin, and her son, Alex, is my nephew."

Elena obeyed Dimitri's instructions and said nothing, because she wasn't willing to lie.

"So where is your husband?" asked the officer, his pen poised.

"He was—" began Dimitri.

"The question was addressed to Mrs. Karpenko, not you," the officer said equally firmly.

"The KGB killed my husband," said Elena, unable to hold back the tears.

"Why?" demanded the officer. "Was he a criminal?"

"No!" said Elena, raising her head in defiance. "Konstantin was a good man. He was the works supervisor at the Leningrad docks, and they killed him when he tried to set up a trade union."

"They kill you for that in the Soviet Union?" said the officer in disbelief.

"Yes," said Elena, bowing her head once again.

"How did you and your son manage to escape?"

"My brother, who also worked on the docks, helped smuggle us onto a ship bound for America."

"With the help of your cousin, no doubt," said the officer, raising an eyebrow.

"Yes," said Dimitri. "Her brother, Kolya, is a brave man, and with God's help we will get him out as well, because he hates the communists every bit as much as we do."

The mention of God's help and hatred of the communists brought a smile to the officer's face. He filled in several more boxes.

"Are you willing to act as a sponsor for Mrs. Karpenko and her son?" the officer asked Dimitri.

"Yes, sir," responded Dimitri without hesitation. "They will live at my home in Brighton Beach, and as Elena is an excellent cook it shouldn't be too difficult for her to find a job."

"And the boy?"

"I want him to continue his education," said Elena.

"Good," said the officer, who finally turned his attention to Alex. "What is your name?"

"Alexander Konstantinovitch Karpenko," he announced proudly.

"And have you been working hard at school?"

"Yes, sir, I was top of the class."

"Then you will be able to tell me the name of the President of the United States."

Elena and Dimitri looked anxious. "Lyndon B. Johnson," said Alex without hesitation. How could he forget the name of the man Vladimir had described as the Soviet Union's greatest enemy, which only made Alex assume he must be a good man?

The officer nodded, filled in the final box, and added his signature to the bottom of the form. He looked up, smiled at the boy, and said, "I have a feeling, Alex, you'll do well in America."

8

SASHA

En route to London

Sasha was sitting in the corner of the railway carriage when the 3:35 shunted out of Southampton station on its way to London. He stared out of the window but didn't speak, because his mind was far away in his homeland. He was beginning to wonder if they'd made a terrible mistake.

He hadn't said a word since they'd climbed on board, while Elena didn't stop chatting to Mr. Moretti about his restaurant as the train rattled through the countryside toward the capital.

Sasha couldn't be sure how much time had passed before they eventually began to slow down and the train pulled into a station called Waterloo. Sasha immediately thought of Wellington, and wondered if there was a Trafalgar station. When they came to a halt, Sasha took Mr. Moretti's bags off the rack, and followed his mother onto the platform.

The first thing Sasha noticed was how many men were wearing hats: flat caps, homburgs, and bowlers, which his teacher back home had claimed simply reminded everyone of their position in society. He was also struck by how many women were strolling along the platform unaccompanied. Only loose women were unaccompanied in Leningrad, he'd once heard his mother say. He'd had to later ask his father what a loose woman was.

Mr. Moretti handed over three tickets at the barrier, before leading his charges out of the station where they joined the back of a long queue. Something else the British were renowned for. Sasha's mouth opened wide when he caught sight of his first red double-decker bus. He ran up the spiral stairs to the top deck, and took a seat at the front before Mr. Moretti could stop him. He was captivated by the panoramic view that stretched as far as the eye could see. So many cars of different shapes, sizes, and colors that stopped whenever a traffic light turned red. There weren't many traffic lights in Leningrad, but then there weren't many cars.

The bus stopped again and again to allow passengers on and off, but it was still several more stops before Mr. Moretti stood up and headed back down the spiral staircase. Once they were on the pavement Sasha kept stopping every few moments to gaze inside shop windows. A tobacconist that sold so many different brands of cigarettes and cigars, as well as pipes, which brought back memories of his father. In another, a man was sitting in a large leather chair having his hair cut. Sasha's mother always cut his hair. Didn't this man have a mother? A cake shop where he would have liked to take a closer look, but he had to keep up with Mr. Moretti. Another shop that displayed only watches. Why would anyone need a watch when there were so many church clocks all around them? A women's boutique, where Sasha stood mesmerized when he saw his first miniskirt. Elena grabbed him firmly by the arm and pulled him away. He didn't have time to stop again until he saw a sign swaying in the breeze, proclaiming MORETTI'S.

This time it was Elena who peered inside to admire the neatly laid tables with their spotless red and white checked tablecloths, folded napkins, and fine bone china. Waiters in smart white jackets bustled around, attentively serving their customers. But Moretti continued walking until he reached a side door, which he unlocked, and beckoned them to follow. They climbed a dimly lit staircase to the first floor, where Moretti opened another door.

"The flat is very small," he admitted, standing aside to let them in. "My wife and I lived here when we were first married."

Elena didn't mention that it was larger than their unit in Leningrad, and far better furnished. She walked into a front room that overlooked the main road just as a motorbike revved by. She'd never experienced traffic noise or congestion before. She inspected the little kitchen, bathroom, and two bedrooms. Sasha immediately inhabited the smaller one. He collapsed onto the bed, closed his eyes, and fell asleep.

"Time for you to meet the chef," whispered Moretti.

The two of them left Sasha sleeping and returned downstairs. Moretti walked into the restaurant and took her through to the kitchen. Elena thought she'd arrived in heaven. Everything she'd requested when she was in Leningrad, and so much more, was there before her.

Moretti introduced her to the chef, and explained how he'd met Elena while on the return journey to England. The chef listened attentively to his boss but didn't look convinced.

"Why don't you take a couple of days finding out how we do things here, Mrs. Karpenko," the chef suggested, "before I decide where you might fit in."

It only took Elena a couple of hours before she was assisting the sous-chef, and long before the last customer had departed the chef's expression of condescension had turned to one of respect for the lady from Leningrad.

Elena returned to her flat just after midnight, utterly exhausted. She looked in on Sasha, who was still lying on his bed, fully dressed and fast asleep. She took off his shoes and pulled a blanket over him. The first thing she must do in the morning was find the right school for him.

Mr. Moretti even had ideas on that subject.

⊸o⊷

Elena tried to focus, and not think about what was going on in the dining room, even though Sasha's future could well depend on it. She set about preparing Mr. Quilter's favorite dish long before he arrived.

Mr. Moretti guided the gentleman and his wife to a corner table usually reserved for regulars or important customers.

Mr. and Mrs. Quilter were not regulars. They fell into the category of anniversaries and special occasions. However, Mr. Moretti had instructed his staff to treat them as VIPs.

He handed them both a menu. "Can I get you a drink?" he asked Mr. Quilter.

"Just a glass of water for now. I'll choose a bottle of wine once we've decided what we're going to eat."

"Of course, sir," said Moretti. He left them to study their menus and went through to the kitchen. "They've arrived. I've put them on table eleven," he announced.

The chef nodded. He rarely spoke unless it was to bawl out one of his sous-chefs, although, he had to admit, life had become a lot easier since the arrival of their latest recruit. Mrs. Karpenko also rarely spoke as she went about preparing each dish with skill and pride. It had taken less than a week for the normally skeptical chef to admit that a rare talent had appeared at Moretti's, and he warned the boss that he feared it wouldn't be long before she wanted to move on and run her own kitchen.

Mr. Moretti returned to the dining room and whispered to the headwaiter, "I'll be taking the order for table eleven, Gino." When he saw the special guest close his menu, he quickly moved across to their table. "Have you decided what you'd like, madam?" he asked Mrs. Quilter, removing a small pad and pen from his jacket pocket.

"Yes, thank you. I'll start with the avocado salad, and as it's a special occasion, I'll have the Dover sole."

"An excellent choice, madam. And for you, sir?"

"Parma ham and melon, and I'll also have the Dover sole. And perhaps you could recommend a wine that would complement the fish?"

"Perhaps the Pouilly-Fuissé?" said Moretti, pointing to the third wine on a long list.

"That looks fine," said Quilter after checking the price.

Moretti hurried away and told his sommelier that table eleven would have the Pouilly-Fuissé. "Premier Cru," he added.

"Premier Cru?" the waiter repeated, only to receive a curt nod.

Moretti retreated to a corner and watched the sommelier uncork a bottle and pour out some wine for the customer to taste. Mr. Quilter sipped it.

"Magnificent," he said, looking a little puzzled. "I think you'll enjoy this, my dear," he added as the sommelier filled his wife's glass.

Although the restaurant was full that night, Mr. Moretti's eyes rarely left the customers on table eleven, and as soon as the main courses had been cleared away he returned to ask if they would like a dessert.

The smile that appeared on Mr. Quilter's lips after he tasted the first mouthful of Elena's crème brûlée could have left no one in any doubt how much he enjoyed it. "Worthy of Trinity," he mumbled when their empty dishes were whisked away, leaving Moretti none the wiser.

Mr. Moretti remained in a corner of the restaurant until the special guest asked a passing waiter for the bill, at which point he made his way back to table eleven.

"What a wonderful meal," Mr. Quilter said as he ran a finger down the bill. He took out his checkbook, filled in the figures, and added a generous tip. He handed the check to Mr. Moretti, who tore it in half.

Mr. and Mrs. Quilter were unable to hide their surprise. "I don't understand," Mr. Quilter eventually managed.

"I need a favor, sir," said Moretti.

⊸o⊷

Elena straightened Sasha's tie, and stood back to take a careful look at her son. He was dressed in his Sunday best, a recent purchase from a local church jumble sale. The suit may have been a little on the large size, but nothing a needle and thread hadn't taken care of.

Mr. Moretti had given Elena the morning off, although he was just as nervous about the outcome as she was. A red double-decker bus transported mother and son to the next borough, and they got off outside a vast set of wrought-iron gates. They walked through into a courtyard, where Elena asked one of the boys for directions to the headmaster's office.

"How nice to meet you both," said Mr. Quilter, when his secretary ushered them into his study. "Now, I know Mr. Sutton is expecting us, so let's not keep him waiting."

Elena and Sasha obediently followed Mr. Quilter out of the room and into a crowded corridor, full of smartly dressed, exuberant young boys, who immediately stood aside when they saw the headmaster heading toward them. Elena admired their smart blue monogrammed uniforms with dismay.

The headmaster stopped outside a classroom with the words MR. SUTTON MA (OXON) painted on the pebbled glass. He knocked, opened the door, and led the candidate in.

A man wearing a long black academic gown over his suit rose from his desk as they entered his classroom.

"Good morning, Mrs. Karpenko," said the senior mathematics master. "My name is Arnold Sutton, and I'm delighted you were both able to join us today. I'll be conducting the examination."

"How nice to meet you, Mr. Sutton," said Elena as they shook hands.

"You must be Sasha," he said, giving the boy a warm smile. "Please, take a seat and I will explain what we have planned."

"Meanwhile, Mrs. Karpenko," said the headmaster, "perhaps we should return to my study while the test is taking place."

Once the headmaster and Elena had left the room, Mr. Sutton turned his attention to the young applicant.

"Sasha," he said, opening a file and extracting three sheets of paper, "this is the mathematics examination that was taken by those pupils who wished to enter the sixth form of Latymer Upper." He placed the three pages on the desk in front of Sasha. "The time allocated for the test is one hour, and I suggest you read each question carefully before answering it. Do you have any questions?"

"No, sir."

"Good." The schoolmaster checked his watch. "I'll warn you when you have fifteen minutes left."

"You do understand, Mrs. Karpenko," said Mr. Quilter as they walked back down the corridor, "that the exam your son is sitting is not only for pupils hoping to enter the sixth form here at Latymer, but also for those preparing to go on to university."

"That's no more than I would want for Sasha," said Elena.

"Yes, of course, Mrs. Karpenko. But I must warn you that he will have to get sixty-five percent to pass. If he does, we would be delighted to offer him a place at Latymer Upper."

"Then I must warn you, Mr. Quilter, that I couldn't afford the school uniform, let alone the fees."

The headmaster hesitated. "We do offer places for pupils in, shall we say, straitened circumstances. And of course," he added quickly, "we award academic scholarships for exceptionally gifted children." Elena didn't look convinced. "Can I offer you a coffee?"

"No, thank you, Mr. Quilter. I'm sure you must be very busy, so please go back to work. I'm perfectly happy to read a magazine while I'm waiting."

"That's most considerate of you," said the headmaster, "Yes I do have rather a lot of paperwork to be getting on with. But I'll return just as soon as—"

The door was flung open and Mr. Sutton burst in even before the headmaster could finish his sentence. He walked quickly across to Mr. Quilter and whispered in his ear.

"Would you be kind enough to wait here, Mrs. Karpenko?" said the headmaster. "I will be back shortly."

"Is there a problem?" asked Elena anxiously, but the two men had already left the room.

"You say he finished the exam in twenty minutes? That barely seems possible."

"What's even more incredible," said Sutton, almost on the run, "he scored a hundred percent, and frankly looked bored." He opened the door of his classroom to allow the headmaster to enter.

"Karpenko," said Quilter, after he'd glanced at a long row of ticks, "can I ask if you've ever seen this paper before?"

"No, sir."

The headmaster studied the pupil's answers more carefully, before asking, "Would you be willing to answer a couple of oral questions?"

"Yes, of course, sir."

The headmaster nodded to Mr. Sutton.

"Karpenko, if I throw three dice," said Sutton, "what is the probability that the result will be a total of ten?"

The would-be scholar picked up his pen and began to write out various combinations of three numbers. Four minutes later, he put the pen down and said, "One in eight, sir."

"Remarkable," said Sutton. He smiled at the headmaster, who, as a classicist, was none the wiser. "My second question is, if you were offered odds of ten to one that you couldn't throw ten with three dice, would you accept the bet?"

"Of course, sir," said Sasha without hesitation, "because on average, I would win every eight throws. But I would want to place at least a hundred bets before I would consider it to be statistically reliable."

Mr. Sutton turned to Mr. Quilter and said, "Headmaster, please don't allow this boy to go to any other school."

9

ALEX

En route to Brooklyn

Alex gazed into a dark hole that masses of people were rushing into. "Follow me," said Dimitri, as he led his reluctant charges down a narrow flight of steps, before coming to a halt in front of a ticket barrier. He purchased three tickets, then they made their way onto a long dirty platform.

Alex heard a rumbling sound in the distance, like the prelude to a thunderstorm, and then out of a vast cavern at the far end of the platform appeared a train like no other train he'd ever seen before. In Leningrad the stations were carved in green marble, the carriages were clean, and it was only the passengers who were gray.

"You'll get used to it," said Dimitri, as the doors slid open. "Ten stops, and we'll be in Brooklyn." But neither of them was listening, both preoccupied with their own thoughts.

Alex looked around the carriage and noticed that no two people were alike, and they were all chattering away in different languages. In Leningrad, passengers rarely spoke to each other, and if they did, it was always in Russian. He was fascinated. Elena looked overwhelmed.

Alex followed the names of the stations on a little map above the carriage door: Bowling Green, Borough Hall, Atlantic Avenue, Prospect Park, came and went, and he never stopped watching the passengers as they got on and off. When the train finally pulled into Brighton Beach, Dimitri led his two charges out onto the platform. Another escalator took them up, and after they stepped off at the top, Dimitri showed them how to feed their little tokens into a turnstile. They emerged into the sunlight, and Alex was struck by how many people were walking up and down the sidewalk, all of them at a speed he'd never experienced. Everyone seemed to be in such a hurry. The road was just as busy, with cars the size of tanks blasting their horns at anyone who dared to step into their path. Dimitri didn't seem to be aware of the noise. Alex was also mystified by the gaudy colors daubed on walls, even doorways. Graffiti, Dimitri explained, something else he'd never seen in Leningrad. A droning sound caused him to look up, where he spotted a plane that seemed to be falling out of the sky. He stood still, horrified, until Dimitri burst out laughing.

"It's an airplane," he said. "It's landing at JFK, which is only a few miles away." A second plane appeared, which seemed to Alex to be pursuing the one in front. "You'll see one every couple of minutes," said Dimitri.

Elena was more interested in checking out each cafe and restaurant they passed. She couldn't believe how many people were having breakfast. How could they possibly afford it? She wondered what a hamburger was, and who Colonel Sanders could be. The only colonel she'd ever known was the dock commandant, and he certainly didn't own a restaurant. And Coke? Wasn't that something you put on the fire at night to keep warm?

After a few blocks they came to a street market, where Dimitri stopped to chat with a couple of traders he clearly knew. He selected some potatoes, carrots, and a cabbage, which he paid for with cash. Elena picked up some of the fruits and vegetables displayed on the next stall that she'd never seen before. She smelled them, and tried to memorize their names.

"How many would you like?" asked the stallholder.

Elena dropped the avocado and quickly moved on.

Dimitri moved across to another stall, and was happy to take Elena's advice before he chose a chicken, which the stallholder dropped into a brown paper bag.

As they left the market, Dimitri handed a coin to a boy who was yelling something at the top of his voice that Alex couldn't make out.

"More Yanks killed in Vietnam!"

Alex was surprised that the boy selling the newspapers was younger than he, and was not only allowed to handle money, but to work alone.

They turned a corner into a side street, not quite as busy, not quite so noisy, with rows of large houses on either side. Could it be possible that Dimitri lived in one of them?

"I live at number 47," he said. Alex was impressed, until Dimitri added,

"I rent the basement." After a few more yards he led them down a short flight of steps. He put a key in the door, unlocked it, and stepped inside.

Elena followed him into a sparsely furnished front room, and wasn't in any doubt that Dimitri was a bachelor.

"Where are we going to live?" Elena asked, after Dimitri had shown her around.

"Perhaps you could stay with me until you find your own place," said Dimitri. Elena didn't look convinced. "I have an extra mattress, so you can take the spare room, while Alex sleeps on the sofa. As long as he takes his boots off."

"Thank you," said Alex, who felt almost anything would be an improvement on a wooden deck that never stopped pitching and tossing.

Finally Dimitri took Elena into the kitchen. Elena emptied the chicken and vegetables they'd bought at the market onto the kitchen table, then set about preparing the meal. The sink had two taps, and she scalded herself when she turned on the first one. She was even more surprised when Alex opened a small white box and peered inside.

"It's a refrigerator," Dimitri explained. "It makes it possible to keep food for several days."

"I've seen a fridge before," said Elena, "but never in someone's home."

Elena rolled up her sleeves, and an hour later placed three laden plates on the kitchen table, as if she was still serving officers. Once she'd sat down, she couldn't stop talking about their life in Russia. It quickly became clear how much she was missing her homeland.

"That was the best meal I've had in years," said Dimitri, as he licked his lips. "You won't find it hard to get a job in this town."

"But where do I start?" Elena asked as Alex filled the sink with warm water and began to wash the dishes.

"With the *Post,*" said Dimitri, reverting to English.

"The post?" said Elena. "But I'm not expecting any letters."

"The *Brighton Beach Post,*" said Dimitri, picking up the newspaper he'd bought from the boy on the street. "Every day it has a jobs section," he said, turning the pages until he reached the classified advertisements. He ignored accountancy, business opportunities, car sales, only stopping when he reached catering. His finger moved down the column until he came to "Cooks."

"Cook wanted in Chinese restaurant," he read out. "Must speak

Mandarin." They all burst out laughing. "Pastry chef required in an Italian restaurant" sounded more promising, until he added, "must be fully trained sous-chef. Italian preferred." He moved on. "Pizza cook—"

"What's a pizza?" asked Elena, as Alex drained the sink and rejoined them at the table.

"It's the latest thing," said Dimitri. "A dough base, with different toppings, for variety." He checked the location. "And it's only a couple of blocks away, so we could call by tomorrow morning. They're offering a dollar an hour, so you could make as much as forty dollars a week while you look for something better. They'll be lucky to get you," he added.

Elena didn't reply, because her head was resting on a table that didn't move. She was fast asleep.

"The first thing we're going to have to do," said Dimitri after they'd finished breakfast, "is get you some new clothes. No one's going to give you a job dressed like that."

"But we haven't got any money," protested Elena.

"That won't be a problem. Most of the stallholders are happy to give credit."

"Credit?" said Elena.

"Buy now, pay later. Everyone in America does it."

"I don't," said Elena firmly, placing her hands on her hips. "Earn now, and only buy when you can afford it."

"Then we'll have to try the Goodwill shop on Hudson. Maybe they'll be willing to give you something for nothing."

"Charity is for those in real need, not for those capable of doing a day's work," said Elena, reverting to her native tongue.

"I don't think you'll have much chance of being offered a job even in a pizza parlor if you look like a Russian refugee who's just got off the boat," said Dimitri.

Alex nodded his agreement.

Elena was finally silenced.

Dimitri took a five-dollar note out of his pocket and handed it to Elena.

"Thank you," said Elena, reluctantly accepting it. "I'll pay you back as soon as I get a job."

"The Goodwill store opens at nine," said Dimitri. "We must be waiting outside at one minute to."

"Why so early?" asked Alex, determined only to speak English.

"A lot of people clear out their wardrobes at the weekend, so the best deals are always on a Monday morning."

"Then let's get going," said Alex, who couldn't wait to be back on the street. He wanted to see if the boy was still standing on the corner selling newspapers, because he hoped his mother would also allow him to look for a job, perhaps even as a trader on one of the stalls.

"And then we must look for a good school that will take Alex," said Elena, dashing her son's hopes.

"But I want to start working," pleaded Alex, "so we can both earn some money."

"If you hope to end up with a worthwhile position, and eventually earn a proper salary," said Elena, "you'll have to go back to school and make sure you're offered a place at university."

Alex couldn't hide his disappointment, but he knew this was the one thing his mother wouldn't compromise on.

"Then you'll have to make an appointment with the education officer at City Hall," said Dimitri. "But not before you both get some new clothes and Elena's landed that job in the pizza parlor, so we'd better get going."

Once they were back on the street, Alex tried to take in everything that was going on around him. He wondered how long it would be before, like Dimitri, he too melted into the background.

One of the first things Alex noticed was that not all of the men were wearing a suit and hat, while many of the women were dressed in brightly colored clothes, some of them in dresses that didn't even cover their knees. The paper boy was standing on the same street corner, shouting a different headline.

"Bobby Kennedy assassinated!"

Alex wondered if Bobby Kennedy was related to the former president, whom he knew had also been assassinated. If he'd had a dime, he would have bought a paper. Once they were back at the market, Elena would have liked to stop and inspect the freshly baked bread, the oranges, apples, and so many other vegetables, and ask about those she was unfamiliar with. What did an avocado taste like, she wondered, and could you eat the skin?

Alex couldn't resist stopping every few moments to stare into the windows of shops that offered watches, radios, televisions, and gramophone records. He kept being distracted, and then having to run to catch up with Dimitri and Elena.

They finally arrived outside the Goodwill store on Hudson, just as a young woman was turning the CLOSED sign around to read OPEN. Dimitri led them inside, still very much in charge.

Elena spent her time rifling through the shelves and clothes racks before she selected a white shirt and a dark blue tie for Alex. She then turned her attention to a row of suits hanging on a long rail, while Dimitri chatted to the shop assistant. Alex was disappointed when his mother picked out a plain gray suit, which she held up against him to check the size. It was a little large, but she knew it wouldn't be too long before he grew into it. She told him to try it on.

When Alex came out of the changing room, dressed in his new suit, he couldn't help noticing that the girl behind the counter was taking a closer look at him. He turned away, embarrassed. Elena pretended not to notice as she began to pick out some clothes for herself: a simple blue dress and a pleated black skirt. She was beginning to worry that her money must be running out, when she spotted a pair of black leather shoes that would go perfectly with Alex's new suit.

"A man dropped them in on Saturday afternoon," said the girl. "He told me no one wears shoes with laces any longer."

"Perfect," said Elena once Alex had tried them on and walked around the shop a couple of times.

"How much?" Elena asked, gathering up all the goods and placing them on the counter.

"Five dollars," said the girl.

Elena handed over the money, stood back, and admired her son, no longer a child. She didn't notice Dimitri hand the girl another ten dollars, give Alex a wink, and say, "Thank you, Miss Marshall," as the girl handed him a bag full of their old clothes.

"I hope you'll come back soon," said Addie. "We get new stuff in every day."

"Now we have to find the pizza parlor as quickly as possible," said Dimitri, as he left the shop and dropped the bag of old clothes in the nearest trash can. "Can't afford to be late and let someone else get that job."

Elena was about to rescue the bag, when Alex said, "No, Mother." She reluctantly joined her son, and they set off once again at a pace everyone else on the sidewalk seemed to consider normal, and they didn't slow down until Dimitri spotted a red and white sign swinging in the breeze. He crossed the road, dodging in and out of traffic, while Elena and Alex followed, showing none of the same confidence as cars shot past them, horns blaring.

"Leave the talking to me," said Dimitri as he pushed open the door and walked inside. He went straight up to a man standing behind the counter and said, "I want to speak to the manager."

"That's me," said the man, looking up from his booking sheet.

"I've come about the job you advertised in the *Post* for a pizza cook," said Dimitri. "It's not for me, but for this lady, and you'd be lucky to get her."

"Have you worked in a pizza parlor before?" the man asked, turning his attention to Elena.

"No, sir."

"Then I can only offer you a job as washer-up."

"But she's a fully qualified cook," said Dimitri.

"What was your last job?" asked the manager.

"I was the head cook in an officers' club in Leningrad."

"In Queens?"

"No, in Russia."

"We don't employ commies," said the manager, spitting out the words.

"I'm not a communist," protested Elena. "In fact I hate them. I would still be there if . . . but I didn't have any choice."

"But I do," said the manager. "The only job fit for a commie is as a washer-up. The pay's fifty cents an hour."

"Seventy-five," said Dimitri.

"You're hardly in a position to bargain," said the manager. "She can take it or leave it."

"We'll leave it," said Dimitri. He began to walk toward the door, but this time Elena didn't follow.

"Where's the kitchen?" was all she said, rolling up her sleeves.

⊰o⊱

As Elena didn't have to clock on at the pizza parlor before ten, she went straight to City Hall the following morning. After checking the board in the lobby she took the elevator to the third floor. By the time she left a couple of hours later, Elena knew the only school she wanted Alex to attend.

She didn't make an appointment to see the principal, but in her afternoon break sat in the corridor outside his office until he finally gave in and agreed to see her.

Alex reluctantly joined the twelfth grade of Franklin High the following Monday, and it wasn't long before the principal had to admit that Mrs. Karpenko hadn't exaggerated when she suggested he would be top in math and Russian. They weren't the only subjects he excelled in, although Alex was far more interested in several lucrative activities that were not listed on the school's official curriculum.

10

SASHA

London

It was at least a week before the other boys stopped staring at Sasha. Although the lower sixth had experienced their fair share of overseas students, he was the first Russian the boys had set eyes on. What did they imagine would be different about him, Sasha wondered.

As English was his second language, it was assumed that he would have difficulty keeping up with the rest of the class. But within a month, several of his classmates had abandoned trying to keep up with "the Russki," and when it came to math, his third language, Mr. Sutton admitted to the headmaster, "It won't be too long before he realizes there's not much more I can teach him."

While his academic prowess was admired by many, what made Sasha particularly popular with the other boys was his ability to keep "a clean sheet."

"A clean sheet?" said Elena. "But you sleep at home, so how can the other boys know if your sheets are clean?"

"No, Mother, I've just become the school's First Eleven goalkeeper, and we've gone three matches without the opposition scoring." What he didn't tell her was that Maurice Tremlett, the boy he'd replaced as goalkeeper, couldn't hide his anger when he was demoted to the Second Eleven—and it didn't help that Tremlett was school captain.

Toward the end of his first term Sasha felt he was becoming accepted by most of his fellow pupils. But that was before the incident, when overnight he became the most popular boy in the school and also made a friend for life.

It was during a playground kick-about in the mid-morning break that the incident occurred. Ben Cohen, another boy from the lower sixth, who played center-forward for the Second Eleven, was running toward the goal looking as if he was certain to score, when Tremlett came charging out of his goalmouth, so Cohen passed the ball to another boy, who struck it into the open net.

Cohen raised his arms in triumph, but Tremlett didn't slow down, and ran straight into him, knocking him to the ground. "Try that again," he shouted, "and I'll break your neck."

When they kicked off again, Cohen was about to shoot when he saw Tremlett once again heading toward him. He stood aside, and the ball rolled to Tremlett's feet. He ran purposefully toward Sasha in the opposition's goal, with everyone stepping out of his way. Sasha came out of his goal so he could cut down the angle, and when Tremlett entered the penalty box, Sasha threw himself to the ground and pulled the ball safely to his chest. Tremlett didn't break his stride, and kicked Sasha squarely in the back as if he were the ball.

Sasha lay motionless on the ground as the ball trickled out of his hands. Tremlett jumped over him and hammered it into the open goal. He raised his arms in triumph, but no one was cheering.

Cohen ran across to help Sasha to his feet, to find Tremlett was standing over him.

"Not quite as good as you thought you were, are you, Russki?"

"Maybe not," said Sasha, "but if you check next week's team sheet, you'll find it's you who's still in the Second Eleven." Tremlett took a swing at him, but Sasha dodged out of the way, and the blow only brushed his shoulder. "And I don't think you'll make the boxing team either," said Sasha.

Tremlett turned red, and raised his fist a second time, but Sasha was too quick for him, and landed a blow on his nose that caused him to stagger back and fall to the ground. Sasha was about to deliver another punch when Tremlett was saved by the bell, calling them all back to their classrooms.

"Thanks," said Cohen as they left the playground. "But keep your eyes open, because Tremlett likes causing trouble."

"He won't be any trouble," said Sasha. "Trouble is when a KGB officer is pointing a gun at your head."

When Sasha got home that evening, he didn't tell his mother about the incident, as he hadn't considered it that important. He was tucking into a plate of spaghetti when there was a knock on the door.

Elena put down her fork, but didn't move. Knocks on the door meant only one thing. Sasha jumped up and left the table before she could stop him. He opened the front door to find a tall slim man, elegantly dressed in a long black coat with a velvet collar and a trilby, standing in the corridor.

"Good evening, Sasha," the man said, handing him a card.

"Good evening, sir," said Sasha, wondering how the stranger knew his name. He looked at the card, and thought he recognized the name. He certainly knew the address.

"I was hoping to have a word with your mother," said Mr. Agnelli, his accent revealing his heritage.

"Please come in," said Sasha, and led Mr. Agnelli into the kitchen.

"Good evening, Mrs. Karpenko," he said, removing his hat. "My name is Matteo Agnelli, and I'm—"

"I know who you are, Mr. Agnelli."

He smiled. "I'm sorry to disturb you while you're having your supper, so I'll get straight to the point. My chef has handed in his notice as he wishes to return to his family in Naples, and I have been unable to find a suitable replacement. So I would like to offer you the position."

Elena couldn't hide her surprise. She'd only been working for Mr. Moretti for a few months, and had no idea that his greatest rival was even aware of her existence. Before she could reply, Mr. Agnelli solved the mystery.

"One of my regular customers told me he'd recently dined at Moretti's, and that the food had improved beyond recognition, so I decided to find out why. On my instructions, our maître d' had lunch at your restaurant last week, and afterward he warned me that we now had a genuine rival on our doorstep. So I would like to offer you the position of head chef at Osteria Roma."

"But—" began Elena.

"I can't give you a flat above the restaurant, but I would be willing to double your wages, which would allow you to rent a place of your own." Sasha began to listen with greater interest. "Of course, the challenge would be considerable, as we have double the number of covers as Moretti's. But from all I've heard, you seem to enjoy a challenge."

"I'm flattered, Mr. Agnelli, but I'm afraid I'm in debt to Mr. Moretti, who—"

"And if I was willing to cover that debt, Mrs. Karpenko?"

"It's not a financial debt," said Elena, "it's personal. It was Mr. Moretti who made it possible for Sasha and me to come to this country. That is not something I can easily repay."

"Of course, I understand. And how I wish it had been me who'd been traveling on that ship from Leningrad." Mr. Agnelli handed Elena his card. "But should you ever change your mind . . ."

"Not while Mr. Moretti is still alive," said Elena.

"Despite my countrymen's reputation, I hadn't thought of going quite that far," said Agnelli. "But if you insist . . ." All three of them burst out laughing.

"It's been a pleasure to meet you," said Elena, rising from her place and accompanying Mr. Agnelli to the door.

"Will you tell Mr. Moretti about the offer?" asked Sasha, when she returned to the kitchen.

"Certainly not. He has enough problems of his own at the moment, without me threatening to leave."

"But if he knew about the offer, he might offer you a raise, even a percentage of the profits."

"There are no profits," said Elena. "The restaurant's barely breaking even."

"All the more reason to take Mr. Agnelli's offer seriously. After all, you might not get another opportunity like this again."

"You may well be right, Sasha, but loyalty doesn't have a price. It has to be earned. And in any case, Mr. Moretti deserves better than that." Sasha still didn't look convinced. "If you ever have to face a similar dilemma," said Elena, "just think what your father would have done, and you won't go far wrong."

⊸o⊷

"The headmaster wants to see you, Karpenko," said Mr. Sutton as he entered the classroom the following morning. "You're to report to his study immediately."

The tone of his teacher's voice didn't suggest it was anything other than a command. Sasha stood up and left the classroom, painfully aware that all the other boys were staring at him. As he walked along the corridor he wondered what the old man could possibly want. He knocked on the headmaster's door.

"Come," said an unmistakable voice.

Sasha entered Mr. Quilter's study to find him sitting behind his desk, grim-faced. Another man was seated opposite him, who didn't turn around.

"Karpenko, this is Mr. Tremlett," said the headmaster. A large man with thinning red hair, whose sizable paunch meant he couldn't do up the buttons on his double-breasted suit, turned and gave Sasha a smug look that would have told any poker player he had a full house. "Mr. Tremlett tells me you punched his son during a game of football yesterday, and broke his nose. Is that correct?"

"Yes, sir."

"Mr. Tremlett has assured me that his son had done nothing to provoke you, other than to score a goal. Is that the case?"

The meaning of the word "sneak" had been explained to Sasha in his first week at Latymer Upper, along with the consequences.

"It's called collaboration in the Soviet Union," Sasha had told his friend Ben Cohen. "But the consequences there are likely to be a little more serious than being sent to Coventry."

The headmaster waited for an explanation, the expression on his face rather suggesting that he hoped there would be one, but Sasha made no attempt to defend himself.

"In the circumstances," Mr. Quilter said eventually, "you leave me with no choice but to administer an appropriate punishment."

Sasha was prepared for detention, extra prep, even six of the best, but he was shocked by the punishment the headmaster prescribed, especially as it meant the school would suffer every bit as much as he would. But he suspected that wouldn't worry Tremlett. Father or son.

"And should such an incident ever be repeated, Karpenko, I will have no choice but to withdraw your scholarship." Sasha knew that would mean his having to leave Latymer Upper, because his mother certainly couldn't afford the school fees. "Let's hope that's an end to the matter," were his final words.

"Why didn't you tell him the truth?" said Ben Cohen when Sasha explained why he'd been demoted to the Second Eleven for the rest of the season.

"Tremlett's father is a school governor, as well as a local councilor, so who do you think Quilter is more likely to believe?"

"This isn't the Soviet Union," said Ben. "And Mr. Quilter is a fair man. I should know."

"What do you mean?"

"My father is a Jewish immigrant, and several other schools turned me down before Latymer offered me a place."

"I always think of you as English," said Sasha.

"I'm sure you do," said Ben. "But the Tremletts of the world don't, and never will."

⊸o⊷

Sasha didn't tell his mother the reason he was no longer playing in goal for the First Eleven. However, the rest of the school became painfully aware who was responsible for the team no longer having a clean sheet, while the Second Eleven were enjoying a vintage season.

When the headmaster asked to see Sasha at the end of term he couldn't think what he'd done wrong this time, but felt sure he was about to find out. He knocked tentatively on Mr. Quilter's door and waited for the familiar "Come." When he entered the study, he was greeted with a smile.

"Take a seat." Sasha was relieved. If you remained standing, you were in trouble; if you were invited to sit, all was well. "I wanted to have a private word with you, Sasha—" the first time the headmaster had called him by his Christian name. "I've been going over your mock A-level papers, and I think you should consider entering for the Isaac Barrow Prize for Mathematics at Cambridge."

Sasha remained silent. He had no idea what the headmaster was talking about.

"The Isaac Barrow is one of Cambridge's most prestigious awards, and the winner is offered a scholarship to Trinity," Mr. Quilter continued. The fog was slowly lifting, but it still wasn't clear. "As Trinity is my alma mater, it would give me particular pleasure if you were to win the prize. However, I must warn you, you'd be up against pupils from every school in the country, so the competition would be stiff. You'd have to sacrifice almost everything else if you were to have a chance."

"Even playing for the First Eleven next season?"

"I had a feeling you might ask me that," said Quilter, "so I discussed the problem with Mr. Sutton, and we felt you could be allowed just one indulgence, especially as cricket has failed lamentably to capture your imagination, and captaining the school chess team hasn't proved too demanding."

"I'm sure you know, headmaster," said Sasha, "that I've already been offered a place at the London School of Economics, subject to my A-level results."

"An offer that you could still take up should you fail to win the Isaac Barrow Scholarship. Why don't you discuss the idea with your mother, and let me know how she feels?"

"I can tell you exactly how she will feel," said Sasha. The headmaster raised an eyebrow. "She'll want me to enter for the prize. But then she's always been far more ambitious for me than she is for herself."

"Well, you don't have to reach a decision before the beginning of next term. However, it might be wise to give the matter some serious thought before you make up your mind. Never forget the school motto, '*paulatim ergo certe*.'"

"I'll try not to," said Sasha, daring to tease the headmaster.

"And while you're at it, please warn your mother that I'm taking my wife to Moretti's for dinner on Saturday evening to celebrate our wedding anniversary, so I hope it's not her night off."

Sasha smiled, rose from his chair, and said, "I'll let her know, sir."

He decided to take a walk around the school grounds before heading home to tell his mother why the headmaster had wanted to see him. He strolled out onto the close to see that a cricket match was taking place on the square. The school were 146 for 3. Despite his fascination with figures, Sasha hadn't mastered the subtle nuances of the game. Only the English could invent a game where logic couldn't determine which side was winning.

He continued walking around the boundary, occasionally glancing up when he heard the smack of leather on willow. When he reached the other side of the ground, he decided to go behind the pavilion so he wouldn't distract the players. He'd only gone a few yards when his reverie was interrupted by the sound of a girl's voice coming from the nearby copse. He stopped to listen more carefully. The next voice he heard was one he recognized immediately.

"You know you want it, so why pretend?"

"I never wanted to go this far," protested the girl, who was clearly crying.

"It's a bit late to tell me that."

"Get off me, or I'll scream."

"Be my guest. Nobody will hear you."

The next thing Sasha heard was a loud cry that sent the starlings perched on top of the pavilion scattering high into the air. He ran into the copse to see Tremlett lying on top of a struggling girl whose skirt was pushed up around her waist, her blouse and knickers on the ground by her side.

"Mind your own business, Russki," said Tremlett, looking up. "She's only a local tart, so get lost."

Sasha grabbed Tremlett by the shoulders and dragged him off the girl, who let out an even louder scream. Tremlett cursed Sasha as he picked up his shoes and, remembering the broken nose, sauntered off through the copse.

Sasha was kneeling by the girl's side, handing her her blouse, when the cricket master and three boys came running out of the back of the pavilion.

"It wasn't me," protested Sasha. But when he turned around, expecting the girl to confirm his story, she was already running barefoot across the grass, and never looked back.

⊸o⊷

"It wasn't me," repeated Sasha after the cricket master had marched him straight to the headmaster's study and reported what he had witnessed.

"Then who else could it have been?" demanded the headmaster. "Mr. Leigh found you alone with the girl, who was screaming before she ran away. Nobody else was there."

"There was someone else," said Sasha, "but I didn't recognize him."

"Karpenko, you don't seem to realize how serious this matter is. As things stand, I have no choice but to suspend you, and place the matter in the hands of the police."

Sasha stared defiantly at the headmaster and repeated, "He ran away."

"Who did?"

"I didn't recognize him."

"Then you must return home immediately. I strongly advise you to tell your mother exactly what happened, and let's hope she can bring you to your senses."

Sasha left the headmaster's study and made his way slowly home, any thoughts of Trinity or the LSE now far from his mind.

"You look as if you've seen a ghost," said his mother when he walked into the kitchen.

He sat down at the table, head in hands, and began to tell her why he'd come home early that afternoon. He'd reached, "I was kneeling by her side . . ." when there was a loud banging on the front door.

Elena opened it to find two uniformed policemen towering over her. "Are you Mrs. Karpenko?" the first officer asked.

"Yes."

"Is your son, Sasha, with you?"

"Yes, he is."

"I need him to accompany me to the station, madam."

"Why?" demanded Elena, blocking the doorway. "He hasn't done anything wrong."

"If that's the case, madam, he has nothing to fear," said the second officer. "And of course you are welcome to come with us."

Elena and Sasha sat silently in the back of the squad car as they were driven to the local police station. Once Sasha had been signed in by the duty sergeant, they were escorted to a small interview room in the basement and asked to wait.

"Don't say a word," said Elena, once the door had closed. "Being suspended from school is one thing, being sent back to the Soviet Union is quite another."

"But this isn't the Soviet Union, Mother. In England you're innocent until proven guilty."

The door swung open and a middle-aged man in a dark gray suit walked into the room and sat down opposite them.

"Good evening, Mrs. Karpenko, I'm Detective Inspector Maddox. I'm the officer in charge of this case."

"My son is innocent, and—"

"And we're about to give him a chance to prove it," said Maddox. "We would like your son to take part in an identity parade, but as he's a minor, we can't do so without your written permission."

"And if I refuse?"

"Then he will be arrested, and will remain in custody overnight while we continue our inquiries. But if you're convinced he has nothing to hide . . ."

"I have nothing to hide," said Sasha, "so please sign the document, Mama."

The inspector placed a two-page form on the table in front of Elena, and handed her a biro. She took her time reading every word before finally adding her signature.

"Please come with me, young man," said the inspector. He rose from his place and accompanied Sasha out of the room and down the corridor. The detective then stood aside to allow Sasha to enter a long narrow room with a raised platform on one side. Standing on the platform were eight young men, roughly the same age as Sasha, who had clearly been waiting for him.

"You can choose where you would prefer to stand," said the inspector.

Sasha stepped onto the platform and took his place between two lads he'd never seen before, second on the left.

"Will all of you now please turn and face the mirror in front of you."

The inspector left the room and went next door, where a frightened young girl, her mother, and a female police officer were waiting for him.

"Now, Miss Allen," said Detective Inspector Maddox as he drew back the curtain along one wall of the room, "remember that although you can see them, they cannot see you." The girl didn't look convinced, but when her mother nodded, she stared intently at the nine young men. She only needed a few seconds before she pointed to the one who was standing second from the right.

"Can you confirm that is the young man who attacked you, Miss Allen?" asked Maddox.

"No," said the girl, barely above a whisper. "That's the boy who came to my rescue."

⊸o⊷

She rang the doorbell twice. She knew he was at home, because she'd sat in her car for the past two hours waiting for him to return. When he answered the door he looked down at her and said, "What do you want?"

"I've come to see you about your son."

"What about my son?" he said, not budging an inch.

"Perhaps it might be wiser if we were to discuss this inside, councilor," she said, glancing across at an elderly lady who was peeping through the lace curtain next door.

"All right," he said reluctantly, and led her through to his study.

"So what's this all about?" he demanded once he'd closed the door.

"Your son tried to rape my daughter," she said.

"I know all about this," said the man, "and you've got the wrong lad. I think you'll find that the police have already arrested the culprit."

"I think you'll find that they've already released him without charge."

"So what makes you think my son was involved?"

Mrs. Allen opened her handbag, took out a gray sock, and handed it to the councilor.

"This could be anyone's," he said, passing the sock, back to her.

"But it isn't anyone's. A conscientious mother has taken the trouble to sew a Cash's name tape on the inside. Perhaps you'd like to have another look?"

He reluctantly took the sock back and checked the inside, where he found the name TREMLETT neatly sewn in red on a thin piece of white tape.

"I presume you've got the other one."

"Of course I have. But I can't make up my mind if I should hand it over to the police, or—"

"One sock isn't proof."

"Perhaps not. But if your son is innocent, my daughter won't be able to pick him out in an identity parade, will she? Unless, of course, all the others have red hair."

"How much?" said Tremlett.

11

ALEX

Brooklyn

A knock on the door at that time of night meant only one thing to Elena.

"Who can that be?" said Dimitri, getting up from his seat.

Alex didn't take his eyes off the television screen as Dimitri left the room, so neither of them noticed that Elena was trembling.

Dimitri peered through the spyglass in the front door to see two smartly dressed men wearing identical gray suits, white buttoned-down shirts, and blue ties, each carrying a hat. He unbolted the door, opened it, and said, "Good evening. How can I help you?"

"Good evening, sir," said the older of the two men. "My name is Hammond, and I'm with the US Border Patrol. This is my colleague Ross Travis." He took out his identity card and held it up for Dimitri to see. Dimitri said nothing. "We understand that a Mrs. Karpenko is living at this address?"

"She's registered here," said Dimitri, standing his ground.

"We're aware of that," said Travis. "We believe she might have some information that could prove useful to us."

"Then you'd better come in," said Dimitri. He led them through to the front room, walked across to the television, and switched it off.

Alex scowled at the intruders. He'd been looking forward to finding out if James Cagney would escape from the house with the help of his mother without being arrested by the FBI. Why didn't he have a mother like that?

"These gentlemen are with the US Border Patrol," said Dimitri to Elena in Russian. "You don't have to speak English if you don't want to."

"I have nothing to hide," said Elena. "What do you want?" she asked, turning to face the two men, and hoping she sounded relaxed.

"Are you Mrs. Elena Karpenko?" asked Hammond.

"I am," said Elena, a slight tremble in her voice.

Once again the two men introduced themselves, and Alex couldn't take his eyes off them. It was as if they'd stepped out of the television screen straight into their front room.

"There's nothing for you to worry about, Mrs. Karpenko," said Hammond, smiling. Elena didn't look convinced. "We'd just like to ask you a few questions."

"Please sit down," said Elena, not least because she didn't like them towering over her.

"We understand that you and your son escaped from Leningrad. We wondered how that was possible, given that the Soviet Union has such tight border security."

"He thinks you might be a spy," said Dimitri in Russian.

Elena laughed, which puzzled the two men. "My husband was murdered by the KGB," she said, as Travis opened a notebook and began to write down every word. Hammond then asked her a series of questions that had clearly been well prepared.

"Can you recall the names and ranks of any of the KGB officers you cooked for, and their responsibilities?" asked Hammond.

"I could never forget them," said Elena, "especially Major Polyakov, who was the docks' head of security, although my husband told me he reported directly to the dock commandant."

Travis turned the page after underlining "dock commandant." He then wrote down the name and rank of every other officer Elena could remember.

"Only a couple more questions," said Hammond. He opened his briefcase and took out a plan of the docks, which he placed on the table in front of her. "Can you show us where you worked?"

Elena placed a finger on the officers' club.

"So you were nowhere near the submarine base," said Hammond, pointing to the other end of the dockyard.

"No. You had to have special security clearance to work in that part of the yard."

"Thank you," said Hammond. "You could not have been more cooperative." Travis closed his notebook, and Elena assumed the interview was over. "And is this your son?" asked Hammond, turning to Alex. Elena nodded. "I hear you're doing well at school, and had hoped to attend the foreign language school in Moscow."

"Yes, I did," said Alex in Russian, hoping he sounded like James Cagney.

"I wonder if you'd be willing to be interviewed by a specialist officer from Langley," responded Hammond in Russian.

"You bet," said Alex, enjoying the whole experience every bit as much as his mother was detesting it. "Especially if it will help get the men who killed my father."

"I only wish it was that easy," said Hammond. "I'm afraid it's not like the television, where they seem to be able to solve all the world's problems every evening in just under an hour, between commercials."

Elena smiled. "We'll do anything we can to help."

"Do either of you have any questions for us?" asked Hammond.

"Yes," said Alex. "How do I become a G-man?"

"They work for the FBI," said Travis. "If you want to join us at Border Patrol, you'll have to study hard at school and make sure you pass all your exams."

Hammond stood up and shook hands with Elena. "Thank you again for your cooperation, Mrs. Karpenko. We'll be in touch with your son again in due course."

Alex immediately turned the television back on, while Dimitri, who'd hardly uttered a word, accompanied the two men out of the room and into the corridor. Alex thought it strange that Dimitri hadn't questioned them, but he was more interested in the film.

"You were right, Dimitri," said Travis once they were outside on the pavement. "She's a gem. And more important, although he's young, the boy could be an ideal candidate."

"I agree," said Hammond. "Perhaps it's time to tell him about Players' Square."

"I already have," said Dimitri. "So you should have a man posted there on Saturday morning."

"Will do," said Hammond. "Then we'll just have to hope they find each other."

"Believe me, they won't be able to miss each other. They'll be like a magnet and iron filings."

Hammond smiled. "When are you going back to Leningrad?"

"As soon as I can find a ship that needs a third mate. Don't worry, I'll keep you informed. Now I'd better get back before they start to become suspicious." Dimitri shook hands with both men, closed the door, and returned to the front room to find that Elena had gone to bed and Alex couldn't take his eyes off James Cagney.

He looked closely at the young man, and wondered if it was too great a risk.

⊸o⟜

Elena and Dimitri were both up by six the following morning, and were soon discussing their nocturnal visitors.

"Can they be trusted?" asked Elena, taking a couple of three-minute eggs out of a saucepan of boiling water.

"Compared to the KGB, they're angels. But don't forget, they can make or break your chances of becoming an American citizen," said Dimitri as Alex burst into the room.

"OK, you guys, my name is Agent Karpenko, and I'm putting you both under arrest."

"On what charge?" Dimitri demanded.

"Brewing illegal alcohol in the basement of this establishment."

They both burst out laughing.

"Then you'd better drink your milk, Alex, before you go to school. And I need to get moving too, if I'm going to keep my job."

"That job isn't good enough for you, Mama. You ought to be working in a real restaurant, not a pizza joint."

"It's fine for the time being," said Elena. "And it's not a joint. The pay's not bad, and yesterday they let me make my first pizza."

"Real chefs don't make pizzas."

"They do when it's the only job in town."

⊸o⟜

Alex couldn't wait to be interviewed by a special agent from the CIA. He borrowed a book from the library the following morning, entitled *The CIA and Its Role in the Modern World*, and read it from cover to cover, twice. He had so many questions he wanted to ask a real agent.

He was on his way to the market the following Saturday when he saw them for the first time. An assorted group of men and women of various ages and nationalities, all with one thing in common: a love of chess. He recalled Dimitri telling him about Players' Square, so he decided to find out for himself. Their heads were bowed as they studied the boards. There must have been a dozen of them, perhaps more, waiting for their opponents' next move.

Alex hadn't played chess since he'd arrived in America, and like a drug addict who's been deprived of his next fix, he joined the onlookers, moving quickly from game to game until he came across a heavyset middle-aged man dressed in jeans and a sweater, who was seated on his own. None of the other players seemed willing to take the seat opposite him. Alex decided there was only one way to find out why.

"Hi," he said. "My name is Alex."

"Ivan," the man replied. "But before you sit down, have you got a dollar to lose? Because that's what it's going to cost you when I win."

Alex did have a dollar, two in fact, which Elena had given him along with a list of groceries she needed for the weekend.

He sat down, extracted a bill from his pocket, and held it up. "Now let's see yours."

The man chuckled. "You'll only see mine if you beat me." He moved his king's bishop's pawn two squares forward.

Alex immediately recognized an opening often used by Boris Spassky, and countered by moving his queen's pawn forward one square.

The undisputed champion of Brighton Beach gave him a second look before moving his king's knight in front of his pawns. It only took a few more moves for Ivan to realize he would have to concentrate if he was going to defeat his young challenger.

Neither noticed that a small crowd had begun to gather around them, wondering if it could be possible that "the champ" was about to be defeated for the first time in months. It was another forty minutes before a round of applause broke out when Alex delivered the word "checkmate."

"Best of three?" suggested the older man, handing over a dollar.

"I'm sorry, sir," Alex replied, "but I have to go. I have some errands to run for my mother."

It was the way he pronounced the word "mother" that caused Ivan to ask his next question in Russian. "Then why don't you come back tomorrow, around midday, and give me a chance to win my dollar back."

"I'll look forward to that," said Alex, who stood up and shook hands with a man he knew wouldn't be taken by surprise a second time.

Alex couldn't be sure what time it was, but felt certain his mother would be home by now. He hurried out of the square and headed straight for the market, where he bought the vegetables and pork chops his mother had asked for. He had quickly learned which stalls to go to for the finest cuts of meat and the freshest vegetables, but most of all he enjoyed haggling with the stallholders before handing over any cash; something every Russian did from the day they were born, except for his mother.

After he'd paid for a couple of pounds of potatoes, the last item on his mother's list, he began to make his way home. He wouldn't have stopped if he hadn't seen her looking at him through the window. He hesitated for a moment, then marched into the shop as if he had always intended to.

"I need a belt," said Alex, naming the first item of clothing that popped into his head.

"That's not the only thing you need," said the girl, as she selected a nearly new brown leather belt and handed it to him. He tried to give her his winnings. "Save it," she said. "You can take me to a movie tomorrow night."

Alex was lost for words. He'd never asked a girl out on a date, and now the dame was doing the asking. Cagney wouldn't have approved.

"Henry Fonda in *Once Upon a Time in the West*," she said. He'd never heard of Henry Fonda.

"Ah yes," said Alex, "I was looking forward to seeing that movie."

"Well, now you're going to. I'll meet you at the Roxy at six thirty. Don't be late."

"I won't," he said, wondering where the Roxy was. As he turned to leave the shop, she said, "Don't forget your belt."

Alex grabbed it, threw it in one of the bags, and walked casually out of the shop. Once he had rounded the corner, he ran all the way home.

"Where have you been?" his mother asked as he entered the kitchen. "It's gone six."

He wondered whether to tell her about Ivan and the chess game (she would approve), the dollar he'd won (she wouldn't approve), and his second encounter with the girl from the thrift store (he couldn't be sure), going to a movie (he could be sure). Elena opened the brown paper bag, pulled out the leather belt, and asked, "Where did you get this?"

Alex would have told her, but he couldn't remember her name.

⤚o⤙

Alex returned to Players' Square the following morning, but not until his mother had left for work.

Ivan was already sitting at one of the boards, fingers tapping impatiently on the table. He held up two clenched fists even before Alex had sat down. Alex tapped the right hand, and Ivan opened it to reveal a white pawn. He rotated the board and waited for Alex to make the first move.

After an hour, it was clear to those who had congregated around the board to watch the match that there wasn't much to choose between the two players. Ivan won the first game, and Alex had to hand back his hard-earned dollar before the board was reset for the decider. The final game was by far the longest.

Eventually Ivan and Alex agreed on a stalemate. They stood and shook hands, which was greeted by a spontaneous round of applause from the lesser mortals surrounding them.

"Do you want to make some real money, kid?" asked Ivan as the crowd melted away.

"Only if it's legal," replied Alex. "My American citizenship is still only provisional, so I could be sent back to the Soviet Union if I was found guilty of a crime."

"We wouldn't want that, would we?" said Ivan, grinning. "Let's go and have a coffee, then I'll explain what I have in mind."

Ivan guided his protégé to the far side of the square and across the road to a small diner. He strolled in, said "Hi, Lou" to the man behind the counter, and headed for what was evidently his usual booth. Alex slipped into the seat opposite him.

"What would you like?" asked Ivan.

"I'll have the same as you," said Alex, hoping it wasn't too obvious he'd never been in a diner before.

"Two coffees," Ivan told the waitress. He then took some time explaining to Alex how they could make some extra cash the following weekend.

"And which role would I play?" asked Alex.

"You'll be the blind man, and I'll tell you the moves your opponent makes."

"But you're as good a player as I am, probably better."

"I won't be by the time I've finished with you. And in any case, you're still only seventeen."

"Nearly eighteen."

"But you look about fifteen, which will make the punters all the more confident they can beat you."

"When do we start?" asked Alex.

"Next Saturday morning, eleven sharp."

"Can I ask a favor?"

"Of course. We're partners now."

"Can I have my dollar back?"

"Why?"

"I'm taking a girl to the movies tonight, and that was meant to pay for our tickets."

Alex was standing outside the movie theater fifteen minutes before they'd agreed to meet. He walked nervously up and down the sidewalk, occasionally pausing to study the poster advertising the film. He was wondering how you ever got to meet someone as beautiful as Claudia Cardinale, when he felt a tap on his shoulder.

He swung around to see Addie smiling at him. She took his hand and led him up to the box office.

"Two for *Once Upon a Time in the West,*" she said, and stood aside to allow Alex to pay. Lesson number one in the courting manual. She then grabbed his hand again and took him inside the dimly lit cinema.

Although the film seemed to be incidental to what Addie had in mind, it was Henry Fonda, not Claudia Cardinale, who Alex couldn't take his eyes off. He wanted to talk like that, walk like that, even dress like that. He decided he would have to see the film again during the week when he wouldn't be distracted, because he no longer wanted to be James Cagney.

Alex didn't want Addie to realize it was his first visit to a cinema, so when the man seated in front of him put his arm around his girlfriend's shoulder, he copied him. She snuggled up closer. He was enjoying the film, when a hand reached across, pulled him toward her, and he experienced his first kiss. There wasn't time for a second, because a few moments later the words THE END appeared on the screen and the lights went up.

"Let's get a Coke," suggested Alex. "I know a great little diner not far from here."

"Sounds good," said Addie.

This time Alex took her hand and led Addie across the square to the diner Ivan had taken him to earlier that day. Alex marched in, waved to the man behind the counter, and said, "Hi, Lou," before heading straight for Ivan's table as if he was a regular.

"Two Cokes, please," said Alex when the waitress appeared.

During the next half hour Alex learned far more about Addie than she did about him. In fact he knew her entire life history by the time the waitress asked if they'd like another Coke. He would have said yes, but he'd run out of money.

Addie didn't stop talking while Alex walked her home. When they reached her front door she stood on her toes, put her arms around his neck, and kissed him. A second kiss. A very different kiss.

He walked home in a daze, crept into the house, and went straight to bed, not wanting to wake his mother.

"I've been given another raise," said Elena triumphantly, when Alex joined her for breakfast the following morning. "I'm now on a dollar fifty an hour. I'm going to suggest to Dimitri that it's time for us to start contributing to the rent."

"Us?" said Alex. "I don't contribute anything, Mama, as you well know. But that could change if you'd allow me to earn some extra cash on the weekend."

"Doing what?"

"There are always odd jobs going at the market," said Alex, "especially on weekends."

"I'd allow you to look for a weekend job but only if you can assure me it won't interfere with your school work. I'd never forgive myself if you didn't get a place at NYU."

"It didn't prevent my father—"

"Your father wanted you to go to college every bit as much as I do," she said, ignoring the interruption. "And if you were to get a degree, who knows what you could achieve, especially in America?" Alex decided this wasn't the time to let his mother know exactly what he had in mind for when he left school.

⊸o⊷

Although he worked hard at school during the week, Alex couldn't wait for Saturdays, and the chance to make some real money.

"Will you clear up?" Elena asked as she put on her coat. "I don't want to be late for work."

Once he'd finished drying the dishes, quickly left the house, and started running down the road. As he approached Players' Square that Saturday morning, he could hear the banter and cries of the basketball players on the nearby courts. He stopped and watched them for a few minutes, admiring their skill. He wished the Americans played football, something else he hadn't thought about when he climbed into the crate. He hadn't realized that there were no goalkeepers in American football. He put it out of his mind as he made his way across to the patch of grass set aside for chess players.

The first thing he saw was Ivan standing legs apart, hands on hips, wearing an unkempt sweater and faded jeans, with a black scarf around his neck.

"You're late," he said in Russian, glowering at him.

"It's only a game," said Alex, "so why not keep them waiting?"

"It's not a game," hissed Ivan. "It's business. Never be late when it's business. It gives your opponents an advantage." Without another word he moved across to a row of six chessboards that had been lined up next to each other with an empty chair behind each board.

Ivan clapped his hands, and once he had caught the crowd's attention, announced in a loud, clear voice, "This young man is willing to challenge any six of you to a game." One or two potential opponents looked interested. "And to make it more interesting, he will be blindfolded. I will tell him each move his opponents make, and then wait for his instructions."

"What odds are you offering?" demanded a voice from the crowd.

"Three to one. You put up a dollar, and if you beat him, I'll give you three."

Several challengers immediately stepped forward. Ivan collected their money and recorded their names in a little notebook, before allocating a chair to each of the six contestants. Several people looked disappointed not to have been chosen, and one of them shouted, "Any side bets?"

"Of course. Same odds, three to one. Just tell me which player you're backing." Several other names entered his little notebook. "The book's closed," said Ivan once the last person had placed his bet. He walked across to Alex, who was staring down at the six boards, removed the scarf from around his neck, placed it over Alex's eyes, and tied it with a firm knot.

"Turn him around so he's not facing the boards," demanded a disbeliever.

Alex swung around even before Ivan had a chance to respond.

"You first," said Ivan, pointing to a nervous-looking young man who was seated at board number one. "Pawn to queen's bishop 3," said Ivan in English, and waited for Alex's instruction.

"Pawn to queen 3," he responded.

Ivan nodded to an older man who was peering down at board number two through thick-rimmed glasses. "Pawn to king 3," he said, and moved on to the third board once Alex had responded.

The crowd huddled around the players and studied all six boards intently, while whispering among themselves. Board number four admitted defeat within thirty minutes, and after another hour only one board was still in play.

A burst of applause broke out when board number three knocked his king over. Ivan removed the scarf from around Alex's eyes before he turned to face the crowd and took a bow.

"Will we get a chance to win our money back?" demanded one of the losing players.

"Of course," said Ivan. "Come back in a couple of hours, and to make it even more interesting, my partner will play ten boards." Alex tried not to show the anxiety he felt. "Let's go, kid," said Ivan once the crowd had dispersed, "and have that pizza your mother promised."

When they entered Mario's Pizza Parlor it was clear that Elena was no longer doing the washing up. She was standing at a large wooden table, kneading a lump of fresh dough until it was flat and even. She was so skillful that she produced a new base every ninety seconds.

Another chef then moved in and checked the order, before he covered the dough with the next customer's chosen ingredients. It was then scooped up on what looked to Alex like a flat wooden spade and placed into an open wood-burning oven by a third chef, who took it out three minutes later and shoveled it onto a waiting plate. Alex calculated that they were producing a piping hot pizza every six minutes. Americans clearly didn't like to be kept waiting.

Elena smiled when she looked up and saw her son.

"This is Ivan," said Alex. "We work together at the market."

Elena pointed to one of the few unoccupied tables.

"How much did we make?" asked Alex once they'd sat down.

Ivan checked his notebook. "Nineteen dollars," he whispered.

"Then you owe me nine dollars and fifty cents," said Alex, holding out his hand.

"Not so fast, kid. Don't forget you've got a bigger challenge this afternoon, so we'll settle up at the end of the day."

"If any of them are as good as the guy on board three, we might even lose the odd match."

"Which wouldn't be a bad thing," said Ivan, as a waitress placed two pizzas and a couple of Cokes in front of them.

"How come?"

"If you lose the occasional game, the suckers become more interested. It's a gambler's weakness. If they see someone else win, it convinces them it's their turn next," said Ivan, before he devoured a large slice of pizza. "Must remember to thank your mother," he said, looking at his watch.

Alex glanced around at Elena, who hadn't stopped turning out perfect pizza bases since they'd arrived. He wondered how long it would be before she was giving the orders.

"Right," said Ivan, "let's get back to work."

When Alex arrived back home for dinner that night, he was surprised to find that Dimitri wasn't sitting in his usual place.

"He was offered a job on a merchant ship bound for Leningrad," Elena explained. "He had to leave on the first tide."

"Do you sometimes wonder if Dimitri is too good to be true?"

"I judge people by their actions," said Elena, raising an eyebrow, "and he couldn't have been kinder to us."

"I accept that. But why did he take such an interest in two Russians he didn't know who might well have been criminals?"

"But we're not criminals."

"He had no way of knowing that. Or did he? And was it just a coincidence that he joined us on deck the first night we were on board?"

"But he's a Russian, just like us," protested Elena.

"Not just like us, Mama. He wasn't born in Russia, but in New York. And I can tell you something else. His parents are very much alive."

Elena turned to face Alex. "What makes you say that?"

"Because when he helps you with the washing up, he sometimes takes off his watch, and engraved on the back are the words, 'Happy 30th, love, mom and dad,' dated 2-14-68. Only last year. So perhaps . . ."

"Perhaps you should remember that without Dimitri's help, we wouldn't have a roof over our heads, and there would be no possibility of you going to university," she said, her voice rising with every word. "So I'll say this once, and once only. You will stop spying on Dimitri, because if you don't, you could end up just like your friend Vladimir, a lonely, sick individual with no morals and no friends."

Alex was so shocked by his mother's words that he didn't speak for some time. He bowed his head and apologized, telling her he would never raise the subject again. After she left for work, he once again thought about her outburst. She was right. He couldn't have done more for them, but what he hadn't told his mother was that he feared that Dimitri was working for the KGB.

12

SASHA

London

Although Sasha worked hard when he returned to school for his final year, once the last football game had been played he hung up his goalkeeping gloves and began a strict regimen that even impressed his mother.

He rose at six every morning, and had already done two hours' work before breakfast. He ran to and from school—almost the only exercise he took—and while the other boys were in the playground enjoying French cricket, he remained in the classroom, turning another page of another book.

Once the bell sounded at the end of the day, and everyone else had gone home, Sasha remained at his desk and, with the help of Mr. Sutton, tackled yet another past Isaac Barrow exam paper. Finally he would run home and eat a light supper, before going to his room to do his prep, often falling asleep at his desk.

As the day of the exam drew nearer, he somehow managed to work harder still, finding hours even his mother wasn't acquainted with.

"The exam will be conducted in the Great Hall at Trinity," the headmaster told him. "It might be wise if you were to travel up to Cambridge the night before, so you don't feel rushed or under any unnecessary pressure."

"But where would I stay?" asked Sasha. "I don't know anyone in Cambridge."

"I've arranged for you to spend the night at my old college."

"Perhaps I should take the day off and come up to Cambridge with you," Elena suggested.

Sasha managed to talk his mother out of the idea, but he couldn't stop her buying him a new suit that he knew she couldn't afford. "I want you to look as smart as your rivals," she said.

"I'm only interested in being smarter than my rivals," he replied.

Ben Cohen, who had just passed his driving test, drove Sasha to King's Cross. On the way, he told him about his latest girlfriend. It was the word "latest" that made Sasha realize just how much he'd missed out on during the past year.

"And my dad's going to buy me a TR6 if I get into Cambridge."

"Lucky you."

"I'd swap it for your brain any day," said Ben, as he turned off the Euston Road and parked on a yellow line.

"Good luck," he said, as Sasha climbed out of the car. "And don't come home with a clean sheet."

Sasha sat in the corner of a packed carriage, staring out of the window as the countryside rattled by, not wanting to admit that he wished he'd agreed to let his mother come with him. It was his first journey outside London, unless you counted away matches, and he was becoming more nervous by the minute.

Elena had given him a pound note to cover any expenses, but as it was a clear fine day when the train pulled into Cambridge station, he decided to walk to Trinity. He quickly learned only to ask people wearing gowns for directions to the college. He kept stopping to admire other buildings he passed on the way, but when he first saw the great gates above which Henry VIII stood, he was transported into another world, a world he suddenly realized how much he wanted to be part of. He wished he'd worked harder.

An elderly porter accompanied him across the court and up a flight of centuries-worn stone steps. When they reached the top floor he said, "This was Mr. Quilter's room, Mr. Karpenko. Perhaps you'll be its next occupant." Sasha smiled to himself. The first person ever to call him Mr. Karpenko. "Dinner will be served at seven in the dining room on the far side of the court," the porter said, before leaving Sasha in a little study that wasn't much bigger than his room above the restaurant. But when he looked out of the mullioned window, he saw a world that appeared to have ignored the passing of almost four hundred years. Could a boy from the backstreets of Leningrad really end up in a place like this?

He sat at the desk and once again went over one of the questions Mr. Sutton had thought might come up in the exam. He was just starting another when the clock in the court chimed seven times. He left his books, ran down the stone staircase, and into the court to join a stream of young men chatting and laughing as they made their way around the outside of a manicured grass square, on which not one of them stepped.

When Sasha reached the entrance to the dining room he peeped inside, to see rows of long wooden tables laden with food, and benches occupied by undergraduates who obviously felt very much at home. Suddenly fearful of joining such an elite gathering, he turned around, and made his way out through the college gates and onto King's Parade. He didn't stop walking until he saw a queue outside a fish and chip shop.

He ate his supper out of a newspaper, aware that his mother wouldn't have approved, which only caused him to smile. When the street lights flickered on, he returned to his little room to revise two or three more possible exam questions, and didn't climb into bed until just after midnight. He only slept intermittently, and was horrified when he woke to hear the clock in the court chime eight times. He was just thankful it wasn't nine. He jumped out of bed, washed and dressed, and ran all the way to the dining hall.

He was back in his room twenty minutes later. He went to the lavatory at the end of the corridor four times during the next hour, but was still standing outside the examination hall thirty minutes early. As the minutes ticked by, a trickle of candidates joined the queue, some talking too much, others not at all, each displaying his own particular level of nervousness. At 9:45, two masters dressed in long black gowns appeared. Sasha later learned they were not masters, but dons, and that the title of Master was reserved for the head of house. So many new words to learn—he wondered if the college had its own dictionary.

One of the dons unlocked the door and the well-disciplined flock followed the shepherd into the examination hall. "You'll find your names on the desks," he said. "They are in alphabetical order." He then took his seat behind a table on the dais at the end of the hall. Sasha found KARPENKO in the middle of the fifth row.

"My colleague and I will now hand out the examination papers," said the invigilator. "There are twelve questions, of which you must answer three. You will have ninety minutes. If you can't work out how much time you need to allocate for each question, you shouldn't be here." A ripple of nervous laughter spread around the room. "You will not begin until I blow my whistle." Sasha immediately recalled Mr. Sutton's first law of exams: *the person who finishes first won't necessarily be the winner.*

Once an examination paper had been placed face down in front of each candidate, Sasha waited impatiently for the whistle to blow. The shrill, piercing blast sent a shiver down his spine as he turned the paper over. He read slowly through the twelve questions, immediately placing a tick by five of them. After considering them a second time, he was down to three. One was similar to a question that had come up seven years ago, while another was on his favorite topic. But the real triumph was question 11, which now had two ticks by it, because it was one he'd tackled the night before. Time for Mr. Sutton's second law of exams: *concentrate.*

Sasha began to write. Twenty-four minutes later he put his pen down and read through his answer slowly. He could hear Mr. Quilter's voice: *remember to leave enough time to check your answers so you can correct any mistakes.* He made a couple of minor emendations, then moved on to question 6. This time, twenty-five minutes, followed by another read-through of his submission, before he moved on to question 11, the double tick. He was writing the final paragraph when the whistle blew, and he only just managed to finish before the papers were gathered up. He was painfully aware that he hadn't left any time to double-check that answer. He cursed.

Once the candidates had been dismissed, Sasha returned to his room, packed his small suitcase, headed downstairs, and walked straight to the station. He didn't look back, fearing he would never enter the college again.

On the journey to London, he tried to convince himself that he couldn't have done any better, but by the time the train pulled into King's Cross, he was certain he couldn't have done any worse.

"How do you think it went?" Elena asked even before he'd closed the front door.

"It couldn't have gone better," he said, wanting to reassure her. He handed his mother eleven shillings and sixpence, which she put in her purse.

When Sasha returned to school the next morning, Mr. Sutton was more interested in studying the examination paper than in finding out how his pupil felt he'd done, and although he smiled when he saw the ticks, he didn't point out to Sasha that he'd missed a question on a theorem they had gone over in great detail only a few days before.

"How long will I have to wait for the results?" asked Sasha.

"No more than a couple of weeks," replied Sutton. "But don't forget, you still have to take your A-levels, and how you do in them could be just as important."

Sasha didn't like the words "could be just as important," but he returned to his slavish routine. It worried him that he found the A-level papers a little too easy, like a marathon runner on a six-mile jog. He didn't admit as much to Ben, who felt it had been far tougher than any marathon, and no longer expected to be the proud owner of a TR6.

"You could always be a bus driver," said Sasha. "After all, the pay's pretty good and so are the holidays."

"You'd get longer holidays if you go up to Cambridge," said Ben, revealing his true feelings. "By the way, I'm holding an end of exams party at my place on Saturday night. Mum and Dad are away for the weekend, so make sure you don't miss it."

Sasha put on a freshly ironed white shirt, school tie, and his new suit. As soon as he arrived at Ben's home he realized that he'd made a dreadful mistake. But then, he had assumed the party would be just a few of his classmates, who would down pints of beer until they fell over, fell asleep, or both.

He discovered his next mistake as he walked into a hallway that was larger than his flat. There were just as many girls as boys at the party, and none of them were wearing school uniform, so he'd removed his tie and unbuttoned his shirt long before he reached the drawing room. He looked around and smiled, quite unaware that everyone seemed to know who he was. But he didn't talk to a girl until more than an hour had passed, and she evaporated almost as quickly as she'd appeared.

"He's from another planet," he heard her tell Ben.

"Only wish I occupied it," his friend replied.

Sasha wished he had Ben's ability to casually chat to a girl, and make her feel she was the only woman in the room. He settled down in a comfortable chair from which he could observe the scene as if he were a spectator watching a game where he didn't know the rules.

He froze when he saw a particularly attractive girl heading in his direction. How long would this one last before she too evaporated?

"Hi," she said. "My name's Charlotte Dangerfield, but my friends call me Charlie." She'd broken the ice, but he still froze. She made a second attempt. "I'm hoping to go up to Cambridge in September."

"To read maths?" asked Sasha hopefully.

She laughed, a gentle laugh followed by a captivating smile. "No, I'm an art historian. Or at least that's what I'd like to be." *What's my next line?* thought Sasha, trying not to make it too obvious that he was staring at her legs as she perched on the arm of his chair.

"Everyone says you're going to win the Isaac Barrow Prize. And as I'm no better than a borderline case, I've got everything crossed, including my toes."

Sasha was desperate to keep the conversation flowing, but as he'd never visited an art gallery in his life, all he could manage was, "Who's your favorite artist?"

"Rubens," she said without hesitation. "Particularly the early paintings he did in Antwerp, when we can be certain he alone was responsible for the entire canvas."

"You mean someone else painted his later pictures?"

"No," she said. "But once he became famous and even the Pope wanted to commission him, he allowed his more talented pupils to assist him. Who's your favorite artist?"

"Mine?"

"Yes."

"Leonardo da Vinci." The first name that came into his head.

She smiled. "That's hardly surprising, as, like you, he was a mathematician. Which of his paintings do you particularly like?"

"The *Mona Lisa*," said Sasha. It was the only one he knew.

"I'm visiting Paris with my parents in the summer," said Charlie, "and looking forward to seeing the original."

"The original?"

"At the Louvre."

Sasha was trying to think what to say next, when she slipped down into the seat beside him, leaned across, and gently kissed him. Neither of them said a great deal during the next hour, and although Sasha was clearly untutored, she didn't treat him as if he'd come from another planet.

When some of his friends began to leave just after midnight, Sasha plucked up the courage to ask, "May I walk you home?" His mother had told him that was what a gentleman did when he really liked a girl. *You can hold her hand during the walk, but when you reach her front door, you should only kiss her on the cheek and say, "I hope we'll meet again," so she knows you care about her. If it's gone really well, you can ask for her telephone number.*

"Thank you," she said.

⊸o⊷

When Charlie took a key out of her bag, he leaned toward her, intending to follow his mother's advice. Her lips parted, and he thought he would explode.

"Why don't you pick me up next Saturday morning around nine," Charlie said as she turned the key in the lock. "Then I'll take you to the National Gallery and introduce you to Rubens," she added before disappearing inside.

As Sasha walked home, he was certainly on another planet, and for a change, Newton wasn't occupying it.

⊸o⊷

Charlie did most of the talking on the tube journey from Fulham Broadway to Trafalgar Square, and almost all of the talking once they'd climbed the steps to the National Gallery.

What Sasha had originally considered no more than an excuse to spend some time with Charlie, turned out to be the beginning of a love affair. He was courted by the Dutch, beguiled by the Spanish, mesmerized by the Italians, and enchanted with Charlie.

"Are there any other galleries in London?" he asked as they walked back down the steps and joined the pigeons in Trafalgar Square.

Charlie didn't laugh, as she already knew it wouldn't be too long before Sasha was asking her questions she couldn't answer.

When they arrived back in Fulham, Sasha wanted to take her to lunch at Moretti's, but the fact that he couldn't afford it wasn't the only reason they ended up at a local coffee shop. Charlie would need a little more time before she was introduced to his mother.

⊸o⊷

Charlie was still on Sasha's mind on Monday morning when the headmaster rang him at home and asked him to drop by and see him. "Drop by" made him laugh.

He thought his legs might give way as he walked through the school gates and down the corridor toward the headmaster's study, like a punch-drunk boxer about to face the final round.

Mr. Quilter answered his knock with the familiar "Come!" Sasha opened the door, but learned nothing from the expression on the headmaster's face. He declined the offer to sit down, preferring to remain standing until he'd heard the verdict.

"*Proxime accessit,*" said Quilter. "Many congratulations." Sasha's heart sank. He didn't consider coming second was worthy of praise. "You were beaten by a boy from Manchester Grammar School who got one hundred percent, while you managed ninety-eight. Of course," the headmaster continued, "you'll be disappointed, and understandably so. But the good news is that, after assessing your A-level papers, Trinity is still willing to offer you a scholarship."

"But you just said I came second."

"In maths, yes. But no one got anywhere near you in Russian."

His first thought was, *I hope Charlie . . .*

13

ALEX

Brooklyn

Ivan handed over twenty-three dollars to Alex and said, "Another good day. I can't see any reason why we shouldn't go on milking this cow for a lot longer. So I'll see you next Saturday at eleven sharp."

"Why wait until then," said Alex, "when we could make money like this every day?"

"Because then we'd only milk the cow dry. And in any case, if your mother were to find out what you're up to, she'd certainly put a stop to it."

Alex stuffed the crumpled notes in the back pocket of his jeans, shook hands with his partner, and said, "See you next Saturday."

"And try and be on time for a change," said Ivan.

As he walked toward the market, Alex began to whistle. He felt like a millionaire—which he'd already told his mother he would be by the age of thirty. He handed over ten dollars to her every Sunday evening, explaining that it came from the odd jobs he did in the market over the weekend. The truth was that the market had become his second home, and in the afternoons after school, and while Elena was still at work, he would hang around the stalls watching the traders, quickly learning who could be trusted and, more important, who couldn't. He always bought his fruit and vegetables from Bernie Kaufman, who never short-changed a customer or sold them yesterday's wares.

"I need two pounds of potatoes, Bernie, some runner beans, and a couple of oranges," said Alex, checking his mother's shopping list. "Oh yes, and a beetroot."

"Three dollars, Mr. Rockefeller," said Bernie, handing over two paper bags. "And I'd just like to say, Alex, how much I've enjoyed having you as a customer, and I have no doubt you will do well if you go to NYU."

"Why would I go anywhere else for my fruit and vegetables?"

"You'll have to in the future, because I'll be giving up my stall in a couple of weeks."

"Why?" asked Alex, who'd assumed Bernie was a permanent fixture in the market.

"My license comes up for renewal at the end of the month, and the owner's demanding eighty dollars a week. At that price, I'd be lucky to break even. In any case, I'm nearly sixty, and I don't enjoy the long hours anymore, especially in winter." Alex knew Bernie got up at four o'clock every morning to go to the market, and rarely went home before five in the afternoon.

Alex couldn't accept that his friend would disappear overnight. There were a dozen questions he wanted to ask Bernie, but he needed some time to think. He thanked him and began to walk home.

He was walking past the thrift store deep in thought, when Addie opened the door and shouted after him, "Come back, Alex, I've got something special for you."

When Alex joined her in the shop, she took what looked like a brand-new suit off the rack and said, "Why don't you try it on."

"How did you get hold of this?" asked Alex as he slipped on the jacket.

"A regular customer who goes on shopping sprees, a few days later often gives us something he no longer wants."

Alex tried to imagine what it must be like to be that rich. "What's this made of?" he asked, feeling the cloth.

"Cashmere. Do you like it?"

"What's not to like? But can I afford it?"

"Yours for ten dollars," she whispered.

"How come?"

"It will have been in and out of the store before my boss even sees it."

Alex pulled off his jeans, put on the trousers—they even had a zipper—and studied himself in the full-length mirror. Beige wouldn't have been his first choice, but it still looked like a hundred-dollar suit.

"Just as I thought," said Addie. "A perfect fit. It could have been made for you."

"Thank you," said Alex, handing over ten dollars.

"Are we still going to the movies next Saturday?" Addie asked as he pulled his jeans back on.

"John Wayne in *True Grit*. I'm looking forward to it," he said as she folded up the suit and slipped it into a bag. "I don't know how to thank you," he added.

"I'll think of something," said Addie as he left the store.

As he walked back home, Alex's thoughts turned to how he could possibly get his hands on the eighty dollars a week he needed to rent Bernie's stall. He was making around twenty dollars from chess games at the weekends, but he had no idea how he could make up the shortfall. He knew his mother didn't have that sort of spare cash, even though she'd just been given another raise. But what about Dimitri, who'd just come back from his most recent trip to Moscow? He must surely have some spare cash.

Alex had prepared his pitch long before he reached home, and when he opened the door, he could hear Dimitri singing out of tune. He joined him in the kitchen, and listened to what he had been up to on his Moscow trip.

"A fascinating city," said Dimitri. "Red Square, the Kremlin, Lenin's tomb. You should visit Moscow one day, Alex."

"Never," said Alex firmly. "I'm not interested in Lenin's tomb. I'm an American now, and I'm going to be a millionaire."

Dimitri didn't look surprised, but then he'd already heard the claim many times before. But on this occasion, Alex added another sentence which did take him by surprise. "And you could be my partner."

"What do you mean?" said Dimitri.

"How much spare cash do you have?" asked Alex.

Dimitri didn't reply immediately. "About three hundred dollars," he said eventually. "There's not a lot to spend your money on while at sea."

"How would you feel about investing it?"

"In what?"

"Not in what, but in who," said Alex. He filled the sink with warm water, and by the time they'd finished washing up, he'd explained why he needed three hundred and twenty dollars, and why he would be getting up at four in the morning.

"How does she feel about this?" was Dimitri's only comment.

"I haven't told her yet."

⊸o⊷

Alex found it difficult to concentrate in class the following Monday, but as there were only half a dozen boys who could keep up with him when he was half-awake, no one noticed except his teacher.

When the bell rang at four o'clock, Alex was the first out of the classroom, and he ran all the way to the market. He headed straight for Bernie's stall. Once he'd caught his breath, he began firing questions at the old trader while he served his customers.

"If I rented the stall," said Alex, "would you be willing to go on working?"

"I'm trying to get off the treadmill, and you'd only want to speed it up," grinned Bernie.

"But if I always went to the market in the mornings, you wouldn't have to start work until eight, and I could take over after school."

Bernie didn't reply.

"I'd pay you forty dollars a week," said Alex as Bernie handed a customer a bag of grapes.

"I'd have to think about it," said Bernie. "But even if I agreed, you'd still have a problem."

"What?" said Alex.

"Not what, but who. Because there's someone else who will have to go along with your plan."

"Who?" demanded Alex. "Because I'm not going to tell my mother until you agree."

"It wasn't your mother I was worried about."

"Then who?"

"The man who owns my stall, and most of the others in the market. You're going to have to convince Mr. Wolfe that you're good for the money, because only he can grant you a license."

"So where do I find this Mr. Wolfe?"

"His office is at 3049 Ocean Parkway. He starts work at six every morning, and never goes home before eight in the evening. And let me warn you, Alex, he's one mean son of a bitch."

"See you same time tomorrow afternoon," said Alex, before setting off for home. "By then, I'll own your stall."

Dimitri winked when Alex dashed in and joined him at the kitchen table. They chatted about everything except what was really on his mind, while Alex waited impatiently for his mother to leave for work.

"You've barely eaten anything," said Elena, checking her watch.

"I'm just not that hungry, Mama."

"Are you working tonight?" she asked. For a moment Alex thought he'd been caught out, and then he realized what she meant.

"Yes, I've got to write an essay on the Founding Fathers. I'm learning about Hamilton and Jefferson, and how they came together to write the Constitution."

"That sounds interesting. If you leave your essay on the kitchen table I'll read it when I get home tonight," said Elena as she put on her coat.

"She's no fool, your mother," said Dimitri when he heard the front door close. "If she finds out you're more interested in Rockefeller and Ford than you are in Hamilton and Jefferson, you could be in real trouble."

"Then she'd better not find out."

As he walked along Ocean Parkway, Alex once again went over what he would say to Mr. Wolfe, while at the same time trying to anticipate his questions. He was wearing his new suit, and could only hope he looked like someone who could afford eighty dollars a week. He was so preoccupied that he walked straight past number 3049 and had to turn back. When he reached Wolfe's office door, he took a deep breath and marched in, to find a prim, middle-aged woman seated behind a counter. She couldn't hide her surprise when she saw the young man.

"I want to see Mr. Wolfe," Alex said before she could speak.

"Do you have an appointment?"

"No, but he'll want to see me."

"What's your name?"

"Alex Karpenko."

"I'll see if he's in." She rose from her desk and went into the next room.

"Of course he's in," mumbled Alex, "otherwise you would have said he wasn't." He paced around the room like a caged tiger while he waited for the ringmaster to return.

Eventually the door opened, and the receptionist reappeared. "He can spare you ten minutes, Mr. Karpenko," she said. The first person ever to address him as Mr. Karpenko—was that a good sign? "But no longer," she added firmly, standing aside to allow him to enter.

Alex straightened his tie and marched into Mr. Wolfe's office, hoping he looked older than his years. The landlord looked up from behind his cluttered desk. He was wearing an olive green three-piece suit and an open-neck brown shirt. A few thin strands of hair had been combed across his head in an attempt to disguise his baldness, and a surplus of chins suggested he rarely left the office, other than to eat. "What can I do for you, kid?" he said, a half-smoked cigar bobbing up and down in his mouth.

"I want to take over Bernie Kaufman's stall when his license expires."

"And where would you get that kind of money?" asked Wolfe. "My stalls don't come cheap."

"My partner will supply the money, that is if we can agree on a price."

"I've already set the price," said Wolfe. "So the only question is, can you afford it?"

"How long would the license run for?" said Alex, trying to gain back the initiative.

"Five years. And the contract would have to be signed by someone who isn't a minor."

"Two hundred and fifty dollars a month, cash in advance," said Alex, "and you've got yourself a deal."

"Three hundred and twenty a month, kid." The bobbing cigar never left Wolfe's mouth. "And only then when I see the cash."

Alex knew he couldn't afford it, and should have walked away, but like a reckless gambler he still believed that somehow he'd come up with the money, so he nodded. Wolfe took the cigar out of his mouth, opened a drawer in his desk, and pulled out a contract, which he handed to Alex. "Read it carefully before you sign it, kid, because no smart-assed lawyer has managed to break it yet, and you'll find the penalty clauses are all in my favor."

The cigar returned to Wolfe's mouth. He inhaled deeply, blew out a cloud of smoke, and said, "Make sure you get here real early tomorrow morning, cash in hand, kid. I wouldn't want you to be late for school."

If this had been a gangster movie, James Cagney would have filled Wolfe with lead and then taken over his empire. But in the real world, Alex slunk out of the office and slowly made his way back home, wondering where he'd get the second month's rent if the stall didn't make a big enough profit.

Although Dimitri had already handed over three hundred and twenty dollars to cover the first month's rent, Alex still needed his mother's blessing, and he knew exactly what she would demand in return. He was all too aware that he hadn't been working hard enough at school recently, and had been winging it for the past few months, although he'd still managed to stay among the top half dozen in his class. But while most afternoons were spent with Bernie learning the trade, and every weekend was taken up with trying to earn enough extra cash with Ivan to survive, he wasn't surprised when, a couple of weeks later, the principal asked to see him on Saturday morning concerning a private matter.

Alex was standing outside the principal's office at one minute to ten, having already been to the market at four that morning, and done an hour's work on the stall before Bernie took over at eight. He knocked on the door and waited to be asked to come in.

"Are you still hoping to make it to NYU, Karpenko?" the principal asked before he'd even sat down.

Alex wanted to say, *No, I plan to build an empire that will rival Sears, so I won't have time to go to university*, but he simply replied, "Yes, sir." Alex had promised his mother he'd work harder at school, and make sure he achieved the grades he needed to get into university.

"Then you're going to have to devote far more time to your school work," said the principal, "because your recent efforts have been less than impressive, and I don't need to remind you that your entrance exam is less than six months away, and the examiner won't be interested in the price of a pound of apples."

"I'll work harder," said Alex.

The principal didn't look convinced, but nodded to indicate that he could leave.

"Thank you, sir," said Alex. Once he'd left the principal's office, he didn't stop running until he reached Players' Square. He realized he must have been a few minutes late when he saw Ivan pacing up and down looking at his watch. Twelve punters were already seated behind their boards, waiting impatiently to make their first move.

"What's your excuse this time?" Ivan asked.

⊸o⊷

Whenever one of Dimitri's chosen vessels tied up in Leningrad, he headed straight for the dockside pub where Kolya could be found most evenings.

Once eye contact had been made, Dimitri would leave and make his way across town to Moskovsky station. He would buy a ticket for a local train, then go to the waiting room between platforms 16 and 17. By the time Kolya appeared he would have secured a corner seat, well away from the window and any prying eyes. Few people other than the occasional tramp hung about in the waiting room for more than fifteen minutes, by which time they would be thrown out.

Kolya and Dimitri also limited themselves to fifteen minutes in case an observant porter, or worse, an off-duty KGB officer—they were never really off duty—might spot them and become suspicious. The rules of encounter had been established during their first meeting. Both would have their questions ready, and often several of the answers as well. This time, Dimitri knew that in their first meeting since Elena and Alex's escape, Kolya would be desperate to know how his sister and nephew were progressing in the New World.

As soon as Kolya arrived, he took the seat next to Dimitri and opened his newspaper. They never shook hands, resorted to small talk, or bothered with any pleasantries.

"Elena is still working at a pizza parlor called Mario's," said Dimitri. "She's been promoted three times already, and is now deputy manager. Even Mario is becoming nervous. Her only problem is she thinks she's putting on weight. It seems that wasn't something she ever had to worry about when she worked at the officers' club."

"Any men in her life?"

"Other than Alex, none that I'm aware of."

"Alex?"

"Alexander. He now insists on being called Alex. More American, he tells me."

"And how's he doing at school?"

"Well enough, but not as well as he could do. He's already been offered a place at New York University in the fall, to study economics. But if he had the choice, he'd skip college and start working straight away. Sees himself as the next John D. Rockefeller."

"Rockefeller?"

"He's an American tycoon—they've even named a building after him," said Dimitri.

Kolya smiled as he turned a page of his newspaper. "But if I know Elena, she'll still want the boy to go to college, and then get what she'd call a proper job."

"No doubt about that," said Dimitri. "But he's hell-bent on becoming a millionaire. He even talked me into investing three hundred and twenty dollars in his latest venture."

"Does he know why you can afford it?"

"No, I just told him there's not much to spend my pay on while I'm away at sea."

"It can only be a matter of time before he finds out. But I have to admit I'd invest in the boy myself, if I had any money," said Kolya. "He's got his father's self-confidence and his mother's common sense. Whoever this Rockefeller is, he'd better watch out."

Dimitri laughed. "I'll keep you briefed on how my investment turns out."

"I can't wait," said Kolya. "Give them both my love."

"Of course. And is there anything you'd like me to pass on to my friends?"

"Yes, it looks as if I might be the next convener of the dockers' union and therefore follow in Konstantin's footsteps, though without the same size shoes."

"He'd have been proud of you."

"Not quite yet. There are still a few more problems to surmount, not least Polyakov, who has his own candidate for the job. A fully paid-up party member who would report directly to him."

"So despite Polyakov being at the docks when Elena and Alex escaped, he somehow managed to keep his job?"

"He actually turned the whole disaster to his advantage," said Kolya. "Told the commandant that he didn't go to the cup final because he'd been tipped off that someone might be trying to escape."

"Then why didn't he arrest both of them?"

"Said he was on his own when a dozen men took him by surprise, and that if it hadn't been for him, a lot more dissidents would have been on that ship."

"And they believed him?"

"Must have. But I hear he's unlikely to be promoted in the near future."

"Did he try to pin anything on you?"

"No, he couldn't. I was back at the stadium well in time to watch the second half of the match. I drifted around the north terrace for the next hour, so by the time the final whistle went, over a thousand of my workmates were able to confirm they'd seen me, so I was in the clear."

"That's a relief."

"Not altogether," said Kolya. "Polyakov remains unconvinced, which is another reason why he's so determined to stop me becoming convener of the trade union."

"And who won?"

"Won what?"

"The cup final. Alex keeps asking me to find out."

"We beat Moscow two to one, despite the referee being a KGB officer."

Dimitri laughed. "Anything else you want to tell me?" he asked, aware that their time was running out.

"Yes," said Kolya, turning another page of his newspaper. "Alexander might be interested to know that his old school friend Vladimir has been elected to the committee of the university Komsomol. Don't be surprised if he's chairman by the next time we meet."

"One last thing," said Dimitri. "Elena wants to know, if I was able to fix a visa for you, would you consider coming to New York and living with us?"

"Thank her for her kindness, but Polyakov would make sure I was never granted a visa. Perhaps you could try and explain to my dear sister that I've still got important work to do here." He folded his newspaper, the sign that he had nothing more to say, just as a train shunted into platform 17 and screeched to a halt.

Dimitri rose from his place, joined the jostling passengers now crowding the platform, and began the long walk back to the ship, making the occasional detour to be sure no one was following him. He couldn't help worrying about Kolya, and the risks he was willing to take because he detested the communist regime. Unlike most of Dimitri's other contacts, Kolya never asked for money. Some men can't be bought.

14

SASHA

University of Cambridge

Once Sasha had read through his essay and made a couple of alterations, he glanced at his watch, then hurriedly pulled on his long black scholar's gown, ran downstairs, and across the court. He charged up another staircase, stopping at the third floor, just as he heard the first of ten chimes.

He couldn't be even a minute late for Dr. Streator, who began his supervisions as the great courtyard clock struck, and finished them when it chimed again an hour later. Sasha caught his breath, knocked on the door, and walked in on the tenth chime, to find the two other scholars already sitting in front of the fire enjoying toasted crumpets.

"Good morning, Dr. Streator," said Sasha, handing over his essay.

"Good morning, Karpenko," said Streator in Russian. "You've missed out on the crumpets, but then, being on time doesn't appear to be one of your strengths. However, I can still offer you a cup of tea."

"Thank you, sir."

Streator poured a fourth cup before he began. "Today, I want to consider the relationship between Lenin and Stalin. Lenin not only didn't have any respect for Stalin, he actively despised the man. However, he recognized that if the revolution was to be a success, he needed money to make sure that his political opponents were removed one way or another. Enter a young thug from Georgia who was only too happy to carry out both tasks. He raided banks, and didn't give a second thought about murdering anyone who got in his way, including innocent bystanders."

Sasha took notes while Dr. Streator continued his discourse. It hadn't taken him long to realize how little Russian history he actually knew, and that his teachers in Leningrad had parroted words from a book that had been vetted by the KGB in a blatant attempt to rewrite history.

"I am only interested in proven facts," said Streator, "with reliable evidence to back them up; not mere propaganda, endlessly repeated until the gullible have accepted it as the truth. Stalin, for example, was able to convince an entire nation that he was in Moscow in 1941, leading from the front at a time when the German army were within twenty miles of the city. Whereas it's far more likely that he actually fled to Kuybyshev, and only returned to Moscow once the Germans were in retreat. Why do I say far more likely? Because I don't have irrefutable proof, and for a historian, odds of ninety percent should not be good enough."

Sasha enjoyed his twice-weekly supervisions, and never missed a lecture, although Ben Cohen kept trying to persuade him there was a life beyond academia. Ben had recently joined the Union and begun to take an interest in politics. After much arm-twisting, Sasha had agreed to attend the next debate with him. Sasha rarely ventured beyond the walls of Trinity unless it was to spend time with Charlie in Newnham. But then, Dr. Streator had made it clear at their first supervision that he expected all three of them to be high Wranglers. Nothing less would be acceptable. While others excelled on the playing fields, Streator considered it his duty to stretch his students' minds, not their muscles. However, Sasha felt a trip to the Union couldn't do any harm.

The hour went by so quickly, that when the clock chimed again, Sasha closed his notebook and reluctantly gathered up his papers. He was about to leave when Streator said, "Can you spare me a moment, Karpenko?"

"Yes, of course, sir."

"I wondered if you had anything planned for this evening?"

"I was going to the Union."

"This house would not fight for Queen and country."

"Yes, sir. Will you be there?"

"No, I've had enough of war," said Streator, without explanation. "But when you've got a free evening, perhaps you could join me after supper for a game of chess, where kings, queens, and knights are not imprisoned, executed, or assassinated, but simply moved across a board and occasionally removed." Sasha smiled. "But I must warn you, Karpenko, I have an ulterior motive. I'm the don in charge of the university chess team, and I want to find out if you're good enough to be selected for the match against Oxford."

⊸o⊷

"Have you slept with her yet?"

"Ben, you're the crudest individual I've ever come across."

"That's only because you've led such a sheltered life. Now answer the question. Have you slept with her?"

"No, I haven't. Frankly I'm not even sure how she feels about me."

"How can you be so clever and so stupid at the same time, Sasha? Charlie adores you, and you must be about the only person who doesn't realize it."

"But it still wouldn't be easy," said Sasha, "because Newnham doesn't allow their undergraduates to have a man in their room after six, and even then, if I recall the regulations, he has to keep both feet on the floor at all times."

"This may come as a surprise to you, Sasha, but people have been known to have sex before six o'clock, and even with both feet on the floor." Sasha still didn't look convinced. "But that isn't the reason I wanted to see you. Are you still coming to the debate tonight?"

"This house would not fight for Queen and country," said Sasha. "Yes, even though it's a ridiculous motion, which I assume will be overwhelmingly defeated."

"I wouldn't be so sure of that. There are an awful lot of Bolshies around who'd happily support the idea of the Queen living in a council house. But there's another reason I want you to come. So you can meet my latest girlfriend."

"Have you slept with her yet?" asked Sasha, grinning.

"No, but it shouldn't be long now, because I know she's got the hots for me."

"Ben," said Sasha in disgust, "English is the language of Keats, Shelley, and Shakespeare, in case you hadn't noticed."

"You clearly haven't read Harold Robbins."

"No, I haven't," said Sasha, letting out an exaggerated sigh. "However, if for no other reason than to meet this unfortunate lady who's got what you so elegantly describe as the hots for you, I'll come along."

"Actually, she's also quite bright."

"She can't be that bright, Ben. Think about it."

"And she's the only woman on the Union committee," said Ben, ignoring the gibe.

"Then she must be out of your league."

"There is no league once you get them into bed."

"Ben, you have a one-track mind."

"Why don't you invite Charlie along, and we can all have supper together afterward?"

"OK, I give in. Now go away. I've got a supervision in an hour's time, and I need to check through my essay."

"I haven't even written mine."

"I didn't realize writing was a prerequisite for anyone studying Land Economy."

It was Sasha's first visit to the Union, but as soon as the two of them walked into the debating chamber, it was clear that Ben was already a fixture. He grabbed two free places on a bench near the front of the room, and immediately joined in the noisy chatter emanating from the benches around them. It only ceased when the Union's officers walked in and took their places in the three high-backed chairs on a raised platform at the front of the hall.

"The one seated in the center," Ben whispered, "is Carey. He's the current president of the Union. I'm going to be sitting in that chair one day." Sasha smiled, as Carey rose and said, "I will now ask the vice president to read the minutes of the last meeting."

While Chris Smith read the minutes, Sasha looked around the packed hall and up into the gallery, which was crowded with eager students leaning over the railings, waiting for the debate to begin.

When the minutes had been read and the vice president had sat down, the president rose again. "Ladies and gentlemen, I shall now call upon the Right Honorable Mr. Anthony Wedgwood Benn MP to propose the motion, that this house would not fight for Queen and country."

As Mr. Benn rose from his place, he was greeted by loud, enthusiastic cheers. Sasha could see, as he looked around the hall, that he appeared to be supported by the majority of students present.

"Mr. President, I'm delighted to have been invited to propose this motion," Benn began. "Not least because we all know Britain isn't a democracy. How could anyone claim it is when our head of state isn't even elected? How can we consider our fellow men and women to be equals in the law, when our second chamber is dominated by seven hundred hereditary peers, most of whom have never done a day's work in their lives, and whose sole contribution is to turn up and vote whenever their birthright is threatened? Yet these are the very people who can decide if you should go to war with whom they consider to be their enemy."

Benn's speech was frequently interrupted by cries of "Hear, hear!" and "Shame!" shouted with equal vehemence, and although Sasha didn't agree with a word he said, it was undeniable that Benn had captured the attention of the whole house. When he resumed his place, the room reverberated with even louder cheers and cries of shame than before.

Admiral Sir Hugh Munro, a Conservative Member of Parliament, rose to oppose the motion. The gallant gentleman pointed out that if Britain had not fought for King and country in the Second World War, it would be Adolf Hitler who was sitting on the throne in Buckingham Palace, and not Queen Elizabeth II. This was greeted by hear, hears from that section of the audience who'd remained silent throughout Mr. Benn's speech. Once the admiral had sat down, the two seconders spoke with equal passion, but it still looked to Sasha as if those in favor of the motion were going to carry the day.

He had listened carefully to all four speeches, still amazed that such diverse views could be expressed so openly without fear of any repercussions. In Leningrad, half the students would have been arrested by now, and at least two of the speakers sent to prison, if not shot.

The president rose from his seat once again, and invited members to speak from the floor, before a vote would be taken. "Two minutes only," he said firmly.

One after another, a succession of undergraduates declared that they would never fight for Queen and country, while others asserted that they would die on the battlefield rather than be subjected to foreign rule. It was after a speech by a Mr. Tariq Ali, a former president of the Oxford Union, that Sasha found he could no longer restrain himself. Without thinking, he leaped up when the president called for the next speaker, and was shocked when Mr. Carey pointed in his direction.

Sasha was already regretting his decision as he walked slowly up to the front of the hall. The house fell silent, unsure which side he was going to support. He gripped the dispatch box to stop himself shaking.

"Ladies and gentlemen," Sasha began almost in a whisper. "My name is Sasha Karpenko. I was born in Leningrad, where I spent the first sixteen years of my life, until the communists murdered my father." For the first time, a silence fell upon the assembled gathering, and every eye in the room remained fixed on Sasha. "His crime," he continued, "was to want to form a trade union so that his fellow dockworkers could enjoy rights that you in Britain take for granted. That is one of the privileges of living in a democracy. As Winston Churchill reminded us, *Democracy is the worst form of government, except for all the others*. I refuse to apologize for not having been born in this country, but I am grateful to have escaped the tyranny of Communism, and be allowed to attend this debate, a debate that could never take place in Russia. Because if it had, Mr. Wedgwood Benn would have been shot and Mr. Tariq Ali sent to the salt mines in Siberia."

A few roars of hear, hear, good idea, were followed by raucous laughter. Sasha waited for silence to return before he continued. "You may laugh, but if we were in the Soviet Union, everyone who spoke in favor of this motion tonight would have been arrested, and every student who even attended the debate would have been expelled and sent to work in the docks. I know, because that's what happened to me." Sasha was quite unaware of the effect his words were having on his fellow students.

"My mother and I were able to escape from that totalitarian state, and were fortunate enough to end up in England, where we were welcomed as refugees. But I must tell this house, I would return to the Soviet Union tomorrow to fight that despotic regime, and be willing to die if I thought there was the slightest chance that the communists could be driven out and replaced by a democratic state in which every one of my countrymen would have a vote."

The cheer that followed gave Sasha a chance to gather his thoughts. Only when he had complete silence did he continue. "It's been fun to debate this motion without fear or favor, to have a vote, and then be allowed to join your friends in the bar. But had I made this speech in my country, I would have ended up *behind* bars, and spent many years, perhaps the rest of my life, in a labor camp. I beg you to defeat this motion, because supporting it will only give succor to those evil despots around the world who consider dictatorship a better system than democracy, just as long as they're the dictator. Let us send a message from this house tonight, that we would rather die in defense of our country and its values than be subjected to tyranny."

As Sasha made his way back to his place, the whole house rose to acknowledge him. He was touched to see both Mr. Wedgwood Benn and Mr. Ali on their feet joining in the ovation. When everyone had finally settled, the president stood again and invited the house to divide and cast their votes.

Twenty minutes later, the vice president rose from his place and declared that the motion had been defeated by 312 votes to 297. Sasha was immediately surrounded by a throng of students, congratulating him and wanting to shake his hand, while Ben sat back and basked in his triumph. A member of the committee leaned across and whispered in his ear. "The president wondered if you and your friend would care to join him for a drink in the committee room."

"You bet," said Ben, who led Sasha out of the hall and up a wide staircase to join the presidential party.

The first person to walk across and congratulate him was Mr. Wedgwood Benn.

"A magnificent contribution," he said. "I can only hope you're considering a career in politics. You have a lot to offer."

"But I might not sit on your side of the house, sir," said Sasha.

"Then I would consider you a worthy opponent, sir."

Sasha was about to respond when they were joined by a young woman who also wanted to offer her congratulations.

"This is Fiona," said Ben. "The only woman on the Union committee."

Sasha was impressed, not only with the achievement, but also by her radiant beauty, which didn't require any announcement.

"I'm surprised we haven't seen you before, Sasha," she said, touching his arm.

"He rarely abandons his books to join us lesser mortals," said Ben, who didn't notice that Sasha couldn't take his eyes off her.

"I was hoping to be able to convince you to join CUCA."

"CUCA?" repeated Sasha.

"The University Conservative club," said Ben. "It was Fiona who recruited me."

⊸o⊷

"I hear your speech at the Union went down rather well," said Streator, moving a rook to protect his queen.

"The British are such a civilized people," said Sasha, as he studied the board. "They allow anyone to express their views, however ridiculous or ill-informed they might be. I'm sure it won't come as a surprise to you, sir, that we didn't have a debating society at my school in Leningrad."

"Dictators don't care too much for other people's opinions. Mind you, even the Duke of Wellington, after chairing his first Cabinet meeting as Prime Minister, was surprised to find that his colleagues didn't seem willing simply to carry out his orders, but actually wanted to discuss the alternatives. It was some time before the Iron Duke was prepared to accept that his fellow Cabinet ministers might have opinions of their own."

Sasha laughed, and moved his bishop.

"But be warned, Sasha, civilized as the British are, you shouldn't assume that just because you're clever, they will accept you as one of them. There are many who are suspicious of a first-class mind, while others will make a judgment based not on the words you say, but the accent in which they're pronounced, and some will be against you the moment they hear your name. However, should you choose to remain at Trinity once you've taken your degree, you will only come up against such prejudice if you were foolish enough to venture outside these hallowed walls."

It had never crossed Sasha's mind that he might stay at Trinity and teach the next generation. Only a few days ago a Cabinet minister had encouraged him to consider a political career, and today his supervisor was suggesting that he should remain at Cambridge. He moved a pawn.

"You're a natural," said Streator, "and I'm sure the college will want to hold on to you." He moved his rook again. "But I suppose you might consider us a pretty dull lot, and think there's a far more exciting world out there for you to conquer."

"I'm flattered that my future has even crossed your mind," said Sasha as he picked up his queen.

"Do keep me informed of any plans you might have," said Streator, "either way."

"I only have one plan at the moment, sir. Checkmate."

The phone on Dr. Streator's desk began to ring, but he ignored it.

"The decision to divide Berlin into four Allied sectors following the Second World War was nothing more than a political compromise." The phone stopped ringing. "And when those people living in what in 1949 became East Germany began to flee to the West in droves, the government's reaction was to panic and build an eleven-foot-high barrier which became known as the Berlin Wall. This concrete monstrosity topped with barbed wire stretches for over ninety miles, with the sole purpose of preventing the citizens of East Germany escaping to the West."

The phone began to ring again.

"Over a hundred people have lost their lives attempting to climb that wall. As a monument to the virtues of Communism, it has proved a public relations disaster."

The phone stopped ringing.

"I hope that in my lifetime, and certainly in yours," continued Streator, "we shall see it torn down, and Germany once again united as a single nation. That is the only way to guarantee a lasting peace in Europe."

There was a loud rap on the door. Streator sighed, reluctantly rose from his place, and walked slowly across the room. He had already prepared his first sentence for the intruder. He opened the door to find the senior porter standing there, flushed and clearly embarrassed.

"Perkins, I am in the middle of a supervision, and unless the college is on fire, or about to be invaded by Martians, I would be obliged—"

"Worse than Martians, sir, far worse."

"And what, pray, could be worse than Martians, Perkins?"

"Nine men from Oxford are lurking in the porter's lodge, intent on doing battle."

"With whom?"

"With you, sir, and the members of the Cambridge chess team."

"Typical of that lot to turn up on the wrong day," said Streator. He returned to his desk, opened his diary, and said, "Bugger."

Sasha had never heard the Senior Tutor swear before, and had certainly never known him lost for words.

"Bugger," Streator repeated a few moments later. "I apologize, gentlemen," he said, slamming his diary shut, "but I am going to have to cut this supervision short. I owe you," he checked his watch, "nineteen minutes. Your essay this week will be on the role Konrad Adenauer played as the first chancellor of West Germany following the Second World War. I recommend that you read A. J. P. Taylor and Richard Hiscocks, who have differing opinions on the subject. I believe neither of them to be wholly correct, but don't let that influence you," he said as he headed out of the room. "Karpenko," he added, almost as an afterthought, "as you're a member of the Cambridge team, I suggest you join me."

The porter hurried down the steps at a speed he only considered in grave emergencies, followed by the Senior Tutor, with Sasha bringing up the rear. When Streator entered the porter's lodge, he was greeted with a warm smile by his opposite number, Gareth Jenkins, a Welshman he'd never really cared for, and eight Oxford undergraduates who were trying hard not to smirk.

"I'm so sorry, Gareth," said Streator. "I thought the match was next week."

"I think you'll find that it's scheduled for four o'clock this afternoon, Edward," said Jenkins, handing over the letter of confirmation, with the Senior Tutor's unmistakable signature scrawled along the bottom.

"Could you give me an hour or so, old chap, so I can rustle up the rest of my team?"

"I'm afraid not, Edward. The match is in the fixture list for four o'clock this afternoon, which leaves us," he said, checking his watch, "sixteen minutes before play will commence. Otherwise it will be recorded as a whitewash." The Oxford team were already celebrating.

"But I can't possibly round up my entire team in sixteen minutes. Do be reasonable, Gareth."

"Can you imagine what the reaction would have been had Montgomery said to Rommel, 'Can you hold up the battle of El Alamein for an hour or so, old chap, I've got the wrong day and my men aren't ready?' "

"This is not El Alamein," replied Streator.

"Clearly not for you," was Jenkins's response.

"But I've only got one member of my team on hand," said Streator, sounding even more frustrated.

"Then he'll have to take on all eight of us," said Jenkins, who paused before adding, "at the same time."

"But—" protested Streator.

"That's fine by me," said Sasha.

"This should be amusing," said Jenkins. "Not so much El Alamein as the Charge of the Light Brigade."

Streator reluctantly led the Oxford team out of the lodge and across the court to the Junior Combination Room, where two college servants were quickly setting up a row of chessboards on the refectory table. Streator kept looking at the clock and then glancing toward the doorway in the hope that at least one other member of the team might turn up. But all he saw was a mass of undergraduates flooding in to witness the forthcoming annihilation.

The eight Oxford players took their places at the boards, ready for combat. Sasha, like Horatio, stood alone on the bridge, while Streator and Jenkins, as match referees, took up their positions at either end of the table.

As the clock on the wall struck four, Jenkins declared, "Time. Let the matches commence."

Oxford's top board moved his queen's pawn two squares forward. Sasha responded by advancing his king's pawn one square, just as the Cambridge captain came rushing into the hall.

"Sorry, sir," he said, catching his breath. "I thought the match was next week."

"Mea culpa," admitted Streator. "Why don't you take the second board, as the match has only just begun?"

"I'm afraid that won't be possible," said Jenkins. "Our man has already made his first move, so the match is under way. Therefore your captain is no longer eligible to take part."

Streator would have complained if he hadn't thought Field Marshal Montgomery's name would have been taken in vain a second time.

The Oxford second board made his opening move. Sasha countered immediately, as more undergraduates wandered into the hall to watch the challenger as he moved on to the next board. Within a few minutes, two more members of the Cambridge team had appeared, but they were also obliged to watch the encounter from the sidelines.

Sasha defeated his first opponent within twenty minutes, which was greeted with a warm round of applause. The next dark blue king fell eleven minutes later, by which time the whole of the Cambridge team were present, but as the hall was so packed they had to watch the proceedings from the balcony above.

The third and fourth Oxford men took a little longer to surrender to Sasha's particular skills, but they nonetheless fell within the hour, by which time there was standing room only in the hall and the balcony was heaving with undergraduates, and even a few elderly dons.

The next three Oxford players kept Sasha occupied for another half hour, but eventually they too succumbed, leaving only their top board remaining on the battlefield. *Be patient,* Sasha could hear his father saying. *Eventually he'll make a mistake.* And he did, twenty minutes later, when Sasha sacrificed a rook and the Oxford captain left an opening that he would regret in another seven moves when Sasha declared, for the eighth time, "Checkmate."

Oxford's top board rose from his place, shook hands with Sasha, and bowed low. "We are unworthy," he said, which was greeted with spontaneous applause.

"I do believe that's a whitewash," said Streator once the applause had died down. "And I think it's only fair to warn you, Gareth, that young Karpenko is a freshman, and I'll make sure I get the right date when we visit you next year."

⊸o⊷

Sasha wondered if he'd ever get used to a woman paying for a round of drinks. "Have you considered standing for the Union committee?" Fiona asked him as she handed him a lager.

He took a sip, which gave him time to think about his response. "What would be the point?" he eventually said. "I can't even make up my mind which party I support, so who would even consider voting for me?"

"Far more people than you realize," said Ben before taking a long draft. "After your rousing speech in the Queen and Country debate, and then trouncing the entire Oxford chess team single-handed, they'd vote for you if you stood as a Russian Separatist."

"Will you be standing, Ben?" Sasha asked.

"You bet. And Fiona's put her name down for vice president."

"Well, you're guaranteed at least two votes from a couple of your most devoted admirers," said Sasha.

"Thank you," said Fiona. "But there are plenty of men, including some in my own party, who still think a woman's place is in the kitchen."

"Shame on them," said Ben, raising his glass.

"Not to mention those members of the Labour Party who consider me to be somewhere on the right of Attila the Hun."

Ben placed his empty glass on the table. "Another round?"

"No, thanks," said Sasha. "I need an early night if I'm going to explain to Dr. Streator why I think he's wrong about the Soviet people being best suited to living under a totalitarian regime, even a tsar."

"Heady stuff," said Ben. "I wouldn't dare to disagree with my supervisor."

"Would he even recognize you if you ever turned up to one of his supervisions?" said Sasha.

Ben ignored the comment. "What about you, Fiona, will you join me for another round?"

"Much as I'd love to, Ben, I also need to get to bed. I don't want to fall asleep during tomorrow's Torts lecture."

"I'd join you," said Ben, "but I've just spotted a group of Liberals who I need to butter up if I'm to have any chance of being elected to the committee."

"Remember to put in a good word for me," said Fiona. "And don't forget you'll be disqualified from standing if you buy them a drink this close to the election."

"Ben's right, you know," she said to Sasha as they headed out of the Union bar and down the cobbled path to King's Parade.

"Right about what?"

"That you should stand for the committee," said Fiona. "You might not be elected first time, but you'd be putting down a marker."

"A marker for what?"

"Higher office."

"I don't think so. I'll leave that to you."

"You should at least consider it. Because once you've decided which party you support, you could even end up as Union president."

"I thought that was the job you were after."

"I am. But as there's a new president every term, why shouldn't we both achieve it?"

"I hadn't considered standing for the committee," said Sasha, "let alone president."

"Then it's time you did. Are you going to walk me back to my college?"

"Of course."

"You're so wonderfully old-fashioned," Fiona teased, as she took his hand.

Once again Sasha was taken by surprise that it was a woman who'd made the first move. Queen's pawn advances one square.

As they walked hand in hand toward Fiona's college, he couldn't help thinking about Charlie. He knew she didn't care much for the Union, and Fiona in particular.

"Will you be able to find your way home, Sasha?" Fiona asked when they reached the entrance to Newnham. But before he could reply, she added, "Perhaps you'd like to come up to my room for a drink?"

"How would I get past the porter's lodge?" said Sasha, looking for a way out.

Fiona laughed. "Come with me." Once again she took his hand, and led him around to the back of the building. "You see the fire escape? The window on the third floor is my room. When you see the light go on, come up and join me." Without another word she left him standing there.

Sasha tried to collect his thoughts. He was thinking about going straight back to Trinity when the light on the third floor went on. She pushed the window open and smiled down at her unwitting Romeo.

Sasha mounted the fire escape and climbed to the third floor. He scrambled inside, and saw Fiona standing by the bed, unbuttoning her blouse. She moved across to join him, slipped his jacket off his shoulders, and began to kiss his neck, his face, his lips. When he pulled away, he found she had already discarded her blouse.

"But I thought you and Ben were an item," said Sasha.

"It suits my purpose for him to think so," said Fiona, pulling him toward the bed. "But my only interest in Ben is his ability to pull in the Jewish vote."

Sasha immediately stood up and pushed her away.

"What did I say?"

"If you don't know, Fiona, I wouldn't be able to explain it to you." He picked his jacket up from the floor and headed for the window. He looked back, and had to admit that even though Fiona couldn't hide her anger, she still looked beautiful. It was after he'd climbed down the fire escape and was walking back to Trinity that he decided he would stand for the Union committee.

15
ALEX
New York University

When Alex ran out of money, he wasn't sure whom he could turn to to bail him out.

Most young men going to university as freshmen could take a few weeks to become accustomed to the routine before they settled in, but Alex didn't have a few weeks. Bernie's stall, as the locals still thought of it, was just about breaking even. Although Alex had found ways of cutting costs, the Wolfe at the door was still demanding his three hundred and twenty dollars a month—and, as he regularly reminded Alex, in advance, as agreed in the contract. But Alex didn't have three hundred and twenty dollars, and if he couldn't hand over the money by Monday morning, he would no longer have a stall. Whom could he possibly ask for another short-term loan?

He sat at the back of the theater scribbling on a notepad. Those undergraduates seated around him assumed he was writing down the lecturer's thoughts, but he was too preoccupied with how to hold on to the stall. He had assured Elena at breakfast that morning that his grades were always good enough to put him in the top half of his class, but knew he couldn't share his other worries with her.

"Could the Wall Street crash have been avoided, and should the financial experts have spotted the signs far earlier, or were they all just . . ."

Alex looked down at his notes and thought about his options: Mama, Dimitri, Ivan. He considered each of them in turn. His mother only knew half the story, and it was the better half. She'd never met Mr. Wolfe, and only ever saw Ivan from a distance when he joined Alex for lunch at Mario's. A shadowy figure whom she didn't like the look of, she'd told her son on more than one occasion.

Recently, Alex had begun to wonder if she might be right. Elena had assumed that Ivan worked in the market, although she'd never seen him there. She frequently made it clear that she hoped her son would not end up as a market trader, but would become a lawyer, or an accountant, with an air-conditioned office in Manhattan, who went home every evening to his wife and three children, and resided on the Upper East Side, rather than in Brooklyn.

Dream on, Alex would have told her. But he knew she would never accept that he was one of life's street traders who, when he put on a suit, became an entrepreneur. He struck a line through her name.

Dimitri? He had proved to be a giver, not a taker. A man whose trust and generosity seemed to know no bounds. He had been responsible for Alex and his mother having a roof over their heads, and had supplied the original loan for his stall, which Alex still hadn't repaid. To make matters worse, Dimitri was away at sea again and wasn't expected back for another ten days.

Alex still thought Dimitri was hiding a secret. But perhaps his mother was right, and he was simply one of the good guys. Alex reluctantly put a line through his name, leaving only one person on the list.

Ivan. Their relationship had become increasingly fraught. His partner would often fly into a temper if Alex was even a few minutes late for a chess match, and recently Alex had begun to suspect that he wasn't getting his fair share of the profits from their weekend games. Ivan never let him see what he'd entered in his notebook, and while the side bets were being placed his eyes were always covered with a blindfold.

During the past year, Alex had learned very little about Ivan. He didn't know what his day job was, other than that he ran a small import and export business on the side. Despite this, Ivan was fast looking like the only prospect of keeping his agreement with Mr. Wolfe.

Alex slowly circled his name, and decided that as in chess, the best form of defense was attack. He would raise the subject of a loan during their lunch break on Saturday.

"I want you to write an essay over the weekend," said the lecturer, "on whether President Roosevelt's first hundred days in office were the turning point . . ."

That wasn't how Alex planned on spending his weekend.

⊸o⊷

"Let me try and understand your problem," said Ivan in Russian, as a large pizza was placed in front of him. "You are currently renting a stall—"

"I have a five-year license."

"For three hundred and twenty dollars a month, and you're only making a small profit."

"Not enough to cover next month's rent."

"But you think the problem would be solved if only you were given enough time?"

"Especially if I could get my hands on a second stall."

"Even though you can't afford the one you already have?"

"That's true, but if you and I were to become partners, I'm confident—"

"Forget it," said Ivan, cutting him short. "If you were to rent a second stall, the only thing that would double would be your losses."

Alex bowed his head and looked down at his untouched pizza.

"However," said Ivan, after he'd picked up a second slice, "if it's simply a cash flow problem, I might be able to help."

"I'll do anything."

"Last week I had to sack one of my couriers, and I'm looking for a reliable replacement."

"But that would mean I'd have to drop out of NYU. If I did that, my mother would disown me."

"Perhaps you could have the best of both worlds," said Ivan, "because I'd only need you two or three times a week, and then just for a couple of hours."

"But there's no way I could earn enough to cover—"

"As long as you're always on call, I'd pay you a hundred dollars a week, which would leave you with a few dollars over."

"What would you expect me to do in return?"

"Nothing too demanding. Don't forget, I'm an immigrant, just like you," said Ivan. "I may not have got off the last ship that docked, but I haven't been here that long. However, I've managed to build up a small import and export business that's doing fairly well, and I'm always on the lookout for good lieutenants."

"I won't have anything to do with drugs," said Alex firmly. That would be the surest way back to the Soviet Union.

"And neither would I," said Ivan. "Although I confess the business is not quite what the Jewish would call kosher, so perhaps it's best you don't know too much."

"Are the goods stolen?"

"Not exactly, but from time to time a few cartons of cigarettes might fall off the back of a truck on its way out of the docks, or the occasional crate of whiskey might not appear on the manifest after being unloaded from a ship."

"But I wouldn't be willing—"

"And you wouldn't be expected to. That isn't a side of the business you'd be involved in. All I'm looking for is a courier to deliver messages to my workers in the field. That shouldn't be too demanding for someone of your intelligence."

"But how could that possibly be worth a hundred dollars a week?" asked Alex.

"You're bilingual, and most of my couriers only speak Russian," said Ivan. He took a wad of hundred-dollar bills out of his back pocket, peeled off four, and handed them to Alex, which stopped him asking any more questions.

Elena watched from behind the counter as the cash changed hands. No one paid out that kind of money if it was legitimate. What made her even more suspicious was that Alex hadn't touched his favorite pizza.

⊸o⊷

To begin with, Ivan was not too demanding. It was as if he was testing out his new recruit, asking him only to deliver innocuous messages to various contacts across the city. Alex rarely got much more than a grunt in return from his fellow countrymen, and when they did speak, it was always in Russian. But Ivan explained that they were all immigrants who, like him, had escaped the tyrannies of the KGB and didn't trust anyone. Alex couldn't pretend he liked the people he was dealing with, but he hated the KGB even more, and equally important, Ivan never failed to pay his wages on time. Most of the money was passed on to Mr. Wolfe the following morning, who seemed to be the only person making a profit.

Alex would leave NYU at around four in the afternoon, and be back at the market in time to relieve Bernie at five. He rarely shut up shop much before seven, when he would walk across to Mario's and join his mother for supper. He would always carry a couple of books under his arm, leaving the impression that he was a hardworking student who'd just come from a lecture. Although he didn't mind admitting to Elena that he was enjoying the economics course far more than he'd expected.

Over supper he would read a chapter of Galbraith or Smith, and when he returned home he'd write extensive notes before going to bed. A routine a Jesuit would have approved of, while disapproving of what Alex was trying to achieve.

⊰o⊱

By the time Alex returned to university for his sophomore year, he was renting three stalls. Fruit and vegetables, jewelry (three times the markup), and clothes, which he purchased from Addie, who put aside anything that didn't look second-hand, which would then turn up in Alex's stall the following morning at double the price. He spent every Saturday evening with Addie, occasionally staying overnight, which wasn't always appreciated, as he had to be back at the market by 4 a.m., in order to make sure he didn't get second-best. Five o'clock, and you ended up with the leftovers.

By the end of his sophomore year, Alex had paid back every penny of his debt to Dimitri, and had bought his mother a fur coat for the New York winters; a thrift store bargain of the month at sixty dollars. He was even thinking about getting himself a second-hand delivery van so he could speed up deliveries and save time, but not until he'd graduated.

Although Alex was working sixteen hours a day, he was enjoying a lifestyle no other undergraduate at NYU would have thought possible. But the real bonus was that his three stalls were now producing a large enough profit to make it possible for him to buy a fourth (cut glass, the latest rage).

Everything was going to plan, until he was arrested.

16

SASHA

University of Cambridge

"When do you think we'll hear the result?" asked Sasha.

"The ballot closed at six o'clock," said Ben, "so the returning officer and his team will be counting the votes now. My bet is that we'll know in about half an hour, possibly sooner."

"But how will we find out?" asked Sasha, not wanting to admit how nervous he felt.

"The outgoing president will announce the names of the new officers along with those who've been elected to the committee, and then we either celebrate or drown our sorrows."

"Let's hope we both make it onto the committee."

"You're a shoo-in," said Ben. "I'm just hoping to scrape into fourth place."

"If you do make it, how will you celebrate?"

"I'm going to have one last crack at getting Fiona into the sack. If she makes VP, I must be in with a chance."

Sasha took a sip of his lager.

"And what have you got planned?" asked Ben.

"Either way I'm going to see Charlie, and try to make up for all the time I've been spending in this place."

"She's been pretty preoccupied herself since she joined Footlights," said Ben. "Perhaps you should have become an actor, not a politician. Then you could have played Oberon opposite her Titania."

"Lucky Oberon."

A sudden silence fell over the room as the outgoing president of the Union made his entrance. He came to a halt in the center of the room, coughed, and waited until he had everyone's attention. "The result of the ballot for officers of the Union in the Michaelmas term is as follows. President, with seven hundred and twelve votes, Mr. Chris Smith of Pembroke College."

A loud cheer followed as Smith's supporters raised their glasses. Carey didn't speak again until silence had been restored.

"The treasurer will be Mr. R. C. Andrew of Caius, with six hundred and ninety-one votes," which allowed the members of the Labour Club to join in the cheering.

"And the vice president, with four hundred and eleven votes," continued Carey, to a hushed audience, "will be," he paused, "Miss Fiona Hunter, of Newnham College." Half the room leaped up, while the other half remained seated.

"She'll be the next president," said Ben.

"Elected as members of the committee," said Carey, turning to a separate sheet of paper, "Mr. Sasha Karpenko with eight hundred and eleven votes, Mr. Norman Davis with five hundred and forty-two votes, Mr. Jules Huxley with five hundred and sixteen votes, and Mr. Ben Cohen with four hundred and forty-one votes."

"Congratulations," said Ben, shaking Sasha warmly by the hand. "It can only be a matter of time before you become president. But for now, let's go and fall at the feet of our new VP."

Sasha reluctantly followed his friend across the room, where Fiona was surrounded by admirers. She gave Ben a warm hug, but when she saw Sasha, turned her back on him.

"We should celebrate," said Ben. "Will you join us for supper?"

"No, thanks," said Sasha. "I'm off to see Charlie. I'm hoping she'll give me a second chance."

"Good luck," said Ben, "and congratulations on climbing to the top of the greasy pole."

Sasha made his way slowly across the crowded room, having to stop several times to shake hands with well-wishers, although he was already thinking about Charlie, and hoping she would want to share in his triumph. He knew how he'd like to celebrate. The last time he'd seen her was for tea in her room just over a week ago. He'd been horrified to discover that Charlie's room was on the second floor, directly below Fiona's. She had been preoccupied—perhaps it was the thought of playing

Titania, with the opening night only a few days away. Or maybe he'd gone on just a little too much about the Union.

Sasha broke into a jog as he passed Trinity, and ran all the way to Newnham, where he made his way around to the back of the building.

Although the curtains were drawn, Sasha could see a light shining in Charlie's room. He grabbed the bottom rung of the fire escape and quickly climbed up to the second floor. He was about to tap on the window when he noticed a gap in the curtains. He peeped through to see Titania was in bed with Oberon.

⤙o⤚

The intermittent sound of a piercing siren accompanied by flashing blue lights caused the traffic on the Fulham Road to pull over and allow the ambulance to continue on its journey.

Elena had rushed out of the kitchen the moment she heard Mr. Moretti had collapsed. She'd immediately instructed the headwaiter to phone for an ambulance, while she knelt by his side and checked his pulse. It was weak, but he was still alive. Gino asked for the nearest phone.

"They'll be here any minute," Elena said, holding his hand tightly. She wasn't sure if he could hear her, but then his eyes opened and he attempted a smile.

It felt like hours before she heard the welcome sound of an approaching ambulance, although in fact it was only seven minutes.

A moment later two young paramedics were kneeling by Moretti's side. While one checked his pulse, the other placed an oxygen mask over his face. They then lifted the gray-faced old gentleman onto a stretcher, and carried him out of the restaurant as concerned customers stood aside to allow them through.

"Phone his wife, Gino," said Elena as she accompanied them out onto the street, still holding Mr. Moretti's hand. He was lifted into the ambulance and strapped in. A few seconds later they were speeding toward the hospital.

Elena tried to remain calm, while praying to a god of whose existence she was no longer certain. The paramedic in the back of the ambulance went through a routine he had carried out countless times; first, wrapping a pad around the patient's right arm and attaching a lead to a small screen that traced a line showing little mountains and valleys bobbing up and down. Suddenly, without warning, the mountains and valleys became a flat uninterrupted desert. The paramedic immediately switched into emergency mode, thumping the patient's chest every few seconds, pausing occasionally to check the monitor. After several minutes, when there was still no response, he finally gave up.

"We've lost him," he said quietly, and slumped back, aware that any further attempt at resuscitation would serve no purpose.

"No!" cried Elena, not wanting to accept his words. Something else he'd experienced many times.

"Was he your father?" he asked sympathetically, as he placed a sheet over Mr. Moretti's face.

"No. But no father could have done more for his daughter."

"Did you see Charlie in *Dream*?" asked Ben, as they sat at the bar.

"All eight performances," admitted Sasha. "Even the matinees."

"That bad?"

"I'm afraid so."

"So what are you going to do about it?"

"There's not much I can do while Oberon is continuing his amorous performance offstage as well as on. I seem to be cast in the role of Bottom."

"I think you'll find he's already moved on to his next part."

"But I saw them—" Sasha stopped in midsentence.

"That was before the critics hailed Rory as a future star, while Charlie barely got a mention."

"But I thought she was wonderful," said Sasha. "Every bit as good as him. Better in fact."

"Pity the critics didn't agree with you," said Ben. "But then, they weren't to know she was in love with someone else."

"There's someone else?"

"No, idiot. Honestly, I sometimes wonder how such a clever man can be so dumb. Every time I see Charlie, she only talks about you. So go and cheer her up. Start by telling her how wonderful you thought she was as Titania."

"I don't think she'd welcome that from me."

"Sasha, for God's sake, wake up, get off your backside and do something about it."

It was another twenty-four hours before Sasha got off his backside and did something about it.

⊸o⊷

Sasha found he couldn't concentrate during his morning supervision. He didn't eat lunch, and skipped his afternoon lecture, before finally taking Ben's advice and setting off in the direction of Newnham.

This time, when he arrived at the college, he didn't creep around the back and climb up the fire escape, but walked through the front gate. He registered his name with the porter before making his way slowly up the stairs to the second floor. Several times he nearly turned back, and might have done so, if he hadn't heard Ben's voice in his ear repeating "Pathetic idiot." He hesitated once again when he reached Charlie's door, then took a deep breath and knocked.

He was about to give up, when the door opened. For a few moments the two of them just stared at each other.

"Et tu, Brute," Charlie eventually managed.

"Wrong play," said Sasha. "I came to tell you there is nothing so fair in all Verona."

"But you climbed onto someone else's balcony before mine."

"You saw me?" said Sasha, turning scarlet.

"Both times. And it didn't improve my love life when I jumped out of bed and ran to the window only to find you'd already disappeared."

Sasha burst out laughing.

"Rory left almost as quickly as you did. But come in," she said, taking his hand, "because that was only a dress rehearsal."

⊸o⊷

When Sasha returned to his college a couple of hours later, no one could have failed to notice the satisfied grin on his face, except perhaps for the porter.

"Telephone message for you, Mr. Karpenko," he said, handing him a slip of paper.

Sasha unfolded it, and once he'd read the single sentence, he asked when she had phoned.

"Just over an hour ago, sir. I tried your room but you weren't there, and no one seemed to know where you were, as you'd missed your afternoon lecture."

"No, I was . . . If anyone asks, please tell them I've had to go to London at short notice, and I don't expect to be back for at least a couple of days."

"Of course, sir."

Within an hour, Sasha was stepping onto the platform at King's Cross. When he arrived back at the little flat above the restaurant in Fulham, he found his mother more distressed than he'd seen her since his father's death. She had taken the evening off, something he'd never known her to do before.

-o-

The large turnout for the funeral held at St. Mary's, Fulham, the following week, bore testimony to just how popular Mr. Moretti was, far beyond the boundaries of the local community. Sasha's moving eulogy led Mr. Quilter to remark, "As they say in Yorkshire, lad, you did him proud."

After the ceremony was over and the coffin had been lowered into the ground, Sasha accompanied his mother back to the restaurant, where family, friends, and customers came to pay their respects. Many of them swapped stories of personal kindnesses they'd experienced, none more touching than Elena's.

When the last guest had departed, Elena accompanied the grieving widow home.

"You must go back to work, Elena," said Mrs. Moretti when the light began to fade. "Salvatore would have expected nothing less."

Elena reluctantly rose from her chair and gave the old lady one last hug before putting her coat back on. She was just about to leave when Mrs. Moretti said, "Would you be kind enough to drop by sometime tomorrow, my dear? I think we ought to discuss what I have planned for the restaurant."

-o-

Sasha didn't return to Cambridge the following day, but headed in the opposite direction, arriving at Oxford well in time to join his teammates at Merton, who had all double-checked the date, time, and place.

But the Oxford team had licked their wounds, and were lying in wait for them. By the time Sasha had worked out what they were up to, it was too late, and Cambridge lost the match 4½ to 3½. Sasha explained to Dr. Streator on the journey back to the Fens how Jenkins had beaten them even before they made their opening moves.

"He did what?" said Streator.

"Mr. Jenkins broke with the convention of playing their best player against our best player. He put their weakest player up against me, clearly willing to sacrifice that game. So their strongest player played our second board, and they were at an advantage for the other seven games."

"The Welsh bastard," said Streator.

"Don't worry, sir. They won't get away with those tactics next year, because I'll make sure it's us who are lying in wait."

"Good. And, Sasha, I intend to make you captain next year, so it will be your last chance for revenge. But I suspect that won't be your biggest challenge, if you're still planning to stand for president of the Union, and get a first."

"I do sometimes wonder if I can do both," said Sasha. "Charlie never says anything, but I know she'd prefer me to give up the Union and concentrate on my work."

"I hear she's given up the theater for the same reason," said Streator. Sasha made no comment. "If you do stand for the presidency, who do you think will be your biggest rival?"

"Fiona Hunter, the current vice president."

"If she's her father's daughter, she'll be a formidable opponent."

"You know Sir Max Hunter?"

"Knew would be more accurate. Max and I were contemporaries at Keble. I never liked him. He was always looking for a shortcut. A bent man, bent on politics."

"He made it to the Cabinet."

"Not for long," said Streator. "He'd trampled on too many people on the way up, so when he finally fell from grace, none of them were there to support him on the way down. I can only repeat, if Fiona is her father's daughter, keep your eyes wide open, because she'll make Gareth Jenkins look like a gentleman."

"I can't believe she's quite that bad," said Sasha.

⤙o⤚

"Milk and sugar, my dear?"

"Thank you," said Elena. "Just milk."

"I wanted to see you because I had an unexpected call from my accountant last week," said Mrs. Moretti. "He's received an offer for the restaurant that he considers fair. More than fair, if I remember his exact words."

Elena put down her cup and listened carefully.

"So I agreed to have a meeting with the prospective buyer, who assured me he was a great admirer of yours. He assured me that he'd want to keep you on in your present position, and had no objection to your continuing to live in the upstairs flat."

Elena couldn't hide her relief. She hadn't admitted even to Sasha that she was anxious about what would happen to the restaurant now that Mr. Moretti was no longer around to look after his extended family.

"May I ask the name of the new owner?" Elena asked, hoping it might be a customer she knew, or perhaps someone she had worked with in the past.

Mrs. Moretti put her glasses back on, picked up the recently signed agreement, and checked the name on the bottom line. "A Mr. Maurice Tremlett," she said, dropping another sugar lump into her tea. "He seemed such a nice young man."

Elena's tea went cold.

⤙o⤚

Maurice Tremlett marched into the kitchen and shouted above the bustle and noise, "Which one of you is Elena Karpenko?"

Elena put down her carving knife and came out from behind the long steel counter. Tremlett stared at her for some time before saying, "I want you off the premises immediately, and I mean immediately. And you have twenty-four hours to clear all your possessions out of my flat."

"That's not fair," said Betty, taking off her rubber gloves and stepping forward to stand by her friend.

"Is that right?" said Tremlett. "Then you're sacked as well. And if anyone else wants to join them, be my guest." Although one or two of the other kitchen staff shuffled around nervously, no one spoke. "Good, then that's settled. But be warned, should any of you speak to either of these two again," he said, pointing at Elena and Betty as if they were criminals, "you can also start looking for another job." He turned and left without another word.

Elena took off her whites, left the kitchen, and made her way upstairs to the flat without speaking to anyone. The first thing she did once she'd closed the front door was to look up the number of the porter's lodge at Trinity. For only a second time, she was going to break her golden rule of never disturbing Sasha during term time. However, she decided this was, without question, an emergency. She picked up the phone, and was about to dial the number when she heard a long buzzing sound. The phone had already been cut off.

⊸o⊷

A firm rap on the door caused Dr. Streator to pause in midsentence.

"Either the college is on fire," he said, "or once again I've got the wrong day for the match against Oxford."

The three undergraduates dutifully laughed as their supervisor rose from his place by the fire, walked slowly across the room, and opened the door, to find a stern-looking man and a uniformed police officer standing in the corridor.

"I apologize for disturbing you, Professor Streator," (he was flattered by the promotion) said the young man in a gray suit and a college tie that the Senior Tutor thought he recognized. "I'm Detective Sergeant Warwick," he said, holding up his identity card. "Is a Mr. Sasha Karpenko with you?"

"Yes, he is. But may I ask why you want to see him?"

Warwick ignored the question, and stepped past the don and into his study, followed by the constable. He didn't need to ask which of the three students was Karpenko, because Sasha immediately stood up.

"I need to ask you a few questions, Mr. Karpenko," said Warwick. "Given the circumstances, it might be more convenient if you were to accompany me to the station."

"What are the circumstances?" demanded Streator.

"I'm not at liberty to say, sir," replied Warwick, as the constable took Sasha firmly by the arm and led him out of the room.

Streator left his puzzled students and followed Sasha and the two policemen out of his study, down the staircase, across the courtyard, and onto the street. Several undergraduates looked on curiously as Sasha climbed into the back of a waiting police car and was whisked away.

BOOK THREE

17

ALEX

Brooklyn

Alex was left alone in a small dark room below a naked lightbulb that barely illuminated the table where he was seated. Two empty chairs that stood on the other side of the table were the only other pieces of furniture in the room. A large mirror covered the wall in front of him, and he wondered how many people were standing on the other side observing him.

His brain began to work overtime. Why had he been arrested? What were they charging him with? What law had he broken? Alex couldn't believe the police were interested in the small pickings he made playing chess on the weekends, and although he now owned four stalls, and was making a reasonable profit, it surely wouldn't have been enough to interest even the lowliest tax inspector. And there was no way they could know about the hundred dollars a week Ivan was paying him, because it was always in cash. It couldn't be anything to do with the university, because they had their own security, and in any case, the dean had recently suggested that he should apply for a place at Harvard Business School. Although he was flattered by the idea, Alex rather hoped he'd end up as a case study, not a student.

His thoughts were interrupted when the door suddenly opened and two well-dressed men entered. He recognized them both immediately, but said nothing. They sat down opposite him. He had never forgotten their first meeting, and wondered which of them would be playing the good cop. At least it couldn't be worse than the Soviet Union, where they only had a bad cop, bad cop routine. He waited for one of them to speak.

"My name is Matt Hammond," the older man said, "and this is my colleague, Ross Travis. You might recall that we met at your home some time ago."

"When you claimed to work for Border Patrol," said Alex, more calmly than he felt.

"We're with the CIA," said Hammond, producing his badge, "and hoped you'd be able to help us with an assignment we're currently working on."

Assignment, not investigation, thought Alex. Wasn't *I need to see my lawyer* always the first sentence uttered by criminals when faced with this situation in the movies? But he wasn't a criminal, so he remained silent. The next sentence Hammond delivered took him completely by surprise.

"We're hoping you'll feel able to work alongside us, Mr. Karpenko." Alex thought back to their first meeting. "For the past six months," continued Hammond, "two of our agents have been watching you day and night while you've been working as a courier for a man known as Ivan Donokov, who we've had under surveillance for some time."

"But Ivan assured me he wasn't dealing in drugs," said Alex.

"And he isn't," said Hammond.

"Then what?" asked Alex, feeling nervous for the first time.

"Donokov is a senior KGB operative, who runs a network of agents right across the country."

A long silence followed, until Alex said, "But he hates the communists even more than I do."

"He knew that was exactly what you wanted to hear."

"But we met playing chess . . ."

"It wasn't a coincidence," said Travis, "that Donokov was sitting at a chessboard with an empty seat opposite him when you first walked into Players' Square."

"How could he possibly have known that—"

"We think Major Polyakov tipped him off after you and your mother escaped from Leningrad."

"But he didn't know that I played chess, and—" Alex stopped in mid-sentence.

"No, it was probably your friend Vladimir who supplied Polyakov with that piece of information," said Hammond.

Another long silence, that neither Hammond nor Travis interrupted.

"What a complete fool I've been," said Alex.

"To be fair, Donokov is an old pro who's been around for a long time, and once you got yourself into debt, frankly you were willing to believe anything he told you."

"Am I going to be sent back to Leningrad?"

"No, that's the last place we need you to be," said Hammond.

"So what do you expect me to do?"

"Nothing too demanding to begin with. After all, we don't want to let your friend Donokov know that we're on to him. Keep delivering his messages, and occasionally one of my agents will make discreet contact with you. Just let him know what that day's message is, and then carry on as normal."

"But Ivan's no fool. It won't take him long to work out what you're up to, and then he'll drop me like the proverbial hot potato."

"Or worse," said Hammond. "Because I have to make it clear that your life would be in danger if Donokov were to discover that you were working with the CIA."

"But on the other hand," Travis added, "with your help, we might just be able to break the ring and put Donokov and his gang behind bars for a very long time."

"What makes you think I'd even consider taking such a risk?"

"Because it was Ivan Donokov who ordered your father's death."

"No, you're wrong about that," said Alex. "I can prove it was Polyakov."

"Polyakov is just a pawn on the KGB's chessboard. Donokov moves the pieces."

Alex was speechless, then said, almost to himself, "That would explain why he's always so well informed." It was some time before he asked, "How did you blow his cover?"

"We have an agent working for us in Leningrad who detests the KGB even more than you do."

⊸o⊷

Alex returned home later that evening. Now he had yet another secret he couldn't share with his mother, or even Dimitri. Could it be possible that Dimitri was also working for Donokov? He had, after all, recommended he visit Players' Square. Or was he a CIA operative? One thing Alex knew for certain—he couldn't risk asking him.

He tried to continue working for Ivan as if nothing had happened, but of course it had, and he was sure it would only be a matter of time before he was found out.

It was about a fortnight after his meeting with the two CIA agents that the first interception took place. Alex was standing on the platform at Queensboro Plaza, waiting for a train to Lexington Avenue, when a voice behind him said, "Don't look around."

Alex obeyed the simple command, although his whole body was shaking. A few moments later the voice whispered, "What's today's message?"

"A package will be arriving from Odessa on Thursday, dock seven. Make sure you pick it up."

The man left without another word. Alex delivered Donokov's message as usual.

For the next few weeks, agents would appear on the subway, on buses, and once when he was crossing a busy intersection. He always passed on whatever message Ivan had given him that day, and then, like the morning mist, they evaporated into thin air, never to be seen again.

Alex could only wonder how long it would be before Ivan worked out that he was serving two masters. But he had to admit, if only to himself, he enjoyed the challenge of trying to convince the KGB man that he had no idea what he was really up to, although he accepted that Ivan was as good a chess player as he was, and his queen was exposed.

He couldn't have missed him. In fact it worried Alex just how obvious he was, standing on the subway platform wearing a smart charcoal gray suit, white shirt, and blue tie. He even smelled CIA.

Perhaps it was just a coincidence. Never believe in coincidences, Hammond had warned him. He smiled at Alex, something no other agent had ever done, which only made him more suspicious. Perhaps he was mistaken, and it was just someone who thought he recognized him.

Alex moved away, but the man followed him down the platform. His first mistake. If he had been a CIA agent, he would have disappeared, assuming he'd been spotted. Alex looked down and noticed his second mistake. Although his shoes were highly polished, they were slip-ons, frowned upon by the CIA, who insisted on laces. Such a trivial error.

Alex heard the rumble of an approaching train, and decided to try the jump on/jump off routine, to see if he could lose his shadow. As the train emerged from the tunnel, Alex moved toward the edge of the platform and waited. Suddenly, without warning, he felt two massive hands in the middle of his back, and with one tremendous shove he was propelled toward the track.

He had no way of stopping himself from falling in front of the train. If anything flashed through his mind at that moment, it was that he was about to die, and not a pleasant death. He didn't notice a young black man racing toward him, who tackled him at the last possible moment, as if he was trying to prevent a touchdown.

The young CIA agent left Alex spreadeagled on the platform, while he set off in pursuit of the assailant. Another tackle, as he felled the man halfway up the steps. A moment later a second agent pinned him to the ground and handcuffed him. The assailant turned and looked at Alex, who was pushing himself up from the platform. Despite the noise and clamor of the train doors opening and the passengers streaming off, Alex didn't need to translate his mouthed words, "You're dead."

18

SASHA

Cambridge

Sasha sat alone in a small, badly lit basement room that he'd previously only read about in a Harry Clifton novel. He wanted to turn the page and find out what was going to happen next.

The door swung open and DS Warwick, accompanied by a female officer, entered the room. They took their places on the opposite side of the table.

"I need to ask you a few questions," said Warwick, switching on a tape recorder by his side. "A serious allegation has been made against you, but I want to hear your side of the story before I decide how to proceed."

The one thing Sasha did remember from Harry Clifton novels was that Derek Matthews, the bent barrister whose regular clients were all too familiar with this predicament, always instructed them to say nothing until he arrived. But Sasha wasn't a criminal, and he had nothing to hide. He waited impatiently to discover what the "serious allegation" was, aware that by withholding that vital piece of information, the detective was trying to make him feel uneasy and nervous. He was succeeding.

"A Miss Fiona Hunter," said Warwick eventually, "has made a statement that on Thursday, November the sixteenth—last Thursday—you climbed the fire escape outside her room in Newnham College around ten o' clock, entered her study on the third floor, and stole a confidential file." He stared directly at Sasha. "What do you have to say about this accusation?"

"What's in the file?" said Sasha.

The detective ignored the question. "Miss Hunter claims that she has proof you entered the country illegally after escaping from prison, having murdered a police officer."

"I did escape," said Sasha, "from the biggest prison on earth. I didn't murder the KGB officer, but only wish I had."

"That may all be true, Mr. Karpenko, but as Miss Hunter has made such a serious accusation, we are bound to follow it up. So to start with, where were you on Thursday evening around ten o'clock?"

Sasha knew exactly where he'd been on Thursday night. After attending a debate in the Union, he'd accompanied Charlie back to Newnham, and while she'd entered the college by the front door and gone straight up to her room, he'd made his way around to the back of the building, climbed the fire escape to the second floor, and spent the night with her.

He had woken just before five the following morning, and after they had made love again, he had got dressed, climbed down the fire escape, and walked back to Trinity. He was in his room just before six, and spent the next couple of hours working on an essay that needed to be polished in time for his morning tutorial.

The only problem with Sasha's cast-iron alibi was that if Charlie was to confirm his story, under Newnham College regulations she would automatically be rusticated, and sent home for the rest of term, making it impossible for her to sit her finals until a full investigation had been carried out, which was bound to conclude that she had indeed broken the rules. Not least because Fiona would be happy to report what she had seen, should her other ruse fail.

"Last Thursday evening," said Sasha, "I attended a debate at the Union, and after I'd accompanied Mr. Anthony Barber to the University Arms, where he was staying overnight, I returned to my college just before eleven. I went down to breakfast around eight the following morning."

"So none of the fingerprints we've found on the fire escape of Newnham College will match yours?" said Warwick, raising an eyebrow.

Sasha suddenly wished he'd obeyed Derek Matthews's golden rule, and remained silent. He pursed his lips and said, "I have nothing more to say until I've spoken to a lawyer."

Warwick closed his file. "In that case, Mr. Karpenko, I will require a set of your fingerprints before you leave. You will report back to this station with or without your lawyer at nine o'clock tomorrow morning."

Sasha was surprised when, after turning off the tape recorder, Warwick added, "That should give you more than enough time to sort this out."

The next surprise came when Sasha left the interview room to find Dr. Streator sitting on the narrow wooden bench in the corridor waiting for him.

"Don't say anything," he said, "until we're in my car." He led his pupil out of the police station and across the road, where an ancient Volvo was parked. "Now," he said, once Sasha had closed the passenger door, "tell me what this is about, and don't spare me the gory details."

Sasha had almost come to the end of his story by the time they reached the fellows' car park at Trinity.

"Clearly the detective sergeant doesn't believe a word of Miss Hunter's story, otherwise he wouldn't have released you. I suspect Miss Hunter spotted you climbing into Miss Dangerfield's bedroom and saw an opportunity to derail your chances of becoming president of the Union," Streator said, as they climbed the steps to his study.

"Could Fiona really be that ruthless?" said Sasha.

"Don't think of her as Fiona, but as Sir Max Hunter's daughter, and then you'll know the answer to that question. But all is not lost. No doubt Miss Dangerfield will corroborate your story, which will make Miss Hunter look extremely foolish." Streator was clearly enjoying the prospect.

"But I've already lied to Warwick in order to protect Charlie," said Sasha. "Why would he believe me if I suddenly change my story?"

"He'll be enough of a man of the world to understand why you did that," said Streator as he opened his study door.

"But I don't want Charlie to be rusticated, and unable to sit her exams."

"I expect Fiona was well aware of that, but if you don't tell Warwick the truth, it will be you who's rusticated, which will mean Fiona Hunter will have knocked out her only rival for the presidency. And even when you're eventually proved innocent, there will always be those who believe there's no smoke without fire, especially if you're considering a career in politics."

"But I have to protect Charlie."

"You say you left her room around five thirty?" said Streator, ignoring the comment. "And returned to college immediately?" Sasha nodded. "Did you see anyone you knew on the way?"

"No. There weren't too many people around at that time in the morning."

"Didn't Mr. Perkins spot you when you sneaked back into college?"

"I'm afraid not. He was fast asleep, which I was pleased about at the time."

"Was he indeed?" The phone on Streator's desk began to ring. He picked it up and listened for a few moments before saying, "It's Perkins. He says he needs to have a word with you."

Sasha grabbed the phone as if it were a lifeline.

"Sorry to disturb you, Mr. Karpenko," said Perkins. "But your mother has just called and says she needs to speak to you urgently."

⊸o⊷

"It's all over the Union," said Ben, as he sat down on the end of the bed in Sasha's study.

"Don't spare me."

"You were arrested during a supervision this morning, handcuffed, dragged out of Dr. Streator's study, thrown into the back of a police car, driven to the nearest nick, charged with breaking and entering a female undergraduate's room and stealing a confidential file, and left to rot in a prison cell while you await trial."

"Then this must be the cell," said Sasha.

"Fair point. Which is why we need to go straight to the Union and be seen having a pint at the bar together, looking as if you haven't got a care in the world."

"I don't think that will be possible."

"It has to be if you're going to have any chance of becoming president of the Union."

"I'm sorry," said Sasha, "but I have to go to London. My mother needs to see me urgently."

"What could possibly be more urgent than gathering evidence to prove you're innocent of any charge?"

"I don't even know what the problem is," admitted Sasha, "but the last time my mother used the word 'urgent' was when Mr. Moretti died."

"Then at least let me tell Charlie what's happened, so we can expose Fiona for what she is and clear your name."

"Now listen carefully, Ben. You are not to go anywhere near Charlie, unless you want to find out just how close that KGB officer got to having his throat cut."

Ben froze, and it was some time before he managed, "Just be sure you're back by nine tomorrow, because you can't afford to miss your appointment with Sergeant Warwick. Otherwise you could be the first president of the Union to be elected while in prison."

⊸o⊷

When Elena heard the knock on the door she assumed it must be Sasha. She was already regretting phoning during term time, and bothering him with her problems. It would be just like him to drop everything and try to help. She stopped packing and opened the door to find Gino standing there.

"I'm so sorry," he said as he embraced her. "I just wanted you to know that I've handed in my notice, along with five of the kitchen staff and three of my waiters."

"You mustn't do that, Gino. I don't want to be responsible for you all being out of work."

"Most of us realize we wouldn't have survived too long with that bastard Tremlett. And in any case, my motives aren't entirely pure, as I've already been offered another job."

"Who with?"

"Matteo Agnelli."

"The enemy!" said Elena, laughing.

"No longer. There's an old Italian saying: *My enemy's enemy is my friend*. But Mr. Agnelli only offered me the job on one condition."

"And what was that?"

"That you'll come with me."

"And Betty?"

"I'm sure he'd agree to that."

"But where would I live?" asked Elena. "Because there isn't a flat above Mr. Agnelli's restaurant."

"You can always come and shack up with me until you find your own place."

"But what about your partner?"

"He'd only object if you were a man," said Gino. "So, are you willing to cross the road and join me at Osteria Roma?"

"You should have been christened Coriolanus," said Elena.

"Corio . . . who?"

⊸o⊷

Sasha had to admit that losing both one's job and the roof over one's head could certainly be described as an emergency. He only wished he'd known about Gino's proposal before he got on the train. But he'd been left with no choice once the operator told him his mother's phone had been cut off. He spent a sleepless night on Gino's sofa, and took the first train back to Cambridge the following morning. He had to fork out almost a pound on a taxi to make sure he arrived at the police station at 8:54 a.m. A young constable took him straight through to Detective Sergeant Warwick's office, and not an interview room.

"Miss Hunter has withdrawn her allegation," said Warwick, once Sasha had sat down.

"Please tell me Charlie hasn't been to see you."

"Charlie who?" asked Warwick innocently. "No, it was a simple piece of detective work that caused Miss Hunter to have second thoughts. We were able to point out to her that your fingerprints on the fire escape stopped at the second floor, and as she also claimed that you left her room within minutes of stealing the file, it's difficult to explain why it took you five and a half hours to get back to your college, unless of course you were tucked up in bed on the floor below."

"But the college porter, Mr. Perkins, wouldn't have been able to confirm the time I returned to college, because he was fast asleep."

"Turned a blind eye, would be a more accurate description," said Warwick. "If you'd been seen coming in at five thirty in the morning, he would have had to enter your name in his log book for breaking college regulations, and then you would have needed to explain to the proctors where you'd been all night."

"So has Fiona got away with it?"

"Not entirely. Miss Hunter has been cautioned for wasting police time. Frankly, I'd have banged her up overnight if her father hadn't had a word with the chief constable. Still, you'd better be off, as I understand you have a busy day ahead of you."

⊸o⊷

"As you know, Elena, I've wanted you to join me for some time," said Mr. Agnelli, "but you made it clear that there was no point in asking while you were still working for Mr. Moretti."

"And there still might not be any point," said Elena.

"My previous offer still stands. I'd make you head chef, and I can promise that you'll never see me in the kitchen. I'll double what Mr. Moretti paid you, and you'll also receive ten percent of the restaurant's profits. But you'd have to find your own accommodation."

"And can Betty join me?" asked Elena. Agnelli nodded. "And will Gino be the maître d'?"

"Yes. I'd already agreed that with him. Is there anything else you were hoping for?"

After listening to Elena's final request Mr. Agnelli said, "I'll need to think about it."

"It's a deal-breaker," said Elena, repeating Sasha's exact words.

⊸o⊷

When Sasha left the police station, he ran all the way to the Union, where he found his campaign manager trying to explain to a voter where the candidate had been for the past forty-eight hours.

"The voting's already started," said Ben, after Sasha joined him at the bar and told him the latest news. "We haven't got a moment to waste, because Fiona's been telling everyone you've spent the past two days in a police cell. You've got to admire her nerve."

"Not to mention her timing."

"Pity Warwick didn't lock her up for the day. That would certainly have helped our chances. But we can still win."

They began to work the room. Several members shook Sasha's hand warmly, while others turned their backs on him—one or two of whom he'd considered supporters, even friends. He tried to speak to everyone who hadn't yet voted, even if he knew they had no intention of backing him. It was clear that some people still believed Fiona's story, or wanted to, while others admitted to him that their own fingerprints might well be on that fire escape. Sasha didn't stop until the last vote had been cast at six o'clock, when he joined Ben and Charlie at the Union bar. Fiona's supporters occupied one side of the room, while Sasha's filled the other half.

"When will you find out the result?" asked Charlie as she sipped a lager.

"Around seven," said Ben. "So not long to wait."

Ben's prediction turned out to be wrong, because it was nearer eight when the retiring president, Chris Smith, entered the bar and made his way to the center of the room, a single sheet of paper in his hand. He waited for complete silence before he spoke.

"I would like to begin by explaining why we've taken so long to announce the result. Three recounts were required before the tellers were able to agree on the outcome. So I can now tell you that, by a majority of three votes, the next president of the Cambridge Union will be . . ."

19

ALEX

Vietnam, 1972

Alex read the letter a second time, before he showed it to his mother. Elena wept, because she knew exactly what her son would do.

"If only we'd gone to England, this would never have happened," she said, and couldn't help thinking they'd climbed into the wrong crate.

Many young men who were reading the same letter that morning would already be on the phone to their fathers' lawyers, or paying a visit to the family doctor, while others would simply tear up the draft, hoping the problem would go away. But not Alex.

Elena wasn't the only person who cried. Addie begged him to at least try and get a deferral, pointing out that as he was in his final year at NYU, they would surely allow him to complete his degree. Although she cried all night, Alex wasn't persuaded.

He still had one pressing problem that needed to be solved before he could pack his bags and leave home. His eleven stalls were now making a handsome profit, and he certainly didn't want to sell any of them. But who could run his burgeoning empire while he was away? To his surprise, it was his mother who came up with the solution.

"I'll give up my job at Mario's, and Dimitri and I will take them over until you come back."

No one raised the subject of what would happen if he didn't return.

Alex happily accepted their offer, and on February 11, 1972, he boarded a train for Fort Bragg, North Carolina, to begin an eight-week course of basic training, before being shipped out to Vietnam.

⊸o⊷

The lights went on. "Up, up, up!" shouted a staff sergeant at the top of his voice as he marched down the corridor between the sleeping recruits, his baton striking the end of every bunk. One by one the young men were rudely awakened, and, unaccustomed to the hour, blinked and rubbed their eyes, with one exception. By four in the morning, Alex would already have been on his way to the market.

"The Vietcong are charging toward you," yelled their instructor, "and they'll kill the last man who puts his feet on the ground!"

Alex was already heading toward the showers, towel in hand. He turned on a tap that offered no choice between cold and cold.

"Anyone who hasn't showered, shaved, and dressed in fifteen minutes, won't be fed before lunch." Suddenly bodies were racing toward the showers.

Alex was the first to be seated on one of the long wooden benches in the mess hall. He had quickly become aware how his mother had spoiled him over the years. It wasn't until the third morning, by which time he'd become so desperate, that he accepted a breakfast of lumpy porridge, greasy bacon, burned toast, and a hot black liquid the army called coffee.

When he was introduced to the parade ground, followed by the gym, route marches, and wading across a freezing river holding a rifle above his head, he quickly discovered he wasn't quite as fit as he'd imagined. However, he did manage to stay a yard or two ahead of most of his fellow recruits, who until then had considered Saturday evenings were for drinking and Sunday mornings for sleeping it off. The staff sergeant gently reminded them that the Vietcong didn't take the weekends off.

While Alex continued to hold his own in the gym, on the shooting range, and in the hills during night operations, he excelled in the classroom, where the education officer attempted to explain why America had become embroiled in a war in the Far East.

Alex became fascinated by the history of Vietnam, and how the north and south had been united since AD 939, but were now at each other's throats.

"But why are we sacrificing our soldiers' lives for a small country on the other side of the world?" asked Alex.

"Because if the communists in the north took control of the whole of Vietnam, who would fall next?" replied the education officer. "Laos?

Cambodia? And would the enemy even stop when they reached Australia? It's the domino effect. Allow one to topple, and others will follow."

"But Vietnam is still on the other side of the world," said Alex.

"You can't be sure of that," said the EO. "With Cuba in the hands of Fidel Castro, the communists are only a stone's throw from the US coast, and if they were to get their hands on anything other than bows and arrows, Florida could be next in line."

Alex didn't ask any more questions, as he was well aware of how the Red Army had occupied the whole of Eastern Europe while the Allies sat and watched.

Alex quickly made friends among his fellow recruits, some of whom were, like him, first-generation immigrants. He helped them write letters to their families and girlfriends, fill in forms, and even taught one of them how to tie his shoelaces. However, there was one—there's always one—who took against Alex from the first bugle call.

Big Sam, also known as the Tank, was 6 foot 4, and the scales didn't stop until they'd reached 226 pounds, most of it taut muscle. He certainly didn't consider Private Karpenko the unit's natural leader. Most of the other recruits avoided Big Sam, and even one or two of the staff sergeants were wary of him. Alex also kept his distance, but he couldn't avoid Big Sam when, during one gym session, the two of them were ordered into the boxing ring for a friendly bout. Big Sam didn't do friendly. All the other recruits crowded around to witness the inevitable slaughter.

"I am the greatest," Alex whispered without conviction as he climbed through the ropes, hoping the words of Cassius Clay would inspire him, and he might at least survive the three three-minute rounds.

For the first round, Alex danced nervously around the ring while his opponent threw punch after punch, none of them hitting the target. Alex somehow made it to the end of the second round, even hitting Big Sam a couple of times, not that he noticed. But Alex's legs were quickly turning to lead. This wasn't a slow waltz at a local dance hall with a young lady as your partner.

About halfway through the third round Sam managed to land a glancing blow on the side of Alex's head. Alex wobbled long enough for Sam to hit him a second time, on the chin, when he collapsed in a heap onto the canvas. A wiser man might have stayed put. But not Alex. He attempted to haul himself to his feet as the referee counted, "Five, six, seven . . ."

He was still only resting on one knee when the next punch landed squarely on his nose. All he could see in front of his eyes were stars and stripes, and far more than fifty. Big Sam would have been disqualified if it had been a championship bout but, as the staff sergeant pointed out, no one would have time to explain the Queensberry Rules to the Vietcong.

When he came around a few moments later, Alex was horrified to see Big Sam standing over him. He braced himself for the next blow, but Big Sam took off his glove and helped Alex to his feet; his new best friend.

In week two, they were introduced to the rifle range and stationary targets.

"Tomorrow the targets will move," said the staff sergeant. "And once you've got used to that, they'll shoot back."

During week three, day became night. No food, no sleep, and if you weren't dead, you wished you were. Week four was hand-to-hand combat, but only after they hadn't eaten or slept for fourteen hours. When they were finally allowed to collapse onto their bunks, they hadn't even fallen asleep before they were ordered back on their feet and told the Vietcong had just launched a counter-attack. "And don't forget, for them, it's a home game."

No one was surprised when in week five, Alex was made up to corporal and put in charge of a dozen of his fellow recruits. He immediately chose Big Sam as his second in command.

By the end of the sixth week, Alex's squad were regularly outperforming their rivals. Every one of them would have followed him over a cliff.

In the seventh week their platoon commander, Lieutenant Lowell, took Alex to one side after morning parade.

"Karpenko, have you considered applying for a transfer to officer training school? Because if you did, I'd be happy to support your application." He was disappointed by Alex's reply.

"I'm a street trader, sir. I have no desire to be an officer. I'll stay and fight with my unit, if that's all right with you."

Over the next few weeks Lieutenant Lowell made several attempts to get Karpenko to change his mind, but he always received the same uncompromising response.

On their final day at Fort Bragg, Alex's platoon received a commendation from the commanding officer. Big Sam accepted the award on their behalf.

"You're one of the finest units I've ever had under my command," said the general as he handed over the pennant.

"Show me the others," said Big Sam. The general burst out laughing.

On June 5, 1972, Lieutenant Lowell, Corporal Karpenko, and the enlisted men of the 116th Infantry Division climbed aboard a dozen trucks in the middle of the night before being shipped out of Fort Bragg and driven to an airport that didn't appear on any map. Fourteen hours later, after three brief stops when the plane was refueled and they weren't, the troops finally landed on a heavily guarded runway somewhere in South Vietnam. They were no longer recruits, but trained infantrymen ready for war.

Not all of them would return.

⊸o⊷

The 116th spent a couple of weeks settling into their makeshift barracks, and another fortnight preparing for their first assignment. By then, every one of them was more than ready. But ready for what?

"Our orders are clear," said Lieutenant Lowell at his morning briefing. "We've been assigned to patrol the area along Long Binh. The Vietcong occasionally stray close by in the hope of finding a weak spot in our defenses. If they're foolish enough to do so, it's our job to make sure they regret it, and send them packing."

"And will we get the chance to take the fight to them?" asked Alex.

"It's unlikely," said Lowell. "That's left to the professionals—the Marines and the US Army Rangers. Only in exceptional circumstances would we be called on to assist them."

"So we're no more than traffic cops," said the Tank.

"Something like that," admitted Lowell. "*They also serve who only stand and wait.*" Alex would have to look up the quote when he was next in a library, which might not be for a couple of years. "The good news," continued Lowell, "is that every six weeks you'll have a few days' R and R, when you can visit Saigon."

A small cheer went up.

"But you can't afford to relax even then. You'll have to assume that anyone who approaches you is a Vietcong agent. Be particularly wary of attractive young women, who'll offer you sex in the hope of extracting what you might consider a trivial piece of information."

"Couldn't we just have the sex and keep our mouths shut?" suggested a soldier.

Lowell waited for the laughter to die down. "No, Boyle," he said firmly. "Whenever you're tempted, just remember it might cause the death of one of your comrades."

"I'm not sure I can go six weeks without a woman," said Boyle. Although the rest of the unit burst out laughing, they clearly agreed with him.

"Don't worry, Boyle," said Lowell. "The army's made a provision for soldiers like you. We have our own designated brothel on the outskirts of the camp. It's run by a lady called Lilly, and all the girls have been carefully vetted. On the only occasion that Lilly discovered one of her girls was working for the Vietcong, she was found floating in the river the next morning. Every unit in the camp has been allocated one night a week on which its men can visit Lilly's establishment. Ours is Wednesday."

No one needed to make a note.

Alex found patrolling boring at best, and pointless at worst. It was five weeks before they spotted a Vietcong patrol. Lieutenant Lowell immediately gave the order to advance and fire at will, but they failed to hit anything other than the odd tree, and within seconds the enemy had melted back into the jungle.

When Alex described the incident in a long letter to his mother, he tried to reassure her that he was more likely to be killed crossing Brighton Beach Avenue than on patrol. This observation was redacted by the censors.

Alex received regular letters from his mother. Bernie had finally retired, and Elena confessed that since he'd left, they were just about breaking even. Alex didn't have to read between the lines to realize that neither his mother nor Dimitri was a natural trader. Elena told him they couldn't wait for him to get back, although Alex had to accept that it wouldn't be for some time. As the long weeks turned into longer months, he wondered if he shouldn't have taken Addie's advice and applied for a deferral. He would have completed his final year at NYU and, more importantly, asked Addie to be his wife. He even had the ring.

20

SASHA

London, 1972

"I would like to request your permission, sir, to ask for your daughter's hand in marriage."

"How gloriously old-fashioned," said Mr. Dangerfield. "But, Sasha, don't you think you're both a little young to be considering marriage? Shouldn't you wait a little longer before you make such an irrevocable decision?"

"Why wait, sir, when you've found the one woman you want to spend the rest of your life with?"

"I'd ask if you were confident my daughter feels the same way about you, if I didn't already know the answer." Sasha smiled, well aware that Charlie was sitting in the next room. "So, as your prospective father-in-law, I think I'm meant to ask about your prospects?"

"I've had three job offers for when I leave Cambridge, sir. My problem is that I can't make up my mind which one to choose."

"An embarrassment of riches," said Mr. Dangerfield.

"Without any guarantee of riches," admitted Sasha. "And what makes it worse, none of them is what I really want to do."

"Now you do have me intrigued."

"Trinity has offered me a prize fellowship, provided I get a first."

"Congratulations."

"Thank you, sir. But I don't think I'm cut out to be a don. I prefer the battlefield to the classroom."

"Any particular battlefield?"

"A mandarin from the Foreign Office has approached me and suggested I sit their entrance exam. But I'm not sure if they want me to be a diplomat or a spy."

"I didn't realize there was a distinction," said Dangerfield. "But I've no doubt you'd do both well. And the third job?"

"Mr. Agnelli, the owner of Elena's restaurant, where my mother is head chef, has asked me to join him. He has no children of his own, and has hinted that in time I could take over."

"Cambridge don, spymaster, or restaurateur. You couldn't have a more eclectic choice, although a restaurateur would be the closest to the battlefield, and probably the best paid."

"Not only would it be better paid, but I'm quite well qualified for the job. For the past five years I've worked in a restaurant during my holidays. I started out as a washer-up, moved on to laying tables, before having spells as a barman and a waiter. It sometimes felt as if I was taking two degrees at the same time."

"But you say that none of the three jobs is what you really want to do."

"No, sir. Like my father, I'm a politician at heart, and Cambridge has only made me more determined to become a Member of Parliament."

"And have you decided yet which party's colors you will be flying under?"

"No, I haven't, sir. The truth is, I've never cared for either extreme. I prefer the center ground, as I often find myself agreeing with the other person's point of view."

"But you'll eventually have to jump one way or the other if you're hoping to pursue a political career," suggested Dangerfield. "Unless of course you decide to join the Liberals."

"No, sir," laughed Sasha. "I don't believe in lost causes."

"Neither do I, and I've voted Liberal all my life."

Sasha turned bright red, and said, "I apologize, sir."

"No need, dear boy. I think you'll find my wife agrees with you."

"Before I make a complete fool of myself, sir . . ."

"Susan's a lifelong Conservative, although she sometimes has to hold her nose when she goes to the polls. So she's even worse than you. But didn't Charlie tell me that after you failed to become president of the Union, you promised her you would never stand again?"

"Never lasted for about a week, sir. Much to her dismay I'll be standing for president again next term."

"But being practical for a moment," said Dangerfield, "if you were to take up Mr. Agnelli's offer, where would you and Charlie live?"

"My mother has recently bought a large flat in Fulham, with more than enough room for the three of us."

"Enough for four, possibly five?" said Dangerfield, raising an eyebrow.

"Both of us feel we should be established in our careers before we think about starting a family. Once Charlie has her PhD, she hopes to find a job that will make it possible for us to earn enough for two, never mind three, or four. Only my mother disagrees with me."

"I look forward to meeting her. She sounds quite formidable. But tell me, how does she feel about her only son getting married at such a young age?"

"She adores Charlie, and doesn't approve of us living in sin."

"Ah, so that's where you've inherited those old-fashioned values."

⊸o⊷

"It would help if you knew which party you belonged to," said Ben. "Although I'm confident you can still win as an independent, it would make my life a lot easier if you joined either the Tories or the Labour Party. Preferably the Tories."

"That's the problem," said Sasha. "I still don't know which party I support. By nature I believe in free enterprise, and less state intervention, not more. But as an immigrant, I feel more at home with the philosophy of the Labour Party. The only thing I'm certain of is that I'm not a Liberal."

"Well, don't tell anyone that, until the last vote has been cast. As an independent, you'll need the support of voters from all three parties."

"Do you have *any* beliefs or convictions?" asked Sasha.

"One can't afford such luxuries until after you've won the election."

"Spoken like a true Tory," said Sasha.

⊸o⊷

"I'm glad we're spending the weekend with my parents," said Charlie, "because I know my father has something he wants to ask your advice about."

"What could I possibly advise him on? I know nothing about antiques, and he's considered a leader in the field."

"I'm just as interested to find out as you are. But I did warn him that you don't know the difference between Chippendale and Conran."

"I know which one I can afford," said Sasha.

"You should read more Oscar Wilde," said Charlie, "and less Maynard Keynes. By the way, will your mother be joining us? You know how my parents are looking forward to meeting her."

"She plans to come on Saturday morning. Which should give me enough time to warn them that she's already chosen the names of our first three children."

"Have you warned her that that might not be for some time?"

⊸o⊷

When Ted Heath sat down at the end of the debate, Sasha was no nearer to deciding which party he felt more in sympathy with. The Prime Minister's speech had been competent and workmanlike, but lacked passion, even though he was speaking on a subject he felt passionately about. Despite the recent success of his campaign to secure Britain's membership in the Common Market, some people were unable to stifle the occasional yawn, including one or two of his own supporters.

Michael Foot, who opposed the motion on behalf of the Labour Party, was in a different class altogether. His brilliant oratory mesmerized the undergraduates, although he clearly didn't have the same detailed knowledge of the subject as the proposer of the motion.

Sasha, like Heath, believed in a stronger Europe as a counterforce to the communist bloc, so he ignored Ben's advice and voted for the motion, not the man.

"I thought Heath was brilliant," said Ben as they left the building following the post-debate dinner.

"No, you didn't," said Sasha. "He may have known the subject backward, but Foot was by far the more persuasive of the two."

"But who would you rather have running the country?" demanded Ben. "A brilliant orator or a—"

"A grocer?" said Sasha. "The jury's still out, so I'll stand as an independent."

"Then we've got a busy weekend ahead of us."

"Doing what?"

"Delivering your manifesto to every college, putting up posters on all the noticeboards, and when no one's looking, removing your rivals'."

"You can forget that, Ben. As you well know, it's against Union rules to take down or deface your opponents' posters. If you were stupid enough to do that, I could be disqualified. And I wouldn't put it past Fiona to produce a photograph of you caught in the act, because nothing would give her greater pleasure than to see me fail a second time."

"Then we'll have to be satisfied with putting your posters on top of your opponents'."

"Ben, you're not listening, and what's worse, I won't be around to keep an eye on you."

"Why not?"

"Charlie and I are spending the weekend with her parents to celebrate our engagement, and my mother will be meeting them for the first time."

"Where's this historic meeting taking place?"

"Why do you ask?"

"Because I've only experienced your mother's cooking once, and I can't wait to be invited to sample it a second time."

"You won't have long to wait, because you're going to be best man at our wedding."

Sasha enjoyed the rare experience of his closest friend being lost for words.

⤙o⤚

"Call me Mike," said Mr. Dangerfield.

"That may take a bit of getting used to, sir," said Sasha, as his host closed the study door and ushered him to a seat by the fire.

"I'm glad to be able to have a moment alone with you, Sasha, because I need to seek your advice."

"I hope it's nothing to do with antiques, sir, because I've only recently learned how old a piece has to be before it can even be described as an antique."

"No, it doesn't concern an antique, but a client of mine who may be in possession of what we in the trade call a once-in-a-lifetime discovery." Sasha was intrigued, but said nothing. "I recently had a visit from a Russian countess, who offered to sell me a family heirloom that, if it's genuine, would set the antique world alight." Mr. Dangerfield rose from his chair, crossed the room, and bent down in front of a large safe. He turned the dial first one way, and then the other, before he pulled open its heavy door, reached inside, and extracted a red velvet box that he placed on the table between them. "Open it, Sasha. Because I can assure you, you won't need any knowledge of antiques to realize you're in the presence of genius."

Sasha tentatively flicked up the clasp and opened the box to reveal a large golden egg encrusted with diamonds and pearls. His mouth fell open, but no words followed.

"And that's only the wrapping," said Mr. Dangerfield. He leaned forward and split the egg open to reveal an exquisite jade palace, surrounded by a moat of blue diamonds.

"Wow," Sasha managed.

"I agree. But is it, as the countess claims, an original Fabergé, or a brilliant copy?"

"I have no idea," said Sasha.

"I didn't think you would. But after meeting her, you might be able to tell me if the countess is an original or a fake."

"The Anastasia problem," said Sasha.

"In one. I've already visited the British Museum, the V&A, and the Soviet Embassy, and there's no doubt that the original egg was owned by a Count Molenski. But is the countess really his daughter, or just an accomplished actress trying to palm me off with a copy?"

"I can't wait to meet her," said Sasha, unable to take his eyes off the egg.

"And even if she convinces you she's the real thing," said Dangerfield, "why would she have chosen me, a small trader from Guildford, when she could have gone to any number of leading specialists in the West End?"

"I presume you've already asked her that question, sir."

"I did, and she told me that the London dealers were not to be trusted, and she feared they'd form a cartel to act against her."

"I'm not sure I understand what she's suggesting," said Sasha.

"A cartel is when a small group of traders join together at an auction with the sole purpose of keeping the price of a valuable object down so one of them can purchase it for less than its real value. They then resell the piece for a handsome profit, and split the proceeds between them. It's sometimes referred to as a concert party."

"But surely that's against the law?"

"It most certainly is. But such cases rarely end up in the courts, because if there aren't any witnesses, it's almost impossible to prove."

"If this is the original," said Sasha, his eyes returning to the egg, "are you able to put a value on it?"

"The last Fabergé egg to come on the market was auctioned at Sotheby Parke Bernet in New York, and the hammer price was just over a million dollars. And that was a decade ago."

"And if it's a fake?"

"Then she'll be lucky to get more than a couple of thousand pounds for it, possibly three."

"When do I get to meet her?"

"She's joining us for tea tomorrow afternoon." Mr. Dangerfield looked at the egg once again. "If she's the real thing, the time may have come for me to do something quite out of character."

"And what might that be, sir?"

"Take a risk," said Mr. Dangerfield.

Ben spent his weekend pinning VOTE KARPENKO posters on all twenty-nine college noticeboards, and even on the occasional fence along the way, despite being aware that Sasha's opponents could legally tear down any fly postings.

As he moved from college to college, he grew more confident that Sasha was going to win, because whenever anyone stopped to chat, they either gave him a thumbs-up, or assured him that they would be supporting his candidate this time. No one raised the subject of Fiona's false accusations at the last election, and one or two admitted they now regretted not voting for Sasha the last time around. Just two of you would have been enough, Ben wanted to remind them.

He reluctantly had to admit, to everyone except Sasha, that Fiona had turned out to be a rather good Union president. Thanks to her father's connections in the House of Commons, the list of guest speakers had been impressive, and her firm chairing of the committee, coupled with some innovative ideas, had been acknowledged by friend and foe alike.

Although she and Sasha rarely spoke, Fiona had recently suggested to Ben that the three of them should have dinner, and let bygones be bygones.

"An olive branch?" suggested Ben.

"More like a fig leaf," said Sasha. "So you can tell her not until I'm sitting in the president's chair."

21

ALEX

Vietnam, 1972

"What do you plan to do when you get back home?" asked Lieutenant Lowell as he and Alex sat in a dugout and shared what passed as lunch.

"Complete my economics degree at NYU, and then build an empire to rival Rockefeller's."

"My godfather," said Lowell matter-of-factly. "I think you'd like him, and I know he'd like you."

"Do you work for the great man?" asked Alex.

"No, I'm chairman of a small bank in Boston that bears my family name. But to be honest, I'm chairman only in name. I prefer to concentrate on my first love, politics."

"Do you want to be president one day?" asked Alex.

"No, thanks," said Lowell. "I'm not as ambitious as you, corporal, and I'm well aware of my limitations. But when I get back to Boston I plan to run for Congress, and possibly one day for the Senate."

"Like your grandfather?" Lowell was taken by surprise and certainly wasn't prepared for Alex's next question. "Why didn't you try to defer? You must have all the right connections to make sure you didn't end up in this hellhole."

"True, but my other grandfather was a general, and he convinced me a spell in Vietnam wouldn't do my political career any harm, especially as most of my rivals will have made sure they avoided the draft. But you're right, every other member of my year at Harvard found some excuse not to be called up."

Alex dug the last bean out of the bottom of the can, and devoured it slowly, as if it was one of his mother's most delicious morsels.

"Well, I guess it's time to go in search of the enemy," said Lowell.

"Some hope," said Alex.

⸻

On Wednesday evenings, while the rest of the unit went off to Lilly's, Alex could be found in the canteen, his only companion a book. He had already exhausted Tolstoy, Dickens, and Dumas in their own languages, and had recently turned his attention to Hemingway, Bellow, and Cheever.

Addie wrote every week, and Alex hadn't realized just how much he would miss her. He would have proposed, but not in a letter. However, once he was back . . .

Big Sam kept pressing him to join the boys on the brothel bus, but Alex continued to resist, even showing the Tank a photo of Addie.

"You wouldn't have to tell her," said Sam, with a huge grin.

"But I would have to tell her," said Alex, as Presley crooned away on the canteen jukebox: *You were always on my mind.*

"I think you'd like Kim," said Big Sam, refusing to give up.

"I had no idea you liked Kipling," said Alex, returning his grin.

⸻

"Do you ever give any thought to the futility of war?" asked Alex.

"Not if I can help it," said Lowell. "It might weaken my resolve, which wouldn't help the men under my command if we ever had to face a real battle."

"But there must be young North Vietnamese soldiers sitting in dugouts nearby who, like us, just want to go home and be with their families. Doesn't history teach us anything?"

"Only that politicians should think a lot more carefully before they commit the next generation to war. How's your mother coping without you?" asked Lowell, wanting to change the subject.

"As well as can be expected," said Alex. "My eleven stalls are just about breaking even, but the truth is, she can't wait for me to come home. It's almost time to renew my licenses, and my mother will be no match for Mr. Wolfe."

"Who's he?"

"My landlord."

"Can't Dimitri deal with him? He sounds like a pretty tough guy."

"Frankly, he's way out of his depth. Dimitri's much happier when he's on the high seas."

"Well, you've only got a few more months before we'll be demobbed, which will please everyone except the Tank."

"Why? Doesn't he want to go home?"

"No, he's requested a transfer to the Marines, which I will happily support. He wants to stay in the military when his year is up. If he had your brain, he'd end up a general."

"If we had to go into battle," said Alex, "I'd rather have him by my side than any general."

⊸o⊷

The platoon were on a routine patrol when the order came through. They only had seventeen days to serve before they would be shipped back to the States, having completed their tour of duty.

Lieutenant Lowell asked HQ to repeat the order before he put down the field phone and gathered his men around him. "There's been a skirmish nearby. One of our patrols was ambushed, and we've been ordered to go and support them."

"At last," said the Tank. His comrades didn't look quite so convinced. Like Alex, they had been ticking off the days.

"Three Huey helicopters are already on their way to the combat area with orders to evacuate the wounded and transport the dead back to HQ." The word "dead" heightened Alex's awareness that the 116th was about to take part in its first serious mission.

The Tank was first on his feet, with Corporal Karpenko only a yard behind, while the rest of the platoon quickly formed a crocodile, with Private Baker bringing up the rear.

"No one speaks except me," said Lowell as they entered no-man's-land. "Even a cough could alert the enemy and put the whole unit in danger."

For an hour they edged slowly and cautiously through the undergrowth and into enemy territory. Lieutenant Lowell checked his compass against the grid reference on his map every few minutes. Suddenly, the sound of gunfire made the map redundant. They fell to the ground and crawled on their bellies toward the battlefield.

Alex looked up to see the first of the three Hueys circling above, searching the dense tropical forest for a patch of flat ground on which they could land.

On, on they crept. Never in his life had Alex felt so alert. Even so, he couldn't help wondering where he might be in an hour's time. At least he no longer felt he'd wasted a year of his life.

He suddenly spotted the enemy about a hundred yards ahead of him. They hadn't seen the approaching American platoon, because their attention was focused on the helicopter onto which the first of the wounded were being carried on stretchers by the medevac team, who were completely unaware that the Vietcong were hidden in the undergrowth only yards away from them.

Lowell raised his hand to indicate that the platoon should change direction, and circle the enemy. Each one of them knew that surprise was their best weapon. But as they edged closer and closer, Baker knelt on a fallen twig. It snapped, producing a noise that sounded like a firecracker. The soldier bringing up the rear of the Vietcong unit swung around and stared into Lowell's eyes.

"*Kẻ thù!*" he cried.

The lieutenant leaped to his feet and began firing his M16 as he charged toward the enemy, with the rest of his unit following closely behind. Almost half the Vietcong were killed before they could return fire, but the lieutenant was hit, and fell face down in the marshy swamp. Alex immediately took his place, with the Tank by his side.

The battle, if that's how you could describe it, only lasted for a few minutes, and the Vietcong unit had been wiped out by the time the first helicopter rose slowly into the air and headed back to base. The second was still hovering overhead, waiting to take its place.

Alex remembered his hours of training. First, make sure the enemy are no longer a threat. He and the Tank checked the sixteen bodies. Fifteen were dead, but one lay writhing in agony, blood pouring from his mouth and stomach, aware that death was only moments away. Alex remembered the second order; he raised his gun and pointed it directly at the young man's forehead, but although it might have been described in the handbook as a mercy killing, he couldn't pull the trigger.

The third order was to check your own men, and evacuate the wounded, followed by the dead, who must be returned to their homeland and buried with full honors, not left to rot on a foreign field. And then the final order. The officer in command and any non-commissioned officers must be the last to leave the battlefield.

Alex left the dying North Vietnamese soldier and rushed to Lowell's side. The lieutenant was unconscious. Alex checked his pulse, a faint beat. The Tank lifted him gently onto his shoulder and carried him through the undergrowth to the waiting helicopter, before coming back to assist the walking wounded to safety. When he returned to the scene of the battle, he found Alex kneeling over the bodies of Baker and Boyle. They were the last to be placed aboard the second helicopter before it rose into the air.

The rest of the unit struggled up the hill toward a small open space as the third helicopter came in to land. Alex waited until everyone was on board, before he turned around to make a final check of the battlefield.

That was when he saw him. Somehow the one surviving Vietcong had managed to haul himself onto his knees and was aiming his rifle directly at Alex.

The Tank leaped off the helicopter and ran down the hill toward him, firing at the same time. Alex could only watch as the lone Vietcong soldier was jolted backward, a full clip of bullets hitting him, but he still managed to pull the trigger once.

As if he was watching in slow motion, Alex saw the Tank fall to his knees and collapse on the ground next to the dead Vietcong soldier. Moments later Alex was bending over his friend. "No!" he screamed. "No, no, no!"

It took four men to carry the lifeless body back up the hill and place it inside the third helicopter. Alex was the last to climb on board and felt ashamed that he had allowed his closest friend to die.

22

SASHA

London

When the elderly lady entered the drawing room, few would have doubted that Countess Molenski was a genuine aristocrat. Her long black pencil skirt and high-necked jacket were of another age, but it was her bearing and demeanor that could not have been taught, even at drama school. She was simply old-school, and both Sasha and Mike rose automatically when she entered the room. As did Elena.

Mr. Dangerfield had choreographed the meeting so that nothing would be left to chance. The countess was guided to the only empty place, on the couch next to Sasha, while Elena and the rest of the family were seated on the other side of a table on which the egg was displayed. Once Mrs. Dangerfield had poured the countess a cup of tea, and offered her a slice of Madeira cake, which she declined, Sasha opened by asking her in her native tongue, "How long have you been living in England, countess?"

"More years than I care to remember," she replied. "But it's always a joy to come across a fellow countryman. May I ask where you are from?"

"Leningrad. And you?"

"I was born in Saint Petersburg," replied the countess, "which rather shows my age."

"Did you live in one of those magnificent palaces on the hill?"

"There are no hills in Leningrad, Mr. Karpenko, as you well know."

"How silly of me," said Sasha. "I apologize."

"No need. But as you've clearly been sent on a fishing expedition, are there any more hoops you'd like me to jump through?"

Sasha was so embarrassed he couldn't think of a reply.

"Shall I begin by telling you about my dear father, Count Molenski?

He was a close personal friend of the late Tsar Nicholas the Second. Not only did they share private tutors in their youth, but several mistresses in later years."

Once again, Sasha was silenced.

"But what I'm sure you really want to know," continued the countess, "is how I came into possession of the masterpiece you see before you, and even more important, how I am certain it was fashioned by the hand of Carl Fabergé, and not an impostor."

"You're right, countess, I would be fascinated to know."

"There is no need for you to address me quite so formally, Mr. Karpenko. I long ago accepted that those days are over, and that I must now live in the real world, and like anyone else who finds herself in impoverished circumstances, recognize that I have no choice but to part with some of my family heirlooms if I hope to survive." Sasha bowed his head. "My father's private art collection was acknowledged as second only to the tsar's, although Papa only owned one Fabergé egg, as it would have been considered disrespectful to attempt to outdo the tsar."

"But how can you be sure that this particular egg was executed by Fabergé himself, and is not, as I believe several experts claim, a fake?"

"Several experts with a motive," said the countess. "The truth is, I can't prove it, but I can tell you that the first time I saw the egg was when I was twelve years old. Indeed, it was my youthful clumsiness that was responsible for a tiny scratch on the base, which is almost invisible to the naked eye."

"Assuming that it is the original," said Sasha, looking at the egg, "I'm bound to ask why you offered the piece to Mr. Dangerfield, whose expertise couldn't be more English—Sheraton, Hepplewhite, and Chippendale are his daily fare, not Fabergé."

"Reputation is not easily acquired, Mr. Karpenko, but has to be earned over many years, and honesty can no longer be taken for granted, which is why I allowed the egg out of my possession for the first time in twenty years. Had I entrusted it to one of our countrymen, they would have only needed a few days to replace my masterpiece with a fake. I have become aware that such a thought would never cross Mr. Dangerfield's mind. So it is his advice that I shall be taking."

Sasha folded his arms, the agreed sign that his mother should take his place, and continue the conversation in Russian. He stood up, gave the countess a slight bow, and walked across the room to sit between Charlie and her father.

"Well?" said Mr. Dangerfield, once the countess was deep in conversation with Elena. "What do you think?"

"I have no doubt that she's exactly who she claims she is," were Sasha's opening words.

"How can you be so sure?" said Mr. Dangerfield, whose tea had long since gone cold.

"She speaks a form of Russian court language that is frankly from another age, and that you rarely come across today outside the pages of Pasternak."

"And the egg, is that also out of the pages of Pasternak?"

⊰o⊱

Sasha seemed to be the only person who was surprised when he was elected—by a landslide—as the next president of the Union.

Fiona clearly didn't enjoy having to read out the result to a packed audience. Ben finally made treasurer, and he and Sasha spent their Christmas holiday planning the next term's debates. They were delighted when the Education Secretary, Mrs. Thatcher, agreed to speak in defense of the government's policies for the opening debate, because there were several leading politicians who were only too happy to oppose the "milk snatcher."

Full terms at Cambridge are eight weeks long, and although Sasha attempted to survive on as little sleep as possible, he still couldn't believe how quickly his fifty-six days in office as president passed. No sooner had he stepped down from the high chair, than his supervisor reminded him that finals were fast approaching.

"And if you're still hoping for a first," Dr. Streator reminded him, "I suggest you now devote the same amount of energy to your studies as you did to becoming president of the Union."

Sasha heeded Dr. Streator's advice, and continued to survive on six hours' sleep a night while he spent every waking hour revising, studying past examination papers, translating long passages of Tolstoy, and rereading his old essays right up until the moment he climbed the steps of the examination hall to sit his first paper.

Charlie and Ben joined him for a quick supper every evening to discuss their own efforts, and what they thought might come up the following day. Sasha would then return to his room and continue revising, often falling asleep at his desk, and feeling less and less confident as each day passed.

"The harder I work," he told Ben, "the more I realize how little I know."

"That's why I don't work at all," said Ben.

When Sasha handed in his final paper to the examiners on Friday afternoon, the three of them opened a bottle of champagne and celebrated long into the small hours. Sasha ended up in bed with Charlie, although it had proved quite an effort to climb up the fire escape, and he fell asleep even before she'd turned out the light.

There then followed that agonizing period when undergraduates have to wait for the examiners to decide which class of degree they consider them worthy of. A fortnight later, the three of them trooped across to the Senate House to learn their fate.

As 10 a.m. struck, the senior proctor, in his long black gown and mortarboard, walked sedately along the corridor, bearing the results in his hand. A hush descended on the undergraduates, who parted to allow him to pass, as if he were Moses approaching the Red Sea.

With considerable ceremony, he pinned several sheets of paper to the noticeboard, before turning and progressing as slowly as before in the opposite direction, only just avoiding being trampled in the stampede that followed.

Sasha protected Charlie as they made their way toward the front. Ben didn't move, remaining at the back of the scrum, not at all sure he wanted to know the examiners' opinion of his efforts.

Long before Sasha had reached the front, several new graduands who passed him on their way back doffed their mortarboards, while a few even applauded. A starred first was rare enough in any subject, and only one name appeared at the head of the list for the Modern and Medieval Languages tripos.

Charlie threw her arms around Sasha, having checked his result before looking for hers. "I'm so proud of you," she said.

"And what did you get?" he asked.

"An upper second, which is about as much as I could have hoped for. It means I'll still have a chance of being offered a research post at the Courtauld."

They looked around to see that Ben still hadn't moved. Charlie turned back and ran a finger down the Land Economy list. It was some time before she reached the name Cohen.

"Will you tell him," she said, "or shall I?"

Sasha marched up to his friend, shook him firmly by the hand, and said, "You got a third." He didn't add that the name of Cohen, B. S., appeared near the foot of the table.

Ben let out a sigh of relief. "Should anyone ever ask," he said, clutching the lapels of his jacket, "I shall tell them I graduated with honors, and will be joining my father at Cohen and Son."

Their laughter was interrupted by raucous cheers coming from a small group on the other side of the hall, who were throwing their mortarboards in the air and toasting their heroine with champagne.

"Fiona obviously got a first," said Ben. "I have a feeling you two will continue to be rivals long after you've left Cambridge."

"Especially as I've decided to join the Labour Party," said Sasha.

23

ALEX

Brooklyn

Alex looked out of the cabin window as the plane began its slow descent over Manhattan. A break in the clouds allowed him a fleeting glance at the Statue of Liberty, and as they'd never been properly introduced, he gave her a mock salute.

When he'd first sailed up the Hudson, he'd been unable to pay his compliments to the lady as he and his mother had been locked in the ship's galley. But thanks to a resourceful Chinese man and the courage and determination of Dimitri, they had escaped and been able to begin a new life in America.

Staff Sergeant Karpenko had sat at the back of the plane and spent most of the flight home thinking about what he would do once he was back on American soil. If only to please his mother, he would complete his studies at NYU. She had made so many sacrifices to make sure he graduated. Although in truth, he knew that the path he wanted to tread was not one that required any letters after his name, not that he would ever be able to explain that to his mother.

He would have to devote every spare moment to his eleven stalls, and make sure they were quickly back up to scratch, and then find out if any more were available. When he had left for Vietnam they had been making a handsome profit, and expansion had been uppermost in his mind. Perhaps one day he would buy out Mr. Wolfe and own the whole of Market Square.

And then there was Addie. Had she missed him as much as he'd missed her?

Troop plane after troop plane landed on a runway that even New Yorkers didn't know existed.

The 116th Infantry Division, together with a thousand of their comrades, disembarked and assembled on the tarmac for their final parade. Along with many of his comrades, when he stepped onto the runway Alex fell to his knees and kissed the ground, relieved to be back home.

It was the first time he'd thought of America as home.

They all waited to be dismissed so they could return to their homes across the United States, civilians once again. But there was to be a surprise that morning that Alex hadn't anticipated.

When Colonel Haskins had finished his speech of welcome, he called out one name. Staff Sergeant Karpenko marched up, came to a halt in front of his commanding officer, and saluted.

"Congratulations, sergeant," said the colonel, as he pinned the Silver Star on his uniform.

Before Alex could ask what for, the colonel announced to the assembled gathering that at the height of the battle of Bacon Hill, Staff Sergeant Karpenko had taken the place of his unit commander after he had fallen, led an attack that wiped out an enemy patrol, and been responsible for saving the lives of several of his comrades.

And caused the death of my closest friend, was Alex's only thought as he marched back to join his unit.

He had wanted to protest that the award should have been given posthumously to the Tank, who had made the ultimate sacrifice. Alex would visit Arlington National Cemetery in Virginia, and lay a wreath on the grave of his friend, Private First Class Samuel T. Burrows.

Once the parade had been dismissed, Alex was surrounded by his comrades, who congratulated him, while they all celebrated friendships forged by war. He wondered if he would ever see any of them again, after they'd disappeared in fifty different directions.

As the men broke up, they went in search of their families and friends who had been waiting patiently behind a barrier at the far end of the airfield. Alex hoped Addie would be among them. Her letters hadn't been quite as frequent recently, but Alex had no doubt that along with his mother they would both be among those waving and cheering. His mother had dutifully written to him every week, and although Elena never once complained, it was clear that she and Dimitri were not enjoying their roles as temporary entrepreneurs. Now Elena could return to what she did best, and Dimitri could sign on for the next ship bound for Leningrad.

Alex joined an excited group of exuberant young men as the impatient crowd broke ranks and began running toward them.

He searched the vast crowd for Addie and his mother. But with so many people jumping up and down, waving flags, and pointing, it was some time before he spotted Elena making her way through the dense mob, Dimitri a pace behind, but no sign of Addie.

Elena threw her arms around her son and clung on to him, as if wanting to make sure he was real. When she finally released him, he shook hands with Dimitri, who couldn't take his eyes off the Silver Star.

"Welcome home," he said. "We're all so proud of you."

There were so many questions Alex wanted to ask, and so many things he needed to tell them, that he didn't know where to begin. As they walked away from the crowded runway, it was hard to hear anything above the joyful, exuberant noise that was coming from every direction.

It wasn't until they had settled into the back of a bus bound for Brooklyn that Alex noticed that all the joy had disappeared from his mother's face, and Dimitri's head was bowed, like an errant schoolboy who'd been found playing truant.

"It can't be that bad," said Alex, in an attempt to cheer them up.

"Worse," said Elena, "far worse than you can possibly imagine. While you've been away fighting for your country, we've lost almost everything you'd managed to build."

Alex took her hand. "It can't be worse than seeing your closest friend killed in front of you. So tell me, what should I expect when I get home?"

Elena offered a weak smile. "We only have one stall left, and it's barely making a profit."

"How can that be possible?" said Alex. He knew from her letters that Elena and Dimitri had been experiencing difficult times, but he hadn't realized things were quite that bad.

"I'm to blame," said Dimitri. "I wasn't always around when your mother most needed me."

"Yes he was," said Elena. "I wouldn't have survived without his wages while you were away."

"But surely that was enough to get by until . . ."

"Not nearly enough for Mr. Wolfe."

"So what's the old crook been up to in my absence?"

"Whenever one of your licenses expired, he doubled the rent," said Elena. "We simply couldn't afford to pay what he was demanding, so we ended up losing all but one of the stalls. The final license comes up for renewal in a couple of months, and recently he's been tripling the price for a new one."

"It's been the same for everyone," said Dimitri. "When you get home, you'll see that the market has become a ghost town."

"But that doesn't make any sense," said Alex. "Those stalls are Wolfe's main source of income, so why . . ." but he didn't finish the sentence.

"What makes it even more strange," said Elena, "is that he's agreed to extend the license on Mario's pizza house with a reasonable rent increase."

"That's the first clue," said Alex.

"I don't understand," said Elena.

"Mario's isn't in Market Square."

⊸o⊷

Once Alex had discarded his uniform, taken a bath, and put on his only suit, he left the house and headed straight for the Goodwill store. Addie couldn't hide her excitement when he walked in, although she was shocked by his crew cut.

"Your news first or mine?" said Alex, as he threw his arms around her.

"Mine. Your mother has kept me well informed of what you've been up to. I'm just relieved you made it back alive."

"I shouldn't have," said Alex without explanation.

"Come with me," she said, taking his hand. "I have a surprise for you." She led him through to the storeroom at the back of the shop. Alex wasn't sure what to say when his eyes fell on a rack of suits, jackets, and a blazer as well as a smart black topcoat. "I've already had the trousers altered, so they should fit perfectly. Mind you," she added, taking a closer look at him, "you've lost some weight."

"How can I begin to thank you?" he said. He hoped he also had a surprise for her, although it would have to wait until his mother agreed.

"That's only the beginning," said Addie, as she pointed to a shelf behind the clothes rack, piled high with a dozen shirts that hadn't been taken out of their boxes, a dark green cashmere sweater, three pairs of leather shoes, and half a dozen ties that looked as if they'd never been worn.

"What more could a man ask for?" said Alex.

"Wait, it's not over yet," said Addie, picking up a brand-new leather attaché case. "Just what an up-and-coming businessman needs when attending important meetings."

"Where's all this come from?"

"Everything came from the same source, a man who, frankly, has more than enough."

"How much do I owe you?"

"Not a penny. It's no more than a conquering hero deserves. We're all so proud of you being awarded the Silver Star."

"Well, the least I can do is take you to dinner tonight," said Alex, leaning down to kiss her. But just as their lips were about to touch, Addie turned away, and he ended up brushing her cheek.

"I'm afraid I'm not free tonight," she said.

"Tomorrow night then?"

"Tonight or any other night." She began to fold up the clothes and pack them into bags.

"Why not?"

"Because I'm going to marry the man who has too many suits," said Addie, holding up her left hand.

◄o►

Alex was coming out of a lecture at NYU when he saw them standing in the corridor, conspicuously failing to blend in. They would have been hard to miss, dressed in their dark, well-cut suits and polished shoes among a group of students wearing faded jeans, scruffy T-shirts, and well-worn sneakers.

Alex recognized one of them straightaway. Not a man he could easily forget.

"Good morning, Mr. Karpenko," said Agent Hammond. "You'll remember my partner, Agent Travis. Could we have a word with you in private?"

"Do I have a choice?"

"Yes, of course," said Hammond.

Alex placed his hands behind his back and whispered, "Arrest me. Handcuff me, and read me my rights."

"What are you talking about?" said Travis.

"It will at least give me some credibility with this lot," dissed Alex, as several students stopped to stare at them.

"If you're not going to cooperate, Karpenko, you'll have to come with us," said Travis at the top of his voice. He then grabbed Alex by the arm and marched him down the corridor to accompanying jeers and cheers. They stopped at a door with the word DEAN stenciled in black on its pebbled-glass window. Travis opened the door and pushed Alex inside.

There was no sign of the dean or his secretary. The CIA did seem to have a gift for making people disappear, thought Alex. Travis released him the moment the door had closed behind them, and they sat down at a small square table in the center of the room.

"Thank you," Alex said. "Now at least one or two of them might still talk to me."

"What's their problem?" asked Hammond.

"If you've served in Vietnam, don't take drugs, never get drunk, and actually hope to come out of this place with a degree, not many of them want to know you. So what can I do for you gentlemen?"

"First," said Hammond, extracting the inevitable files from his briefcase, "we'd like to bring you up to date on what happened to your former chess partner, Ivan Donokov, while you were away in Vietnam."

At the mention of Donokov's name, Alex felt sick, and tried to stop himself trembling.

"Thanks to you, we were able to arrest him, along with several of his associates. They're now all safely behind bars."

"For how long?"

"Ninety-nine years, in Donokov's case," said Travis, "without parole."

"Let's hope his cell mate's a Grand Master, otherwise he's going to get very bored," said Alex. The three men laughed for the first time. "That can't be the only reason you wanted to see me."

"No, it isn't," said Hammond. "We felt we owe you one. We know you're now down to your last market stall, and its license comes up for renewal next month. We also know that the landlord, Mr. Wolfe, will try to extract a price you can't afford."

"But more important," said Alex, "do you know why?"

"Yes," said Hammond. "Our colleagues in the FBI have a cabinet full of files dedicated to Mr. Wolfe, but they've never been able to lay a finger on him. However, they've passed on some information that might be of interest to you." He nodded toward his colleague, who proceeded to explain exactly why Wolfe needed to be in possession of the licenses for every stall in Market Square by midday on June 17. "And yours is now the only one left."

"Thank you," said Alex. "Although I should have worked it out for myself."

"And, by the way," said Travis, "there's something else you've probably worked out by now."

"Dimitri is one of the good guys," said Alex.

Alex put on one of the suits Addie had given him, along with a white shirt and a blue silk tie he would never have been able to afford. He opened the attaché case and checked that everything was in place, before glancing at his watch. This was one meeting he wasn't going to be late for.

He couldn't resist whistling as he walked slowly along Brighton Beach Avenue. He reached 3049 Ocean Parkway a few minutes before nine, opened the door, and walked into the reception area to be greeted by Molly, the long-suffering receptionist, known among the market traders as the devil's gatekeeper.

"Have a seat, Mr. Karpenko. I'll let Mr. Wolfe know you've arrived."

"Don't bother," said Alex, not breaking his stride or stopping to knock before he marched into Wolfe's office.

Wolfe looked up from his desk. He didn't attempt to hide his annoyance at being taken by surprise. "I'll have to call you back," he said, slamming down the phone. "Good morning, Mr. Karpenko," he said, pointing to the seat opposite him. Alex remained standing. Wolfe shrugged. "I've drawn up the new license for your stall."

"How much?"

"A thousand dollars a week for the next three years," said Wolfe matter-of-factly. "And of course, I'll expect a month's payment in advance. Should you fail at any time to pay the full amount, the license will automatically revert to me." He smiled, confident that he knew exactly what Alex's response would be.

"That's grand larceny," said Alex. "I don't need to remind you of the clause in our contract that says any rise in rent must reflect current market conditions."

"I'm glad you mentioned that particular clause," said Wolfe, allowing himself a wry smile, "because another stallholder recently took me to court claiming I was overcharging and cited that clause as proof. I'm happy to say the judge came down in my favor. So precedent has been set, Mr. Karpenko."

"How much did that cost you?"

Wolfe ignored the comment as he pushed a familiar document across the table and, pointing to a dotted line, said, "Sign there, and the stall will be yours for another three years."

Once again he looked as if he knew what Alex's response would be. But to his surprise Alex sat down and began to read slowly through the contract clause by clause. Wolfe leaned back, selected a cigar from the box in front of him, lit it, and had taken several puffs before Alex picked up the pen on his desk and signed the agreement.

The cigar fell out of Wolfe's mouth and landed on the floor. He quickly picked it up and brushed some ash off his trousers before saying, "Don't forget that will be four thousand dollars in advance."

"How could I forget," said Alex. He opened his attaché case and extracted forty hundred-dollar bills. Every cent he, his mother, and Dimitri possessed. He placed the cash on the blotting pad in front of Mr. Wolfe, then put the contract in his attaché case, stood up, and turned to leave. He was just about to open the door when Wolfe spluttered, "Don't be in such a rush, Alex. Let's talk this over like reasonable people."

"There's nothing to talk over, Mr. Wolfe," said Alex. "I'm looking forward to operating my stall for the next three years, and whatever the rent is when this license expires, I'll pay it." He touched the door handle.

"I'm sure we can come to an arrangement, Alex. What if I were to offer you fifty thousand dollars to tear up the contract? That's far more than you could hope to make even if you were running a dozen stalls."

"But nowhere near as much as the million dollars a year rent you'd be raking in if I were to tear the contract up." Alex opened the door.

"How did you find out?" said Wolfe, glaring at his back.

"It's not important how I learned that the council will be granting you planning permission for a new shopping mall on June the seventeenth, only that I did. In the nick of time, I might add."

"How much do you want?"

"I won't settle for anything less than a million," said Alex. "Otherwise the bulldozers won't be making their way onto your site for at least another three years."

"Half a million," said Wolfe.

"Seven hundred and fifty thousand."

"Six hundred."

"Seven hundred."

"Six fifty," blurted Wolfe.

"Agreed."

Wolfe managed a half smile, feeling he'd still got the better of the bargain.

"But only if you throw in the freehold for Mario's Pizza Parlor on the corner of Players' Square," added Alex.

"But that's daylight robbery," Wolfe protested.

"I agree," said Alex. He sat down, opened his attaché case, and took out two contracts. "If you sign here, and here," he said, pointing to a dotted line, "the builders can start work on the super-mall next month. If not . . ."

24

ALEX

Brooklyn

"Do you think I'm capable of that?" said Elena.

"Of course you are, Mama. Your problem is that you've spent your whole life underestimating yourself."

"That's certainly never been one of your problems."

"Frankly, you're too good to be working in a pizza parlor," said Alex, ignoring her reprimand. "But with my help we could build the brand, turn it around, sell it on, and then set you up in your own restaurant."

"Great restaurants aren't run by chefs, Alex, but by first-class managers, so before you risk one cent of your money on me, you must find an experienced manager."

"Good managers are two a penny, Mama. Great chefs are a far rarer commodity."

"What makes you think I'm a great chef?"

"When you first got the job at Mario's, I could always get a table, at any time of day. Now there are queues outside from eleven o'clock in the morning. And I can assure you, Mama, they are not queuing to meet the manager."

"But it would be such a risk," said Elena. "Perhaps you'd be wiser to put your money on deposit in a bank."

"If I did that, Mama, the only one making a profit would be the bank. No, I think I'll risk a little of my newfound wealth on you."

"But not before you find a manager."

"Actually, I've already got someone in mind."

"Who?" demanded Elena.

"Me."

⊸o⊷

Elena stared at the gold-embossed invitation card that Alex had put on the mantelpiece for all to see.

"Who's Lawrence Lowell?" she asked as he sat down for breakfast.

"You remember Lieutenant Lowell. He was the officer in command of my unit in Vietnam. Frankly I'm surprised he even remembered my name, let alone found out where I lived."

"Aren't we coming up in the world?" Elena teased, as she poured him a cup of coffee. "I don't suppose there'll be that many pizza parlor managers among his guests. Will you accept?"

"Of course I will. I'm the manager of Elena's, the most exclusive pizza house in New York."

"Exclusive in this case means there's only one."

Alex laughed. "Not for much longer. I've already got my eye on a second site a few blocks away."

"But we're not making a profit at the first one yet," Elena reminded him as she put two eggs on to boil.

"We're breaking even, so it's time to expand."

"But—"

"But," said Alex, "my only problem is what to buy a man who has everything for his thirtieth birthday—a Rolls-Royce, a private jet?"

"A pair of cuff links," said Elena. "Your father always wanted a pair of cuff links."

"I have a feeling Lieutenant Lowell just might have several pairs of cuff links."

"Then make them personal."

"What do you mean?"

"Have a pair made with his family crest, or his club's emblem, or even your old regiment."

"Good idea, Mama. I'll have a pair engraved with a donkey."

"Why a donkey?" asked Elena, as the egg timer buzzed to indicate four minutes.

⊸o⊷

"Are you sure?" said Alex as he looked at himself in the full-length mirror.

"Couldn't be more sure," said Addie. "It's all the rage. By this time next year, everyone will be wearing wide lapels and bell bottoms. You'll be the toast of Broadway."

"It's not Broadway I'm worried about, but Boston, where I suspect it still won't be the fashion even the year after next."

"In which case you'll be a trend setter, and all the other guests will envy you."

Alex wasn't convinced, but he still bought the suit, and a frilly sky-blue shirt that Addie insisted went with it.

⊰o⊱

The following morning Alex rose early, but instead of heading straight for the market to select the day's toppings, he went to Penn Station, where he bought a return ticket to Boston. Once he'd found a seat on the train, he placed his small suitcase in the overhead rack and settled down to read *The New York Times*. The stark headline shouted: NIXON RESIGNS.

By the time the train pulled into South station four hours later, Alex was wondering if President Ford would pardon the former president. He grabbed a cab and asked the driver to take him to a sensibly priced hotel. Despite his newfound wealth, Alex still considered it a waste of money to pay for a suite when you could sleep just as well in a single room.

Once he'd checked into the Langham, he took a shower before trying on the two suits he'd brought with him. In one, he felt like Jack Kennedy; in the other, he looked like Elvis Presley. But on the cover of *Vogue* on his bedside table was a photo of Joan Kennedy wearing a sky-blue ballgown, which *Vogue* was predicting would be this year's color. Alex changed his mind yet again. One last check of the time on the invitation, 7:30 for 8:00 p.m. He left the hotel just after seven, hailed a cab, and told the driver the address.

After driving around the Common, Alex noticed that as they climbed higher toward Beacon Hill, the houses became grander. They came to a halt at the entrance of a magnificent town house, where he was met by two security guards, who gave him a long hard look before demanding to see his invitation.

"Maybe he's part of the cabaret," one of them said, loud enough for Alex to hear as the cab turned into the long driveway and continued on its journey up to the front of the house.

Alex knew he'd made a mistake the moment he stepped into the oak-paneled hall and joined a long queue of guests waiting to be greeted by their host. He wanted to turn around, go back to his hotel, and change into the more conservative suit, but then he would have been late. He wasn't sure which would cause more offense. He couldn't help noticing that several of the guests were turning to take a second look at him.

"It's wonderful to see you again, Alex," said Lowell, when he finally reached the front of the queue. "I'm so glad you could make it."

"It was kind of you to invite me, sir."

"Lawrence, Lawrence," his host whispered, before turning to greet his next guest. "Good evening, senator."

Alex made his way through to a large drawing room packed with guests, almost all of the men wearing dinner jackets. He grabbed a glass of champagne from a passing waiter before disappearing behind a large marble pillar in one corner of the room, from where he stared at a painting by someone called Pollock. He didn't move or attempt to speak to anyone, until a gong sounded, when he made sure he was among the last to enter the dining room. He was surprised to find he'd been placed on the top table, between an Evelyn on his left and a Todd on his right.

Alex quickly sat down, relieved that at least no one could now see his bell-bottom trousers.

"How do you know Lawrence?" asked the young woman on his left, after grace had been delivered by the Cardinal Archbishop of Boston.

Alex found himself stuttering for the first time in his life. "I served . . . I served under Lieutenant Lowell in Vietnam."

"Ah yes, Lawrence mentioned that he'd invited you, but he wasn't sure if you'd come."

Alex was already wishing he hadn't.

"And what do you do now, Alex?"

"I own a string of pizza parlors," he blurted out, immediately regretting his words.

"I've never eaten a pizza," she said, which Alex didn't find hard to believe. After a long silence, he asked, "And how do you know Lieutenant Lowell?"

"He's my brother." Another long silence followed before Evelyn turned to the person on her left and began telling him when she would be returning to her villa in the south of France.

When the first course was served, Alex was uncertain which knife and fork to pick up from the large array in front of him. He followed Evelyn's lead, before turning to the man on his right, who said, "Hi, Todd Halliday," and shook him by the hand.

"How do you know Lawrence?" asked Alex, hoping he wasn't his brother.

"We were at Choate together," said Todd.

"And are you also in banking?" asked Alex, as he had no idea who or what Choate was.

"No. I manage a small investment company that specializes in start-ups. And you?"

"I own a couple of pizza parlors, and have my eye on a third site. We're not Pizza Hut yet, but it can only be a matter of time."

"Are you looking for any capital?"

"No," said Alex. "I've just sold my old company for over a million, so I won't be needing any outside finance."

"But if you're hoping to rival Pizza Hut, the right partner could speed the whole process up, and if you were interested . . ."

Todd wasn't able to complete his sentence as he was interrupted by a familiar figure whom Alex immediately recognized, who rose from his place to propose Lawrence's health. Alex admired the relaxed way the senior senator from Massachusetts addressed the gathering, without once referring to a note, but he couldn't take his eyes off the woman seated next to the senator, whom he'd just seen on the cover of a glossy magazine in his hotel. He only wished he looked half as good in sky blue.

When the senator sat down to warm applause, Lawrence rose to reply. "I'm delighted," he began, "that so many of my family and friends have been able to join me this evening to celebrate my thirtieth birthday. I'm particularly honored that Teddy was able to break away from his busy schedule to propose my health. I hope that one day, and in the not too distant future, he'll consider running as the Democratic candidate for president."

Several of the guests joined in the applause, which allowed Lawrence the chance to turn to the next page of his speech.

"I am equally delighted to welcome to my home the man who made tonight possible, because if he hadn't saved my life, one thing is for sure, this party would not be taking place. As you all know, when I was serving in Vietnam, I was wounded and could have been left for dead, but fortunately my second in command didn't hesitate to take my place, and because of his leadership and courage, not only was an entire Vietcong unit wiped out, but he didn't leave the battlefield until every American soldier had been rescued. As a result of his actions that day, Staff Sergeant Alex Karpenko was not only awarded the Silver Star, but made it possible for me to deliver this speech tonight."

Lawrence turned to Alex as he raised his glass, and everyone in the room stood and joined in the applause, although Alex's immediate thought was of the Tank, and the fact that he still hadn't visited his grave in Virginia.

There was an even louder cheer when Lawrence announced that he would be running for Congress as a Democratic candidate at the next election. When he finally sat down, the assembled guests broke into a raucous, out-of-tune rendition of "Happy Birthday, dear Lawrence . . ."

Once the laughter and applause had finally died down, Todd turned to Alex and continued where he'd left off. "If you do decide to expand, keep in touch. Yours is just the sort of company I like backing." He took a business card out of his wallet and handed it to Alex, who was about to ask what sum he had in mind, when he was distracted by a hand resting on his thigh.

"Do tell me more about your little empire, Alex," said Evelyn, leaving her hand in place.

For a second time he found himself struggling for words as he stared into her green eyes.

"I've just sold it."

"I do hope you got a good price."

"Just over a million," he said, enjoying the attention.

"Are you going to introduce me, Evelyn?" said a voice from behind him.

Alex leaped to his feet when he saw the senator standing by his chair. Evelyn introduced them, and Teddy Kennedy immediately put him at ease as they chatted about Vietnam.

"You know, Alex," Kennedy whispered, "if you could spare a little time to help Lawrence during his campaign, it might make all the difference, and I know he'd appreciate it."

It had never crossed Alex's mind that he could actually help Lawrence do anything. "I'd be only too happy to do whatever I can, senator," he heard himself saying.

"That's good of you, Alex. Let's keep in touch."

Kennedy's words gave Alex a little more confidence, and made him more determined to press Todd on how much he might consider investing in Elena's, and what he would expect in return. But when he looked around, he saw Todd standing behind him, deep in conversation with Evelyn. Alex felt he couldn't interrupt them.

When he sat back down he was surprised to find a queue of guests had formed, all of them wanting to speak to him and shake his hand. He answered every one of their questions, not least because it ensured he wouldn't have to venture onto the dance floor and make a complete fool of himself. When he noticed the first guests departing just before midnight, Alex decided that after he'd had a word with Todd, he'd also slip away, but first he asked a passing waiter where the restroom was.

"Follow me," said Evelyn, who'd appeared from nowhere.

Alex happily obeyed. She took his hand and led him up a wide marble staircase to the second floor, and opened a set of double doors into a bedroom that was larger than Alex's flat in Brighton Beach.

"Use my private bathroom," she said, gesturing toward a door on the far side of the room.

"Thank you," said Alex, as he disappeared into a room that had a bath and a shower. He smiled as he washed his hands and straightened his tie, now confident enough to ask Evelyn if she would call a taxi to take him back to his hotel. But when he returned to the bedroom, he couldn't see her. He assumed she must have gone back downstairs to the party, until he heard a voice say, "I'm over here, Alex." He swung around to see her sitting up in bed, her magnificent ballgown lying on the floor. "Come and join me," Evelyn said, tapping the covers.

Alex couldn't believe what was happening, but after hesitating for a moment, he nervously discarded his suit and shirt, and climbed into bed beside her. She immediately took him in her arms and began kissing him. He wondered if it was obvious that she was only the second woman he'd ever slept with. She finally leaned back, let out a loud sigh, and said, "I can see why the enemy didn't have a chance."

Moments later she fell asleep in his arms.

When Alex woke the following morning, and looked at Evelyn lying beside him, he still couldn't believe this beautiful and sophisticated woman had given him a second look. He feared that the moment she woke, the bubble would burst and he would have to return to the real world.

He began to gently stroke her long red hair. She slowly woke and lazily stretched her arms, before pulling him toward her. After they'd made love a second time, Evelyn rested her head on his shoulder.

"Can I ask you something?" said Alex.

"Anything, my darling," she replied.

"What can you tell me about Todd Halliday, the guy who was seated on the other side of me last night?"

"Extremely wealthy, old money, but he likes to invest in new companies."

"Do you think he might be interested . . ."

"I suspect that's why Lawrence put him next to you," said Evelyn.

"But my company is so small—"

"Todd likes to get in at the beginning. He says that's how the real money is made. I only wish I'd listened to him when he told me to invest in Coca-Cola, McDonald's, and Walt Disney."

"What sort of sum does he usually invest?"

"Ten, fifteen million, and I've even known him to put up as much as twenty-five if he really believes in the person, and I could see he was impressed by you."

"But what would he expect in return?"

"I've no idea," said Evelyn, "but I'm not going to miss out this time."

"What do you mean?"

"I shall be among the first to back."

"You'd be willing to invest in my company?"

"Not in your company," said Evelyn, "in you. Todd always says there are bullshitters and bulls, and he wasn't in any doubt which you were, so I asked him to put me down for half a million. In fact," she added as she stepped out of bed and put on a silk dressing gown, "if Todd is willing to back you, I'm going to have to sell the Warhol my grandfather left me in his will." Evelyn stood in front of a portrait hanging on the wall. "It's known as the Blue Jackie, and it captures that poignant moment when she realized her husband was dead."

"I couldn't let you do that," said Alex as he followed her into the bathroom.

"Don't give it a second thought," said Evelyn as her robe fell to the floor and she stepped into the shower. "It's worth over a million, and there are several New York dealers who'd be only too happy to give me half a million, possibly more. And I'll let you into a little secret, I've never really liked it."

Alex couldn't concentrate when she turned on the shower and handed him the soap. Another first. It wasn't until he was drying himself that he said, "I couldn't let you sell the Warhol, not least because Lawrence would never forgive me."

"I won't tell him if you don't," said Evelyn, as she strolled back into the bedroom and opened a walk-in wardrobe to reveal row upon row of dresses, skirts, blouses, and shoes. She took her time selecting an outfit. Alex didn't enjoy putting his old clothes back on as he watched her getting dressed.

"Why don't we cut out the dealers?"

"Can you zip me up, darling?"

Alex walked across the room, zipped up the dress, and bent down to kiss her on the shoulder as he did so.

"I'm not sure I understand," said Evelyn, turning to face him.

"I'll act as the dealer, but with a difference. I'll buy the picture for half a million, which you can then invest in my company, and I'll return the Warhol when you repay me."

"But why take the risk?" said Evelyn.

"There's no risk, while the picture's worth a million," said Alex.

"And you wouldn't tell Lawrence?"

"Not a word."

"Then we have a deal," said Evelyn as she removed the small painting from the wall.

"No, I won't need to take it until the deal is closed."

"Then it won't be possible, because I'm off to the south of France for six weeks, and if I know Todd, he'll have closed a deal with you long before I get back." Evelyn handed over the picture. "I trust you enough to keep your end of the bargain."

Alex reluctantly took the painting, sat down, wrote out a check for five hundred thousand dollars, and handed it to Evelyn.

"Thank you," she said, leaving it on the bedside table. "Why don't you come back to Boston next weekend? We can go sailing, and celebrate our new partnership," she added before kissing him gently on the lips.

Alex couldn't believe she wanted to see him again, and simply said, "I'd like that."

"I think it's time for us to have some breakfast," said Evelyn. "But not a word to Lawrence about our little deal."

"I'd rather not, dressed like this," said Alex. "It was embarrassing enough last night, and it would be even worse at breakfast. In any case, are you sure you want your brother to know I stayed the night?"

"I don't think he'd give a damn."

"But I do."

"You're so beautifully old-fashioned," said Evelyn. "But if you insist, you can slip down the back stairs and out of the tradesmen's entrance. That way no one will see you."

"I do insist."

Evelyn shrugged her shoulders and walked across to the bedroom door. She opened it, looked up and down the corridor, and beckoned to Alex to join her. She pointed to a staircase at the far end of the corridor. "Don't forget the painting," she said, handing over the Warhol.

He reluctantly took it, and headed to the far end of the corridor.

"Look forward to seeing you next weekend then, darling," Evelyn said as they went in opposite directions.

Once he was out of sight, Evelyn strolled down the broad staircase to the dining room and joined Lawrence for breakfast.

"Good morning, Evelyn," he said as she walked in. "I hope you slept well."

On the train back to New York, Alex couldn't resist the occasional glance at the painting. Of course he'd heard of Warhol, but he'd never imagined he would ever own one, even if it was only for a short time. He already felt guilty about holding on to a picture that Evelyn's grandfather had left her in his will. He couldn't wait to give it back once she returned his half a million.

When he arrived at Penn Station, he took a cab to Brighton Beach, as he certainly wasn't going to travel on the subway with a Warhol. Even before he showed his mother the painting, he told her, "I've met the woman I'm going to marry."

Evelyn arrived at the Mayflower Hotel just after eleven. Todd immediately rose from his place in the alcove and waved. She walked quickly across to join him. Like the Cheshire Cat, she couldn't stop grinning.

"From the expression on your face, my darling, I assume you've sampled the cream," said Todd as she sat down opposite him.

"A large dollop," said Evelyn, handing him a check for five hundred thousand dollars.

"Bravo," he said after pocketing it. "Any problems?"

"None. You'd set him up perfectly. But we can't hang about, because if my brother were to find out . . ."

"I'm booked onto a two forty-five flight out of Logan that lands in Geneva just before seven tomorrow morning. I'll present the check the moment the bank opens its doors."

"Just be sure you ask for immediate clearance, and call me the moment the money's been transferred into my account. Then I'll fly over and join you in Monte Carlo, and we can celebrate."

"What are you going to do for the next couple of days while I'm away?"

"Make sure I'm available whenever Alex calls. At least until the check's cleared."

Todd leaned over and kissed his wife. "You're so clever," he said.

That afternoon, Alex phoned Evelyn, and they chatted for nearly an hour. He had to assure her several times that nothing would stop him joining her in Boston for the weekend.

On Tuesday morning, he caught her just before she left the house to go shopping. She promised to call back, and it was only later that he remembered she didn't have his number. On Wednesday he rang her first thing in the morning—first thing in the morning for her, at least, because he'd already been to the market and selected the freshest vegetables and the finest cuts of meat before delivering them to Elena's.

She was full of news. Todd was thinking of investing at least ten million, possibly fifteen, in his company, and would be in touch with him later in the week. Evelyn wondered if he'd like to go sailing on the weekend. "We could visit my uncle Nelson in Chappaquiddick, and enjoy the finest clam chowder on earth."

"Sounds great. What should I wear?" he asked, not wanting to admit that he'd never been on a yacht.

"Don't worry, I've already been shopping and picked out a couple of outfits for you."

Later that morning, Alex's bank manager called to say they'd received a check made payable to cash for five hundred thousand dollars, with a request for immediate transfer. As it was such a large amount, the manager said, he was checking to make sure Alex wanted it cleared.

"Immediately," said Alex without hesitation.

"It will leave your current account with a balance of seventeen thousand two hundred and sixty-nine dollars," said the manager.

Which will soon be several million, Alex wanted to tell him, but he satisfied himself with, "Please clear the check immediately."

Evelyn picked up the phone.

"The money has been transferred and I'll be taking the next plane down to Nice. When do you think you'll be able to join me?"

"With a bit of luck I'll be in Monte Carlo in time for dinner tomorrow evening," said Evelyn. "But first I have to let my brother know the sad news."

"One does have to feel a little sorry for Mr. Karpenko," said Todd.

"But not too sorry. I have a feeling he'll cope just fine in jail, and then we can forget all about him. By the way, Todd, don't forget to book our usual table."

The butler hadn't seen Evelyn running down the stairs since she was a small child.

"Have you seen my brother?" she shouted long before she'd reached the bottom step.

"He's just gone in to breakfast, Miss Evelyn," Caxton said, hurrying across the hall to open the dining-room door for her.

"Whatever's the matter, Eve?" asked Lawrence as his sister burst into the room.

"Have you moved the Warhol from the Jefferson bedroom?" she asked, still out of breath.

"What are you talking about?" said Lawrence, putting down his coffee.

"The Warhol, it's gone. It's not there."

Lawrence leaped up from his place and walked quickly out of the room. He took the stairs up to the first floor two at a time, before making his way along the landing and into the Jefferson room. He found a bare hook on the wall where the Warhol had once hung.

"When did you last see it?" he asked as Evelyn stared at the faint outline of where the picture had been.

"I can't be sure. I've just got so used to it being there. But I do recall seeing it on the night of your party." A long silence followed before she added, "I feel ashamed, Lawrence, because I think it could be my fault."

"I'm not sure I understand."

"I got a little drunk on the night of your party, and allowed someone to join me in my room."

"Who?"

"Your friend Alex Karpenko."

"Did he stay the night?"

"Certainly not. He'd left by the time I woke in the morning. I just didn't think . . ."

"You never do," said Lawrence. "But if anyone's to blame, it's me."

"Perhaps I should try and contact him, and see if I can get the picture back?"

"That's the last thing you should do. If anyone's going to speak to Alex, it will be me."

"Will you have to inform the police?"

"I don't have any choice," said Lawrence. "As you well know, the picture doesn't belong to me, it's part of our grandfather's bequest, and as it's worth a million, possibly more, I'll have to report the theft to the police, as well as to the insurance company."

"But he saved your life."

"Yes, he did. So if he returns the painting immediately, perhaps I won't press charges."

"I'm so sorry," said Evelyn. "He seemed such a nice guy."

"You never can tell about anyone, can you?" said Lawrence.

That afternoon, Alex called Evelyn, and the phone was picked up by the butler, who told him Miss Lowell had left the house around eleven, and he couldn't be sure when she would be returning. She didn't call back, so Alex rang again in the evening. This time Lawrence answered the phone.

"What a wonderful party, Lawrence. You're a great host, and I'm looking forward to seeing you and Evelyn tomorrow."

"I didn't know you were coming to Boston for the weekend."

"Didn't Evelyn tell you?"

"Evelyn left this morning for her home in the south of France, and I'm visiting my mother in Nantucket."

"But we'd agreed that I should join you both for dinner on Friday evening, and go sailing on Saturday." There was such a long silence, Alex thought the line must have gone dead. "Are you still there, Lawrence?"

"I apologize for asking you this, Alex, but when you left the house on Sunday morning, the butler said you were carrying a package under your arm."

"A Warhol," said Alex, without hesitation. "Somewhat reluctantly, I might add. But Evelyn insisted I take it as security."

"Security for what?"

"I loaned her half a million to invest with Todd Halliday, who intends to back my company."

"Todd Halliday is her husband, and doesn't have a penny to his name."

"Evelyn is married?"

"Has been for years," said Lawrence.

"But she told me Todd specializes in start-ups."

"Todd only specializes in breakdowns that always involve other people's money," said Lawrence. "Yours on this occasion."

"But Evelyn assured me he was considering investing ten, possibly fifteen million in Elena's."

"I'm not sure Todd could afford to invest ten dollars, let alone ten million, in anything. I hope you haven't given him any money."

"Her," said Alex. "My check was cashed this morning." Lawrence was glad Alex couldn't see the expression on his face.

"But don't worry, I still have the Warhol as security," Alex added.

Another long silence followed before Lawrence said, "That picture wasn't hers to give. It's part of the Lowell family collection, which is held in trust, and always left to the firstborn son, who then passes it on to the next generation. I inherited the collection when my father died a couple of years ago, and although Evelyn is next in line, until I have a son, my father made it clear in his will that if I were to die in Vietnam, the collection was to be bequeathed to the Boston Fine Arts Society, and not a single work was to go to Evelyn."

"I'll return the painting immediately," said Alex.

"And I'll pay you back your half a million dollars," said Lawrence.

"No, you will not," said Alex firmly. "My agreement was with Evelyn, not you. Let's give her the benefit of the doubt and assume she's invested my money in a blue-chip company."

"The only blue chips that woman ever invests in are to be found in casinos. In future, whenever she comes to stay, I'll have to nail every picture to the wall. But that doesn't stop us working as a team just as we've done in the past, and see if we can find a way of getting your money back."

"I'll do anything I can to help," said Alex. "And of course I'll return the painting. I'm only sorry to have caused you so much trouble."

"You should have left me to die on the battlefield, Alex. Then you would never have met my sister."

"Mea culpa," said Alex. "Jezebel, Lucrezia Borgia, Mata Hari, and now Evelyn Lowell. She knew a sucker when she saw one."

"You're not the first, and you probably won't be the last. What's more, I'm afraid I'll be away for the next month, as Mother and I always spend August in Europe. Why don't I send you a check now, and you can return the painting as soon as I get back. Then we can go sailing, and leave Evelyn on dry land."

"No," said Alex. "You can give me the check but only when I return the painting."

"If you insist. Just make sure you don't lose it, because if you do, Evelyn will deny ever having given it to you."

"Lawrence, can I ask why you assumed I was the innocent party, and you didn't immediately take your sister's side?"

"Form. When I was nine, Evelyn used to steal my pocket money, and when she was caught red-handed she blamed it on our nanny, who got the sack. And after a string of similar incidents at school, my dear father had to build a new library to prevent her being expelled."

"But that doesn't prove I'm innocent. Don't forget, I've still got a painting that's worth over a million."

"True, but Evelyn made a mistake when she cast you as nanny on this occasion."

"How come?"

"She told me you'd left the house before she woke on the morning after the party, despite the fact that she joined me for breakfast at around eight thirty."

"You've lost me."

"But you hadn't left, because you asked Caxton to call a cab around that time to take you back to your hotel. Much as I admire your nerve, courage, chutzpah, call it what you will, Alex, even you wouldn't have the gall to walk out of the house with a Warhol under your arm and expect the butler to hold open the door of a taxi for you."

Alex laughed. "So what are you going to do about your sister?"

"I'll wait for her to make her next mistake," said Lawrence, "which, given her past record, shouldn't be too long."

25

SASHA

London

"I now pronounce you man and wife," said the vicar. "You may kiss the bride."

Sasha took Charlie in his arms and kissed her as if they were on a first date. The congregation of nearly a hundred people burst into applause.

The bride and groom progressed slowly down the aisle and out into the churchyard, where a photographer, tripod already set up, awaited them. The first picture he took was of the new Mr. and Mrs. Karpenko, followed by group shots with their parents, the rest of the bride's family, and finally with the best man and the ushers.

The newlyweds were then driven back to Barn Cottage in a Rolls-Royce. On the way, Sasha admitted to his wife that he was a little nervous about his speech.

"I'd be a lot more nervous about Ben's speech, if I were you," said Charlie. "When I heard him rehearsing it in the kitchen before supper last night, I felt quite sorry for you."

"That bad?" said Sasha. When they arrived back at the house, they were surprised to find Elena already checking the canapés.

"How did she get here before us?" whispered Charlie as she straightened her husband's tie, and removed a hair from his jacket.

"Silly question," said Sasha, as the guests began to arrive in dribs and drabs before making their way through to the marquee for lunch.

Sasha quite forgot about the speeches until the plates had been cleared, coffee had been served, and Ben rose to deliver his offering.

"My lords, ladies and gentlemen," he began.

"Where are the lords?" shouted one of the ushers.

"Just thinking ahead," said Ben, placing a hand on Sasha's shoulder.

"Hear, hear!" cried some of his Cambridge Union contemporaries.

"You may ask," said Ben, "how a pathetic illegal immigrant from Leningrad could possibly have captured the heart of a beautiful English girl. Well, he didn't. The truth is that Charlie, being a good-hearted thing, took pity on him when they first met at a party given at my home to celebrate the end of our school days. Because Charlie is a liberal and therefore a supporter of lost causes, Sasha was in with a chance. But even I didn't think he'd get that lucky, and end up marrying such a bright and beautiful creature.

"But there's a downside, Sasha, that I must warn you about. Charlie was captain of hockey at Fulham High School, and I'm reliably informed that with stick in hand she thought nothing of mowing down any opponent within reach. So stick to chess, old friend. And don't forget that while the queen can range freely around the board, the king can only move one square at a time."

Ben waited for the laughter and applause to die down before he continued. "To say I was proud to be invited to act as Sasha's best man would be an understatement, because I have known for some time that I was destined to walk in this man's shadow, and just occasionally be allowed to bask in his limelight. I have watched in awe as he won a scholarship to Cambridge, became president of the Union, captained the varsity chess team, and ended his time at Trinity with a starred first. But put all of those things together, and still they're nothing compared to capturing the heart of Charlie Dangerfield. Because with her by his side, it will be possible for him to scale even higher mountains. But then, behind every great man . . . is a surprised mother-in-law."

Once again, Ben waited for the laughter to die down before he said, "But I have not entirely given up hope for myself, as none of you can have failed to notice the four beautiful bridesmaids who accompanied Charlie down the aisle. I've already asked three of them out."

"And all three turned you down!" shouted another usher.

"True," said Ben, "but don't forget there are four, so I still live in hope."

"Not if she's got any sense!"

"Despite that, I ask you to rise and toast the health of Sasha and Charlie."

Everyone stood, raised their glasses, and cried, "Sasha and Charlie!"

"Would you be kind enough to remain standing," continued Ben, "so that I can always remind Sasha in the years to come, that when I gave the best man's speech at his wedding, I received a standing ovation."

The applause that followed made Sasha realize just how hard his old friend had worked on the speech that he was now expected to follow. He understood why Charlie had warned him he should be nervous.

He rose slowly to his feet, aware that his friend had raised the bar.

"I would like to begin by thanking Mr. and Mrs. Dangerfield, not only for their generosity in being such wonderful hosts, but even more for welcoming this pathetic refugee into their antique English family. This, despite the fact that I have yet to visit Wimbledon, Lord's, or Twickenham, and don't know the meaning of foot-fault or leg-before, let alone hooker. Not only that, I'm still not sure if you should pour the milk into a cup before or after the tea. And will I ever get used to warm beer, waiting patiently in queues, and Maypole dancing? Remembering all this, you may well ask how I got so lucky as to marry the quintessential English rose, who blossoms in all seasons.

"The answer is that there has always been another, equally remarkable, woman in my life. I am referring of course to my mother, Elena, without whom none of this would have been possible."

The prolonged applause allowed Sasha to gather his thoughts. "Without her, I would have had no moral compass, no guiding star, no path to follow. I never thought I would meet her equal, but the gods"—he looked up to the sky—"were to prove me wrong, and excelled themselves when they introduced me to Charlie."

"It wasn't the gods," interrupted Ben, "it was me!" Which was met with raucous laughter.

"Which reminds me," continued Sasha, "to warn the fourth bridesmaid, who seems to be a sensible and charming young lady, to emulate her three colleagues and reject Mr. Cohen out of hand. She can do so much better." Hear, hears echoed around the room. "But I can't," concluded Sasha, raising his glass, "so I invite you all to join me in a toast to the bridesmaids."

"The bridesmaids!"

It was some time before the audience resumed their seats.

Ben leaned across to Sasha. "Well done," he said. "Especially as you had such an impossible act to follow." Sasha laughed and raised a glass to his friend. "As soon as you're back from your honeymoon," continued Ben, suddenly sounding more sober, "we have to start to plan the next move on your journey to the House of Commons."

"That might not be so easy for a pathetic refugee," said Sasha.

"Of course it will—especially if you have me as your campaign manager."

"But you're a member of the Conservative Party, Ben, just in case you've forgotten."

"And will remain so in every other constituency, apart from the one in which you're standing. With Charlie by your side, nothing can stop you. And I have another little piece of information to share with you before you disappear off to Venice. I know Charlie won't thank me for discussing business on your wedding day, but a surprise package turned up on my desk yesterday, which could turn out to be an unexpected wedding gift." Sasha put down his glass. "The freehold for 154 Fulham Road has come on the market."

"Tremlett's restaurant? How come?"

"As you probably know, it's been losing money for the past couple of years. I suspect his old man has finally had enough, and decided to cut his losses and sell up."

"How much?"

"Four hundred thousand."

Sasha took another sip of champagne. "Way out of our league," he eventually managed.

"That's a pity, because I've no doubt your mother would only have to cross the road to turn the place around in no time."

"I agree, but it's still too soon for us."

"Well, at least you can be thankful that your greatest rival has bitten the dust. And at that price, it's unlikely to be another restaurant that will replace it. Help," he said, "I see a formidable woman bearing down on me, clearly not pleased that I've been monopolizing the groom. Forgive me while I disappear!"

Sasha laughed as his friend leaped up and melted into the crowd. He stood as the elderly lady approached.

"What a magnificent occasion," said the countess, sitting down in Ben's empty chair. "You are indeed a lucky man. Thank you for inviting me."

"We were delighted you could join us," said Sasha. "My mother was particularly pleased."

"She's even more old-fashioned than I am," whispered the countess. "But there's another reason I wanted to speak to you." Sasha didn't refill his glass. "As you know, my Fabergé egg comes up for auction at Sotheby's in September. I wonder if you'd be kind enough to pay me a visit when you return from your honeymoon, as there's something I need to discuss with you."

"I'd be delighted to," said Sasha. "Any clues?"

"I think," said the countess, "that between the two of us we might just be able to defeat both the Russians and the English. But only if you felt able to . . ."

"Damned good speech, Sasha. But then, I wouldn't have expected anything less," said a voice behind him, who clearly hadn't left his glass unfilled.

"Thank you," said Sasha, trying to recall the name of Charlie's uncle. By the time the man had moved on, so had the countess. But her instructions couldn't have been clearer.

Sasha mingled with the guests while his wife—he wondered how long it would take him to get used to that—went up to her room to change into her going-away outfit. When she reappeared on the staircase forty minutes later, he was reminded of the first moment he'd seen her at Ben's party nearly four years ago. Did she have any idea how he had prayed that she was heading toward him? Only recently she'd confessed to Ben that she'd been hoping he wouldn't turn up at the party with another girl.

It was another half hour before they were able to bid their final farewells and climb into Sasha's old MG, having abandoned the Rolls-Royce. They arrived at Victoria station only just in time to board the Orient Express for Venice.

They both burst out laughing when they discovered that their sleeping compartment only had two narrow single beds.

"We ought to claim half our money back," said Sasha, as he squeezed in alongside his wife and turned out the light.

"There's only one thing I insist on," said Tremlett once his son had fully briefed him on the sale of 154 Fulham Road.

"And what's that, Dad?"

"Under no circumstances will you allow the property to fall into the hands of the Karpenkos."

"That's unlikely to happen with the price at four hundred thousand."

"Agnelli could afford it."

"At his age, Agnelli's a seller, not a buyer," said Maurice. "Besides, I know he hasn't been well of late."

"I'm glad to hear that," said Tremlett. "Because I need you to handle the sale while I concentrate on getting planning permission for the block of flats in Stamford Place."

"Any more news on that front?"

"Councilor Mason tells me there'll be an announcement next week, which is why I've invited him to join us on our yacht at Cannes for the weekend."

"That should clinch the deal," said Maurice.

"Especially as the unfortunate man is going through an unusually messy divorce case. For the second time."

Mr. and Mrs. Karpenko returned from Venice a fortnight later, and among the first things Sasha did on arriving back in London was to phone the countess. She invited him to join her for tea the following afternoon.

He knocked on the door of her basement flat in Pimlico just before three, not quite sure what to expect. The door was opened by a maid who was almost as ancient as her mistress. She led him through to the sitting room, where the old lady was seated in a winged armchair, with a rug over her lap.

The flat was spotless, and every surface was crowded with silver-framed sepia photographs of a family who would never have considered living below stairs. She waved Sasha into the seat opposite her and asked, "How was Venice?"

"Wonderful. But if we'd stayed any longer, I'd be bankrupt."

"I visited it several times as a child," said the countess. "And often I enjoyed a chocolate gateau and a glass of lemonade in Saint Mark's Square—the drawing room of Europe, as Napoleon once described it."

"It's now crowded with tourists like myself whom I feel sure Napoleon would not have approved of," said Sasha as the maid reappeared carrying a tray of tea and biscuits.

"Another man who underestimated the Russians, and lived to regret it."

Once the maid had poured the tea and departed, the countess moved on to the purpose of the meeting.

Sasha listened attentively to every word she had to say, and couldn't help feeling that if this formidable woman had been born in the twentieth century, she would have been a leader in any field she had chosen. By the time she came to the end of her audacious proposal, he wasn't in any doubt that the Russian ring had met their match.

"Well, young man," she said. "Are you willing to assist me in my little subterfuge?"

"Yes, I am," said Sasha without hesitation. "But don't you consider Mr. Dangerfield is far better qualified to pull it off?"

"Possibly. But he has the British weakness of believing in fair play, a concept we Russians have never really grasped."

"My timing will need to be spot on," said Sasha.

"It most certainly will," said the countess. "And more importantly, knowing when to stop will be the biggest decision. So let's run through the details again, and don't hesitate to interrupt if there's something you don't fully understand, or think you can improve on. Before I begin, Sasha, do you have any questions?"

"Yes. Where's the nearest telephone box?"

⊸o⊷

The auction house was almost full by the time Mr. Dangerfield and the countess took their reserved seats in the third row.

"Your egg is lot eighteen," said Dangerfield after turning several pages of the catalog. "So it won't come up for at least half an hour. But then it should only be a few moments before we discover if the experts consider it a fake or a masterpiece." He turned and glanced at a group of men who were standing in a huddle at the back of the room. "They've already decided the answer to that question," he added. "But then, it suits their purpose."

"It doesn't help that the Soviet ambassador issued a press statement this morning claiming that the egg was a fake and the original is on display at the Hermitage," said the countess.

"A piece of propaganda that even Goebbels would have been embarrassed by," said Mr. Dangerfield. "And you'll notice that despite his words, His Excellency is sitting a couple of rows behind us. Don't be surprised if he tries to pick up your egg at a reduced price, and then overnight it's suddenly recognized as a long-lost masterpiece."

"The revolution may have killed my father," said the countess, turning around to glare at the ambassador, "but its heirs are not going to steal my egg."

The ambassador didn't acknowledge her presence.

"What does POA mean?" the countess asked, looking back down at her catalog.

"Price on application," explained Dangerfield. "As Sotheby's are unwilling to offer an opinion on its value, they will leave it to the market to decide. I'm afraid the ambassador's intervention won't have helped."

"Bunch of cowards," said the countess. "Let's hope they're all left with egg on their faces." Mr. Dangerfield would have laughed, but he wasn't sure if the pun had been intended. "So what happens next?" she asked.

"At seven o'clock precisely, the auctioneer will climb the steps to the podium, and open proceedings by offering lot number one. Then I'm afraid you'll have a rather long and anxious wait before he reaches lot eighteen. At that point it will be in the hands of the gods. Or possibly," he added, glancing around at the ring, "the infidels."

"Who are those casually dressed men behind that rope near the podium?"

"The gentlemen of the press. Pencils poised, hoping for a story. You'll either make the front pages or be relegated to a footnote in the arts column."

"Let's hope it's the front pages. And the smartly dressed ones on the platform to our right?"

"That's the home team. It's their job to help the auctioneer spot the bidders. That also applies to those assistants manning the phones to your right, who will be bidding on behalf of clients who are either calling from abroad, or wish to remain anonymous."

At precisely seven o'clock a tall, elegantly dressed man wearing a dinner jacket and black bow tie entered the auction room from a door behind the podium. He slowly climbed the steps, and smiled as he surveyed the packed audience.

"Good evening, ladies and gentlemen. Welcome to the Russian sale. I shall start proceedings with lot number one in your catalog. *A Winter's Evening in Moscow* by Savrasov. I shall open the bidding at ten thousand pounds. Do I see twelve?"

Although the countess considered the work inferior to the Savrasov that had hung in her father's library, she was nevertheless pleased when the hammer came down at twenty-four thousand pounds, well above its high estimate.

"Lot number two," declared the auctioneer. "A watercolor by . . ."

"I was hoping that Sasha might be joining us," said Mr. Dangerfield. "But he did warn me that he had a party booking at the restaurant and wasn't sure if he'd be able to get away in time."

The countess made no comment as she turned the page of her catalog to lot three, which didn't make the low estimate. Mr. Dangerfield glanced around, to see that the ring was celebrating its first killing. He looked back to find the countess tapping her fingers agitatedly on her catalog, which surprised him, because he'd never known her to show any emotion.

"That picture belonged to an old family friend," she explained. "He needed the money."

When the auctioneer offered the next painting, Mr. Dangerfield noted that the countess was becoming more and more nervous as each lot was offered up for sale. He even thought he spotted a bead of sweat on her forehead by the time the auctioneer had reached lot sixteen.

"A pair of Russian dolls. Shall I open the bidding at ten thousand?" No one responded. The auctioneer stared down at the impassive sea of faces and suggested, "Twelve thousand," but Mr. Dangerfield knew he was plucking bids off the wall. "Fourteen thousand," he said, trying not to sound desperate. But there was still no response, so he brought down his hammer and mumbled, "Bought in."

"What does that mean?" whispered the countess.

"There was never a bidder in the first place," said Mr. Dangerfield.

"Lot number seventeen," said the auctioneer. "An important portrait by the distinguished Russian artist Vladimir Borovikovsky. Do I see a bid of twenty thousand?" No one responded until a member of the ring shouted, "Ten thousand!"

"Do I see twelve thousand?" asked the auctioneer, but still no one else took any interest, so he reluctantly brought down his hammer and said,

"Sold, for ten thousand pounds, to the gentleman at the back," although he wasn't entirely sure which gentleman.

Dangerfield felt this didn't bode well for his client, but he didn't proffer an opinion.

"Lot number eighteen." The auctioneer paused to allow a porter to enter the room carrying the egg on a velvet cushion. He placed it on a stand beside the podium, and withdrew. The auctioneer smiled benevolently down at his attentive audience, and was about to suggest an opening price of fifty thousand pounds when a voice from the back of the room shouted, "One thousand pounds," which was followed by laughter and a gasp of disbelief.

"Two thousand," said another voice, before the auctioneer could recover.

"Ten thousand," said someone two rows behind the countess. The bewildered auctioneer looked hopefully around the room, and was just about to bring his hammer down and say, "Sold to the Russian ambassador," when out of the corner of his eye he saw the hand of one of the assistants on the platform to his left shoot up. He turned to face a young woman on the phone, who said firmly, "Twenty thousand."

"Twenty-one thousand," said the first voice from the back of the room.

The auctioneer looked back at the young woman, who appeared to be deep in conversation with her telephone client.

"Thirty thousand," she said after a few seconds, which had felt like a lifetime to the countess.

"Thirty-one thousand." The same voice from the back.

"Forty thousand," said the assistant on the phone.

"Forty-one thousand," came back the immediate response.

"Fifty thousand," the assistant.

"Fifty-one thousand," the man at the back.

There was another long silence as everyone in the room turned toward the young woman on the phone.

"One hundred thousand," she said, causing a loud outbreak of chattering, which the auctioneer studiously ignored.

"I have a bid of one hundred thousand pounds," he said. "Do I see one hundred and twenty-five thousand pounds?" the auctioneer inquired as his eye returned to the leader of the ring, who stared back at him in sullen silence.

"Do I see one hundred and twenty-five thousand?" the auctioneer asked a second time. "Then I'll let it go to the phone bidder for one hundred thousand pounds." He was just about to bring down his hammer, when a hand in the fifth row rose reluctantly. Clearly the Russian ambassador now accepted that his press statement had failed to achieve the desired result.

A flurry of bids followed, once the ambassador had acknowledged the egg had indeed been crafted by Carl Fabergé, and was not a fake. When the price reached half a million, Mr. Dangerfield noticed that the young woman on the phone was having an intense conversation with her client.

"The next bid will be six hundred thousand," she whispered. "Do you want me to continue bidding on your behalf, sir?"

"How many bidders are left?" he asked.

"The Russian ambassador is still bidding, and I'm fairly sure the deputy director of the Metropolitan Museum in New York is showing an interest. And a dealer from Asprey is tapping his right foot, always a sign that he's about to join in."

"Fine, then I'll wait until you think we're down to the final bidder."

When the bidding reached one million, the young woman whispered into the phone, "We're down to the last two, the Russian ambassador and the deputy director of the Met."

"One million, one hundred thousand pounds," said the auctioneer, turning his attention back to the Russian ambassador, who sullenly folded his arms and lowered his head.

"We're down to one," she whispered over the phone.

"What was the last bid?"

"One million one."

"Then bid one million two." Her right hand shot up.

"I have one million two on the phone," said the auctioneer, looking back down at the deputy director of the Met.

"What's happening?" asked the voice on the other end of the line. He sounded quite anxious.

"I think you've got it. Congratulations."

But she was wrong, because the hand of the Met's representative rose once again, if somewhat tentatively.

"No, wait. There's a bid of one million three. But I'm confident it would be yours if you were to bid one four."

"I'm sure you're right," said the voice on the other end of the line, "but I'm afraid I've reached my limit. Thanks anyway," he said before he put the phone down. He stepped out of the telephone box, and dodged in and out of the traffic as he crossed Bond Street.

The auctioneer continued to stare hopefully at the young assistant, but she shook her head and put the phone down. The auctioneer brought down his hammer with a thud, and said, "Sold, for one million three hundred thousand pounds to the Metropolitan Museum in New York."

The audience burst into spontaneous applause, and even the countess allowed herself a smile as Sasha came dashing into the room. He walked quickly down the aisle and took the only empty seat, next to his father-in-law.

"I'm afraid you've missed all the drama," said Mr. Dangerfield.

"Yes, I know. Sorry, I got held up."

Sasha leaned across and congratulated the countess. She gave his hand a gentle squeeze and said, "Thank you, Sasha," as she turned to the next page of her catalog.

"Lot number nineteen," said the auctioneer once the audience had settled. "A fine marble bust of Tsar Nicholas the Second. I have an opening bid of ten thousand pounds."

"Eleven," said a familiar voice from the back of the room. The countess didn't bother to turn around, but simply raised her gloved hand slowly. When she caught the attention of the auctioneer she said, almost in a whisper, "Fifty thousand," which was followed by a gasp from all those around her. But then she considered it a small price to pay for a masterpiece she'd last seen on the desk in her father's study. She also knew which member of the family had put it up for sale, and accepted that he needed the money even more than she did.

26

SASHA

London

"You're looking very smart, Mama," said Sasha. "Is that a new suit?"

Elena didn't look up from the reservations book.

"And as it's three in the afternoon, you must either be meeting a friend for tea or going for a job interview."

Elena pulled on a pair of gloves, while continuing to ignore her son.

"I hope it's not a job interview," teased Sasha, "because frankly we couldn't run the place without you."

"I'll be back long before we open this evening," said Elena tersely. "Is the first sitting fully booked?"

"Except for tables twelve and fourteen."

Elena nodded. Although the restaurant was often booked out days in advance, Mr. Agnelli had taught Sasha to always keep two of the best tables in reserve for regulars, and not to release them before seven o'clock.

"Have a good time, Mama, wherever it is you're off to." In fact he had already worked out exactly where she was going.

Elena left the restaurant without another word. She walked for a hundred yards down the road before turning right at the corner and hailing a taxi. She didn't want Sasha to see her being extravagant. She would normally have caught a bus, but not in her smart new Armani outfit, and in any case, there are no bus stops in Lowndes Square.

"Forty-three Lowndes Square," she told the cabbie.

Elena had been touched when the countess had sent a handwritten note inviting her to tea, which would give her the opportunity to see the new flat. The Fabergé egg had changed all their lives. Mike Dangerfield had split his commission with Sasha and Charlie, which had allowed them to buy a flat just around the corner from the restaurant.

Elena was sad that they no longer lived with her, but she understood that a young married couple would want a home of their own, especially if they were planning to start a family.

Sasha worked all the hours in the day, and several during the night, as he attempted to juggle working in the restaurant with attending the course he'd signed up for at the London School of Economics, not to mention, or at least not to Charlie or Elena, that he had recently joined the local Labour Club. Chess nights had bitten the dust.

Elena's was going from strength to strength, not least because when Tremlett's restaurant closed, Elena had been able to pick up their best waiters and kitchen staff. The Tremletts, père and fils, had moved to Majorca and opened an estate agency soon after Councilor Tremlett had resigned, citing ill health following an inquiry into the council's decision to grant planning permission for a proposed new block of flats in Stamford Place. Sasha didn't need to read between the lines of the local paper's report to realize they wouldn't be coming back.

While Elena oversaw the kitchen, and Gino ran front of house, Sasha kept a tight rein on income and expenditure, an area where his mother was completely at a loss, although he had tried to explain to her the difference between tax avoidance and being tax efficient. He plowed most of the profits back into the business, and they had recently acquired two double-decker freezers, an industrial dishwasher, and sixty new linen tablecloths and napkins. He planned to build a bar at the front of the restaurant, but not until they could afford it.

As she sat in the back of the taxi, Elena thought about the countess, whom she hadn't seen recently. Her unsocial hours at the restaurant meant that she had little time for a private life, so the invitation to tea was a pleasant break from her normal routine. And she was looking forward to seeing the new apartment.

When the taxi drew up outside number 43 Lowndes Square, Elena gave the cabbie a handsome tip. She had never forgotten Mr. Agnelli telling her, you can hardly expect to be tipped yourself, if you're not generous to those who give you service.

She checked the four names printed neatly beside the doorbells, before pressing the button for the top floor.

"Please come up," said a voice that was obviously expecting her.

A buzzer sounded, and Elena pushed open the door and made her way to the lift. When she stepped out on the fourth floor, she saw a maid standing by an open door.

"Good afternoon, Mrs. Karpenko. Let me take you through to the countess."

Elena tried not to stare at the photographs of the tsar and tsarina on holiday with the countess's family on the Black Sea, as she was taken through to a drawing room full of the most beautiful antique furniture. A marble bust of Tsar Nicholas II rested on the center of the mantelpiece.

"How kind of you to take the time in your busy life to visit me," said the countess, waving her guest to a large comfortable chair opposite her. "There's so much we have to talk about. But first, some tea."

Elena was pleased to find the countess was now living in luxury, compared with the cramped basement flat in Pimlico.

"And how is Sasha?" was the countess's first question.

"When he's not working in the restaurant, he's studying accountancy and business management at the LSE, which can only benefit our burgeoning business."

"Not burgeoning for much longer, I'm told. When I last saw Sasha, he mentioned rumors that—"

"But only rumors, countess," said Elena, "although Gino's sure he spotted two of the judges having lunch at the restaurant quite recently. But we've heard nothing definite."

"I'll keep my fingers crossed," said the countess as the maid returned bearing a large silver tray laden with tea, biscuits, and a chocolate cake, which she placed in the center of the table.

"Milk, no sugar, if I remember correctly," said the countess as she began to pour.

"Thank you."

"Sasha also tells me he's considering standing for the local council. I hear a vacancy has arisen recently."

"Yes, he's been shortlisted for the seat, but he's not confident they'll select him."

"Be assured, Elena, Fulham Council will be nothing more than a stepping stone on his inevitable path to the House of Commons."

"Do you really think so?"

"Oh yes. Sasha has all the qualities and failings necessary to make an excellent Member of Parliament. He's bright, resourceful, cunning, and not averse to taking the occasional risk if he believes the cause is worth it."

"But don't forget he's an immigrant," said Elena.

"Which may even be an advantage in the modern Labour Party."

"Don't let him know," said Elena, "but I've always voted Conservative."

"Me too," admitted the countess. "But in my case I don't think it would come as much of a surprise. Enough of Sasha, how is Charlie getting on at the Courtauld?"

"She's almost completed her thesis on 'Krøyer: The Unknown Master.' So it won't be too long until she's Dr. Karpenko."

"And are there any signs of—"

"Unfortunately not. It appears that the modern generation think it's important to establish a career before you have children. In my day . . ."

"I do believe, Elena, you are more old-fashioned than I am."

"Sasha certainly thinks so."

"My dear, I can assure you, he admires you above all women," said the countess, offering her guest a slice of Black Forest gateau. She paused and took a sip of tea, before saying, "Now, I must confess, Elena, that I had an ulterior motive for asking to see you."

Elena put down her fork and listened carefully.

"The truth is, I have a secret I want to share with you." She paused for effect. "Thanks to Mr. Dangerfield's diligence and expertise, and your son's ingenuity, I received far more for my egg than I had originally thought possible."

"I had no idea Sasha was involved," said Elena.

"Oh yes, he played a crucial role, for which I will be eternally grateful. Not only did the sale allow me to purchase a short lease on this charming flat, but also to buy several fine pieces of furniture from a certain antique dealer from Guildford." Elena smiled. "However, I still have the problem of how to invest the rest of the money, because there is a considerable amount left over. My father used to say, always invest in people you can trust, and you won't go far wrong. So I've decided to invest in you."

"I'm not sure I understand," said Elena.

"For the past month, I've been negotiating the purchase of a freehold property in the Fulham Road."

Elena's hand was shaking so much she spilled her tea. "I'm so sorry," she said.

"It's of no importance," said the countess, "compared to finding out if you would feel comfortable with the idea of running two restaurants at the same time."

"I'd have to talk to Sasha before I can make a decision."

"No, I'm afraid you can't," said the countess firmly. "In fact, you must never mention our conversation to Sasha, for reasons I will explain. The seller I've had to deal with is a Mr. Maurice Tremlett, so you can't say anything to Sasha as I got the strong impression that he and your son are not on good terms. He is clearly envious of the success you've made of Elena's."

"It goes back a lot further than that," said Elena, "to the days when they were at school together, and Sasha was the First Eleven goalkeeper."

"No doubt Tremlett was relegated to the Second Eleven, which doesn't surprise me, as that's exactly what I intend to do with him, once the contract has been signed. During our negotiations Tremlett asked me twice, if not three times, if I was a front for Mr. Karpenko, and I was able to truthfully say no. So please don't say anything to Sasha until I've put down the deposit. If Tremlett were to find out what I was up to, I've no doubt the deal would be off. Now, I have to ask again, Elena, do you think you can run two establishments at the same time?"

"I've run that restaurant once already, so it shouldn't be difficult to get it back up to scratch, especially as I'm already employing the only good kitchen staff and waiters they ever had."

"And you're confident you could do that while running Elena's at the same time?"

"It will just be a hundred and thirty covers instead of seventy. Of course I may have to build a bridge or dig a tunnel under the Fulham Road between Elena One and Elena Two."

"Then that's settled," said the countess.

"Can I ask what you'll expect in return for your investment?"

"I would become a fifty-fifty partner in the new restaurant, and be allowed to dine at either establishment whenever I wish, at no charge. There are several Russian émigrés in London who appreciate fine cooking, Elena, but no longer experience it as regularly as they used to. However, you have my word that I will only bring them along one at a time."

"In that case you must have your own table at both restaurants," said

Elena, "which no one else will be allowed to book. So when can I tell Sasha?"

"Not until the contract has been signed and the ink is dry, because I must tell you, Elena, if Mr. Maurice Tremlett had been born in the Soviet Union, he would undoubtedly be working for the KGB."

Elena shuddered, but couldn't disagree. "Thank you for tea," she said, "and, more important, thank you for your confidence in me. Now I must get back to the restaurant, as I like to be in the kitchen a full hour before the first customer arrives."

"What a good investment I'm about to make," said the countess. "And I have one more request of you before you leave."

"Anything, countess."

"That in future, you'll call me Natasha." Elena looked uncertain. "If you don't, I'll make it a condition of the contract."

27

SASHA

London

"Do we know anything about them?" asked Elena. "The name Rycroft doesn't mean anything to me."

"Only that the lady who called, a Mrs. Audrey Campion, told me there would be three of them traveling up from Surrey to discuss a private matter."

"Then it's probably a special birthday or anniversary party of some kind that they wish to celebrate. What time are you expecting them?"

"In about ten minutes," said Sasha, glancing at his watch. "Do you want to join us for the meeting, Mama?"

"No, thank you," said Elena. "You're so much better at these things than I am. Just be sure to check both diaries."

"I already have," said Sasha. "Elena One is fully booked for March the thirteenth."

"And Elena Two?"

"If it's for twenty or less, we could just about manage it."

"It seems as if you have everything covered, so I'll get back to work. I need to discuss today's specials with the sous-chef."

Sasha smiled, well aware that his mother would do almost anything to avoid having to deal directly with customers, but was transformed the moment she entered the kitchen. How different she was from him. He avoided the kitchen at all costs, so the division of labor suited them both ideally.

Sasha was considering which menu options he should offer when the front door bell rang.

He sat down at the popular alcove table at the back of the room as Gino opened the door to let the three of them in. As he accompanied them over to the table, Sasha tried, as he always did, to assess his potential customers.

From their ages, they could have been father, mother, and son, but not from their pedigrees. He rose to greet them, taking a closer look at the younger man, whom he could have sworn he'd seen somewhere before.

"Good morning, I'm Sasha Karpenko."

"Alf Rycroft," the older man replied, shaking him firmly by the hand.

"And I'm Mrs. Campion," said the woman. "You'll remember I called you," she added, sounding as if she was used to getting her own way.

"Indeed I do."

"Hi," said the younger man, "I'm—"

And then Sasha remembered. "Nice to see you again, Michael. How are you?"

"I'm well, thank you. And touched that you remember me. But then, I told Alf and Audrey on the journey up to London how you demolished the entire Oxford chess team single-handed, so perhaps I shouldn't be surprised that you could recall my name."

"So what are you up to now?" asked Sasha. "Didn't you read Jurisprudence?"

A waiter appeared, and once they'd ordered coffee, Michael answered Sasha's question.

"I'm a solicitor in Merrifield. But that isn't the reason we wanted to see you."

"Of course not. So let me start by asking what sort of party you had in mind."

"The Labour Party," said Alf.

Sasha looked puzzled.

"Allow me to explain," said Audrey Campion, in the same no-nonsense voice. "As I'm sure you know, until recently the Member of Parliament for Merrifield was Sir Max Hunter."

"Fiona's father," said Sasha. "How could I possibly forget? I saw that he died of a heart attack while out fox hunting."

"That's correct. But what you won't know is that last night the local Conservative Association selected his daughter to fight the by-election."

Sasha remained silent for some time before muttering, "So Fiona will be the first of my contemporaries to sit on the green benches."

"You can hardly be surprised by that," said Michael, "because we all assumed it would be either you or her who would be the first to climb the greasy pole."

"But I still don't understand why you've come all this way to tell me something I can read about in tomorrow's papers."

"I'm the association chairman of the Merrifield Labour Party," said Alf Rycroft. "And Audrey is the party agent."

"Unpaid, I might add," she said firmly.

"And my committee," continued Alf, "couldn't think of anyone better qualified to take on Miss Hunter."

"But surely it would be wiser to select someone with more experience, who has at least some knowledge of the constituency."

"We don't have the time to go through the normal selection procedure," said Alf. "We assumed the Conservatives would at least have the decency to wait until Sir Max was buried before they announced the date of the by-election, but they took advantage of the fact that we don't have a candidate in place."

"How typical of Fiona," said Sasha as the waiter returned with their coffee, which allowed him a moment to gather his thoughts. "I'm flattered," he said once the waiter had left, "but my problem is I simply don't have the time . . ."

"The by-election will be held three weeks from today, on Thursday, March the thirteenth," said Alf. "And as Sir Max had a majority of twelve thousand two hundred and fourteen, you have absolutely no chance of winning."

"Then why should I waste my time?"

"Because," said Mrs. Campion, "if you were to reduce the majority in a Tory stronghold, it would look good on your CV when you eventually apply for a seat that you might actually win."

"But you're a local man, Michael, why don't you stand?"

"Because Fiona Hunter always terrified the life out of me, but if she discovered that you're the Labour candidate, she'll be the one who's on the back foot for a change. Besides which, you know more about her than any of us."

"I'll need a little time to think about it," said Sasha. "How long have I got?"

"Ten minutes," said Alf.

"The motion before the association is that Sasha Konstantinovitch Karpenko be selected as the Labour Party candidate for the constituency of Merrifield. Those in favor?" said the chairman, looking around the assembled gathering. Twenty-three hands shot up. "Those against?" Not a single hand was raised. "Then I declare the motion carried unanimously," Alf Rycroft announced to as loud an ovation as twenty-three people could manage.

By the time Sasha boarded the last train back to London, he knew all twenty-three of their names, and not one of them thought he had a chance of winning.

"Another woman?" said Charlie as he crept into the bedroom just after midnight, determined not to wake her.

"Just over twenty-eight thousand of them," said Sasha, as he placed his head on the pillow and explained why he'd traveled down to Merrifield that morning and returned in the evening as the Labour candidate for a by-election. "So you won't be seeing much of me during the next three weeks."

"Congratulations, darling," said Charlie. She switched on the bedside light, and threw her arms around him. "What do you know about your opponent?"

"Everything."

"How come?"

"It's Fiona Hunter."

Charlie caught her breath and sat bolt upright before saying, "You have to beat her this time."

"Not possible, I'm afraid. They don't count the Conservative votes in Merrifield, they weigh them."

"Not this time, they won't," said Charlie, "because I'll be on that train with you tomorrow morning, so she'll have to beat both of us."

"But you've got your thesis to finish."

"I handed it in last week."

"And you didn't tell me?"

"I wanted to wait until I heard the result." She leaned across and kissed her husband. "Sleep well, my darling," she said, before placing her head back on the pillow. "You must be exhausted."

But Sasha couldn't sleep, as his mind was racing with all that had happened in such a short space of time. He'd thought he was preparing for a party booking, and had ended up being booked by a party.

⤙o⤚

Sasha and Charlie caught the 6:52 from Victoria to Merrifield the following morning, and arrived at the local Labour Party headquarters just before 8 a.m.

The chairman was sitting outside in his Ford Allegro waiting for them.

"Jump in," he said, once Sasha had introduced his wife. "Nice to meet you, Charlie, but we've no time to waste." He put the car into first gear, set off at a leisurely speed, and gave a running commentary as they drove down the high street and out into the countryside.

"There are twenty-six villages in the Merrifield constituency. They're the people who give the Tories their majority, and Fiona Hunter has a branch office in every one of them."

"How about us?" asked Charlie.

"We have one branch office," said Alf, "and the chap who runs it is seventy-nine. But the town of Roxton, with its population of sixteen thousand and a paper mill, guarantees that we never lose our deposit."

"Any good news?" asked Sasha.

"Not a lot," admitted Alf. "Although Sir Max wasn't universally popular in the constituency, he built a reputation for having the ear of the minister, and being able to get things done. He had a gift for finding out what was about to happen, and then taking the credit for it. Classic example, the building of a new hospital, which was part of the last Labour government's long-term infrastructure program, but just happened to be completed during a Conservative administration. By the time the health minister opened the hospital, you'd have thought it was Sir Max's idea in the first place, and he'd personally laid the first brick."

"A gift his daughter has inherited," said Charlie, with some feeling. "So how's she going down?"

"They like her," admitted Alf, "but then they've known her since the days when she was wheeled around the constituency in a pram. Rumor has it that her first words were 'Vote Hunter!,' and it wouldn't surprise me if Sir Max had left her the constituency in his will. It doesn't help our cause that the same name will appear on the ballot paper."

"So what's my line when the locals accuse me of being a carpetbagger?"

"Labour has never had a better chance of winning the seat," said Alf.

"But you've already admitted we haven't got a hope in hell," said Sasha.

"Welcome to the world of realpolitik," said Alf, "or at least the Merrifield version of it."

⤙o⤚

"So what's your first impression?" asked Michael when Sasha and Charlie joined the rest of the team for lunch at the Roxton Arms.

"The Conservatives may have all the best constituencies, but Labour still have all the best people," he said as he ate a ham sandwich that his mother wouldn't have given plate space to.

"Right," said Mrs. Campion after Sasha had devoured a pork pie, washed down with half a pint of Farley's. "The time has come to foist you upon an unsuspecting public. Our posters and leaflets haven't been printed yet, so we'll have to wing it for the first couple of days. And just remember, Sasha, there's only one sentence you have to deliver again and again until you're repeating it in your sleep," Audrey added, as she pinned a large red rosette to his lapel.

Sasha, accompanied by his chairman, agent, and a couple of party workers, ventured out onto the high street. When he encountered his first constituent, Sasha said, "My name's Sasha Karpenko, and I'm the Labour candidate for the by-election on Thursday, March the thirteenth. I hope I can rely on your vote?" He thrust out his hand, but the man ignored him and kept on walking. "Charming," muttered Sasha.

"Shh!" said Mrs. Campion. "It doesn't necessarily mean he won't be voting for you. He could be deaf, or in a hurry."

His second attempt was a little more successful, because a woman carrying a bag of shopping at least stopped to shake hands.

"What are you going to do about the closing of the cottage hospital?" she asked.

Sasha didn't even realize Roxton had a cottage hospital.

"He'll do everything in his power to get the council to reverse their decision," said Alf, coming to his rescue. "So make sure you vote Labour on March the thirteenth."

"But you haven't got a hope in hell," said the woman. "A donkey wearing a blue rosette would win Merrifield."

"Labour has never had a better chance of winning the seat," said Sasha, trying to sound confident, but the woman didn't look convinced as she picked up her bag and walked off.

"Hello, I'm Sasha Karpenko, and I'm the Labour candidate—"

"Sorry, Mr. Karpenko, I'll be voting for Hunter. I always do."

"But he died last week," protested Sasha.

"Are you sure?" said the man, "because my wife told me to vote Hunter again."

"Is it true that you were born in Russia?" asked the next man Sasha approached.

"Yes," said Sasha, "but—"

"Then I'll be voting Conservative for the first time," the man said, not breaking his stride.

"Hi, I'm Sasha Karpenko—"

"I'm voting Liberal," said a young woman pushing a pram, "and even we'll beat you this time."

"Hi, I'm Sasha—"

"Good luck, Sasha, I'll be voting for you, even though you haven't got a chance."

"Thank you," said Sasha. Turning to Alf he said, "Is it always this bad?"

"Actually, you're doing rather well compared to our last candidate."

"What happened to him?"

"Her. She had a nervous breakdown a week before the election, and didn't recover in time to vote." Sasha burst out laughing. "No, it's true," said Alf. "We've never seen her since."

"And to think I was the only man you wanted!" said Sasha.

"You'll be grateful to us when you find a safe seat, and become a minister," said Audrey, ignoring the sarcasm. It was the first time Sasha had considered he might one day be a minister.

"Look who I see on the other side of the road," said Charlie, nudging Sasha in the ribs.

Sasha looked across to see Fiona, surrounded by a team of supporters who were handing out leaflets and holding up banners that declared VOTE HUNTER FOR MERRIFIELD.

"They haven't even had to print new posters," said Alf bitterly.

"It's time to confront the enemy head-on," said Sasha and immediately marched across the high street, dodging in and out of the traffic.

"My name's Fiona Hunter, and I'm—"

"What are you going to do about the Roxton playing fields being turned into a supermarket, that's what I want to know."

"I have already spoken to the leader of the council concerning the issue," said Fiona, "and he's promised to keep me informed."

"Just like your father, full of promises, with bugger-all results."

Fiona smiled and moved on, leaving a local councilor to deal with the problem.

"Will the Tories increase my pension?" said an old woman, jabbing a finger at her. "That's what I want to know."

"They always have in the past," said Fiona effusively, "so you can be sure they will again, but only if we win in the next election."

"Jam tomorrow should be your slogan," said the woman.

Fiona smiled when she saw Sasha heading toward her, hand outstretched.

"How nice to see you, Sasha," she said. "What are you doing in Merrifield?"

"My name's Sasha Karpenko," he replied, "and I'm the Labour candidate for the by-election on March the thirteenth. I hope I can count on your vote?"

The smile was wiped off Fiona's face for the first time that day.

28
ALEX
Brooklyn

"When you return the Warhol to Lawrence and he gives you back your money, are you still sure you ought to be investing even more in Elena's?"

"Yes I am, Mother," said Alex. "But after making such a fool of myself, I've decided to go back to school."

"But you already have a degree."

"In economics," said Alex, "which is fine if you want to be a bank manager, but not an entrepreneur. So I've signed up for night school. I'll be doing an MBA at Columbia, so that when I come across another Evelyn, I won't make the same mistake. Meanwhile, I'm going to get a job at Lombardi's in Manhattan."

"But why support the opposition?"

"Because Lawrence told me they make the best pizzas in America, and I intend to find out why."

September was a busy month for Alex. He enrolled at night school to do his MBA, and despite working during the day at Lombardi's, he never once missed a lecture. His essays were always handed in on time and he read every book on the set texts list, and many that weren't. Ironically, Evelyn had managed to achieve what his mother hadn't.

His learning also progressed during the day, because Paolo, the manager of Lombardi's, showed him how the restaurant had earned its reputation. With Paolo to advise him, Alex began to make some small changes to Elena's, and later some larger ones. He would have liked to purchase a rollover oven from Antonelli in Milan, which would have made it possible to produce a dozen fresh pizzas every four minutes, but he couldn't afford it until he'd returned the picture and Lawrence had handed over the half million. He would miss her. The Warhol, not Evelyn.

⊸o⊷

Alex was on his way to night school when he saw her for the first time.

She was standing on the platform at 51st Street wearing a smart blue suit and carrying a leather briefcase. It was her neatly cropped auburn hair and deep brown eyes that captivated him. He tried not to stare at her, and when she glanced in his direction, he quickly looked away.

When the train pulled into the station, he found himself following the vision and sitting in the empty seat beside her even though she was going in the wrong direction. She opened her briefcase, took out a glossy magazine, and began reading. Alex glanced at the cover to see a painting by an artist called de Kooning. He could have sworn he'd seen a similar one in Lawrence's home, but decided *I own a Warhol* wouldn't be a good chat-up line.

"Did de Kooning paint the same subject again and again?" he asked, his eyes remaining fixed on the picture.

She looked at Alex, then at the cover of her magazine, before saying, "Yes, he did. This one is from his *Woman* series."

Her clipped accent reminded him of Evelyn, although nothing else did. He hesitated before saying, "Could I have seen one in a private collection?"

"It's possible. Although there are very few in private hands. There are several examples of his work in MoMA, so there's a chance you might have seen one there."

"Of course," said Alex, although he'd never entered the Museum of Modern Art, and only had a vague idea where it was. "You're right, that's where I must have seen it." When the train pulled into the next station, he hoped she wouldn't get off. She didn't.

"Who's your favorite artist?" he ventured as the doors closed.

She didn't respond immediately. "I'm not sure I have a favorite among the Abstract Expressionists, but I think Motherwell is underrated, and Rothko overrated."

"I've always admired Pollock's *Moon Woman*," said Alex, rather desperately. The painting he'd had to stare at for half an hour while he hid behind a pillar at Lawrence's birthday party.

"It's supposed to be one of his best, but I've only ever seen a photograph of it. Not many people have been lucky enough to see the Lowell Collection."

The train pulled into the next station, and once again, she didn't get off. *Lawrence Lowell is a personal friend of mine, so if you'd like to see his collection* . . . he wanted to say, but he was afraid she'd think she was sitting next to a lunatic.

"Do you work in the art world?" he ventured.

"Yes, I'm a very junior assistant in a West Side gallery," she said, closing her magazine.

"That must be fun."

"It is." She put the magazine back in her briefcase, and stood up as the train pulled into the next station.

He leaped up. "My name's Alex."

"Anna. It was nice to meet you, Alex."

He stood there like a statue as she got off the train. He waved as she walked down the platform, but she didn't look back.

"Damn, damn, damn," he said as the doors closed and she disappeared from sight. He'd have to get off at the next stop, turn around, and go back to 51st Street. It would be the first time he'd missed a lecture.

"Paolo, I need some advice."

"If it's about how to run a pizza joint, there's not much more I can teach you."

"No, I have a woman problem. I only met her once, and then I lost her."

"You're way ahead of me, kid. Better you start at the beginning."

"I met her on the subway. Well, met would be an exaggeration, because my attempt to open a conversation with her was pathetic. And just as I got going, she left me standing there. All I can tell you is her first name, and that she's an assistant in an art gallery on the West Side."

"OK, let's start with the station where you first saw her."

"Fifty-first Street."

"Expensive shops, lots of galleries. Let's try and narrow down the field. Do you know which period the gallery specializes in?"

"Abstract Expressionism, I think. At least that's what it said on the cover of her magazine."

"There must be at least a dozen galleries that specialize in that period. What else can you tell me about her?"

"She's beautiful, intelligent . . ."

"Age?"

"Early twenties."

"Build?"

"Slim, elegant, classy."

"Then what makes you think she'd have any interest in you?"

"I agree. But if there was the slightest chance, I—"

"You're a much better catch than you realize," said Paolo. "You're bright, charming, well educated, and I suppose some women might even find you good-looking."

"So what should I do next?" Alex asked, ignoring the sarcasm.

"First, you have to realize that the art world is a small community, especially at the top end. I suggest you visit the Marlborough on Fifty-seventh Street, and talk to an assistant who's about the same age. There's a chance they'll know each other, or at least have met at some opening."

"How come you know so much about art?"

"The Italians," said Paolo, "know about art, food, opera, cars, and women, because we have the best examples of all five."

"If you say so," said Alex. "I'll start first thing tomorrow morning."

"Not first thing, that would be a waste of time. Art galleries don't usually open before ten. The sort of clients who can afford to pay half a million dollars for a picture aren't early risers like you and me. And another thing, if you turn up looking like that, they'll think you've come to collect the trash. You'll have to dress and sound like a prospective customer if you want them to take you seriously."

"Where did you learn all this?"

"My father is a doorman at the Plaza, my mother works in Bloomingdale's, so I was educated at the university of life. And one more thing. If you really want to impress her, perhaps you should . . ."

⊰o⊱

Alex was up, dressed, and bargaining in the vegetable market by four thirty the following morning. Once he'd delivered his purchases to the restaurant, he returned home and had breakfast with his mother.

He didn't tell her what he had planned for the rest of the morning, and waited for her to leave for work before he took a second shower and selected a dark gray, single-breasted suit, white shirt, and a tie his mother had given him for Christmas. He then carefully took the Warhol down from the wall and wrapped it in some brown paper before placing it in a carrier bag.

He took a taxi into Manhattan, a necessary expense as he couldn't risk carrying such a valuable painting on the subway, and asked the driver to take him to West 57th Street.

When he arrived at the Marlborough Gallery, the lights were just being switched on. He studied the painting displayed in the window, which was by an artist called Hockney. When a young woman sat down behind the desk, he took a deep breath and strolled in.

Don't be in a hurry, Paolo had told him. *The rich are never in a hurry to part with their money.* He walked slowly around the gallery, admiring the paintings. It was like being back in Lawrence's home.

"Can I help you, sir?" He turned to find the assistant standing by his side.

"No, thank you. I was just looking."

"Of course. Do let me know if I can help you with anything."

Alex fell in love for a second time, not with the assistant, but with a dozen women he wished he could take home and hang on his bedroom wall. After being mesmerized by a small canvas by Renoir, he remembered that he had originally come in for a reason. He walked across to the assistant's desk.

"I recently met a girl called Anna who works at a gallery on the West Side that specializes in Abstract Expressionism, and I wondered if you'd come across her?"

The young woman smiled and shook her head. "I only began working here a week ago. Sorry."

Alex thanked her, but didn't leave the gallery until he'd taken another look at the Renoir. He didn't waste his or her time asking the price. He knew he couldn't afford her.

He moved on to a second gallery, and then a third, and spent the rest of the morning fruitlessly entering a dozen other establishments, and asking a dozen other young assistants the same question, but with the same result. When the bells of St. Patrick's Cathedral rang out once, he decided to take a break for lunch before continuing his quest. He spotted a small queue waiting outside a sandwich bar, and headed toward it, still clutching his Warhol. And then he saw her through a restaurant window.

She was sitting in a corner booth, chatting to a handsome man who looked as if he knew her well. His heart sank when the man leaned across the table and took her hand. Alex retreated to a nearby bench, where he sat despondently, no longer feeling hungry. He was just about to go home, when they came out of the restaurant together. The man leaned over to kiss her, but Anna turned away, not smiling. Then she walked off and left him standing there without another word.

Alex jumped up from the bench and began to follow her along Lexington, keeping his distance until she disappeared into an elegant art gallery. As he walked past N. Rosenthal & Co. he looked inside and saw her taking a seat behind a desk. He waited for a few moments before turning back. He then sauntered into the gallery without even glancing in her direction. A customer was speaking to her, and he pretended to be interested in one of the paintings. Eventually the chatty woman left, and Alex walked across to the desk. Anna looked up and smiled.

"Can I help you, sir?"

"I hope so." He took the Warhol out of the carrier bag, removed the wrapping, and placed it on the desk. Anna took a careful look at the painting, and then at Alex. A flicker of recognition crossed her face.

"I was hoping you might be able to value this picture for me."

She studied it once again before asking, "Is it yours?"

"No, it belongs to a friend of mine. He asked me to get it valued."

She took a second look at him before saying, "I don't have enough experience to give you a realistic valuation, but if you'd allow me to show the painting to Mr. Rosenthal, I'm sure he could help."

"Of course."

Anna picked up the painting, walked to the far end of the gallery, and disappeared into another room. Alex was admiring a Lee Krasner called *The Eye is the First Circle,* when a distinguished-looking gray-haired gentleman wearing a double-breasted dark blue suit, pink shirt, and red polka-dot bow tie emerged from his office carrying the painting. He placed it back on Anna's desk.

"You asked my assistant if I could value this picture for you?" he said, looking closely at Alex. The words "slow" and "measured" came to mind. This was not a man in a hurry. "I'm afraid I have to tell you, sir, that it's a copy. The original is owned by a Mr. Lawrence Lowell of Boston, and is part of the Lowell Collection."

I'm well aware of that, Alex wanted to tell him. "What makes you think it's a copy?" he asked.

"It's not the painting itself," said Rosenthal, "which I confess had me fooled for a moment. It was the canvas that gave it away." He turned the painting over and said, "Warhol couldn't have afforded such an expensive canvas in his early days, besides which, it's the wrong size."

"Are you certain?" asked Alex, suddenly feeling first angry and then sick.

"Oh yes. The canvas is an inch wider than the original one in the Lowell Collection."

"So it's a fake?"

"No, sir. A fake is when someone attempts to deceive the art world by claiming to have come across an original work that is not recorded in the artist's catalog raisonné. This," he said, "is a copy, albeit a damned fine copy."

"May I ask what it would have been worth had it been the original?" Alex asked tentatively.

"A million, possibly a million and a half," said Rosenthal. "Its provenance is impeccable. I believe Mr. Lowell's grandfather bought it directly from the artist in the early sixties, when he couldn't even pay his rent."

"Thank you," said Alex, having quite forgotten why he'd originally come into the gallery.

"If you'll excuse me," said Rosenthal. "I ought to get back to my office."

"Yes, of course. Thank you."

Rosenthal left them, and after a moment Alex realized Anna was staring at him. "We met on the subway, didn't we?" she said.

"Yes," he admitted. "Why didn't you say something when I first showed you the painting?"

"Because for a moment I wondered if you were an art thief."

"Nothing quite so glamorous," said Alex. "During the day I work at Lombardi's, and spend most evenings at business school."

"Lombardi's margheritas were my staple diet before I graduated."

"My mother cooks a mean calzone," said Alex, "if you'd like to give it a try."

"I would," said Anna. "Then you can tell me how you came into possession of such a fine copy of a Blue Jackie Kennedy."

"It was just an excuse to see you again."

29

ALEX

Brooklyn

"Now tell me," said Anna, "did you follow me onto that train?"

"Yes, I did," admitted Alex, "even though it was going in the wrong direction."

She laughed. "How romantic. So what did you do when I got off?"

"Traveled on to the next station, and as I was too late for my evening class, went home."

A waiter came across and handed them both a menu.

"What do you recommend?" Anna asked. "After all, you own the joint."

"My favorite is the pizza capricciosa, but you choose, because they're so big we can share."

"Then let's order one. But you're not off the hook, Alex. So after your lamentable failure at trying to pick me up, you decided like Antony to come in search of me."

"I spent the morning checking out half the galleries in Manhattan. Then by chance I spotted you having lunch in an expensive restaurant with a handsome older man."

"Not that much older," said Anna, teasing him. "Then you followed me to the gallery with the excuse that you wanted your painting valued, when surely you must have known it was a copy."

Alex said nothing as the waiter placed a large pizza between them in the center of the table.

"Wow, it looks great."

"My mother will have cooked this one herself," said Alex, cutting off a slice and putting it on Anna's plate. "I should warn you, she won't be able to resist coming over to meet you. So you'll have to tell her it's simply the best."

"But it is," said Anna after taking a bite. "In fact I think I'll bring my boyfriend here." Alex couldn't hide his disappointment, but then Anna grinned. "Ex-boyfriend. You saw him at the restaurant." Alex wanted to learn more about him, but Anna changed the subject. "Alex, it was obvious when Mr. Rosenthal told you your painting was a copy, that you were surprised. So I'm curious to know how it came into your possession."

Alex took his time telling her the whole story—well, almost the whole story—glad to at last have someone to share his secret with. By the time he'd come to their meeting in the gallery, Anna had almost finished her half of the pizza, while his remained untouched.

"And why would your friend give you half a million for a painting that can't be worth more than a few hundred dollars?"

"Because he doesn't know it's a copy. Now I'll have to tell him the truth, and what makes it worse, I can't see Evelyn returning one cent of my money."

Anna leaned across the table, touched his hand, and said, "I'm so sorry, Alex. Does this mean you won't be able to open the second Elena's?"

"Very few entrepreneurs don't have setbacks along the way," said Alex. "According to Galbraith, the wise ones chalk it up on the blackboard of experience and move on."

"Is it possible that your friend Lawrence was in on the scam, and deliberately placed you next to his sister at his party?"

"No," Alex said firmly. "I've never known a more decent, honest man in my life."

"I'm sorry," said Anna, "that was rude of me. I don't even know your friend. But I must confess, I'd love to see the Lowell Collection."

"That would be easy enough," said Alex, "if you could . . ."

"You must be Anna," said a voice. Alex looked up to see his mother standing over them.

"You have a gift for timing, Mother, that the Marx Brothers would be proud of."

"And he never stops talking about you," said Elena, ignoring him.

"Mother, now you're embarrassing me."

"I'm so glad he eventually found you. But wasn't he stupid not to have followed you off the train in the first place?"

"Mother!"

Anna burst out laughing.

"How was the pizza?" Elena asked.

"Simply the best," said Anna.

"I told her to say that," said Alex.

"Yes, he did," admitted Anna, leaning across the table and taking his hand. "But he needn't have bothered, because it is the best."

"Then can we hope to see you again?"

"Mother, you're worse than Mrs. Bennet."

"And why have you eaten hardly anything?" she asked, as if he was still a schoolboy.

"Mother, go away."

"Has Alex told you about his plans for a second restaurant?"

"Yes, he has." Alex was uncomfortably aware that he hadn't told his mother the whole story. "It sounds very exciting, Mrs. Karpenko."

"Elena, please," she said as Alex stood up, clutching his knife. "Well, I'd better get back to the kitchen, or the boss might sack me," she added, smiling at them. "But I hope I'll see you again, then I can tell you how Alex won the Silver Star."

Alex raised the knife above his head, but she had already scurried away. "I apologize, she's not normally so—"

"There's nothing to apologize for, Alex. She's just like her pizzas, simply the best. But do tell me how you won the Silver Star," she said, suddenly serious.

"The truth is, it should have been awarded to the Tank, not me."

"The Tank?"

Alex told her everything that had happened when his unit had come across the Vietcong patrol on Bacon Hill. How the Tank had not only saved Lawrence's life, but his as well.

"I would love to have met him," said Anna quietly.

"I don't suppose you'd consider . . ."

"Consider what?"

"Coming to Virginia with me? I've wanted to visit his grave for so long, and—"

"What girl could refuse such an offer?" Alex looked embarrassed. "Of course I'll come with you." She burst out laughing. "Why don't we go on Sunday?"

"Lawrence has just arrived back from Europe, so I'll have to go and see him in Boston this weekend, and tell him what Mr. Rosenthal had to say about the Warhol. But I'm free the following weekend."

"Then it's a date."

Alex stepped off the train in Boston carrying an overnight case and a large carrier bag. He hailed a yellow cab and gave the driver Lawrence's address.

As each mile passed, Alex became more and more anxious. He knew he had no choice but to tell his friend the truth.

Lawrence was standing on the top step waiting to greet his guest as the taxi drove up the long driveway and came to a halt outside the house.

"I see you've brought the picture back," he said as they shook hands. "Let's go to my study, complete the exchange, and then we can relax for the rest of the weekend."

Alex said nothing as he followed him across the hall. When he walked into Lawrence's study, he remained speechless.

Almost every inch of the oak-paneled walls was filled with paintings and photographs of his family and friends. Alex's eyes settled on Nelson Rockefeller, which made Lawrence grin as he took his place behind the desk and ushered Alex into the seat opposite him.

When he unwrapped the painting, a large smile appeared on Lawrence's face. "Welcome home, Jackie," he said, and immediately pulled open a drawer in his desk and extracted a checkbook.

"You won't be needing that," said Alex.

"Why not? We made a deal."

"Because it isn't a Warhol. It's a copy."

"A copy?" Lawrence repeated in disbelief as he took a closer look at the painting.

"I'm afraid so. And that's not my view, but the opinion of no less an authority than Nathanial Rosenthal."

Lawrence remained calm, but said almost to himself, "How did she manage it?"

"I don't know, but I can guess," said Alex.

Lawrence looked at the picture. "Once again she must have known all along." He opened his checkbook, took the top off his pen, and wrote out the figure $500,000.

"There's no way I'm ever going to cash your check," said Alex. "So you needn't bother signing it."

"You must," said Lawrence. "It's clear that my sister's deceived both of us."

"But you didn't know," said Alex, "and that's all that matters."

"But without the money you won't be able to open Elena Two."

"Then it will have to wait. Anyway, I learned more in one weekend with your sister than I've done in a year at business school."

"Perhaps we should consider an alternative plan," Lawrence suggested.

"What do you have in mind?"

"In exchange for my five hundred thousand, I get a ten percent stake in your company. The one that's going to end up bigger than my godfather's."

"Fifty percent would be fairer."

"Then let's compromise. I'll take fifty percent of your burgeoning empire, but the moment you return my half a million, it will fall to ten percent."

"Twenty-five percent," said Alex.

"That's more than generous of you," said Lawrence as he signed the check.

"It's overgenerous of you," said Alex. When Lawrence handed him the check, they shook hands for a second time.

"Now I understand," said Lawrence as he placed his checkbook back in the drawer, "why Todd Halliday slipped away so soon after dinner on my birthday. Originally he was meant to be staying overnight."

"The Empress Catherine herself would have been proud of your sister," said Alex. "She knew the only way I was going to see the Warhol was if I spent the night with her."

"Five hundred thousand," said Lawrence. "An expensive one-night stand. However, I've already been working on a plan to make sure she pays back every penny. Let's have supper."

⊸o⊷

Lawrence waited until Alex had checked over the questions a second time. He only added the words *insurance company?* before he handed the crib sheet back. Lawrence nodded, took a deep breath, picked up the phone, and dialed an overseas number.

He once again studied the list as he waited for one of them to answer the phone. He had chosen his time carefully: 12 noon in Boston, 6 p.m. in Nice. They should be back from lunch at La Colombe d'Or, but not yet have left for the casino in Monte Carlo.

"Hello?" said a familiar voice.

"Hi, Eve, it's me. Thought I'd bring you up to date on the Warhol."

"Have the police found it?"

"Yes, it was hanging above the mantelpiece in Karpenko's apartment in Brighton Beach. They could hardly miss it."

"So is it now safely back in the Jefferson room?"

"I'm afraid not. The Boston police department decided to have the picture valued before they pressed charges, and, here's the surprise, it turns out to be a copy."

"Why are you surprised?" asked Evelyn, a little too quickly.

"What do you mean?" asked Lawrence innocently.

"He obviously substituted a copy for the real thing. My bet is the original will have been smuggled out of the country. It's probably somewhere in Russia by now."

Somewhere in the south of France is more likely, thought Lawrence. "The insurance company agree with you, Eve," said Lawrence, checking his list, "and they wondered when you'd be back in Boston, as you were the last person to see Karpenko before he left for New York."

"I wasn't planning on returning for some months," said Evelyn. "I assume the police have arrested your friend Karpenko."

"They did, but he's out on bail. He claims he gave you a check for five hundred thousand dollars to invest with Todd in a start-up company, and you offered him the picture as security."

"The exact opposite is true," said Evelyn. "He begged me to invest some money in his pizza company, and I refused and sent him packing."

"But he's produced the check," said Lawrence. "So it would be helpful if you could come and tell the police your version of the story."

"My version of the story?" said Evelyn, her voice rising. "Whose side are you on, Lawrence?"

"Yours of course, Eve, but the police are refusing to press charges until they've interviewed you."

"Then they'll have to wait, won't they?" said Evelyn, slamming down the phone.

Lawrence replaced the receiver, turned to Alex, and said, "I have a feeling she won't be returning for some time," a broad smile appearing on his face.

"But you've lost your Warhol," said Alex.

"I confess I'll miss Jackie," said Lawrence, "but not Evelyn."

⊸o⊷

"I only heard one side of the conversation," said Todd Halliday, handing his wife a glass of whiskey after she'd slammed the phone down. "Am I right in thinking that Lawrence now realizes the Warhol's a copy, and Karpenko's produced the check?"

"Yes," said Evelyn, emptying the glass. "I forgot that checks were returned to the issuing bank."

"But it was made out to cash, so they won't be able to trace it back to you."

"True, but if Lawrence were ever to discover—"

"If he does," said Todd, "we'll just have to revert to plan B."

⊸o⊷

When Alex returned to New York, he had to explain to his mother why he'd come back with a check for five hundred thousand dollars even though he'd told Lawrence the Warhol was a copy. He was surprised by her only question.

"Have you asked Anna to marry you yet?"

"Mama, I've only known her for a week."

"Your father proposed to me twelve days after we met."

"Then I've still got another five days," said Alex, smiling.

⊸o⊷

Alex stepped off the train at 14th Street just after midday, and headed straight for Lombardi's. He took a seat, but didn't order anything. When the manager appeared he handed him the contract. Paolo sat down and took his time checking over every clause. There were no surprises. Everything Alex had promised had been included, so he happily signed on the dotted line.

"Welcome on board, partner," said Alex as they shook hands. "You'll be managing Elena One, while I concentrate on getting Elena Two up and running."

"I'm looking forward to working with you," said Paolo.

"See you at five to eight on Monday morning, because it's high time you met my mother. Mind you, it's probably a good thing you didn't before you signed the contract. I've got to run. I'm having lunch with someone I can't afford to be late for."

"So you found her?"

"Sure did."

Alex arrived at Le Bernardin only moments before Anna appeared.

"How did Boston go?" was her first question after they placed their orders.

"It couldn't have gone better," he said, and explained why he would still be opening Elena 2 on time.

"What a remarkable friend you have in Lawrence," said Anna. "So where's the Warhol?"

"The real one, or the copy?"

"The copy to start with."

"Back in the Jefferson room."

"And the original?"

"Lawrence thinks it's probably in the south of France. Which is another reason Evelyn won't be coming back to Boston in a hurry."

"Don't count on it," said Anna. "The man you've described would never allow his sister to go to jail."

"You know that, and I know that, but can Evelyn risk it? Anyway, what did you get up to while I was away?"

"I had lunch at Lombardi's."

"Traitor."

"And although your mother cooks a far superior pizza, their menus are in a different class," she said as their food was served.

"I've never noticed."

"Don't forget, the customer sees the menu long before they see their food. As design was part of my degree course, I thought I could come up with something a little more enticing for Elena's." She took half a dozen sheets of paper out of her carrier bag and placed them on the table.

Alex studied the different designs for some time before he said, "Wow, I see what you mean."

"They're only preliminary sketches," said Anna. "I'll have a more polished version by the time we go to Virginia."

"I can't wait," said Alex, as the waiter whisked their empty plates away.

"But you'll have to," said Anna, checking her watch. "Must dash. Mr. Rosenthal will raise his cultured eyebrow if I'm a minute late."

While Anna returned to the gallery, Alex took the subway to Brighton Beach and dropped in to Elena's to let his mother know Paolo would be joining them on Monday.

"And Anna?" said Elena.

"She's fine," said Alex, who quickly left for his other world, before she could remind him he only had three days left to beat his father's record.

He was sitting in the front row of the lecture theater at Columbia only moments before Professor Donovan made his entrance.

"This evening, we will consider the significance of the Marshall Plan," said Donovan, "and the role President Truman played in assisting the Europeans to get back on their feet after the Second World War. The financial instability facing Europe in 1945 was such that . . ."

By the time Alex got home just after ten, he was exhausted. He found his mother in the kitchen chatting to Dimitri, who'd just arrived back from Leningrad.

Alex collapsed into the nearest chair.

"Dimitri tells me that your uncle Kolya has just been made convener of the dockers' union," said Elena. "Isn't that wonderful news?"

Alex didn't comment. He was sound asleep and quietly snoring.

30

ALEX

Boston

"I'd love to hear more about your life in the Soviet Union, and how you ended up coming to America," said Anna, as the train pulled out of Penn Station.

"The sanitized version, or do you want all the gory details?"

"The truth."

Alex began with the death of his father, and everything that had happened to him between then and the day he met her on the subway on 51st Street. He only left out the real reason he'd nearly killed Major Polyakov, and the fact that Dimitri worked for the CIA. When he came to the end, Anna's first question took him by surprise.

"Do you think it's possible your school friend might have been responsible for your father's death?"

"I've thought about that many times," admitted Alex. "I've no doubt Vladimir was capable of such an act of treachery, and I only hope for his sake we never meet again."

"How different it might have been, if you and your mother had climbed into the other crate."

"I wouldn't have met you, for a start," said Alex as he took her hand. "So now you've heard my life story, it's your turn."

"I was born in a prison camp in Siberia. I never knew my father, and my mother died before I could even—"

"Good try," said Alex, placing an arm around her shoulder. She turned and kissed him for the first time. It took him a few moments to recover, before he murmured, "Now tell me the real story."

"I didn't escape from Siberia, but from South Dakota, when I was offered a place at Georgetown. I'd always wanted to go to art school, but I wasn't quite good enough, so I settled for art history, and ended up being offered a job at Rosenthal's."

"You must have done well at Georgetown," said Alex, "because Mr. Rosenthal didn't strike me as someone who suffers fools gladly."

"He's very demanding," said Anna, "but quite brilliant. He's not only a scholar but a shrewd dealer, which is why he's so highly respected in the profession. I'm learning so much more from him than I did at university. Now I've met your indefatigable mother, tell me something about your father."

"He was the most remarkable man I've ever known. Had he lived, I've no doubt he would have been the first president of an independent Russia."

"Whereas his son will end up as president of a pizza company in Brooklyn," she teased.

"Not if my mother has anything to do with it. She'd like me to be a professor, a lawyer, or a doctor. Anything but a businessman. But I still have no idea what I'm going to do after I leave business school. I have to admit, though, that you and Lawrence have changed my life."

"How?"

"While I was searching for you, I dropped into several other galleries. It was like discovering a new world where I kept meeting so many beautiful women. I'm hoping that when we get back to New York, you might introduce me to even more."

"Then we'll have to start at MoMA, move on to the Frick, and if the love affair continues, I'll introduce you to several reclining women at the Metropolitan. And to think I thought it was me you'd fallen for."

"Anna, I fell for you the moment I saw you. If you'd only turned around after you got off that train and given me even the hint of a smile, I would have battered the doors down and chased after you."

"My mother taught me never to look back."

"Your mother sounds as bad as mine, but can she cook a calzone?"

"Not a hope. She's a schoolteacher. Second grade."

"And your father?"

"He's the principal at the same school, but no one's in any doubt who really runs the place."

"I can't wait to meet them," said Alex as Anna rested her head on his shoulder.

Alex had never known a journey to pass so quickly. They swapped stories about their upbringing, and she introduced him to Fra Angelico, Bellini, and Caravaggio, while he told her about Tolstoy, Pushkin, and Lermontov.

They'd only reached the seventeenth century by the time the train pulled into Union Station just after eleven thirty. Alex didn't speak as the taxi drove them to the National Cemetery. When he and Anna walked along the manicured lawns, passing row upon row of unadorned white gravestones, he was reminded of his conversation with Lieutenant Lowell in a dugout and the word "futility" rang in his ears. Not a day went by when he didn't remember the Tank. Not a day went by when he didn't thank whatever god there might be for how lucky he was to have survived.

They stopped when they reached the gravestone of Private First Class Samuel T. Burrows. Anna stood by silently as Alex wept unashamedly. Some time passed before he pulled a handkerchief from his pocket, unwrapped it, knelt down, and placed the Silver Star on his friend's grave.

Alex didn't know how long he stood there. "Good-bye, old friend," he said, when he finally turned to leave. "I will return."

Anna smiled at him so tenderly that he began to weep again.

"Thank you, Anna," he said as she took him in her arms. "The Tank would have loved you, and you would have approved of him being my best man."

"If that was a proposal," said Anna, who couldn't help blushing, "my mother would point out that we've only known each other for two weeks."

"Twelve days was enough for my father," said Alex, as he fell to one knee and produced a small velvet box from his pocket. He opened it to reveal his grandmother's engagement ring.

As he placed the ring on the third finger of Anna's left hand, she delivered a line he would remember for the rest of his life.

"I must be the only girl who's ever been proposed to in a cemetery."

"How do you like the new menus?" asked Alex.

"Classy, like your mother," said Lawrence. "Did she design them?"

"No, Anna did, in her spare time."

"I can't wait to meet this girl. Perhaps I should invite her up to Boston for the weekend to see my art collection."

Alex laughed. "And I can tell you she'd accept, because Anna can't wait to meet you and view the collection. So, Lawrence, as I suspect you didn't fly down to New York just to flatter me, I can only hope you don't want your money back, because I've already spent it."

"But are you ready for me to invest even more?"

"Why would you do that?"

"Because if Elena's is going to expand, the only thing Todd was right about, you'll need an injection of capital."

"And you'd be willing to supply it?"

"You bet. It's in my interest to do so, as I own fifty percent of the business."

"Only until I pay you back."

"Which could take you some considerable time if you agree to my proposal."

Alex laughed. "Your godfather wouldn't approve."

"I can't imagine why. One of his first investments was in McDonald's, despite his never having eaten a hamburger in his life. But we do have a problem."

"And what's that?" said Alex, as Paolo returned with the day's special.

"I think I may have found the perfect site for Elena Three in Boston, but how do we duplicate your mother?"

"It will always be her recipes on the menu," said Alex. "And God help any chef who falls below her high standards."

"How do you think she'd feel about spending the first month in whichever city we choose whenever we open a new Elena's?"

"If she was convinced it was your idea," said Alex, "she might just go along with it."

"How are you enjoying today's specials?" asked a familiar voice.

Lawrence stood to greet Elena. "Superb," he said, two fingers touching his lips. Alex recognized the special smile his mother reserved for her favorite customers. "And I wondered, Elena, if you and I could have a private word later, preferably when Alex is not around?"

When Elena 3 opened its doors to the Boston public for the first time, Alex was surprised by the interest shown by the local and national press. But then, he wasn't a politician.

Ted Kennedy, who presided over the opening ceremony, told the assembled gathering that in the past he had opened hospitals, schools, football stadiums, even an airport, but never a pizza parlor. "But let's face it," he continued, "this is an election year." He waited for the laughter to die down before adding, "In any case, Elena's is no ordinary pizza parlor. My good friend, Lawrence Lowell, your Democratic candidate for Congress, got behind this enterprise right from the start. You see he believes in Elena Karpenko and her son, Alex, who escaped from the tyranny of Communism in the belief that they could build a new life in the United States. They personify the American dream."

Alex looked around to see his mother hiding behind a fridge with Anna standing by her side. He wondered if she'd told her yet.

"Ladies and gentlemen," said Kennedy, "it gives me great pleasure to officially declare Elena Three open."

Once the applause had died down, Lawrence stepped forward to thank the senator, adding, "Once I've had today's special, the Congressman pizza—cheesy, a lot of ham with a pinch of salt—I'll be well prepared to set out on the campaign trail."

He waited for the cheers to subside before going on to say, "I also have an important announcement to make. I have invited Alex Karpenko to join my team, as a press liaison officer."

"But he's never been involved in a campaign before," shouted one of the journalists.

"And I hadn't eaten a pizza before I came to America," Alex retorted, which was greeted with more cheers.

Once Lawrence had finished his speech, Alex looked around for Senator Kennedy, so he could thank him. But he'd already left for his next engagement, giving Alex an immediate insight into what the next twelve weeks were going to be like.

⊸o⊷

"Do you think your brother reported the theft of the picture to the police?" asked Todd after the butler had left the room.

"What makes you think he didn't?" said Evelyn, taking a sip of wine.

"The front page of the *Globe* rather suggests he didn't," said Todd, as he passed the paper across to his wife.

Her eyes settled on a photo of a smiling Ted Kennedy standing between Lawrence Lowell and Alex Karpenko. "The bastard," she said as she read the report of Senator Kennedy's speech before he opened Elena 3.

"Perhaps it's time for us to go back to Boston and let everyone know you'll be voting Republican for the first time," said Todd.

"That would be lucky to get a mention on page sixteen of the *Herald*, and wouldn't come as a surprise to many people. No," said Evelyn, "what I have in mind for my brother will make the front page of *The New York Times*."

⊸o⊷

Alex was surprised by how fascinated he became with the whole election process, and how much he enjoyed every aspect of the campaign. For the first time he understood why his father had wanted to be a trade union leader.

He liked the raw contact with the voters on the ground, in the factories, on the doorstep. He reveled in public meetings and was always happy to stand in for Lawrence when the candidate couldn't be in two places at once.

Most of all, he enjoyed the weekly visits to the capital to be briefed by the party leaders on how the national campaign was going, and what the next policy statement would be. In fact Washington became his second home. He even began to wonder, although he didn't mention it to Anna, if one day he might join Lawrence in Washington, as the representative for the Eighth Congressional District of New York.

The only thing he didn't enjoy was the long periods of separation from his fiancée, and he found himself waiting impatiently for her to join him in Boston every weekend. And although the campaign seemed to go on forever, she never once complained.

They'd already set the date for the wedding—for three days after the last vote had been cast—although he hadn't yet told his mother Anna was pregnant. Dimitri would be best man, Lawrence chief usher, and there were no prizes for guessing who would be in charge of the catering.

⊸o⊷

"Do you have photographic proof?" asked Evelyn.

"A dozen or more pictures," said a voice on the other end of the line.

"And his birth certificate?"

"We had that even before we signed him up."

"So what happens next?"

"You just sit back, relax, and wait for your brother to withdraw from the race."

⁂

"The only problem with having you on my team," said Lawrence, "is how many voters are saying you'd make a far better candidate than me. More people are turning up to hear you speak than ever attend my rallies."

"But the Lowell family has had a representative in Washington for over a hundred years," said Alex. "I'm just a first-generation immigrant, fresh off the boat."

"As are many of my supporters, which is why you'd make an ideal candidate. If you ever decide to stand for anything, from dogcatcher to senator, I'd be happy to support you."

⁂

Evelyn and Todd boarded a flight back to Nice that afternoon, as they didn't want to be in Boston when the first editions of the papers hit the streets the next day.

"Did you post the package to Hawksley?" asked Todd, as he fastened his seatbelt.

"Hand delivered it to his headquarters," said Evelyn. "Couldn't risk the mail after what they charged me for those photographs." She smiled as the stewardess offered her a glass of champagne.

"What if Lawrence finds out the truth?"

"It will be too late by then."

⁂

"But you must get a hundred crank calls every day," said Blake Hawksley. "Why take this one seriously?" he asked, pointing at a dozen photographs strewn across his desk.

"I don't get many hand-delivered by a smartly dressed woman with a clipped Brahmin accent," said his campaign manager.

"So what are you advising me to do about it?" asked the Republican candidate.

"Let me share the information with a good contact I have on *The Boston Globe,* and see what he makes of it."

"But the *Globe* always supports the Democrats."

"Perhaps they won't after they've seen these," said Steiner, collecting up the photographs and placing them back in the envelope. "Don't forget their first interest is selling newspapers, and this could double their circulation."

"When they see them, the first person they'll call will be me. So what do I say?"

"No comment."

⁂

Alex read the lead story on the *Globe*'s front page a second time before he passed the paper to Anna. When she finished the article he asked, "Did you know that Lawrence was gay?"

"Of course," said Anna. "Everyone did. Well, everyone except you, it would seem."

"Do you think he'll have to step down as candidate?" said Alex, looking at the photographs spread across the center pages.

"Why should he? Being gay isn't a crime. It might even increase his majority."

"But having sex with a minor is a crime."

"It was obviously a set-up," said Anna. "A street hustler who's fifteen, going on thirty, traps Lawrence, having no doubt been paid handsomely for the part he played. It wouldn't even surprise me if the Republicans are behind it."

"Did you see what Hawksley said when the *Globe* called him?" asked Alex.

"No comment. And you should advise Lawrence to do the same."

"I don't think the voters will let him get away with that. I'd better go over to Beacon Hill immediately, before he says something to the press that he'll later regret." As Alex got up from the breakfast table he smiled ruefully. "It doesn't help that he's addressing the Daughters of the American Revolution at lunch today."

"Give him my love," said Anna, "and tell him to tough it out. He might be surprised how sympathetic people are. We don't all live inside the Washington beltway."

Alex took Anna in his arms and kissed her. "I got lucky when I stepped onto the wrong train."

Urged on by Alex, the cabdriver broke the speed limit several times in an attempt to get to Lawrence's home before the press beat him to it. But his efforts were in vain, because by the time they reached Beacon Hill a marauding pack of journalists and photographers had already pitched their tents on the sidewalk in front of Lawrence's town house, and clearly had no intention of budging until the candidate emerged from his castle and made a statement.

For the past month Alex had been trying to get even one of them to attend one of Lawrence's rallies and give him some coverage, only to be met with, "Why should we bother, when the result's a foregone conclusion?" Now they no longer believed that was the case, they were hovering like vultures who'd spotted a wounded animal attempting to hide in the undergrowth.

"Is Mr. Lowell going to withdraw?" shouted one of the reporters as Alex stepped out of the cab.

"Will you be taking his place?" Another.

"Did you know he had sex with a minor?" A third.

Alex said nothing as he pushed his way through the baying pack, almost blinded by the photographers' flashbulbs. He was relieved when Caxton opened the front door even before he knocked.

"Where is he?" he asked as the butler closed the door behind him.

"Mr. Lowell is still in his room, sir. He hasn't appeared since I took his breakfast up over an hour ago, along with the morning papers."

Alex bounded up the stairs, not stopping until he reached the master bedroom. He paused for a moment to catch his breath, then knocked softly on the door. There was no reply. He knocked a second time, a little louder, but still nothing. Tentatively he turned the handle, pushed open the door, and stepped inside.

Lawrence was hanging from a beam. A Harvard tie his noose.

31

SASHA

Merrifield

"This one's from the butcher," said Charlie. "It's their monthly account."

"Pay it immediately," said Elena. "Sasha insists on paying all our suppliers by return of post; that way we're guaranteed the finest cuts, the freshest vegetables, and bread that's come out of the oven that morning. A week late and you get what's left over from the day before. Two weeks late, and they palm you off with whatever they haven't been able to pass on to their regular customers. A month late, and they'll stop supplying you."

"I'll write out a check now," said Charlie. "Sasha can sign it when he gets back from the constituency, and we can drop it off at the butcher's on the way to the station tomorrow morning."

"It was good of you to take the day off and give me a hand with all this," said Elena, staring despairingly at the stack of post on the table in front of her.

"Sasha's only sorry he's not here to deal with it himself, but he can't afford to take even a couple of hours off at the moment."

"Does that mean he's going to win?" asked Elena.

"No, it does not," said Charlie firmly. "Merrifield is a rock-solid Tory seat. Mother Teresa couldn't hope to win it, even if she was up against the devil himself."

"But Sasha is up against the devil," said Elena.

"Fiona's not quite that bad."

"But if he can't win," said Elena, as Charlie opened the next letter, "why is he bothering, when there's still so much work to be done here?"

"Because he feels he has to win his spurs and prove himself on the field of battle, if he hopes to eventually be offered a safe seat."

"But surely the people of Merrifield can work out that Sasha would make a better MP than Fiona Hunter?"

"I have no doubt that Sasha would win if it was a marginal seat," said Charlie, "but it isn't, so we'll just have to accept he's going to lose this one."

"I'm not sure I'll ever understand English politics. In Russia, they know exactly who's going to win, without bothering to count the votes."

"Just be grateful that cooking is an international language," said Charlie, "that doesn't require translation. Now, this one," she said as she read the next letter, "is a reminder that the dishwasher in Elena Two is now three years old, and the company have recently launched a new model which has double the capacity of the old machine, and can wash everything at twice the speed."

"So when will the by-election take place?" asked Elena.

"Eleven days to go, and then we can all get back to normal."

"No, you can't. Because then Sasha will be a Member of Parliament and your life will be even more hectic."

"Elena, how many times do I have to tell you, he can't win," said Charlie, trying not to sound exasperated.

"Never underestimate Sasha," said Elena under her breath, but although Charlie heard her, she didn't respond, because she had to read the next letter a second time.

"What's the matter?" asked Elena when she saw the look on Charlie's face.

Charlie threw her arms around her mother-in-law, handed the letter to her, and said, "Congratulations! Why don't you read it for yourself, while I go and open a bottle of champagne."

COWARD!

screamed the headline on the front page of the *Merrifield Gazette*.

"But I never said that," protested Sasha.

"I know you didn't," said Alf, "but that's what the journalist assumed you meant when you told him you were disappointed that Fiona wouldn't agree to take part in a public debate."

"Should I complain to the editor?"

"Certainly not," said Alf. "That's the best free publicity we've had in years, and what's more, she'll have to respond, which will give us another headline tomorrow."

"I agree," said Charlie. "Let her worry about you for a change."

"And I see your mother is also making the headlines," said Alf, turning the page.

"She most certainly is," said Sasha, "and it's no more than she deserves, although even I was surprised that both restaurants were awarded a Michelin star."

"Once this is all over," said Alf, "I intend to take the whole team up to London so they can sample your mother's cooking."

"Nice idea," said Charlie. "But be warned, Alf, the only thing she'll want to know is why her son isn't your Member of Parliament."

"So what are we meant to be up to today?" asked Sasha, champing to get back to work.

"There are still a few villages in the constituency that you haven't visited yet. All you have to do is walk up and down the high street, and shake hands with at least one local resident, so no one can say you didn't even bother to visit them."

"Isn't that a bit cynical?"

"And make sure you have lunch at a local pub," said Alf, ignoring the comment, "and tell the landlord you're thinking of buying a house in the constituency."

"But I'm not."

"And then I want you back in Roxton to canvass the council estate between five thirty and seven thirty, when most people will be getting home from work. But you can take a break between seven thirty and eight o'clock."

"Why then?"

"Because you'll only lose votes if you interrupt someone while they're watching *Coronation Street*." Sasha and Charlie burst out laughing. "I'm not joking," said Alf.

"And after that, do I keep on canvassing?"

"No, never knock on anyone's door after eight. I've arranged for you to address another public meeting, this time at the Roxton YMCA."

"But only twelve people bothered to turn up to the last one. And that included you, Charlie, and Mrs. Campion's dog."

"I know," said Alf, "but that's still five more than the last candidate managed. And at least when you sat down, the dog was wagging its tail."

⊸o⊷

Sasha was surprised by the warm welcome he received on the doorsteps and in the streets during the last week of the campaign. Several people commented on the fact that Fiona had refused Sasha's challenge to a public debate on the grounds that she couldn't agree on a date with all the candidates, which produced another favorable headline: ANYTIME SUITS ME SAYS LABOUR CANDIDATE.

"You'll know you've made it," said Alf, "when they replace the words 'Labour candidate' with your name."

"Especially if they get the spelling right," said Mrs. Campion.

Alf nodded toward Charlie, who was chatting to a young man outside the local Jobcentre. "And what's more," said Alf, "if your wife was the candidate and your mother agreed to open a restaurant in Merrifield, we'd have a far better chance."

During the last few days before the vote, Sasha didn't even bother to go home, but slept in Alf's spare room, so he was always up in time to greet the morning commuters.

⊸o⊷

Polling day was one long blur as Sasha rushed around the constituency, knocking on doors that had a tick on the party's internal canvass returns, to remind their supporters to vote. He even drove some of the elderly, lame, and lazy to the nearest polling station, although he wasn't sure that all of them actually voted for him.

When the polls closed at ten o'clock on Thursday evening, Alf told him, "You couldn't have done more. In fact I'd say you're the best candidate we've ever had."

"Thank you," replied Sasha, then whispered to Charlie, "It was a one-horse race."

After half a pint of bitter and a shared packet of crisps in the Roxton Arms, Alf suggested they make their way across to the town hall, where the count was already under way.

When Alf, Sasha, and Charlie entered the main room, they were greeted by rows and rows of long tables, where volunteers were placing ballot papers into separate piles, while others were counting them, first in tens then in hundreds and finally thousands.

They spent the next couple of hours walking around the room, discreetly checking the piles. Alf told Sasha more than once that he couldn't believe what he was seeing. When the town clerk, as returning officer, announced the result just after 3 a.m., a gasp went up from the Conservative ranks, while the Labour Party workers began applauding and slapping Sasha on the back.

Alf wrote down the figures on the back of a cigarette packet and stared at them in disbelief.

Roger Gilchrist (Lib) 2,709
Fiona Hunter (Con) 14,146
Screaming Lord Sutch (Ind) 728
Sasha Karpenko (Lab) 11,365
Janet Brealey (Ind) 37

"I therefore declare that Fiona Hunter has been duly elected as the Member of Parliament for the constituency of Merrifield," announced the town clerk.

Fiona stepped up to the microphone to make her acceptance speech. She began by thanking her party workers and went on to say how much she was looking forward to representing the citizens of Merrifield in the House of Commons, but never once mentioned the names of her opponents. When she stepped aside to allow Sasha to take her place, she received less than enthusiastic applause.

Sasha followed and accepted defeat graciously, congratulating his opponent on her well-run campaign, and wishing her success as Member of Parliament. Once all five candidates had delivered their speeches, Sasha left the stage to rejoin his team, who were celebrating as if they'd won by a landslide.

"You've cut their majority from twelve thousand two hundred and fourteen to less than three thousand," said Alf. "That will look very good on your CV, and God help whoever follows you as our candidate at the general election."

"Won't you want me to stand again?" asked Sasha.

"No, we won't expect you to do that," said Alf. "Not least because

I have a feeling you'll be offered several winnable seats before then, possibly even a safe Labour one."

"I've loved every moment of these last three weeks," said Sasha.

"Well, you don't have to be bonkers to be the Labour candidate in a seat like Merrifield," said Alf, "but it certainly helps. My final responsibility as chairman is to make sure you catch the last train back to Victoria."

"I think you'll find it's the first train to Victoria," said Charlie.

As they walked onto the platform for the last time, Alf kissed Charlie on both cheeks, then shook hands warmly with Sasha.

"You were a fine candidate, sir," he said. "I hope I live long enough to see you take your seat at the Cabinet table."

The four of them met once a quarter. It wasn't formal enough to be described as a board meeting, or casual enough to be thought of as a family get-together. The meeting always took place around a table in the alcove of Elena 1 at four o'clock on a Monday afternoon. Late enough for all the lunch guests to have departed, and early enough to be finished before the first dinner booking arrived.

Sasha always chaired the meeting, while Charlie acted as secretary, preparing the agenda and taking the minutes. Elena, as head chef, and the countess as a fifty percent shareholder, made up the quartet.

As they all saw each other regularly, it was rare for anything on the agenda to take them by surprise. A barman had stolen one bottle of whiskey too many and finally had to be sacked. Elena reluctantly had to change her baker when too many customers rejected the contents of the bread baskets. She had once told *Catering Monthly* that you can produce an award-winning meal only for it to be ruined by a stale bread roll or a lukewarm cup of coffee.

Any other business, the last item on the agenda, usually consisted of agreeing on a date for the next meeting. But not today.

"I picked up a piece of information yesterday," said Sasha, "that I thought I ought to share with you." The other three became unusually attentive. "Luini's are about to announce that they'll be closing their doors after forty-seven years. It seems young Tony Luini isn't a chip off the old block, and since his father's death, they've been steadily losing customers. So the family are putting the restaurant up for sale. Tony approached me and asked if we might be interested."

"What exactly is he selling?" asked Elena. "Because there'll be little or no goodwill."

"A fourteen-year lease with an option to renew."

"Rent and rates?" asked Charlie.

"The rent is thirty-two thousand pounds per year, payable to the Grosvenor Estate, and the rates are around twenty thousand pounds."

"How far away is it from Elena One and Two?" asked the countess, ever practical.

"Just over a mile," said Sasha. "About ten minutes in a taxi."

"If it's not raining," said Charlie.

"My father," said the countess, "used to say never spread your assets too thin. And as we only have one irreplaceable asset, I think Elena's opinion is the one that matters. Especially if you were thinking of naming the restaurant Elena Three."

"Agreed," said Charlie. "And there's another factor we should take into consideration. If Sasha were to become an MP at the next election, he'll find it hard to keep an eye on two restaurants, let alone three."

"Especially if I were selected for a northern seat," said Sasha. "I'd have to spend half my life in a train or car. I've just been invited to attend an interview for Wandsworth Central, but it's such a safe Labour seat I'll be lucky to get shortlisted."

"May I suggest," said the countess, "that we all have lunch at Luini's during the week, and then Elena can let us know if the idea is worth pursuing. Because without her particular brand of magic, we would be wasting our time."

"Agreed," said Sasha. "And on that note, I declare the meeting closed."

The two of them walked down the town hall steps, holding hands.

"Just smile," said Sasha. "Don't say anything until we're in the car."

He opened the car door and waited for Charlie to get in.

"You haven't done that for a while," teased Charlie, as he climbed into the driver's seat.

Sasha waved to Bill Samuel, the local party chairman, before he put the car into first gear. He didn't speak until he'd eased away from the pavement and joined the early evening traffic.

"Well, how do you think it went?" he asked as they headed toward the river.

"You couldn't have done much better," said Charlie. "I'm confident you'll be their candidate by this time next week."

"A week's a long time in politics, as Harold Wilson once reminded us," said Sasha. "So I'm not going to take anything for granted."

"They all but selected you tonight," said Charlie.

"How can you possibly know that?"

"The chairman's wife, Jackie, told me you got one hundred and forty-nine votes, and the other two shortlisted candidates got one hundred and fifty-one between them. If you'd only got two more votes, she said, they would have selected you this evening. So by this time next week!"

"One of the safest seats in the country," said Sasha. "Less than twenty minutes from the House of Commons and only fifteen from our home in Fulham. What more could a man ask for?"

"I'm pregnant," said Charlie.

Sasha slammed on the brakes. There was a cacophony of angry horns coming from behind him, but he ignored them, as he took Charlie in his arms and said, "That's wonderful news, darling. But we must make sure the committee know before they meet next week. Perhaps you should give your new friend Jackie Samuel a call."

"I must confess that wasn't quite the reaction I was expecting," said Charlie.

"Congratulations, darling," said Elena when she heard the news.

"Thank you," said Sasha. "But they haven't actually selected me yet."

"Not you, idiot. I was congratulating Charlie. What are you hoping for, a girl or a boy?"

"A girl of course," said Sasha. "After all, there hasn't been one in the Karpenko family for four generations."

"I don't care," said Charlie, "as long as he or she doesn't want to be a politician."

"But she could end up being Labour's first woman Prime Minister," said Sasha.

"It's not natural for a woman to be Prime Minister," said Elena.

"Don't let Fiona Hunter hear you saying that," said Sasha, "unless you want to be banished to the Tower."

"If that woman ever became Prime Minister, I'd seriously consider returning to Russia," said Elena. "Meanwhile, some of us ought to be getting back to work, especially if we're going to have a Member of Parliament in the family. I'm told they're not very well paid."

"And they don't get any tips either," said Charlie.

"Other than everyone telling them how to govern the country," said Sasha as he ran a finger down the evening bookings, coming to a halt when he noticed a familiar name.

"I didn't know Alf Rycroft was booked in for tonight."

"Yes," said Elena. "He rang this morning, said he hoped both of you would be able to join him for dinner, as there's something important he needs to discuss with you."

"He's probably hoping you'll agree to contest Merrifield again at the general election," said Charlie. "But of course he doesn't know that you're about to be selected for a safe seat."

"He'll be delighted when he hears the news," said Elena, "and so proud that his protégé will soon be a Member of Parliament. How's that Hunter woman getting on?"

"Rather well, actually," said Sasha. "After only a couple of years of sitting on the green benches, she's already been appointed as Parliamentary Private Secretary to the Shadow Minister for Rural Affairs."

"How important is that?" asked Charlie.

"It's the first step on the ladder for MPs who are thought to have a promising career ahead of them."

"It will be interesting to see which one of you gets into the Cabinet first," said Elena.

"Don't let's get ahead of ourselves," said Charlie.

"Agreed," said Sasha. "I've still got to make sure I'm selected for Wandsworth Central, and as I'll have to prepare a completely new speech for the final round you won't be seeing much of me before next Thursday. By the way, Mother, have you given any more thought to whether you want to run a third restaurant?"

"Yes, I have," said Elena, before disappearing into the kitchen.

Sasha opened a bottle of champagne and poured Charlie and himself a glass. "I'll have to pick the right moment," he said. "Preferably before Alf even has a chance to raise the subject of Merrifield."

"And how do you propose to do that?"

"I shall behave like an Englishman for a change. Talk about anything else, even the weather, before touching on the one subject that needs to be discussed."

"He's just coming through the door," whispered Charlie.

Sasha jumped down from his stool at the bar and walked quickly across the restaurant to greet his former constituency chairman.

"Do come and join us, Alf. I've opened a bottle of champagne in your honor."

"Are we celebrating anything in particular?"

"I'm about to become a father."

"And I think I'm the mother," said Charlie, grinning.

"Wonderful news," said Alf, kissing her on both cheeks.

"Thank you," said Charlie as a waiter handed them menus.

"What do you recommend?" asked Alf, not even opening his menu.

"Elena's moussaka is the house special," said Sasha. "Customers travel for miles just to sample it, to quote the *Spectator*."

"Not a magazine I read regularly," admitted Alf, "but I'll take their word for it. In any case, I'm a huge fan of your mother, a remarkable woman."

"I'm surrounded by remarkable women," said Sasha, "and I look forward to a child who will worship me."

"I suspect it will be the other way around," said Alf.

After they had ordered, and Sasha had poured three more glasses of champagne, they discussed the televising of Parliament, the problems in Northern Ireland, and finally the weather, before Sasha suggested they go through to dinner.

"I can't wait to hear what Fiona's been up to," said Sasha after they had taken their seats.

"All in good time," said Alf. "But first, I want to know how you're getting on at the Courtauld, Charlie."

"You are sitting next to Dr. Karpenko," said Sasha, giving his wife a nod.

"Many congratulations. You must be very proud."

"Not as proud as I am of Sasha, who may well be an MP after the next election," said Charlie, coming in bang on cue.

Alf couldn't hide his disappointment. It was some time before he managed, "So you've been selected for another seat?"

"Not quite yet," said Charlie, as Gino served their first course. "But he's on the shortlist for Wandsworth Central, and as he came top in the first round by a fair margin, we're feeling fairly confident."

"Congratulations once again," said Alf. "I can't pretend I'm surprised, because I meant it when I said I hoped to live long enough to see you take your place in the Cabinet, though I confess I'd rather hoped it might be as the member for Merrifield."

"But you told me you wouldn't expect me to stand for Merrifield again. And in any case, now that Fiona has begun to establish herself in the House, we can assume it will go back to being a safe Tory seat at the next general election."

"I would normally agree with you," said Alf, "if it weren't for the recommendations of the boundary commission, which have just been published."

"Am I missing something here?" asked Charlie. "I feel like Alice at the Mad Hatter's tea party."

"That's not surprising, because not many people outside the Westminster hothouse have even heard of the boundary commission. It's an independent body that comes together as and when required to review the parliamentary landscape, so that any anomalies that have arisen over the years can be ironed out. In their wisdom, the Commission has decided that Merrifield's boundaries should be redrawn to include Blandford, a few miles up the road, and form a new constituency that will retain the name of Merrifield."

"Does that mean Merrifield will become a safe Labour seat?" asked Sasha.

"No, I can't pretend it does," said Alf, "but we've done the calculations, and it will certainly be a key marginal. In fact the *Guardian* has listed it as among the seats that will decide who wins the next election."

The waiters cleared away the first course, although Sasha's soup had gone cold. "And how has Fiona reacted to this bombshell?" he asked.

"She appealed, of course, and fought the commission's decision tooth and nail, but she lost, and had to decide whether to look for a safer seat, or stay put and contest Merrifield. I'm told that the chairman of the Conservative Party left Fiona in no doubt what was expected of her, so she's just announced that she'll be defending the seat."

Although the main courses had been served, Sasha's knife and fork remained in place.

"In view of the changed circumstances," said Alf, "I called a meeting of the committee last night and they unanimously agreed that if you'd be willing to stand as our candidate, we wouldn't look elsewhere."

"How long has he got to make up his mind?" asked Charlie.

"I've promised to report back to the committee by the end of the week."

"Before Wandsworth Central select their candidate?" said Sasha.

"You know perfectly well, Sasha, that whoever Wandsworth Central select will win by a landslide, whereas I'm convinced that you're our best hope to capture Merrifield, and therefore give the Labour Party a chance of clinging on to power."

"That sounds to me like a not very subtle attempt at arm-twisting," said Charlie.

"Sometimes known as backroom politics," said Alf, as Elena came bursting out of the kitchen.

Alf immediately stood up. "The moussaka was mouthwatering, my dear," he said. "And there's still your famous banoffee pie to follow."

"Yes, but not before we all have another glass of champagne," said Elena. "I assume Sasha has told you the good news?"

"We've been discussing little else," said Alf.

"And I think you'll find he's already made up his mind."

Alf looked disappointed, Charlie surprised, and Sasha puzzled.

"Oh yes," said Elena. "Konstantin if it's a boy, Natasha for a girl."

Sasha, Charlie, and Alf all burst out laughing.

"What did I say that was so funny?" asked Elena.

Dear Chairman,

It is with considerable regret, and much soul-searching, that I have decided not to allow my name to go forward as the prospective Labour parliamentary candidate for the constituency of . . .

Sasha placed his pen on the desk, leaned back, and thought yet again about the decision he and Charlie had finally agreed on.

Even at this last moment, he considered changing his mind. After all, it was a decision that could change his whole life. And then he thought about Fiona. He picked up his pen and wrote the words "Wandsworth Central."

32

ALEX

Boston

The Cathedral of the Holy Cross was packed for Lawrence Lowell's funeral. This gentle, modest, and decent man would have been touched by how many people had clearly admired him.

Alex was honored when Lawrence's mother, Mrs. Rose Lowell, invited him to deliver one of the three eulogies, especially as the other two orators were Senator Ted Kennedy and Bishop Lomax. Mrs. Evelyn Lowell Halliday sat in the front row, but never once acknowledged Alex.

After the bishop had given the final blessing and the mourners had departed, Alex was approached by two men; one he knew well, the other he'd never met before.

Bob Brookes, the chairman of the Boston branch of the Democratic Party, said he needed to speak to him on a private matter. Alex had intended to return to New York that afternoon, but he agreed to delay his departure by twenty-four hours, and they arranged to meet at his hotel at ten o'clock the following morning. The second man turned out to be the Lowell family lawyer, and he had a similar request. However, Mr. Harbottle was unwilling to discuss such a delicate matter outside his office, so Alex made an appointment to see him following his meeting with Brookes.

Alex returned to the Mayflower Hotel, and called Anna at the gallery to tell her he wouldn't be back until the next day. She sounded disappointed, but confessed she couldn't wait to find out why the two men wanted to see him.

"By the way," she said, "have you told your mother yet?"

"The vote was unanimous," said Brookes.

"I'm flattered," said Alex, "but I'm afraid the answer is still no. Elena's has recently opened two new pizza parlors in Denver and Seattle, and the staff have yet to meet their boss, so you'll have to look for someone else."

"You were the only candidate the committee considered," said Brookes.

"But I'm from New York. My only connection with Boston was Lawrence."

"Alex, I've watched you working with Lawrence during the past six weeks, and after a life in politics, I can tell you, you're a natural."

"Why don't you stand yourself, Bob? You were born and bred in Boston, and everyone knows and respects you."

"I could introduce you to a dozen people who can chair their local party committee," said Brookes, "but only occasionally someone comes along who was born to be the candidate."

"I have to admit," said Alex, "that I have considered politics as a career, but it would make far more sense for me to start out in local government in Brighton Beach, where I went to school and founded my business—and perhaps if I'm lucky enough, one day I'll represent them in Congress. No, Bob, you'll have to find a local man to fight Blake Hawksley."

"But Hawksley isn't in your class, and the Democratic majority is large enough for you to see him off. Once we've got you into Congress, no one will ever prize you out, at least not until you want to become a senator."

Alex hesitated. "I wish it was that easy, but it isn't. So would you be kind enough to thank your committee and say that perhaps in four or five years' time . . ."

"The seat won't be available in four or five years' time, Alex. Politics is about timing and opportunity, and those two stars aren't aligned that often."

"I know you're right, Bob, but the answer is still no. I must get going. I've got an appointment with Lawrence's executor. He asked me to drop by his office on the way to the airport."

"If you should change your mind . . ."

"My name is Ed Harbottle. I'm the senior partner of Harbottle, Harbottle, and McDowell. This firm has had the privilege of representing the Lowell family for over a hundred years. My grandfather," said Harbottle, glancing at an oil painting of an elderly gentleman wearing a dark blue, pin-striped double-breasted suit with a gold fob watch, "administered the estate of Mr. Ernest Lowell, the distinguished banker and fabled art collector. My father was legal adviser to Senator James Lowell, and for the past eleven years I have been Mr. Lawrence Lowell's personal attorney and, I would like to think, friend."

Alex looked at the man seated on the other side of the desk, who was also dressed in a dark blue, pin-striped double-breasted suit and wearing a gold fob watch, which was unquestionably the same one as in the painting. Alex couldn't be sure about the suit.

"We meet in sad circumstances, Mr. Karpenko."

"Tragic and unnecessary circumstances," said Alex with feeling. Harbottle raised an eyebrow. "I hope I live to see the day when people's sexual preferences are considered irrelevant, including for those who wish to serve in public office."

"That isn't the reason Mr. Lowell committed suicide," said Harbottle, "but I shall come to that later," he added, readjusting his half-moon spectacles. "Mr. Lowell instructed this firm to be the sole executor of his last will and testament, and in that capacity, it is my duty to inform you of a certain bequest that has been left to you."

Alex remained silent, trying not to anticipate . . .

"I shall only make reference to the single clause in the will that applies to you, as I am not at liberty to disclose any other details. Do you have any questions, Mr. Karpenko?"

"None," said Alex, who had a dozen questions, but had a feeling that all would be revealed in the fullness of time. Mr. Harbottle's time. Once again, the elderly lawyer adjusted his glasses before turning several pages of the thick parchment document in front of him.

"I shall read clause forty-three of the testament," he announced, finally coming to his purpose. "'I bequeath to Alexander Konstantinovitch Karpenko my entire shareholding of fifty percent in the Elena Pizza Company, of which we are joint partners.'"

Alex was momentarily stunned by the generosity of his old friend, before he managed, "I can't believe that his sister will take that lying down."

"I don't think Mrs. Evelyn Lowell-Halliday will be causing you or anyone else any trouble. On the contrary."

"What are you not telling me, Mr. Harbottle?" said Alex, staring across the table.

The lawyer hesitated for a moment, before removing his glasses and placing them on the desk. "The reasons for his suicide are more complex than the public realize, Mr. Karpenko. Lawrence did not commit suicide because of the press revelations."

"Then why?"

"Lawrence had many worthy qualities, including generosity of heart and pocket, as well as a genuine desire to serve, which made him an ideal candidate for public office. I have no doubt he would have been a very fine congressman."

"But?"

"But," repeated Harbottle, "a different set of skills and expertise are required to run a modern financial institution, and although Lawrence was chairman of the Lowell Bank and Trust Company, he held that position in name only, and allowed others to handle the day-to-day business of the bank. Others who were not of the same moral fiber."

"How bad is it?" asked Alex, leaning forward.

"I'm not acquainted with the finer details of the bank's present financial position, but I can tell you that Douglas Ackroyd, the chief executive, will be announcing his resignation later this afternoon. I'm only relieved that this firm will not be representing that particular gentleman in any forthcoming legal actions that might arise."

"Is there anything I can do to help?" asked Alex.

"I am not in a position to advise you on that matter, Mr. Karpenko. But Lawrence did ask me to give you this letter." He opened the drawer of his desk, took out a slim white envelope, and handed it to Alex.

Alex tore it open and extracted a single sheet of paper, written in Lawrence's clear, unmistakable hand.

My dear Alex,

By now you will know that I have made a complete fool of myself, and more importantly, ruined the good name of my family, earned over a hundred years, and squandered in a generation.

I apologize for burdening you with my problems, but within days of my death, the Lowell Bank and Trust Company will be subject to an investigation by the IRS. Someone will be left with the unenviable task of having to wind up the bank's assets, while at the same time doing everything in their power to ensure that its loyal shareholders and customers suffer the minimum loss.

To that end, I have left all the family assets, including my homes in Boston, Southampton, and the south of France, along with the Lowell art collection, to be disposed of as the new chairman of the company considers fit.

However, that begs the question of who that chairman should be. I can think of no one I would trust more to carry out that onerous responsibility than you, and if you felt able to do so, I would also leave you my fifty percent shareholding in the bank. However, I would understand if you felt unable to take on such a task, especially as it wouldn't be the first time you'd come to my rescue.

For all you have done in the past, my grateful thanks.

As ever,

Lawrence

Alex looked across the table at the lawyer and said, "Has anyone else seen this letter, Mr. Harbottle?"

"I haven't even read it myself, sir."

Once Alex had left Mr. Harbottle's office, he went straight back to his hotel, and told the receptionist that he would be checking out in the morning. But first he needed to make some phone calls before he even thought about visiting the bank. The first was to Anna, to tell her he wouldn't be returning to New York for some time. He then briefed her on the details of Lawrence's will, before asking, "Do you think you and Mr. Rosenthal could come up to Boston as soon as possible and value the Lowell Collection?"

"I'll see if he's free, and then call you back. Are you camping in the Mayflower for the next few days?"

"No, Mr. Harbottle has advised me to move into Beacon Hill as quickly as possible to make sure Evelyn doesn't take up residence and claim the property as next of kin."

"How generous of Lawrence to leave you his fifty percent of Elena's, especially as he didn't know if you'd agree to become chairman."

"And he's made my task of attempting to keep the bank afloat a little easier by also leaving me his fifty percent shareholding if I agreed to be chairman. That means no one can overrule me other than Evelyn, who owns the other fifty percent."

"Evelyn? Won't that make your job even more difficult?"

"Certainly if I'd been advising Lawrence's father, I would have told him that the law courts are full of warring siblings who each own fifty percent of their father's estate. But Harbottle's convinced that as long as the shares are worthless, she's unlikely to cause any trouble. I'm missing you," he said, suddenly changing the subject. "When do you think you'll be able to join me?"

"It's you who was meant to be coming back to New York, in case you've forgotten. I'll fly up on Friday morning so we can spend the weekend together. I'll need to catalog the collection before Mr. Rosenthal joins us."

"You have a way of making a man feel wanted," said Alex laughing.

His second call was to a local real estate agent with instructions to value Lawrence's properties in Boston, Southampton, and the south of France.

The third call was to Paolo to warn him he'd be running the company for a little longer than he'd originally anticipated.

⊸o⊷

"Two eggs, sunny side up, bacon, and hash browns," said Alex as the waitress poured him a steaming coffee. He was glad that his mother was a couple of hundred miles away in Brooklyn, and couldn't see him.

He took a sip of coffee before turning to the financial supplement of the *Globe*. On the front page was a photograph of Douglas Ackroyd, above a self-serving statement he'd released the previous day.

> I feel the time has come for me to retire as chief executive of the Lowell Bank and Trust Company, which I have served for the past twenty years. Following the tragic death of our distinguished chairman, Lawrence Lowell, I believe the bank should look to new leadership as we move toward the twenty-first century. I will happily remain on the board and serve the new chairman in any capacity he sees fit.

I bet you will, thought Alex. But why did Ackroyd even want to remain on the board? Perhaps because he needed to make sure that it was Lawrence who would shoulder the blame when the bank went under, allowing him to come out of the debacle with his reputation untarnished. Alex was beginning to feel he knew the man, even though he'd never met him.

As soon as he'd had time to study the books, Alex intended to issue his own press statement, so that no one would be in any doubt where the blame really lay. He folded his newspaper, and stared admiringly at the magnificent Georgian building that dominated the far side of State Street, wondering if the bank could still be sold as a going concern. After all, it had been trading for over a hundred years, with an impeccable reputation. But questions like that couldn't be answered until he'd studied the books, and that might take days.

Alex checked his watch as the waitress returned with his order: 8:24 a.m. He planned to enter the building for the first time at 8:55. He looked around the diner and wondered how many of the other customers worked at the bank, and were aware that their new chairman was sitting in one of the booths.

Among the options he'd already considered was to invite one of the larger Boston banks to participate in a merger, with the explanation that as Lawrence didn't have an heir, there was no natural successor. But if the bank's financial plight made that impossible, he would be left with no choice other than to resort to plan B, a fire sale. In which case he'd be back in New York serving pizzas by the end of the month.

At 8:30 he looked across the street to see a smartly dressed man in a long green topcoat and peaked cap emerge from the bank and take his place by the front door. Staff were beginning to trickle into the building: young women in sensible white blouses and dark skirts that fell below the knee, young men in gray suits, white shirts, and somber ties, followed a little later by older men in well-tailored, double-breasted suits and club ties, with an air of confidence and belonging. How long would that confidence last when they discovered the truth? Would he know the answer to that question by the time the bank closed this evening? And would those same doors even open for business tomorrow morning?

At 8:50, Alex paid his bill, left the warmth of the diner, and walked slowly across the square. As he approached the front entrance, the doorman touched the peak of his cap and said, "Good morning, sir. I'm afraid the bank won't be open for a few more minutes."

"I'm the new chairman," said Alex, thrusting out his hand. The doorman hesitated before returning the compliment, and saying, "I'm Errol, sir."

"And how long have you been working for the bank, Errol?"

"Twelve years, sir. Mr. Lawrence got me the job."

"Did he?" said Alex. He left the doorman with an anxious look on his face, stepped inside, and crossed the lobby to the front desk.

"How can I help you, sir?" asked a smartly dressed young woman.

"I'm the new chairman of the bank," said Alex. "Could you tell me where my office is?"

"Yes, Mr. Karpenko, you're on the top floor. Would you like me to accompany you?"

"No, please don't bother. I'll find my own way."

He walked across to the elevators and joined some staff who were chatting among themselves about everything from the Boston Red Sox' third defeat in a row, to the appointment of their new chairman. Both losers in their opinion.

"I'm told Karpenko's never run anything except a pizza joint," said one of them, "and has absolutely no experience of banking."

"Mark my words, Ackroyd will be back as chairman by the end of the week," said another.

"I'm going to open a book on how long he'll last," said a third.

"You might be wise to wait and see how he actually performs before you set the odds," suggested a lone voice. Alex smiled to himself, but didn't comment.

The elevator stopped several times to disgorge its passengers on different floors. By the time its doors finally opened on the twenty-fourth floor, Alex was alone. He stepped out into a deserted corridor and opened the first door he came across, to discover that it was a cupboard. The second was the restroom, and the third a secretary's office, but with no sign of a secretary. At the far end of the corridor he found a door that had CHAIRMAN painted on it in faded gold letters. He walked in, and it took only one glance to know that the room had once been occupied by Lawrence. But not that often. The office was well furnished and comfortable, with a fine display of paintings, including portraits of Lawrence's father and grandfather, but it didn't feel lived in. Alex closed the door, walked across to the window, and looked out onto a magnificent view of the bay.

He sank down into the comfortable red leather chair behind a teak desk, on which rested a blotting pad, a phone, and a silver-framed photograph of a young man he didn't recognize, but thought he might have seen at the funeral. He picked up the phone, pressed a button marked FRONT DESK, and when a voice came on the line, said, "Please ask Errol to join me in the chairman's office."

"The doorman, sir?"

"Yes, the doorman."

While he waited for Errol to appear, Alex wrote down a list of questions on a sheet of paper. He hadn't quite finished when there was a gentle tap on the door.

"Come in," he said. The door opened slowly to reveal Errol silhouetted in the doorway, but he made no attempt to enter. "Come in," Alex repeated. "Take off your hat and coat and have a seat," he added, pointing to the chair on the other side of his desk.

Errol removed his hat, but not his coat, and sat down.

"Now, Errol, you told me earlier that you've worked for the bank for twelve years. That means you're in possession of something I need desperately." Errol looked puzzled. "Information," said Alex. "I'm going to ask some questions that may embarrass you, but will help me do my job, so I hope you'll feel able to assist me." Errol sank back in his chair, not looking as if he wanted to assist the new chairman. Alex changed tack. "You also told me it was Mr. Lowell who got you your job."

"Sure did. Lieutenant Lowell spoke at a Veterans' Association meeting, and when he heard I'd served in Nam—"

"Which division?"

"Twenty-fifth, sir."

"I was with the 116th."

"Mr. Lawrence's division."

"Yes, that's how we met. And, like you, it was Mr. Lowell who got me this job."

Errol smiled for the first time. "If you served alongside Lieutenant Lowell," he said, "I'll do anything I can to help."

"I'm glad to hear that because, like me, you got on well with Mr. Lowell. How about Mr. Ackroyd?"

Errol bowed his head.

"That bad?"

"I've opened his car door every working day for the past twelve years, and I'm still not sure if he knows my name."

"And his secretary?" asked Alex, looking down at his list of questions.

"Miss Bowers. She left with him. But don't worry, sir, no one will miss her." Alex raised an eyebrow. "She was a little bit more than his secretary, if you catch my drift." Alex remained silent. "And, frankly, no one blamed Mrs. Ackroyd when she finally divorced him."

"Do you know Mrs. Ackroyd?"

"Not really, sir, she didn't visit the bank that often, but when she did, she always remembered my name."

"One final question, Errol. Did Mr. Lowell have a secretary?"

"Yes, sir, Miss Robbins. A real gem. But Mr. Ackroyd fired her last week, after twenty years' service."

"Come in."

"You asked to see me, chairman?"

"I did, Mr. Jardine. I need to see the bank's audited accounts for the past five years."

"Any particular version, chairman?" said Jardine, unable to resist a smirk.

"What do you mean, any particular version?"

"It's just that Mr. Lowell preferred to be shown an abbreviated version, which I used to guide him through once a year."

"I'm sure you did. But I am not Mr. Lowell, and I will require a little more detail."

"The summary in the annual report stretches to three pages, and I think you'll find it quite comprehensive."

"And if I don't?"

"I suppose you could study the detailed accounts we prepare for the IRS every year, but they stretch to hundreds of pages, and it would take me two, possibly three, days to put them all together."

"I said I wanted to see the past five years' accounts, Mr. Jardine, not next year's. So make sure that the full IRS version," said Alex, emphasizing the word "full," "is on my desk within an hour."

"It might take a little longer than that, sir."

"Then I might have to find someone who understands how many minutes there are in an hour, Mr. Jardine."

Alex had never seen anyone leave an office as quickly. He was about to call Mr. Harbottle, when the phone on his desk rang.

"I've tracked down Miss Robbins, chairman," said the switchboard operator, "and I have her on the line. Shall I put her through?"

"Please do."

"Good morning, Miss Robbins. My name is Alex Karpenko, and I'm the new chairman of Lowell's."

"Yes, I know, Mr. Karpenko. I read about your appointment in this morning's *Globe,* and of course I heard your moving eulogy at Mr. Lowell's funeral. How can I help?"

"I understand that Mr. Ackroyd fired you last Friday."

"Yes he did, and ordered me to clear my desk by close of business."

"Well, he had no authority to do so. As you were Lawrence's personal assistant, not his. So I was wondering if you'd consider coming back and doing the same job for me."

"That's most generous of you, Mr. Karpenko, but are you sure you wouldn't rather have a younger person to herald in a new era for the bank?"

"That's the last thing I need. I'm sinking under a sea of paperwork, and I have a feeling you might be the one person who knows where the lifeboat is."

Miss Robbins stifled a laugh. "When would you like me to start, chairman?"

"Nine o'clock, Miss Robbins."

"Tomorrow morning?"

"No, this morning."

"But it's already eleven thirty-five, chairman."

"Is it?"

⊸o⊷

"Hi, Alex, I'm Ray Fowler, company secretary. What can I do for you?" he said, thrusting out his hand.

"Good morning, Mr. Fowler," said Alex, making no attempt to rise from behind his desk, or to shake the outstretched hand. "I want a copy of the minutes of every board meeting held during the past five years."

"Not a problem, sir, I'll have them sent up immediately."

"No, you will bring them up yourself, Mr. Fowler, along with any notes you made at the time when you drew them up."

"But they may have been mislaid or destroyed after all this time."

"I'm sure I don't have to remind you, Mr. Fowler, that it's against company law to destroy any material that might later prove relevant in a criminal inquiry."

"I'll do my best to locate them, chairman."

"I seem to remember President Nixon saying something similar when he was ordered to produce the Watergate tapes."

"I hardly think that a fair comparison, chairman."

"I'll let you know how I feel about that, Mr. Fowler, but not until I've read the minutes."

◄o►

"He did what?" said Ackroyd.

"Asked to see the bank's audited accounts for the past five years and all the board minutes with any attached handwritten notes," said Ray Fowler.

"Did he indeed? Then we'll have to be rid of him before he gets his feet under the table, and starts causing any real problems."

"That might be easier said than done," said Fowler. "We're not dealing with Lawrence Lowell any longer. This guy's smart, tough, and ruthless. And don't forget he now has control of fifty percent of the bank's shares."

"While Evelyn owns the other fifty percent," said Ackroyd. "So he can't do anything without our backing, certainly not while we still have a majority on the board."

"But what if he were to find out—"

"Let me remind you, Ray, if the IRS were to discover what you've been up to for the past ten years, I can tell you exactly where the buck will stop, and as I'm not President Truman—it won't be with me."

◄o►

There was a knock on the door.

Alex checked his watch: fifty-eight minutes and twenty seconds. He smiled and said, "Come in, Mr. Jardine."

The door opened and the bank's finance director led six of his staff into the chairman's office, all of them laden down with boxes.

"Here are a few to be getting on with, chairman," said Jardine, making no attempt to hide his sarcasm.

"Put them over there," said Alex, pointing to a long table against the far wall.

The six assistants immediately carried out his orders, while Jardine stood and watched.

"Will that be all, chairman?" he said confidently.

"No, it won't, Mr. Jardine. You said these were a few to be getting on with, so when can I expect the rest?"

"I'm afraid that was my feeble attempt at a little humor, chairman."

"It fell on deaf ears, Mr. Jardine. Could you ensure that no one from your department leaves the building tonight before I do, and that includes you. I have a feeling," he said, glancing across at the stack of files, "I'll be needing several questions answered before I go home."

⁂

"Evelyn, we have a problem."

"Douglas, I expect you to take care of any problems at the bank, especially now you're the chairman."

"But I'm not the chairman," said Ackroyd. "Just before he died, Lawrence appointed some guy called Alex Karpenko to take his place."

"Not him again."

"You know the man?"

"Our paths have crossed," said Evelyn, "and I can tell you, he doesn't take prisoners. But as I now own one hundred percent of the bank's shares, I can remove him whenever—"

"Lawrence also left his fifty percent holding in the bank to Karpenko. The guy's already started digging, and if he were to find out—"

"Do we still have a majority on the board?" asked Evelyn.

"As long as you turn up to vote, we do."

"Then I'll have to fly back for the next meeting, won't I. And, Douglas, the first item on the agenda will be to remove Karpenko from the chair and replace him with you. All I expect you to do is organize the meeting without him working out what we're up to."

"It may not be quite that easy," said Ackroyd. "He's already taken possession of your brother's house, and I suspect your villa in the south of France will be next on his list."

"Over my dead body."

"And he's also given orders to transfer the entire Lowell Collection to the bank as security in case the IRS wants to value it."

"That could be a problem," admitted Evelyn.

"I have to tell you, Karpenko is one tough bastard," said Ackroyd. "You clearly don't know the man."

⊸o⊸

Alex spent the rest of the week studying balance sheets, dividend returns, tax payments, and even junior staff wages. But it wasn't until Wednesday afternoon that he came across an entry that needed to be checked a third time before he was sure that no responsible board would have sanctioned it.

He stared at the item again, thinking it had to be one naught too many. It was tucked neatly in between two other figures of a similar amount so as not to draw attention to the entry. He double-checked the sum and wrote the figure down on a pad by his side. Alex wondered how many more such entries he would come across before he reached the present day.

The following morning, Alex found a similarly large withdrawal appearing on the balance sheet without explanation. Once again, Alex wrote the figure down. It was already dark by the time he came across the third entry, which was for a far larger amount. He added the figure to his growing list, and wondered how she'd been allowed to get away with it.

By Friday, Alex had concluded that Lowell's, by any standards, was trading while insolvent, but he decided not to inform the banking commissioner until Mr. Rosenthal had valued the art collection, and he'd been able to value any other assets the bank might possess.

When the street lights flickered on, Alex decided it was time to leave the office and go home. He couldn't wait to see Anna again. He glanced at the diminishing pile of balance sheets that still needed to be studied, and wondered if he'd ever get through them.

It hadn't helped that Lawrence had been serving in Vietnam for two years when Douglas Ackroyd had brought a new meaning to the words "when the cat's away." He not only paid himself five hundred thousand dollars a year, but claimed another three hundred thousand dollars in expenses, while his two cronies, Jardine and Fowler, only ever traveled first class whenever they climbed aboard his gravy train. But the conductor was clearly Evelyn, who, with her fifty percent of the bank's shares, appeared to have given Ackroyd carte blanche to do as he pleased. Now he'd discovered just how much she'd expected in return.

He was looking forward to spending the weekend with Anna, who was traveling up from New York that afternoon, but it didn't stop him picking up half a dozen more files before he left the office. As he passed Miss Robbins's room, he noticed that her light was still on. He popped his head around the door and said, "Thank you, and have a good weekend."

"I'll see you at six o'clock on Monday morning, chairman," she said, without looking up from a pile of correspondence.

Alex had quickly discovered why Doug Ackroyd had fired her. She was the one person who knew where all the bodies were buried.

As Alex left the building, he had a nagging feeling that he was being watched; a throwback from his days in Leningrad. It brought back memories of Vladimir, and he wondered how far up the KGB ladder he'd crawled by now. *I ought to give him a call and see if he'd like to join the board of Lowell's,* he thought. He was sure Vladimir would have ways of making Ackroyd, Fowler, and Jardine divulge which entries he should be checking more carefully.

Alex gave the driver his address before he sank into the back seat of a taxi and opened another file. If he hadn't read each debit with close attention, he might have missed yet another withdrawal, which could only have been sanctioned by one man. He checked the figure three times, but still couldn't believe it. The final check had been cashed two days after Lawrence's death, and the day before Ackroyd resigned, and was by far the largest amount to date.

Alex added the latest figure to his long list, before he totaled up all the withdrawals Evelyn had made since her father had died and her brother had taken over as chairman of Lowell's. The final figure came to just over twenty-one million dollars, with no suggestion of any repayments. If you added her profligacy to the outrageous salary Ackroyd had paid himself and his four placemen, plus their countless expenses, it was no wonder that Lowell's was facing bankruptcy. Alex began to wonder if he would have to sell off the Lowell Collection in order to make sure the bank was solvent enough to lower its debts and continue trading.

He was considering the consequences as the taxi pulled up outside Lawrence's home. He would always think of it as Lawrence's home.

He climbed out of the car and a huge smile appeared on his face when he spotted Anna standing in the doorway. It evaporated just as quickly when he saw the look on her face.

"What's the matter, darling?" he asked as he took her in his arms.

"You'd better have a large vodka before I tell you." She took his hand, and without another word led him into the house. She poured them both a drink and waited for him to sit down before saying, "It's not just the Warhol that's a copy."

Alex drained his glass before asking, "How many?"

"I can't be sure until Mr. Rosenthal has given his opinion, but I suspect that at least half the collection are copies."

Alex said nothing, while she refilled his glass. After another long gulp, he admitted, "The value of the Lowell Collection is the one thing that's preventing the bank from going under. I don't think I'll be able to sleep until Mr. Rosenthal arrives."

"I called him a couple of hours ago and he's already on his way."

"And my mother?" asked Alex. "How is she?"

"Your mother keeps asking me why we constantly change the date for our wedding," said Anna.

"And what did you tell her?"

"We're still trying to fit it in between rescuing a bank, opening the latest Elena's, and preferably when we're both in the same place at the same time."

"We could have grandchildren by then," said Alex.

33

SASHA

Merrifield

Sasha had always managed to survive on six hours' sleep a night, but once the Prime Minister had visited Buckingham Palace and sought a dissolution of Parliament, he had to learn how to get by on four.

Once again he adopted a daily routine that would have impressed a Bolshoi ballet master, even if it was only for three weeks. He rose every morning at five, and was standing outside Roxton station with a small band of volunteers long before the first commuters arrived. He greeted them with, "Hi, I'm Sasha Karpenko, and I'm . . ."

At 8 a.m. he took a break for breakfast, a different cafe every morning, and twenty minutes later he would walk to party headquarters in the high street—three rooms hired for a month—and check the morning papers. The *Merrifield Gazette* had found several different ways of saying it was neck and neck, a close-run thing, everything to play for, but the morning's headline took him by surprise: HUNTER CHALLENGES KARPENKO TO DEBATE.

"Shrewd move," said Alf. "She didn't wait for you to make the running this time. You have to accept immediately, and then we'll agree later on a date, time, and place."

"Any time, any place," said Sasha.

"No, no!" said Alf. "We're not in any hurry. We need the debate to be in Roxton, and as close to the election as possible."

"Why Roxton?"

"Because more of our supporters are likely to turn up there than anywhere else in the constituency."

"But why hold it off until the last moment?"

"It will give you more time to prepare. Don't forget you're not up against a university student any longer, but a parliamentarian who's lived in this constituency all her life. But for now, you should get back on the street and leave us to worry about the details."

After Sasha had rung the editor of the *Gazette* to say he would be delighted to accept Ms. Hunter's challenge, and couldn't wait to debate with her, he left HQ to join the early morning shoppers, mainly women and young children, and a few old-age pensioners. During the next three hours he shook hands with as many voters as possible, always delivering the same simple message: his name, his party, the date of the election, and a reminder that Merrifield was now a key marginal seat.

Then came a forty-minute break for lunch at one o'clock, when Alf would join him at a local pub and bring him up to date with what Fiona was up to. Sasha always chatted to the publican about licensing hours and the tax on alcohol, while ordering only one course and a half pint of the local beer.

"Always make sure you pay for your own food and drink," said Alf. "And don't buy anything for anyone if they have a vote in the constituency."

"Why not?" asked a heavily pregnant Charlie, as she sipped an orange juice.

"Because you can bet the Tories would try to claim he was attempting to bribe a constituent, and therefore breaking electoral law."

After shaking hands with everyone in the pub, they left for a factory visit, where Sasha usually got more hellos than bugger-offs, followed by the school run from three thirty to four thirty—primary, secondary, and finally the local grammar school. This was when Charlie came into her element, and many mothers confided in her that, unlike their husbands, they would be voting for Sasha.

"She's our secret weapon," the chairman often told the candidate, "especially as, although Fiona claims to be engaged, her fiancé has yet to make an appearance. Not that I'll be mentioning that to anyone, of course," he added with a grin.

Back to HQ around 5 p.m. for a debriefing, before leaving to address two, possibly three, evening meetings.

"But so few people bother to turn up," said Sasha.

"Don't worry about that," said Alf. "It will give you a chance to rehearse a few of the key points and phrases that will need to sound off-the-cuff during the debate."

Back home by midnight and hopefully asleep by 1 a.m. Not always possible, because just like with an actor treading the boards, the adrenaline doesn't conveniently stop the moment the curtain comes down. Four hours' sleep before the alarm goes off, when he started the whole process again, only thankful that it was one day less until the election.

⊸o⊷

On the morning of the debate, one local poll gave Fiona a two-point lead, while another had the two candidates neck and neck. It didn't help steady Sasha's nerves when the local TV station announced that there had been so much interest in the debate that they would be showing it live at prime time.

Charlie selected the suit (gray, single-breasted), shirt (white), and tie (green) that Sasha would wear for the encounter that evening. She didn't interrupt him while he rehearsed salient lines and well-honed phrases whenever they were alone. But if he asked for her opinion, she didn't hesitate to respond candidly, even if it wasn't always what he wanted to hear.

"Time to leave," said Charlie, checking her watch.

Sasha followed her out of party HQ and joined her in the back of a waiting car.

"You look so handsome," she said, as they moved off. Sasha didn't reply. "Don't forget, she's just not in your class." Still no response. "By this time next week, it will be you, not her, who's sitting in the House of Commons." Still nothing. "And by the way," she added, "perhaps this isn't the best time to tell you, but I'm thinking of voting Conservative."

"Then let's be thankful you haven't got a vote in this constituency," said Sasha as the car pulled up outside Roxton Town Hall.

⊸o⊷

"If you win the toss," said Alf, who was standing at the top of the steps waiting to greet them, "you should speak second. Then you can respond to anything Fiona raises in her opening remarks."

"No," said Sasha. "If I win the toss I'll go first, and then she'll have to respond to what I have to say."

"But that would be handing her an immediate advantage."

"Not if I've already made her speech for her. I think I've worked out what her line of attack will be. Don't forget, I know her better than anyone."

"It's a hell of a risk," said Alf.

"The sort of risk you have to take when the polls are this close."

Alf shrugged his shoulders. "I hope you know what you're doing," he said, as they walked onto the back of the stage and the moderator came across to join them.

"Time for the toss," said Chester Munro, the veteran anchorman from Southern News.

Sasha and Fiona shook hands for the photographers, although she never once looked him in the eye.

"Your call, Ms. Hunter."

"Heads," said Fiona as Munro spun a silver coin high in the air. It bounced on the floor before coming to rest to reveal the image of the best-known woman on earth.

"Your choice, Ms. Hunter," said Munro. "Will you open the batting, or put Mr. Karpenko in first?"

Sasha held his breath.

"I shall allow my opponent to speak first," said Fiona, clearly pleased to have won the toss.

A young woman appeared from the wings and powdered Munro's forehead and the tip of his nose, before he marched out onto the center of the stage to warm applause.

⊸o⊷

"Good evening, ladies and gentlemen," said Munro as he looked down at the packed auditorium. "Welcome to the debate between the two main contenders for the parliamentary seat of Merrifield. Fiona Hunter, the current member, is representing the Conservative Party, and her opponent, Sasha Karpenko, is the Labour Party's candidate.

"Each candidate will make a three-minute opening statement, which will be followed by questions from the floor, and then we will end proceedings with both of them making a two-minute closing statement. I will now invite the two candidates to join us."

Sasha and Fiona appeared from opposite wings of the stage, each of them greeted with rapturous applause from their own supporters. Sasha wished he was back in the Fulham Road enjoying one of his mother's moussakas and a glass of red wine, but then he spotted Charlie and his mother smiling up at him from the front row. He smiled back, as Munro said, "I shall now call upon Mr. Karpenko to make his opening statement."

Sasha walked slowly forward, placed his notes on the lectern, and waited for the audience to settle. He glanced down at the opening sentence, although he knew the entire speech by heart. He looked up, aware that he only had three minutes in which to make a lasting impression. No, Alf had told him to think of it as 180 seconds, that way you'll make every second count. For the first time, Sasha wondered if Alf might have been right when he suggested that whoever spoke first would be at a disadvantage.

"Ladies and gentlemen," Sasha began, fixing his eyes on the tenth row of the audience. "You see, standing before you, a carpetbagger."

A palpable gasp went up around the hall. Only Charlie didn't look surprised. But then, she'd already heard the speech several times.

"And if that's not bad enough," continued Sasha, "I'm also a first-generation immigrant. And if you're still looking for an excuse not to vote for me, I was born in Leningrad, not Merrifield."

Alf looked anxiously out from the wings to see that the audience had been stunned into silence.

"But please allow me to tell you something about this particular carpetbagger. I was, as I said, born in Leningrad. My late father was a brave man who won the Defence of Leningrad for defending his homeland against the Nazis during the siege of that city in the Second World War. After the war he worked his way up from dock laborer to become works supervisor in charge of eight hundred men. A position he held until he committed a crime for which he was put to death."

The audience were now hanging on his every word.

"Of course, you will want to know what that crime was. Murder, perhaps? Armed robbery? Fraud, or even worse, was he a traitor who'd betrayed his country? No, my father's crime was that he wanted to form a trade union among his fellow dockworkers so that his comrades could enjoy the same benefits that everyone in this country takes for granted. But the KGB didn't want that, so they had him eliminated.

"My brave mother, who is sitting among you tonight, risked her life so she and I could escape the tyranny of Communism and begin a new life in this great country. I went to school in London and, like Ms. Hunter, won a scholarship to Cambridge, where, again like Ms. Hunter,

I became president of the Union, and was awarded a first-class honors degree."

The first round of applause followed, giving Sasha a moment to relax, look down at his speech, and check the next sentence.

"After coming down from Cambridge, I went to work in my mother's restaurant, while at the same time attending night school, where I studied accountancy and business management. My mother may have won two Michelin stars as one of the finest chefs in this country, but she's rubbish when it comes to balancing the books."

Laughter and warm applause greeted these words.

"I fell in love with and married an English girl, who now works as a research fellow at the Courtauld Gallery. Our first child is due on election day." Sasha looked up to the heavens and said, "Could you possibly make it the day after?"

This time the applause was spontaneous and Sasha smiled down at his wife. A buzzer sounded to indicate that he only had thirty seconds left. He hadn't anticipated such prolonged applause, and needed to speed up.

"When I first came to Merrifield to fight the by-election three years ago, I fell in love for a second time. But you rejected this suitor and gave the prize to my rival, although the margin was slim enough for me to hope that you were perhaps suggesting I should try again. Now I am asking you to have a change of heart." He lowered his voice to almost a whisper. "I want to share a secret with you which I hope will prove how much I care about Merrifield. Before this election was called, I had the opportunity to contest a London seat with a Labour majority of over ten thousand. But I declined that opportunity because I have something else in common with Ms. Hunter. Like her, I want to be the Member of Parliament for Merrifield. I may be a carpetbagger, but I want to be your carpetbagger."

Half the audience rose to hail their standard-bearer, while the other half remained in the seats, but even some of them joined in the applause.

Munro waited for Sasha to return to his seat and the applause to die down before he said, "I call on Ms. Hunter to respond."

Sasha looked across at Fiona to see that she was furiously crossing out whole paragraphs of her prepared speech. Finally she rose and walked slowly toward the lectern. She smiled nervously down at the audience.

"My name is Fiona Hunter, and I have had the privilege of representing you as your Member of Parliament for the past three years. I hope you will feel that I have proved worthy of your support." She looked up, to receive a smattering of applause from her most ardent supporters.

"I was born and brought up in Merrifield. England is my homeland, always has been and always will be," a line she immediately realized she should have left out. She quickly turned the page, and then another. Sasha could only wonder how often the words "carpetbagger," "interloper," "outsider," even "immigrant," had been removed from her script.

Fiona stumbled on, talking about her father, Cambridge, and the Union, all too aware that by allowing her rival to go first, she had given him the opportunity to steal her best lines. When the buzzer went to warn Fiona that she had thirty seconds left, she quickly turned to the last page of her speech and said, "I can only hope you will give this local girl a second chance to carry on serving you."

She returned quickly to her seat, but the applause had faded away long before she'd sat down.

No one could have been in any doubt who had won the first round, but the bell was about to go for the second, and Sasha knew he couldn't let his concentration lapse for even a moment.

"The candidates will now take your questions," said Munro. "Please keep them brief and to the point."

A dozen hands immediately shot up. Munro pointed to a woman seated in the fifth row.

"How do the two candidates feel about Roxton's playing fields being sold off by the council to be replaced by a supermarket?"

Fiona was on her feet even before Munro could say who should respond first.

"I learned to play hockey and tennis on those playing fields," she began, "which is why I raised the issue in the House, at Prime Minister's Questions. I condemned the proposal then, and I will continue to do so if I am reelected. Let us hope that is something else Mr. Karpenko and I have in common, although it seems unlikely, as it was the Labour council that granted planning permission for the supermarket in the first place."

This time she was rewarded with prolonged applause.

Sasha waited for complete silence before he responded. "It is correct that Ms. Hunter spoke against the council's proposal to build a supermarket on the site of Roxton playing fields, when she raised the subject in the House of Commons. But what she didn't mention is that she is the PPS to the Shadow Minister for Rural Affairs, who has never once supported her. Why not? Possibly because the shadow minister would have pointed out to Ms. Hunter that an even bigger sports center is being built three miles down the road at Blandford, with facilities for football, rugby, cricket, hockey, tennis, and a swimming pool, thanks to a Labour government. If I am elected as your member, I will back the council on this issue, as they have had the common sense not to allow arbitrary political boundaries to influence their better judgment. Be assured, I will always support what I believe to be in the best interests of the citizens of Merrifield. Perhaps Ms. Hunter should be elected not to Parliament, but as President of the Not in My Back Yard society. Forgive me if I try to consider the bigger picture."

When Sasha sat down, the audience was still applauding.

Munro next selected a tall, elegant man, dressed in tweed and wearing a striped tie.

"What do the Conservatives feel about the defense cuts proposed by Mr. Healey when he visited the constituency two weeks ago?"

Fiona smiled, but then Major Bennett had been well primed before he put his question.

"Perhaps you should answer this one first, Mr. Karpenko," suggested Munro.

"Defense cuts are a contentious issue for any government," said Sasha. "However, if we are to build more schools, universities, hospitals, and, yes, even sports facilities, either cuts must be made or taxes raised, which is never an easy choice. But it is one that can't be sidestepped. I can only promise that as your representative, I would always weigh up the arguments for any cuts in the defense budget, before coming to a decision." He sat down to a smattering of applause.

"If you could win a battle simply by blowing hot air on your opponents, clearly Mr. Karpenko would be commander in chief of the armed forces," said Fiona. She had to wait for the laughter and applause to die down before she could continue. "Haven't two world wars taught us that we can never allow ourselves to lower our guard? No, the defense of the realm should always be the first priority for any MP, and it always will be for me if you send me back to Westminster."

Fiona basked in the prolonged applause before returning to her seat, leaving Sasha in no doubt who had won that round. The next question came from a woman seated near the back.

"How long are we going to have to wait for the Roxton bypass to be given the green light?"

Sasha realized this was another planted question, as a smile reappeared on Fiona's face, and she didn't even need to glance at her notes.

"The bypass would get the go-ahead tomorrow," said Fiona, "if planning permission wasn't being held up by the current Labour government, which as I don't have to remind you is under Socialist control. I wonder why. Perhaps Mr. Karpenko will enlighten us. But if the Conservatives are elected, I can assure you the bypass will be a priority."

Fiona smiled triumphantly at Sasha as she sat down to even warmer applause than before. But then she knew, if the bypass went ahead, the local council estate would be leveled to make way for it, which would turn Merrifield into a safe Conservative seat once again. She also knew that Sasha couldn't admit that was the real reason he was backing the council on this issue.

"I'm in no doubt," he began, "that Roxton needs a bypass. The only thing under discussion is where the route should be."

"Not in your back yard!" shouted Fiona, to cheers and catcalls.

"I can promise you," said Sasha, "that as your member I would do everything in my power to speed the process up."

The applause, or lack of it, made it clear to everyone in the hall that Fiona had won another round.

Munro finally gave in and pointed to an elderly woman who had jumped up and raised her hand at every opportunity.

"What plans do the candidates have for raising the old-age pension?"

"Every Conservative administration has raised the old-age pension in line with inflation," said Fiona. "The Labour government has always failed to do so, possibly because under their stewardship, inflation has risen on average by fourteen percent per year. So I say to anyone of pensionable age, if you hope to maintain, or improve, your standard of living, make sure you vote Conservative. Actually, I would say the same to anyone below pensionable age as well, because we'll all get there eventually." This suggestion brought a loud cheer from the Tory supporters, who clearly felt their candidate had come fighting back after her earlier setback, and was now ahead on points.

"I sometimes wish," said Sasha, when he rose to reply, "that Ms. Hunter would, just for once, take a long-term view and look beyond next week's election. The present average life expectancy in this country is seventy-three. By the year 2000, it will be eighty-one, and by 2020, when I will be sixty-eight, and eligible for the state pension myself, it is predicted to be eighty-seven. No government—of whatever color—will have the resources to keep raising the old-age pension year on year. Hasn't the time come for Members of Parliament to tell the truth about such difficult and important issues as this, and not to spout platitudes, in the hope that they will scrape home at the next election? I'm an economist by profession, not a lawyer like Ms. Hunter. I will always tell you the facts, while she will always tell you what she thinks you want to hear."

When he sat down, the applause suggested that there was no clear-cut winner of that round.

"There's time for just one more question," said Munro, pointing to a young man seated on the aisle.

"Do either of you think Merrifield United will ever win the FA Cup?"

The whole room burst into laughter.

"I've been a supporter of 'The Merries' since I was a child," said Fiona, "and my father left me his season ticket in his will. But for fear of being told by my opponent that I'm only seeking cheap votes, I'll admit that I think it's unlikely we'll win the cup, but I live in hope."

Sasha took her place. "It was a magnificent achievement for Merrifield to reach the third round of the cup last year," he said. "Joey Butler's goal against Arsenal was a joy to behold, and no one could have been surprised when the Gunners offered him a contract. I was equally delighted that the board decided to use their cup windfall to build a new all-weather stand. But if I'm fortunate enough to become your member, don't be surprised if you still find me standing on the terraces cheering on the home team."

The young man who'd asked the question didn't hide whom he'd be voting for, and Sasha felt the contest was back on an equal footing. Everything now rested on their closing remarks.

"As Mr. Karpenko spoke first at the opening of these proceedings," said Munro, "I shall call on Ms. Hunter to make her closing statement."

Fiona put aside her notes and looked directly at the audience.

"It seems I'm not allowed to mention the fact that I'm a local girl and that my opponent doesn't come from this neck of the woods. I also mustn't remind you that I beat Mr. Karpenko for the presidency of the Cambridge Union, and I beat him again at the by-election following my father's death. And when winning this constituency became a tougher proposition for my party, I didn't run away. But I can tell you, if Mr. Karpenko loses this election, you will never see him again. He will go off in search of a safe seat, whereas you know for certain that I'll be here for the rest of my life. The choice is yours."

Half the audience rose to cheer her, while the other half remained seated, waiting to see if their champion still had any arrows left in his quiver.

Sasha only had a few moments in which to consider how to counter such a brilliant and simple message, although he had no doubt that if Fiona lost, she would also be looking for a safe seat elsewhere. But he couldn't say that, because he couldn't prove it. The packed hall waited in anticipation, one half willing him to succeed, the other half hoping he would stumble.

"Like my father," he began, "I've always believed in democracy, despite being raised in a totalitarian state. So I'm happy to let the voters of Merrifield decide which of us they consider best qualified to represent them in the House of Commons. I only ask that you make that choice based on which candidate you consider will do the better job, and not simply on who has lived here the longest. Naturally I believe that person is me. But if living in Merrifield is proof of commitment, I want you all to know that last week I completed the purchase of a house in Farndale Avenue, and that like Ms. Hunter, I look forward to spending the rest of my life in this constituency."

Chester Munro waited for the applause to die down before thanking both candidates. "And I'd also like to thank you, the audience," he said, but was interrupted by a young woman who appeared from the wings and handed him a slip of paper. He unfolded it and considered the contents before announcing, "I know you will all be fascinated to learn that a TV poll taken immediately following this debate shows Ms. Hunter's support on forty-two percent and Mr. Karpenko also on forty-two percent. The remaining sixteen percent are either undecided or will vote for other parties."

The two candidates rose from their places, walked slowly toward each other, and shook hands. They both accepted that the debate had ended in a draw, and they now only had a week left in which to knock out their opponent.

⊸o⟜

Sasha didn't seem to stand still for a moment during the next seven days, while Alf continually reminded him that the final outcome might be decided by only a handful of votes. He didn't doubt that Fiona would be having the same message hammered home.

On election day, Sasha rose at two in the morning, quite unable to sleep. He'd read all the papers by the time he came down for breakfast. By six o'clock he was back outside Merrifield station imploring the commuters to VOTE KARPENKO—TODAY.

Once the polls opened at seven, he dashed from committee room to committee room in a gallant attempt to thank his legion of dedicated workers, who were refusing to take even a minute off until the last vote had been cast.

"Let's go and have a drink with the rest of the team," he said to Charlie at 10 p.m., after the BBC announced that the polls had closed, and counting was about to begin all over the country.

They walked slowly up the high street to cries of good luck, good-bye, and even, haven't I seen you somewhere before? When they arrived at the Roxton Arms, Alf and the team were already standing at the bar placing their orders.

"And the drinks are on you for a change," said Alf, "now that we're unbribable."

The rest of the team cheered.

"The two of you couldn't possibly have done more," said Audrey Campion as she handed Charlie a tomato juice and Sasha a pint—his first for three weeks.

"Agreed," said Alf. "However, I suggest we all have something to eat before we go across to the town hall and follow the count, as it's unlikely there'll be a result much before two."

"Care to predict that result?" asked Sasha.

"Predictions are for gamblers and fools," said Alf. "The electorate have made their decision. All we can do is wait to find out if they've made the right one. So whatever you say now won't make a blind bit of difference."

"I'd close the cottage hospital, start building the bypass, and cut defense spending by at least ten percent," said Sasha.

Everyone laughed except Charlie, who stumbled forward and clung on to the bar.

"What's the matter?" said Sasha, placing an arm around her.

"What do you think's wrong, idiot?" said Audrey.

"And you've got no one to blame but yourself," said Alf, "because you did implore the Almighty to wait until after the election."

"Stop chattering, Alf," said Audrey, "and ring the hospital. Tell them there's a woman on the way who's about to give birth. Michael, go and fetch a taxi."

Alf scuttled off to the phone at the other end of the bar while Sasha and Audrey supported Charlie as she made her way slowly out of the pub. Michael had already flagged down a passing cab and instructed the driver exactly where he had to go long before Charlie clambered into the back seat.

"Hold on, darling," said Sasha as the taxi moved off. "We don't have far to go," he added, suddenly thankful that the cottage hospital hadn't yet been closed.

Headlights on full, the driver wove in and out of the late night traffic. Alf must have done his job, because when the cab pulled up outside the hospital entrance, two orderlies and a doctor were waiting for them. The doctor helped Charlie from the car while Sasha took out his wallet to pay the fare.

"Have this one on me, guv," said the cabbie. "It'll make up for the fact that I forgot to vote."

Sasha thanked him, but cursed him at the same time as Charlie was eased into a wheelchair. If he lost by one vote . . . He held his wife's hand while the doctor calmly asked her a series of questions. One of the orderlies wheeled her down an empty corridor to the delivery room, where an obstetrics team were waiting. Sasha only let go of her hand when she disappeared inside.

He began to pace up and down the corridor, berating himself for having pushed Charlie so hard during the last few days of the campaign. Alf was right, a child's life was more important than any damned election.

He couldn't be sure how much time had passed before a nurse finally emerged from the delivery room, gave him a warm smile, and said, "Congratulations, Mr. Karpenko, it's a girl."

"And my wife?"

"She's fine. Exhausted, and will need to rest, but you can go and see them both for a few minutes." Sasha followed her into the room, where Charlie was tenderly holding her newborn child. A wrinkled little thing with unfocused blue eyes stared up at him. He hugged Charlie, thanked whatever gods there were for this miracle, and gazed down at his daughter as if she was the first child that had ever been born.

"Pity this didn't happen a week ago," said Charlie.

"Why, my darling?"

"Imagine how many more votes you might have got if you could have told the audience at the debate that your daughter was born in the constituency."

Sasha laughed as a nurse placed a hand on his shoulder and said, "We should let your wife rest."

"Of course," said Sasha, as another nurse gently lifted the baby from her arms and placed her in a cot.

Sasha reluctantly left the room, although Charlie had already fallen asleep. Once he was back out in the corridor, he stopped to stare at his daughter through the window in the door. He waved at her; stupid really, because he knew she couldn't see him. He turned and began to walk toward the stairs, and for the first time in hours, his thoughts returned to what was going on at the town hall. He ran along the corridor and down the steps, wondering if he'd be able to find a taxi at that time of night. He walked across the lobby and was just about to push the door open when a voice behind him said, "Mr. Karpenko?"

He turned around to see a nurse standing behind the reception desk. "Congratulations," she said.

"Thank you. I couldn't be more delighted that it's a girl."

"That wasn't why I was congratulating you, Mr. Karpenko." Sasha looked puzzled. "I just wanted to say how pleased I am that you'll be our next MP."

"You know the result?"

"It was announced on the radio a few moments ago. After three recounts, you won by twenty-seven votes."

34

ALEX

Boston

"I'm sorry to say that Anna was spot on," said Rosenthal. "More than fifty of the pictures are copies, and remembering your own experience with the Warhol, it's not difficult to work out who's got the originals."

"And she's probably sold them all by now," said Alex. "Which means the bank can never hope to recover its losses."

"I wouldn't be so sure of that," said Rosenthal. "The art world is a small, close-knit community, so if a painting from the Lowell Collection were to appear on the market, it would almost certainly be recognized immediately. And we're not talking about one painting, but over fifty. However, now that Mr. Lowell is dead, his sister may well feel confident enough to dispose of them, especially if she believes her only other source of income is about to dry up."

"Which it most certainly is," said Alex with considerable feeling.

"Then the first thing we have to do is find out where the paintings are located."

"Tucked safely away in Evelyn's villa in the south of France would be my bet," said Alex.

"I agree," said Anna. "Because if they were in her apartment in New York, Lawrence couldn't have missed them."

Rosenthal's next question took them both by surprise. "How well do you know Mr. Lowell's butler?"

"Not that well," admitted Alex. "Why do you ask?"

"Do you have any idea where his loyalties lie?"

"When it comes to the Lowell family," said Alex, "you have to support either one faction or the other, as I found out to my cost fairly early on. But I've no reason to believe he's not a member of the home team."

"Then with your permission," said Rosenthal, "I'd like to ask him a couple of questions."

"I can't see why not," said Alex, ringing the bell.

Caxton appeared a few moments later. "You called, sir?"

"Actually, it's me who wanted a word with you, Caxton," said Rosenthal. "I was curious to know if Mr. Lowell's sister ever stayed at the house while he was serving in Vietnam."

"Regularly," said Caxton. "She treated it like a second home."

"And were you always around during those visits?"

"No, sir, not always. Once a month my wife and I like to visit our daughter and grandson in Chicago for a weekend. Sometimes when we returned on a Sunday night, it was clear that Mr. and Mrs. Lowell-Halliday had visited the house in our absence."

"How could you be so sure?" asked Alex.

"There would be beds to make, tables to be cleared, glasses to be washed, and a lot of ashtrays to be emptied."

"So they could have been here on their own for at least forty-eight hours?"

"On several occasions."

"That's very helpful, Caxton," said Rosenthal. "Thank you."

"It's also most important, Caxton," said Alex, "that this conversation remains confidential. Is that understood?"

"In the twelve years I served Mr. Lowell," said Caxton, "he never found it necessary to question my discretion."

"I apologize," said Alex. "That was tactless of me."

No one spoke until the butler had left the room, when Anna said, "Well, that certainly put you in your place, my darling."

"Actually, it was rather reassuring," said Rosenthal. "He would never have considered delivering such a rebuke if he had any intention of contacting Mrs. Lowell-Halliday."

"I agree," said Anna. "But if Evelyn did take several of the pictures to the south of France, how can we prove it?"

"That shouldn't be too difficult," said Rosenthal. "One of the paintings she stole was a Rothko that measures about six feet by four. That isn't something she could carry on board as hand luggage."

Rosenthal rose from his chair and began pacing slowly around the room. Anna, who had become quite used to this habit, glanced at Alex and put a finger to her lips.

"In my opinion," Rosenthal eventually said, "you could not move a painting of that size without the help of a professional art courier, especially if you were sending the picture overseas, as there would have to be export documents and other paperwork to complete. There are only a handful of such specialists on the East Coast, and only one of them is based in Boston."

"Do you know them?" asked Alex hopefully.

"I most certainly do, but I have no intention of contacting them, because immediately after taking my call, he would be on the phone to his client to let her know I'd been making inquiries."

"But he might be our only lead," said Alex.

"Not necessarily, because another company would have had to pick up the packages when they arrived in Nice, and then deliver them to Mrs. Lowell-Halliday's villa in Saint-Paul-de-Vence. It wouldn't surprise me if whoever that was had no idea of the contents, as that's a secret Mrs. Lowell-Halliday wouldn't have wanted to share with anyone else, including the IRS."

"But how do we find out who was collecting the paintings without alerting half the art world?"

"By making sure we remain at arm's length," said Rosenthal. "And I think I know exactly the right dealer in Paris to assist us. May I use the telephone in the study?"

"Yes, of course," said Alex, as Rosenthal poured himself a large whiskey and left the room without another word.

"What's he up to?" asked Alex.

"I can't be sure," said Anna. "But I have a feeling he'll be twisting a few arms, which is why he doesn't want to be overheard."

Rosenthal didn't reappear for another forty minutes, and when he did, although he needed to refill his glass, Anna thought she detected the suggestion of a smile.

"Pierre Gerand will call back as soon as he's tracked down the courier in Nice. He says it's likely to be one of three, and all of them would want to retain his business. Meanwhile, Monty Kessler will set out from New

York first thing tomorrow morning, and anticipates being with us around midday."

Alex nodded. He would have liked to ask who Monty Kessler was, but had already learned when, and when not, to question Mr. Rosenthal.

⊸o⊷

When Alex came down to breakfast the following morning, he found Rosenthal halfway up the stairs, placing little red or yellow stickers on each picture on the wall.

"You'll be glad to hear, Alex, that there are still seventy-one originals left in the collection, including some of the finest examples of Abstract Expressionism I've ever come across. However, I'm in no doubt that fifty-three are copies," he said as the telephone rang.

"Long distance from Paris for Mr. Rosenthal," said Caxton.

Rosenthal walked quickly down the stairs and took the phone. "Good afternoon, Pierre." He said very little for the next few minutes, but never stopped scribbling on a pad by the phone. "I am most grateful," he said finally. "I owe you one." He laughed. "All right, two. And I'll let you know the moment our shipment has left New York," he added before putting down the phone. "I have the name of the French courier," he announced. "A Monsieur Dominic Duval, who over the past five years has delivered a large number of different-sized crates to Mrs. Lowell-Halliday's residence in Saint-Paul-de-Vence."

"But if Pierre phones this Monsieur Duval," said Alex, "won't he contact Evelyn immediately?"

"Not if he wants to go on working for Pierre, he won't. In any case, Pierre has already told him he has an even bigger consignment lined up for him, as long as he can keep his mouth shut."

⊸o⊷

"There's a large, unmarked white van coming up the drive," said Anna, as she looked out of the front window.

"That will be Monty," said Rosenthal. "Caxton, would you be kind enough to open the front door for Mr. Kessler? And be prepared for an invasion of professional art thieves."

"Of course, sir."

Shortly afterward, a small fat balding man marched into the hallway, followed by his six associates, all dressed in black tracksuits with no logos, none of whom would have looked out of place in a boxing ring. Each carried a bag full of the equipment required by any self-respecting burglar.

"Good morning, Monty," said Rosenthal. "I appreciate your coming at such short notice."

"No trouble, Mr. Rosenthal. But I have to remind you that as it's Saturday, we're all on double time. Where do you want me to start?" he asked as he stood, hands on hips, in the middle of the hallway, and looked around at the paintings with the fondness of a doting father.

"I only want you to pack up the ones with yellow stickers on their frames. And once you've done that, I'll tell you where they have to be delivered."

Alex watched with admiration as the seven men fanned out and went about their task with efficiency and skill. While one of them removed a picture from the wall, another covered it in bubble wrap, and a third placed it in a crate ready to be stacked in the van. Mr. Rosenthal had faxed through the exact measurements the previous evening, and another team had worked through the night to have the crates ready in time. All of them on double time.

"They look as if they've done this before," said Alex.

"Yes, Monty specializes in divorce and death. Wives who need to remove valuables after their husbands have left for work and before they return in the evening."

Alex laughed. "And death?"

"Children who want to move paintings and furniture that they agreed with their parents wouldn't be mentioned in the will. It's a thriving business, and Monty is almost always on double time."

"Is there anything I can do to help?"

"I need you to go to the bank and make sure everything is ready by the time Monty and his team turn up, which should be around four o'clock this afternoon. There'll need to be someone waiting at the back door to accompany Monty to a secure vault that's large enough to house seventy-one paintings. Once that's done, please come straight back to the house."

"And will the van also be returning to Beacon Hill?"

"Oh yes. After all, they will only have done half the job."

"Then I'd better get going." There were several questions Alex would have liked to ask Mr. Rosenthal, but he accepted that "need to know" must have been his family motto. As Alex left the house, the first picture was being loaded onto the van.

"And what would you like me to do, Mr. Rosenthal?" asked Anna.

"Double-check the inventory, and make sure they only pack those paintings with yellow stickers. Our real job won't begin until they get back from the bank, when the remaining fifty-three pictures will be loaded onto the van and taken to New York."

"But they're only copies," said Anna.

"True," said Rosenthal. "But they still have to be returned to their rightful owner."

"The Warhol's stowed safely in the hold," said Anna as the plane lifted off. "Has the rest of the collection arrived in Nice?"

"Yes," said Rosenthal. "I called Pierre Gerand again as soon as I got back to New York on Sunday night. He's one of the leading abstract dealers in Paris, and an old friend who's familiar with the Lowell Collection, as his grandfather sold three pictures to Mr. Lowell's father when he was touring Europe in 1947. I told him that a large consignment of paintings was on its way to Nice, and asked him to arrange for Monsieur Duval to collect them and store them until we arrive. He phoned back yesterday to let me know that Evelyn and Mr. Halliday were spotted boarding an Air France flight for Boston that morning. That's when I called to remind you not to forget the Warhol. So by the time we touch down in Nice, everything should be in place. Pierre and Monsieur Duval will meet us off the plane."

"So now all we have to do is get the rest of the collection back," said Anna.

"Which will be no small undertaking. At least we're in the hands of professionals. But should we fail . . ."

"Alex tells me the bank will go bust and we'll be broke."

"So, no pressure," said Rosenthal. "Mind you, I could always offer Alex a job as a runner at the gallery. He'd be rather good at it."

"Or he could have my job, as you'll need someone to fill in for me when the baby is born."

"No, he's not that good," said Rosenthal, as the plane reached forty thousand feet and banked toward the east.

⊸o⊷

"How much notice do you have to give?" said Ackroyd.

"The bank's statutes require fourteen days," said Fowler, "so I was thinking of sending letters to all the directors this morning."

"But the moment Miss Robbins opens the mail, she'll be alerted and tell Karpenko about the emergency board meeting, and if he's half as bright as you say he is, it won't take him long to work out what we're up to."

"I'd thought of that," said Fowler, "and intend to send Karpenko's letter to his apartment in Brooklyn. Now that he's taken up residence in Boston, it will be lying on his doormat until he returns."

"And the motion to replace him as chairman will have been passed before he has a chance to do anything about it. So why don't you post those letters, Ray?"

⊸o⊷

Anna emerged from the plane soon after they'd touched down in Nice, and was greeted by a warm evening breeze. She wished Alex was with her to share her first visit to France. But she knew he couldn't risk being away from his desk for even a few hours.

Once they'd cleared customs and walked into the arrivals hall, a man, dressed in an open-necked floral shirt and a now fashionable light blue suit, rushed up to Rosenthal and kissed him on both cheeks.

"Welcome, *mon ami*. Allow me to introduce you to Dominic Duval, whom I have chosen to mastermind this operation."

When his Citroën joined the early evening traffic heading toward Nice, Duval began to brief his co-conspirators.

"As soon as Mr. and Mrs. Lowell-Halliday left the villa, I called Pierre in Paris to let him know they were on their way to Boston."

"How could you be so sure they were going to the airport?" asked Anna.

"Three suitcases was a minor clue," said Duval.

"It also suggests," said Rosenthal, "that Evelyn intends to remain in Boston for some time."

"I then called Nathanial in New York," said Pierre—the first time Anna had heard anyone call Mr. Rosenthal by his first name—"to tell him they were on the way, and immediately flew down to Nice to make sure we're ready for tomorrow's exchange."

"Why so soon?" asked Rosenthal.

"We have to take advantage of the fact that Thursday is the butler's day off. Otherwise we'd have to wait another week. And Mrs. Lowell-Halliday might well have returned by then."

"Is your team in place?"

"Ready and waiting," said Duval. "First thing tomorrow morning I'll call the villa and tell the maid I have an important package for delivery."

"Do we know anything about the maid?" asked Rosenthal.

"Her name's Maria," said Duval. "She's worked there for several years, and she's the only one who's around on the butler's day off. She's not particularly bright, but she has a heart of gold."

"And as we have a comprehensive list of the paintings that have to be exchanged, we should be able to carry out the whole exercise in less than an hour," said Pierre.

"But you can't pack fifty-three valuable paintings in under an hour," said Rosenthal. "They're not cans of baked beans. It's likely to take at least three or four hours."

"We can't even risk an hour," replied Duval. "We'll remove them as quickly as possible from the villa, then drive to our warehouse, which is only seven kilometers away, where we can pack them properly for the flight. Don't forget, we've already got the crates containing the copies."

"Impressive," said Rosenthal, "but I still worry that the maid might be a problem."

"I have an idea," said Anna.

⊰o⊱

"As it seems I can't even stay in my own home," said Evelyn, "we've had to take a suite at the Fairmont, which doesn't come cheap, so I do hope, Douglas, that you've got everything set up for next Monday's meeting."

"Everything's in place," said Ackroyd. "Although the board's divided, with your vote, we'll still have a majority, so by this time next week Karpenko should be on his way back to New York worrying about pizzas, and I'll be chairman of the bank."

"And I can move back into Beacon Hill and remove the rest of the pictures, before the IRS discovers that Lowell's isn't even a piggy bank."

⊸o⊷

He phoned the villa at ten past eight the following morning.

"Hi, Maria, it's Dominic Duval," he said. "I've got a delivery for Mrs. Lowell that needs to be dropped off at the villa."

"But Mrs. Lowell isn't here, and it's the butler's day off."

"My instructions couldn't be clearer," said Duval. "Madame insisted that the package should be delivered before she returns from America, but if you're in any doubt, please call her in Boston, though I should warn you, it's two o'clock in the morning there." His first risk.

"No, no," said the maid. "When should I expect you?"

"In about an hour's time." Duval put the phone down and joined the rest of the team, who were waiting for him in the van.

"And how's my wife?" he said as he sat next to Anna. She gave him a weak smile.

Duval drove the van out of the warehouse and onto the main road. He stuck to the inside lane, and never exceeded the speed limit. During the journey, he took every member of the team through their roles one last time, especially Anna, Pierre, and Rosenthal.

"And don't forget," he said, "only Anna and I are to leave the van when we arrive."

Forty minutes later they drove through the front gates and up the driveway, and came to a halt outside a magnificent villa. Anna would have loved to stroll through the colorful, well-tended gardens, but not today.

She and Duval walked up to the front door hand in hand. Duval pressed the bell, and moments later the maid appeared. She smiled when she recognized the van.

"One package to be delivered to Mrs. Lowell," said Duval. "If you'll just sign here, Maria, I'll fetch the crate from the van."

Maria smiled, but her expression turned to anxiety when Anna collapsed on the ground at her feet, clutching her stomach.

"Ah, *ma pauvre femme,*" said Duval. "My wife is pregnant, Maria. Do you have somewhere where she could lie down for a few minutes?"

"Of course, monsieur. Come with me."

Duval helped Anna to her feet and they followed the maid into the house and up the wide staircase to a guest bedroom on the first floor, while he studied the pictures on the way.

"I'm sorry to be such a nuisance," said Anna, as Duval helped her onto the bed.

"It's not a problem, madame," said Maria. "Should I call for a doctor?"

"No, I'm sure I'll be all right if I can just rest for a few minutes. But, darling," she said to Duval, "would you fetch my bag from the van, there are some pills I ought to take."

"Of course, darling, I won't be a moment," he said, taking a closer look at the picture above the bed.

"You're so kind," said Anna, clinging on to Maria's hand.

"No, no, madame, I have four children of my own. And men are so useless in these situations," she added as Duval slipped out of the room.

He ran down the stairs to find his team were already in full swing, with Rosenthal acting as ringmaster, while Pierre cracked the whip. One by one the masterpieces were removed from the walls, to be replaced moments later with copies.

"You'll find the Matisse above the fireplace in the drawing room," Rosenthal said to one of the couriers. "The Picasso belongs in the master bedroom," to another, "and the Rauschenberg goes right there," he said, pointing to a large empty space on the wall in front of him.

"I'm looking for a Dalí," said Duval. "It goes in the guest bedroom," he added as a de Kooning disappeared out of the front door.

"There are three Dalís," said Pierre after checking the inventory. "What's the subject?"

"A yellow clock melting over a table."

"Oil or watercolor?" asked Pierre.

"Oil," said Duval as he headed back up the staircase.

"Got it. And don't forget your wife's handbag," said Rosenthal.

"*Merde!*" said Duval, who dashed out of the house, nearly colliding with two couriers coming the other way.

He opened the passenger door of the van, grabbed Anna's handbag, and ran back into the house and up the stairs, taking them two at a time. Pierre was just a pace behind, clutching the Dalí. Duval caught his breath, opened the door, and walked in, assuming a look of concern, while Pierre waited outside in the corridor.

"And the problem with Béatrice," the maid was saying, "is that she's fourteen, going on twenty-three."

Anna laughed as Duval handed her the bag. "Thank you, darling," she said, as she undid the clasp and took out a bottle of pills. "I'm sorry to be such a nuisance, Maria, but could I have a glass of water?"

"Of course," said the maid, bustling into the bathroom.

Anna leaped up, stood on the bed, and quickly lifted the Dalí off its hook. She handed it to Duval, who ran to the door and exchanged it with Pierre for the copy, which he passed to Anna seconds later. Their second risk. She just had time to hang it on the hook and fall back down on the bed before Maria reappeared, carrying a glass of water. She found the two of them holding hands.

Anna took her time swallowing two pills, then said, "I'm so sorry to be holding you up." Her well-trained husband came in bang on cue.

"Maria, where should I put the package for Mrs. Lowell?"

"Leave it in the hall, and the butler can deal with it when he gets back tomorrow."

"Of course," said Duval, "and by the time I return, darling, perhaps you'll have sufficiently recovered for me to take you home."

"I hope so," said Anna.

"Don't worry," said Maria, "I'll stay with madame until you get back."

"How kind of you," said Duval as he left the room. He was running down the stairs when he spotted Pierre handing the Dalí to a courier. "How much longer?" he asked as he joined Rosenthal in the hall.

"Five minutes, ten at the most," said Rosenthal, as a courier showed him a Pollock. "Far side of the drawing room," he said without hesitation.

Duval's eyes never left the bedroom door. He said, "Any problems?"

"I can't find the blue Warhol of Jackie. It's too important not to be in one of the main rooms. But you'd better get back upstairs before the maid becomes suspicious."

Duval walked back upstairs and returned to the bedroom, where the maid was still regaling Anna with tales about her children. He held up five fingers, and as she nodded, he noticed that the Dalí was hanging lopsided.

"Maria was just telling me, darling, about the trouble she's been having with her daughter Béatrice."

"She can't be worse than Marcel," said Duval, sitting on the edge of the bed.

"But I thought you told me this would be your first child?" said Maria, looking puzzled.

"Dominic has a son by his first wife," said Anna quickly, "who tragically died of cancer, which I think is one of the reasons for Marcel's problems."

"Oh, I'm so sorry," said Maria.

"I think I'm feeling a little better now," said Anna, slowly sitting up and lowering her feet onto the carpet. "You've been so kind. I don't know how to thank you." She rose unsteadily and, with Maria's support, began walking slowly toward the door, while Duval knelt on the bed and straightened the Dalí. His third risk. He caught up with them just in time to open the door.

"I'll go ahead and make sure the van door is open," he said—not part of the well-rehearsed script—and he was only halfway down the stairs when he saw Rosenthal and Pierre still in the hallway.

"Where's the Warhol?" Pierre demanded.

"To hell with the Warhol," said Duval. "We're out of here."

Pierre left quickly, followed by Rosenthal, cursing under his breath.

When Anna and Maria reached the hallway a few moments later, they found Duval standing by the front door, one hand resting on a crate.

"Thank you for being so kind to my wife," he said. "Here's the package I was asked to deliver, along with a letter for Mrs. Lowell."

"I'll see madame gets them both as soon as she returns," said Maria.

Duval took Anna gently by the arm and led her out of the house to find the passenger door of the van already open. It was the little details that Rosenthal was so good at.

As the van moved slowly down the drive, Duval wondered if Maria would find it strange that they had used such a large van to deliver one picture.

"Any problems, Anna?" said Rosenthal from the back of the van.

"Other than being pregnant, having two husbands, neither of whom I'm married to, and a stepson I've never even met, nothing in particular."

"Remember to drive slowly, Dominic," said Rosenthal. "We mustn't forget that we have precious cargo on board."

"How thoughtful of you," said Anna, touching her stomach.

Rosenthal had the grace to smile, as Anna leaned out of the window and waved good-bye to Maria. She waved back, a puzzled look on her face.

35

ALEX

Boston

Alex arrived at the bank so early the following morning that Errol hadn't yet taken up his post, and the night security guard had to let him in. Someone else who needed to be convinced that he was the new chairman.

He went up in the elevator alone, and when he stepped out into the corridor on the twenty-fourth floor, he was amused to see that Miss Robbins had left her light on. *Fuelish,* he would tease her. He opened the door, intending to switch the light off, only to be greeted with, "Good morning, chairman."

"Good morning," said Alex, not missing a beat. "Have you been here all night?"

"No, sir, but I wanted to bring the mail up to date before you arrived."

"Anything interesting?"

"There's one letter and a package I thought you ought to see immediately. They're on the top of the pile on your desk."

"Thank you," said Alex, curious to discover what Miss Robbins considered interesting. He walked into his office to find the promised mountain of mail awaiting him.

He took the letter from the top of the pile and read it slowly. He then opened the package and stared in disbelief at the real thing. His hands were still shaking as he put it back in the package. He had to agree with Miss Robbins, the letter was interesting, and she'd offered her opinion without knowing what was in the package.

The second letter was from Bob Underwood, a director of the bank who felt the time had come for him to retire, not least because he was seventy. He suggested that the emergency board meeting on Monday morning would be an ideal time to inform the board of his intention. Alex cursed, because Underwood was one of the few people he had hoped would remain on the board. He seemed perfectly satisfied with the ten thousand dollars a year he received as a non-executive director, he rarely claimed any expenses, and you didn't have to read between the lines of the minutes to realize that he was one of the few board members who was willing to stand up to Ackroyd and his cronies. Alex would have to try and get him to change his mind.

And then his eyes returned to the words, *emergency board meeting on Monday morning.* Why hadn't Miss Robbins informed him about that earlier?

There was a gentle tap on the door and Miss Robbins appeared bearing a cup of coffee, black no sugar, and a plate of digestive biscuits. How did she find out what his favorite biscuits were?

"Thank you," said Alex, as she placed a silver tray that must have been one of Lawrence's family heirlooms on the desk in front of him. "May I ask a delicate question, Miss Robbins? You must have a first name?"

"Pamela."

"And I'm Alex."

"I'm aware of that, chairman."

"I agree with you, Pamela, that Mrs. Ackroyd's letter is interesting. But as I don't know the lady, how would you advise me to respond to her offer?"

"I would accept it in good faith, chairman. After all, it's common knowledge that their recent divorce was acrimonious . . ." Miss Robbins hesitated.

"I don't think we have time to observe the social niceties, Pamela, so spit it out."

"I was only surprised how few women were named as co-respondents."

"That's sure spitting it out," said Alex. "Carry on."

"The latest of his secretaries, a Miss Bowers, may well have hidden attributes of which I am unaware, but she certainly couldn't spell."

"So you feel I should take Mrs. Ackroyd's words at face value?"

"I most certainly do, chairman, and I particularly enjoyed the last paragraph of her letter."

Alex read it again, and indeed it brought a smile to his face.

"Anything else, chairman?"

"Yes," said Alex, "before you go, Pamela, I also read Mr. Underwood's letter and he's under the impression there's an emergency board meeting next Monday. If that's the case, it's news to me."

"As it was to me," said Miss Robbins. "So I made a few discreet inquiries, and it turns out that Mr. Fowler sent out notice of the meeting a few days ago."

"Not to me, he didn't."

"Yes, he did. But he sent the agenda to your apartment in New York, which is registered with the company as your home address."

"But Fowler knows perfectly well that I'm staying at Mr. Lowell's home for the foreseeable future. What's he up to?"

"I have no idea, chairman, but I could try to find out."

"Please do. And see if you can lay your hands on an agenda, without Fowler finding out."

"Of course, chairman."

"Meanwhile, I'll plow on with these files until Mr. Harbottle arrives for his appointment at eleven." As she turned to leave, Alex couldn't resist asking, "What do you think of Mr. Harbottle, Pamela?"

"He's a stuffy, eccentric old buzzard, right out of the pages of Dickens, but let's at least be thankful he's batting for our team, because the enemy are terrified of him, and perhaps even more important, he's like Caesar's wife."

"Caesar's wife?"

"When you have more time, chairman."

"Before you go, Pamela, if I were to ask you for one piece of advice to keep this ship afloat, what would it be?"

"Not what, but who. I'd have a private meeting, very private, with Jake Coleman, who until six months ago was the bank's chief financial officer."

"Why do I remember that name?" said Alex. "Something I read in the minutes?"

"He resigned after a flaming row with Mr. Ackroyd, and like me, he was told to clear his desk by the end of the day."

"What was the row about?"

"I've no idea. Mr. Coleman is far too professional to have discussed the matter with a member of staff."

"Who's he working for now?"

"He hasn't been able to find another job, chairman, because every time he's shortlisted for a major position they call Mr. Ackroyd, and he not only sticks the knife in, but twists it."

"Set up a meeting with him as quickly as possible."

"I'll call him immediately, chairman," said Miss Robbins before closing the door behind her.

As Alex read through the minutes of the previous years' board meetings, it became increasingly evident that although Lawrence might well have attended, even chaired, every one of them, the unholy trinity of Ackroyd, Jardine, and Fowler had simply run rings around him. He had reached September, when there was a knock on the door. Could it possibly be eleven o'clock already?

The door opened and in walked the unmistakable figure of Mr. Harbottle. "Good morning, chairman," said the elderly counsel.

"Good morning, sir," said Alex, standing and waiting for Harbottle to take a seat. He paused to allow Mr. Harbottle to suggest that perhaps they might now call each other by their first names, but no such offer was forthcoming.

"May I begin by thanking you for your excellent advice yesterday," said Alex. "It allowed me to remain a yard ahead of Ackroyd and Jardine, but only a yard, because I've just learned that Fowler has called an emergency board meeting for next Monday."

"Has he indeed?" said Harbottle. He adjusted his spectacles before continuing. "Then I suspect it is their intention to try to replace you as chairman. And they wouldn't have called the meeting unless they're convinced they have a majority on the board."

"If they have, is there anything I can do about it?"

"I won't know the answer to that, chairman, until I have another chance to consult the bank's statutes."

"Another chance?"

"Yes, because I may already have come up with something that will assist you in your efforts."

Alex sank back in his chair, only too aware that Harbottle would take his time.

"While you've been familiarizing yourself with the board minutes and annual accounts, I've been engrossed in the company's statutes—

fascinating bedtime reading—and I think I may have come across something that will be of interest to you." He removed a file from his Gladstone bag.

"Paragraph 33b, no doubt."

Harbottle allowed himself a half-smile. "No, in fact," he said, opening the file, "statute 9, subclause 2. Allow me to enlighten you, chairman," he said, and began to read a passage he had underlined. "No employee or director of the company shall be paid more than the chairman."

Alex's mind began to race, but it quickly became clear that Harbottle had continued to burn the midnight oil.

"Ackroyd paid himself the outrageous sum of five hundred thousand dollars a year as CEO, which also allowed him to reward his inner team with inflated salaries, thereby guaranteeing him a majority on the board."

"So if I were to pay myself a more realistic salary," said Alex, "say—"

"Sixty thousand dollars a year," prompted Harbottle, "while at the same time insisting that all future expenses had to be signed off by you, I suspect that all three of them would resign fairly quickly."

"But that's assuming I survive as chairman."

"Agreed," said Harbottle. "And after what I have to tell you, you may not be certain you want to remain in the post." Alex sat back again. "You asked me to visit the chairman of the Banking Commission, which I did yesterday afternoon. I can't pretend he was in the giving vein. In fact, he made it quite clear after he'd studied the latest balance sheet that the entire Lowell Collection would have to be valued by a recognized dealer and lodged in the bank's vaults before he would consider it as an asset. He will allow you twenty-eight days to fulfill this obligation, and I am to report back to him personally should you fail to do so."

Alex let out a deep sigh. "Anything else?"

"Yes, I fear so. He also made it clear that Mr. Lowell had no right to leave you his fifty percent of the bank's shares, or even his fifty percent of the Elena Pizza Company, and has insisted that those shares also be lodged with the bank as security. He went on to suggest that you might consider including your fifty percent of Elena's, to prove your commitment to the bank. However, he did add that you were under no obligation to do so."

"How very generous of him," said Alex. "Anything in the credit column?"

"Yes. I wrote down his exact words." Harbottle turned a page of his yellow pad. "I am confident that anyone who could escape from the KGB in a crate with only half a dozen bottles of vodka for his passage and go on to win the Silver Star, will surely be able to overcome the bank's current problems."

"How does he know about that?" said Alex.

"You clearly haven't had the time to read today's *Boston Globe*. It's published a glowing profile of you in the business section. It makes you sound like a cross between Abraham Lincoln and James Bond."

Alex laughed for the first time that day.

"But be warned. Ackroyd is every bit as ruthless and resourceful as Blofeld, and I wouldn't be at all surprised if he fed his cat on live goldfish."

"I can't believe that you're . . ."

"Ah, I confess to being an admirer of Mr. Fleming. I've read all his books, although I've never seen any of the films."

The lawyer removed his glasses, placed the file back in his Gladstone bag, and folded his arms; a sign that he was about to say something off the record.

"Dare I ask how Mr. Rosenthal's trip to Nice worked out?"

"It could hardly have gone better," said Alex. "With the exception of one painting, the entire Lowell Collection will soon be safely stored in a secure vault, to which only I and the bank's head of security know the code, and which cannot be opened unless both of us are present, with our keys."

"That is indeed good news," said Harbottle. "But you did say, with one exception?"

"And even that is now in my possession," said Alex, as he handed over Mrs. Ackroyd's letter. Once the lawyer had read it, Alex passed across a small painting to Mr. Harbottle.

"A Blue Jackie by Warhol," said Harbottle. "I must say, this restores one's faith in one's fellow man."

"Or even woman," said Alex with a grin.

"But how did Mrs. Ackroyd get her hands on the painting?" asked Harbottle.

"She says Ackroyd gave it to her as part of their divorce settlement."

"And how did he get hold of it?"

"Evelyn Lowell-Halliday, would be my bet," said Alex. "A reward for services rendered, no doubt."

"Which gives me an idea," said Harbottle. He paused for a moment before saying, "But if I'm to pull it off, I'll need to borrow Jackie for a few days."

"Of course," said Alex, well aware that there would be no point in asking him why.

Harbottle wrapped up the painting, and placed it carefully in his Gladstone bag. "I've wasted enough of your time, chairman," he said as he rose from his seat, "so I'll be on my way."

Alex was unable to resist a smile as he accompanied Mr. Harbottle to the door. But once again, the old gentleman took him by surprise.

"Now we know each other a little better, I think you should call me Harbottle."

⊰o⊱

It wasn't difficult for Alex to work out why Jake Coleman and Doug Ackroyd were never going to be able to work together. Coleman was so clearly an honest, decent, straightforward man, who believed the team was far more important than any individual. Whereas Ackroyd . . .

The two of them met for lunch at Elena 3, as Alex was confident that was the one place in Boston Ackroyd and his cronies would never patronize.

"Why did you leave Lowell's?" asked Alex, once they'd both ordered a Congressman special.

"I didn't leave the bank," said Jake, "I was fired."

"Can I ask why?"

"I felt someone had to inform the chairman that his sister's gambling habit had got out of control, and that if she was allowed to go on borrowing indiscriminately, the bank would surely go bust."

"How did Ackroyd respond?" said Alex as two sizzling pizzas were placed in front of them.

"Told me to mind my own business if I knew what was good for me."

"And you clearly didn't."

"No. I warned Ackroyd that if he didn't inform the chairman of what was going on behind his back, then I would. Which was as good as signing my own death warrant, because I was fired the next day."

"And did you tell Lawrence the truth?"

"I wrote to him immediately," said Jake, "even set up an appointment to see him. But he asked if it could wait until after the election, and as that was only a few weeks away, I readily agreed."

"And you haven't been able to find a suitable position since?"

"No. At least not at the same level I had at Lowell's. Ackroyd made sure of that."

"I'm surprised he still has that sort of influence in banking circles."

"He has enemies, that's for sure, but whenever I applied for a job, the first person they'd contact was the CEO of the last bank I'd worked for."

Alex could almost hear Ackroyd whispering confidentially: *Between you and me, the man can't be trusted.* The one word in banking that would have closed every door.

"So, if I were to offer you a job, would you consider coming back?"

"No. At least not while Ackroyd is still on the board. I don't need to be fired twice."

"But if Ackroyd were to resign?"

"Wild horses won't move him while he still has a majority on the board, and while Evelyn owns fifty percent of the stock, what's the point?"

"You may well be right," said Alex, "because I can't pretend that my own position is all that secure. And even if that were to change, I still can't guarantee the bank will survive. However, I am convinced that if you were to climb back on board, we'd have a lot better chance."

"What makes you so confident of that, when you don't even know me?"

"But I do know Bob Underwood, and Pamela Robbins, and if those two are willing to vouch for you, that's good enough for me."

"That is indeed a compliment. So if you are able to get rid of Ackroyd and his cronies, I will be happy to continue in my old job as the bank's financial officer."

"That wasn't what I had in mind," said Alex. Jake looked disappointed. "I was rather hoping you'd be willing to take over Ackroyd's position, and return to Lowell's as the chief executive."

⊸o⊷

"Good morning, gentlemen," said Alex, looking around the table to see only one unoccupied chair. "I will ask Mr. Fowler to read the minutes of the last meeting."

The company secretary rose from his place and opened the minute book. "The board met on March eighteenth," he began, "and among the matters discussed . . ."

Alex's mind drifted back to the hastily called meeting held in Harbottle's office the previous evening that had lasted until the early hours of the morning. They had both come to the reluctant conclusion that the numbers were stacked against him, well aware that Evelyn was in Boston. He glanced at the empty chair. But if Evelyn didn't turn up, he might still be in with a chance.

By the time Alex had arrived home, Anna was fast asleep. He decided not to wake her and burden her with his news. He placed a hand on his future son or daughter, a little mound of would-be-life keen to get out and join the world. He climbed into bed, desperate for sleep, but his mind didn't rest, even for a moment, like a convicted murderer the night before being strapped into the electric chair.

He snapped back into the real world when Fowler said, "That concludes the minutes of the last meeting. Are there any questions?"

Still no sign of Evelyn.

There were no questions, not least because everyone around that table knew only too well what the first item on the agenda was.

"Item number one is the selection of a new chairman," said Alex as the door opened and Evelyn burst into the room. Alex cursed as he looked at the woman who'd so captivated him when they'd first met. He could see why men fell so completely under her spell, if only for a short time. Jardine and Ackroyd both rose to greet her, and she took the empty place between them.

"I apologize for being late," said Evelyn, "but I needed to consult my lawyer on a personal matter before I attended the meeting."

Which lawyer, Alex wondered, *and what personal matter?*

"I was about to invite nominations for the post of chairman," said Fowler, "following the tragic death of your brother."

Evelyn nodded. "Please don't let me hold you up," she said, smiling warmly at the company secretary.

Mr. Jardine was quickly back on his feet. "I'd like to place on record my admiration for the way Mr. Karpenko has temporarily filled the gap while we looked for a more suitably qualified candidate to be our next chairman. I believe that, for the long-term future of the company, that person is Doug Ackroyd. We will all recall what an outstanding job he did as the bank's CEO."

"Almost brought the company to its knees," muttered Bob Underwood, loudly enough for his fellow board members to hear.

Jardine ignored the sotto voce interruption and plowed on. "I therefore have no hesitation in proposing our former CEO, Mr. Douglas Ackroyd, to be the next chairman of Lowell's Bank."

"Do we have a seconder?" asked Fowler.

"I shall be delighted to second the nomination," said Alan Gates, coming in bang on cue.

"Another of the fifty-thousand-dollar-a-year expenses brigade," said Underwood, "making sure the gravy train rolls on in perpetuity."

"Thank you," said Fowler. "If there are no further nominations, all that is left for me to do is call for a vote. Those in favor of Mr. Doug Ackroyd being elected as our next chairman, please raise your hands."

Six hands were raised.

"On a point of order, Mr. Chairman." The well-organized juggernaut suddenly ground to an unscheduled halt. "I feel I should point out," said Underwood, "that under standing order 7.9 of the bank's statutes, no one standing for the position of chairman can vote for himself."

Alex smiled. Clearly Harbottle wasn't the only person who'd been burning the midnight oil. There was some muttering among the board members while Fowler looked up that particular standing order.

"That appears to be correct," he eventually managed.

"Well, what do you know?" said Underwood. "Our founding fathers weren't that stupid after all."

"However," said Fowler, "Mr. Ackroyd still has five votes. I will now ask if anyone wishes to vote against?"

Five directors immediately raised their hands.

"Any abstentions?"

"Only me," said Evelyn, in her most innocent voice.

Ackroyd was baffled, while Alex couldn't hide his surprise.

"Then the vote is five each, with one abstention," said Fowler.

"So what do we do now?" asked Tom Rhodes, a director who rarely spoke.

"I suggest Mr. Fowler reads standing order 7.10," said Underwood, "and we just might find out."

Fowler reluctantly turned the page and read out, "In the event of a tie, the chairman will have the casting vote."

Everyone turned to face Alex, who didn't hesitate before saying, "Against." Even louder muttering broke out among the board members.

It was some time before Fowler, after once again checking the standing orders, asked, "Are there any other nominations?"

"Yes," said Bob Underwood. "I propose that Mr. Alex Karpenko continue as our chairman, as no one can be in any doubt about the outstanding contribution he has made since he took over the chair."

"I second the nomination," said Rhodes.

Fowler resumed his role as arbitrator. "Those in favor, please raise their hands." Only five hands shot up, as Alex couldn't vote for himself.

Just as Fowler was about to ask for those against, Evelyn slowly raised her hand to join the other five. Fowler couldn't have sounded more dismayed when he had to announce, "I declare Mr. Alex Karpenko to have been elected as the chairman of the Lowell Bank and Trust Company."

Several members of the board burst into spontaneous applause, while Ackroyd was unable to hide first his disbelief, then his anger. He along with four other directors immediately rose from their places and left the room.

"Judas," said Ackroyd, as he walked past Evelyn.

"More like the Good Samaritan!" shouted Underwood before the door slammed shut.

"They'll be back," said Alex with a sigh.

"I don't think so," said Evelyn quietly. She didn't speak again until she was sure she had everyone's attention.

"The reason I was a little late for the board meeting, gentlemen," she said, "was because earlier this morning I had a visit from a senior officer with the Boston police department." Every eye was fixed on her.

"It seems that a Blue Jackie by Andy Warhol was stolen from the Lowell Collection while Lawrence was serving in Vietnam." She paused and took a sip of water, her hand trembling to show how distressed she was.

"When the officer told me the name of the culprit, I was so shocked, I immediately consulted my lawyer, who advised me to attend this meeting and make sure that Mr. Karpenko continues as chairman of the bank. I also felt it nothing less than my duty to assure the chief of police that when Mr. Ackroyd comes up for trial, I will be happy to appear as a state witness."

Some of the directors nodded, while Alex remained puzzled.

"Congratulations," said Underwood. "You single-handedly managed to remove five shits with one shovel."

"But I don't understand," said Alex, once the laughter had died down. "Why would you be willing to support me?"

"Because who am I to disagree with my brother's choice for chairman?" Not one of the remaining board members believed her for a moment, and they were even more surprised by her next statement. "And to that end, I would like to place on record that I am willing to sell my fifty percent holding in the company for one million dollars."

Now Alex understood exactly why she needed Ackroyd out of the way. He was about to respond to her offer, when Miss Robbins burst into the room and handed him a slip of paper. He unfolded it, read the message, and smiled before rising to his feet.

"Wild horses couldn't have dragged me away from this meeting," he said, "but the words 'your wife's gone into labor' certainly can and will." He was already on the move.

A second round of applause followed, and when Alex reached the door he turned and said, "Bob, will you take over the chair? I don't think I'll be back today."

"There's a taxi waiting for you," Miss Robbins said as they went down in the elevator.

The cab sped off as if it was on the front of the grid at Daytona. Alex had to cling on to his seat as the driver swerved in and out of the traffic. Clearly the words "she's in labor" created another gear.

By the time the taxi came to a screeching halt outside the hospital entrance fifteen minutes later, two police motorcycles were on their tail. Alex prayed they were both fathers. He took his wallet out, handed the driver a hundred-dollar bill, and ran inside.

"Your change!" shouted the driver, but Alex had long since disappeared.

He crossed the lobby to the front desk and gave the receptionist his name.

"Maternity unit, 6B, fourth floor," she said, checking her screen and smiling. "Your wife got here just in time."

Alex ran to the elevator, jumped in, and jabbed the number 4 several times, only to discover it didn't make it move any faster. When the doors eventually slid open on the fourth floor, he walked quickly along the corridor until he came to a door marked 6B. He charged in to find Anna sitting up in bed, holding a little bundle in her arms. She looked up and smiled.

"Ah, here's your father. What can have taken him so long?"

"I'm so sorry I wasn't here in time," said Alex, taking her in his arms. "Something unexpected came up at the office isn't much of an excuse, but at least it's true."

"Meet your son and heir," said Anna, handing him over.

"Hello, little fellow. Had a good day so far?"

"He's doing fine," said Anna. "But he's quite anxious to find out what happened at the board meeting."

"No need to be, his father's still the chairman of Lowell's Bank."

"How come?"

"Evelyn gave me her casting vote."

"Why would she do that?"

"Because she's had to accept that the bank can no longer afford to pay out any more money, and perhaps more important, she won't now be able to get her hands on the Lowell Collection."

"But why would she roll over quite so easily?" said Anna.

"Jackie Kennedy came to our rescue," said Alex.

"I'm lost."

"It seems that the police had to arrest either Ackroyd or Evelyn for stealing the Warhol, while allowing the other to turn state's evidence. No prizes for guessing which role Evelyn cast herself in. In fact she's so desperate, she even offered to sell me her shares in the bank."

"For how much?"

"A million dollars. Just a pity I don't have that sort of money at the moment."

"Let's hope you don't live to regret it," said Anna.

There was a tap on the door, and a nurse poked her head into the room. "I'm sorry to bother you, Mr. Karpenko, but there's a traffic policeman outside who says he needs to see the evidence."

BOOK FOUR

36

SASHA

Westminster, 1980

It would have been better if Mr. Sasha Karpenko MP had never left the Soviet Union, was the opening sentence in *The Times'* leader that morning.

Sasha fell in love with the Palace of Westminster from the moment he walked through St. Stephen's entrance, and joined his new colleagues in the Members' Lobby. His mother burst into tears when he swore the oath before taking his place on the opposition back benches. As he held the Bible in his hand with members on both sides staring down at him as if he'd just arrived from another planet, it felt to Sasha like being the new boy at school.

Michael Cocks, the Labour chief whip, told him to keep his head down for the first few years. However, it didn't take the whips long to realize they had a prodigious young talent on their hands who might not always be easy to handle. So when Sasha rose to make his maiden speech even the two front benches remained in their places to hear the member for Moscow, as the Conservatives referred to him. But Sasha had already decided to tackle that problem in its infancy.

"Mr. Sasha Karpenko," called Mr. Speaker Thomas. The House fell silent, as is the tradition when a member delivers his or her maiden speech.

"Mr. Speaker, may I begin by saying what an honor it is for this Russian immigrant to become a member of the British House of Commons. If you had told me, just twelve years ago when I was a schoolboy in Leningrad, that I would be sitting on these benches before my thirtieth birthday, only my mother would have believed it, especially as I had already told my closest school friend that I was going to be the first democratically elected president of Russia."

This statement was greeted by loud cheers from both sides of the House.

"Mr. Speaker, I have the privilege of representing the constituents of Merrifield in the county of Kent, who in their wisdom decided to replace a Conservative woman with a Labour man." He looked across the floor at the Prime Minister seated on the front bench opposite, and said, "That's something my party intends to repeat at the next general election."

Margaret Thatcher gave a slight bow, while those seated on the opposition benches roared their approval.

"My opponent, Ms. Fiona Hunter, served in this House for three years, and will be sadly missed in Merrifield—by the Conservatives. I have no doubt she will eventually return to the benches opposite, but not in my constituency." Hear, hears erupted from those around him, and when Sasha looked up from his notes, there wasn't any doubt that he had captured the attention of the whole House.

"Some members on both sides of the House must wonder where my true allegiance lies. Westminster? Leningrad? Merrifield? Or Moscow? I'll tell you where it lies. It lies with any citizen of any country who believes that the power of democracy is sacred and the right to live in a free society universal.

"Mr. Speaker, I have no time for political labels such as 'left' or 'right.' I am an admirer of both Winston Churchill and Clement Attlee, and the heroes of my university days were Aneurin Bevan and Iain Macleod. With them in mind, I will always attempt to judge every argument on its merits, and every member on the sincerity of his or her views, even when I profoundly disagree with them. I may occasionally shout from the highest mountain, but I hope I will have the good grace to occasionally dwell in the valleys and listen.

"The chief whip's first words to me when I arrived in this place made me feel like Shakespeare's whining schoolboy, with his satchel and shining morning face, creeping like snail unwilling to school." Laughter arose from both sides of the House. "Ah, I can see I'm not the first," he said. This was received by cheers, with only the Labour chief whip remaining silent. "He advised me to speak only on subjects about which I know a great deal . . . so you won't be hearing from me much in the future."

Sasha waited for the laughter to die down before he began his peroration.

"What a compliment it is to the citizens of Merrifield that they could elect a Russian immigrant to sit on these hallowed benches, where he is able to express his opinions on any subject without fear or favor. Does anyone in this chamber believe that an Englishman could take his place in the Kremlin on equal terms? No, of course they don't. But I only hope I live long enough to see you all proved wrong."

He sat down to resounding cheers from both sides of the House. To everyone's surprise, a bespectacled man with a shock of white hair rose from his place on the front bench.

"The leader of the opposition," said the Speaker.

"Mr. Speaker, I rise to congratulate the honorable member for Merrifield on a remarkable maiden speech." Hear, hears echoed around the chamber. "However, I feel I should point out to him that many of those sitting on the benches opposite already think I am the member for Moscow." Cheers and jeers filled the air. "Nevertheless, I'm sure I speak for the whole House when I say we all look forward to the honorable member's next contribution."

Sasha looked up at the visitors' gallery to see Charlie, his mother, Alf, and the countess, all looking down at him with unabashed pride. But it was not until he read *The Times*' leader the following morning that the impact he had made in those few short minutes began to sink in.

It would have been better if Mr. Sasha Karpenko MP had never left the Soviet Union, as he might have played an important role in helping that country embrace the values of democracy.

⊸o⊷

"I'm to blame," said Sasha. "I should have realized it was a step too far."

"No one's to blame," said Elena. "We took a vote and only the countess expressed her reservations."

"I just thought it might be a little too much for Elena to cope with," said the countess.

"And you were proved right," said Sasha, "because, I must warn you, the latest figures don't make pleasant reading."

The rest of the board braced themselves.

"Elena Three has made a loss for the seventh quarter in a row. Even though I'm a born optimist, this is a trend I can't see us reversing."

"What is the financial impact on the business?" asked the countess.

"If you put together the purchase price of the lease, the original set-up costs, and the losses we've sustained so far"—Sasha paused as he added up the figures—"we're down a little over one hundred eighty-three thousand pounds."

Charlie was the first to speak. "Can we survive such a setback?"

"I believe we can," said Sasha, "but it will be a close-run thing."

"What's the bank's attitude?" asked Elena.

"They're still willing to back us if we agree to close Elena's Three immediately, and concentrate our attention on Elena's One and Two. Although they're both still making a profit, they're also suffering from some of the consequences of my decision."

"Well, let's look on the bright side," said Elena. "At least you've got your parliamentary salary to fall back on."

"Not for much longer, I fear," said Sasha, "because if Margaret Thatcher retains her lead in the polls, it will be very hard for me to hold on to Merrifield at the next election."

"Isn't there a personal vote, if your constituents feel you've done a good job?" asked the countess.

"Rarely worth more than a few hundred votes, and usually reserved for rebels who've voted against their own party. And if the company were to go bankrupt, I'd have to resign and leave Fiona to march back onto the field in triumph."

"One should never forget," said the countess, "you have to climb a ladder to success, but failure is a lift going down."

"Then we'll just have to start climbing again," said Elena.

Sasha realized that if Elena's was to survive, his biggest problem would be the taxman. Should the Inland Revenue demand their pound of flesh, the company would have to go into receivership, and dispose of its assets. And if Elena's One and Two were to suddenly come on the market, everyone in business would know it was a fire sale.

Sasha knew if that was the outcome, he would have to abandon his political career and look for a job. What a complete fool he'd made of himself, just when he thought nothing could derail him.

There was no one else to blame, so he decided to face the problem head-on. He phoned the Inland Revenue and made an appointment to see his case officer, Mr. Dark. Even the name filled him with foreboding. He could already visualize the damn man. Short, bald, overweight, coming to the end of an undistinguished career of pen-pushing, who enjoyed nothing more than depositing lives into an out-tray. He probably voted Conservative, and wouldn't be able to resist saying how sorry he was, but he had a job to do, and there couldn't be any exceptions.

⤙o⤚

Sasha parked his Mini in Tynsdale Street, fifteen minutes before the appointed hour, crossed the road, and entered a soulless-looking red-brick building. The royal crest hung above the entrance, and might as well have read, ABANDON HOPE ALL YE WHO ENTER HERE. He gave his name to the lady on the reception desk.

"Mr. Dark is expecting you," she said ominously. "His office is on the thirteenth floor."

Where else? thought Sasha.

Even the lift seemed reluctant to make the upward journey, before disgorging its only visitor. Sasha stepped out into a gray pictureless corridor, and went in search of Mr. Dark's office.

He knocked on the door and entered a room with no windows and a desk covered in red files. Behind the desk—first surprise—sat a man of his own age who greeted him with a warm smile—second surprise. He stood up, and shook hands with Sasha.

"Would you like a cup of tea, Mr. Karpenko?"

An Englishman's idea of putting you at ease before adding a teaspoonful of cyanide.

"No, thank you," said Sasha, wanting the executioner to get on with his job.

"Can't say I blame you," said Dark, before sitting down. "I know you're a busy man, Mr. Karpenko, so I'll try not to waste too much of your time." He opened the top file and studied the contents for a few moments, reminding himself of the salient points. "I've studied your tax returns for the past five years," Dark continued, "and after a long chat to your bank manager, which you authorized"—Sasha nodded—"I think we may have found a solution to your problem."

Sasha continued to stare at the man, wondering what the next surprise would be.

"You currently owe the Inland Revenue one hundred and twenty-six thousand pounds, which your company is clearly unable to pay at the present time. However, contrary to public opinion, we tax collectors get our kicks out of saving companies, not closing them. After all, it's our only hope of getting any of our money back."

Sasha wanted to laugh, but somehow resisted the temptation.

"With that in mind, Mr. Karpenko, we will allow you a year's grace, during which time you will not have to pay any tax. After that, we will require you to return the full amount"—he checked the figure—"of one hundred twenty-six thousand pounds over a period of four years. However, if the company should make a profit during that time, every penny will come to the Inland Revenue." He paused before looking across his desk at Sasha and adding firmly, "I accept that the next five years are not going to be easy for you and your family, but if you feel unable to accept this offer, we will be left with no choice but to take possession of all your assets, as the taxman is always paid in full before any other creditors." He paused again, and looked up at his visitor. "You may wish to spend a few days considering your position, Mr. Karpenko, before you make a final decision."

"That won't be necessary, Mr. Dark," said Sasha. "I accept your terms, and am most grateful to you for giving me a second chance."

"I applaud your decision. So many of my clients go bankrupt, and then open a new business the following day, not bothering about their debts, or anyone else's problems." Mr. Dark opened a second file and extracted another document. "Then all that is left for you to do, Mr. Karpenko, is to sign here, here, and here." He even offered Sasha a biro.

"Thank you," said Sasha, wondering if he was about to wake up.

Once Sasha had signed the agreement, Mr. Dark rose from behind his desk and shook hands with him for a second time.

"I have no politics, Mr. Karpenko," said Dark as he accompanied Sasha out of the room and back down the corridor to the lift, "but if I lived in Merrifield, I would vote for you, and although I have only dined at Elena's on one occasion, I enjoyed the experience immensely."

"You must come again," said Sasha, as the lift door opened and he stepped inside.

"Not until you've paid off your debt in full, Mr. Karpenko."

The lift door closed.

⸻

Sasha's prospects of retaining his seat didn't improve following Mrs. Thatcher's much vaunted triumph in the Falklands, and Michael Foot's stubborn refusal to occupy the center ground.

But then he had a stroke of luck that can change the career of any politician. Sir Michael Forrester died of a heart attack, triggering a by-election in the neighboring constituency of Endlesby. The chance of representing a safe Tory seat for the rest of her life was too tempting for Fiona Hunter, and few people were surprised when she allowed her name to go forward as the prospective candidate. After all, she claimed, Endlesby was half of her old constituency.

Fiona won the by-election by over ten thousand votes, and returned to take her place on the green benches, where Sasha assumed their rivalry would continue. Sasha's second piece of luck came when the Merrifield Conservative Association quarreled among themselves as to who should be their candidate at the next general election, and ended up selecting a local councilor who divided opinion even in his own party.

After the general election, Margaret Thatcher returned to the Commons with an overwhelming majority, despite being spurned by the voters of Merrifield, who decided to hold on to their member, if only by a majority of ninety-one. But as Alf pointed out to Sasha, it was Winston Churchill who said, "One is quite enough, dear boy."

⸻

Neil Kinnock, the new leader of the Labour Party, invited Sasha to join the opposition front bench as a junior spokesman in the foreign affairs team, with special responsibilities for the Eastern Bloc countries.

Sasha's reputation inside and outside Parliament grew, and members on both sides of the House became aware that whenever he rose to take his place at the dispatch box, the ill-prepared lived to regret it.

Fiona was made an undersecretary of state at the Foreign Office, and looked set for a long parliamentary career. However, it was another newly elected Conservative member who caused Sasha to jump with joy—if only in the privacy of his own home.

Sasha accepted that there would be no love lost when they faced each other across the floor of the House, but that wouldn't stop him sharing the occasional half pint in Annie's Bar with The Hon. Member Ben Cohen MP.

37

SASHA

London and Moscow

When the government announced they would be sending an all-party delegation to Moscow to discuss Anglo-Russian relations following the election of Mikhail Gorbachev as General Secretary, no one was surprised that Sasha was chosen to represent the Labour Party.

However, Sasha was not amused to discover that the Conservatives had invited Fiona Hunter to lead the delegation. Was it simply because nothing gave her greater pleasure than to oppose Sasha given any opportunity?

"How long will you be away with that dreadful woman?" Charlie asked when Sasha told her the news.

"Three, four days at most, and we won't exactly have any time for socializing."

"Don't relax, even for a moment, because nothing would give Fiona greater pleasure than to derail your career."

"I think she's more interested in promoting her own at the moment. She's hoping to become a minister of state in the next reshuffle," Sasha said as he came out of the bathroom.

"Don't you believe it," said Charlie. "And before you desert me, have you given any more thought to names for our child, who should be joining us in about six weeks' time?"

"If it's a boy, I've already chosen his name," said Sasha, placing his ear against Charlie's stomach.

"Do I get a vote, or is this a three-line whip?" she asked.

"One line. You can choose between Konstantin, Sergei, and Nicholas."

"Konstantin," said Charlie without hesitation.

Fiona boarded the BA jet bound for Moscow accompanied by a small cadre of civil servants. They took their places at the front of the aircraft while Sasha sat alone near the back. He wished he was leading the delegation, and not just a shadow.

Once the seatbelt signs had been switched off, he leaned back, closed his eyes, and began to think about returning to the Soviet Union for the first time in nearly twenty years. How would the country have changed? Was Vladimir now a senior officer in the KGB? Was Polyakov still stationed in Leningrad? Was his uncle Kolya the docks convener, and would he be allowed to see him?

When the plane touched down at Sheremetyevo airport four hours later, Sasha glanced out of the window to see a small delegation waiting on the runway to greet them. Fiona was first off the plane, making the most of the photo opportunity she hoped would be picked up by the press back home.

She walked slowly down the steps, waving at a group of local people gathered behind a metal barrier, but they didn't return her greeting. It wasn't until Sasha appeared that they suddenly burst into spontaneous applause and began waving. He walked uncertainly toward them, unable to believe the welcome was meant for him until one of them held up a placard with the word KARPENKO scrawled on it. Fiona couldn't hide her displeasure as an embassy official stepped forward to greet her.

Several bunches of flowers were thrust into Sasha's arms, as he walked across to join them. He then tried to answer the multitude of questions being thrown at him in his native tongue.

"Will you come back to lead our country?"

"When will we be allowed contested elections?"

"What chance of a free and fair election next time?"

"I'm flattered you even know my name," said Sasha to a young woman who couldn't have been born when he'd escaped from the Soviet Union.

He glanced around to see Fiona being whisked away in the ambassador's limousine, a Union Jack fluttering from its front wing.

"Can I get a bus into the city?" he asked.

"Any one of us would be proud to drive you to your hotel," said a young man standing at the front of the crowd. "My name is Fyodor," he said, "and we wondered if you'd be willing to address a meeting this evening. That seems to be the only time you'll be free before the conference opens tomorrow."

"I'd be honored," said Sasha, wondering if he would draw a bigger crowd in Moscow than he managed at the Roxton Working Men's Club.

During the journey into the city in a car that neither looked nor sounded as if it could possibly reach its destination, Fyodor told Sasha that his speeches were often reported in *Pravda,* and he even occasionally appeared on Soviet television, all part of the new regime's outreach policy.

Sasha was surprised, although he knew only too well that if the authorities thought there was the slightest chance of him returning to Russia to contest an election, the tap would be quickly turned off. In any case, Gorbachev didn't seem to be doing a bad job. While Sasha remained a novelty that the Communist Party could use as a propaganda tool to show how their philosophy was spreading across the globe, he was in no danger. He could hear them saying, *Don't forget Karpenko came from the docks of Leningrad, won a scholarship to Cambridge University, and became an English Member of Parliament—isn't that proof enough that our system works?*

When they arrived at the hotel there was another group standing outside waiting in the bitter cold. Sasha shook many more outstretched hands, and answered several questions. He finally checked in, and took the lift to his room. It may not have been the Savoy, but it was clear that his countrymen had finally embraced the concept that if foreigners were going to come to Moscow they would have to be provided with at least some of the facilities they took for granted in the West. He showered and changed into his other suit, a fresh shirt, and a red tie before going downstairs, where the same car and driver were waiting for him.

Sasha climbed into the front seat, once again wondering if they would make it. He gazed out of the window as they passed the Kremlin.

"You'll live there one day," said Fyodor as they left Red Square behind them and drove on through the empty streets.

"How many people are you expecting this evening?" Sasha asked.

"We have no way of knowing, because we've never done anything like this before."

Sasha couldn't help wondering if the Russian Alf would be able to muster more than a dozen men and a sleeping dog. He turned his thoughts to what he might say to his audience. If the gathering was small, he decided, after a few opening remarks he'd just take questions, and be back at the hotel in time for dinner.

By the time the car drew up outside the workers' hall, he had a few remarks prepared in his mind. He stepped out onto the pavement to be greeted by a woman dressed in Russian national costume, who presented him with a basket of bread and salt. He thanked her and bowed low, before following Fyodor down a narrow alley and through a back door. When he entered the building he could hear cries of "Kar-pen-ko, Kar-pen-ko!" As he was led up onto a stage, over three thousand people rose as one and continued to chant, "Kar-pen-ko, Kar-pen-ko!"

Sasha stared down at the packed gathering and realized that his youthful boast, meant only for the ears of his friend Vladimir, had become a rallying cry for countless people he had never met, who, for generations, had remained silent about how they really felt.

His speech lasted for over an hour, though because it was interrupted so often by chanting and applause he only actually spoke for about fifteen minutes. When he finally left the stage, the building echoed to the repeated cries of "Kar-pen-ko! Kar-pen-ko!"

Out on the street, his car was mobbed, and it was almost a mile before Fyodor was able to shift into second gear. Sasha suspected that if he tried to describe what had just taken place to Charlie or Elena, neither would believe him.

Sasha had always hoped that he might be able to play some part, however small, in bringing down Communism and ushering in perestroika, but now, for the first time, he believed that he might live to see that day. Would he regret not remaining in his homeland and standing for the Duma? He was still preoccupied by these thoughts when he entered the hotel lobby, and quickly returned to his old world. The first person he saw in the lobby was Fiona.

"Have you had an interesting evening?" he asked.

"The embassy got us tickets for the Bolshoi," she replied. "We called your room, but you were nowhere to be found. Where were you?"

Someone else who wouldn't have believed him if he'd told her, and perhaps more important, wouldn't have wanted to.

"Visiting old friends," he said, picking up his key and joining Fiona as she walked toward the lift.

"Which floor?" he asked as they stepped inside.

"Top."

He thought about telling her that was always the worst floor in the Soviet Union, but decided she wouldn't have understood. He pressed two buttons, and neither of them spoke again until they reached the fourth floor when he said good night.

"Don't be late for the bus in the morning. Nine fifteen sharp," said Fiona as the doors opened. Sasha smiled. Once a head girl, always a head girl.

"The Russians are famous for keeping you waiting," he said as he stepped out into the corridor.

He placed his key in the door of a room that was probably half the size of Fiona's. The only compensation was that it would have half as many bugs. Suddenly he realized he hadn't eaten, and for a moment he thought about room service, but only for a moment. He put on his pajamas and climbed into bed, still hearing the chants of *Kar-pen-ko* as he placed his head on the pillow, pulled the blankets over himself, and almost immediately fell into a deep sleep.

Was the persistent banging all part of his dream, he wondered, but when it didn't stop, he finally woke. He glanced at his watch: 3:07. Surely it couldn't be Fiona? He dragged himself out of bed, put on his dressing gown, and reluctantly padded across to the door.

"Who is it?"

"Room service," said a sultry voice.

"I didn't order room service," said Sasha as he opened the door.

"I wasn't on the menu, darling," said a long-legged redhead, who was also dressed in pajamas and a dressing gown, but hers were in shimmering black silk, and unbuttoned. "I'm tonight's special," she said, holding up a bottle of vodka in one hand, and two glasses in the other. "I did come to the right room, didn't I, darling?" she purred in perfect English.

"No, I'm afraid you didn't," replied Sasha in perfect Russian. "But do come back again at seven thirty, because I forgot to ask the front desk to give me a wake-up call." He gave her a warm smile, said, "Good night, darling," and quietly closed the door.

He climbed back into bed, thinking the KGB's research left a little to be desired. Someone should have told them he'd never cared for redheads. Although they were right about the vodka.

Sasha was among the first to be seated on the bus the following morning, and to his surprise, when Fiona climbed on board, she deserted her minders and sat down next to him.

"Good morning, comrade minister," he teased. "I hope you had a good night's sleep."

"I had rather a bad night, in fact," whispered Fiona. "I met a charming young man in the lounge called Gerald, who told me he worked at the embassy. He came up to my room just after midnight and I should have slammed the door in his face. But I'm afraid I'd drunk a little too much champagne."

"Nothing wrong with that," said Sasha. "You're an attractive single woman, so why shouldn't you enjoy the company of a colleague outside working hours? I can't imagine it would excite much interest beyond a few perverts in the Kremlin recording center."

"It's not the sex I'm worried about," said Fiona, "it's what I might have said après sex."

"Like what?" asked Sasha, enjoying every moment.

Fiona buried her head in her hands and whispered, "Thatcher is a dictator with no sense of humor. Geoffrey Howe is so wet you could wring him out, and I may have told him the names of two or three members of the Cabinet who are having affairs with their secretaries."

"How unlike you, Fiona, to be quite so indiscreet. But I'd hardly describe any of that as front-page news."

"It is when you're lying in the arms of a KGB officer."

"You don't know that."

"But I do know there's no one called Gerald working at the British Embassy. If the story was to get into the hands of the press, I'd be finished."

"Perhaps not finished," said Sasha, "although it might put off the much-heralded promotion that the press keep hinting at. But only until the Blessed Margaret is finally deposed, which I confess doesn't look too imminent. But why tell me all this?"

"Oh, come on, Sasha. Everyone knows you have excellent contacts in the Soviet Union. Do you imagine for one moment that your meeting last night went unnoticed? You must have some influential friends in the KGB."

"Sadly not. You may not have noticed, Fiona, but they're the bad guys."

"Minister?" said the voice of a civil servant, hovering over them.

"I'll be with you in a minute, Gus," said Fiona. Turning back to Sasha, she whispered, "If you could do anything to help, I'd be eternally grateful."

And we all know what your idea of eternity is, thought Sasha as the bus came to a halt in Red Square.

Fiona led her little troop out to be greeted by her opposite number, who would never have guessed from the minister's demeanor that anything was troubling her. *Impressive,* thought Sasha as he followed in her wake.

The delegation was accompanied through a set of vast iron doors sculpted with images of the Siege of Moscow. Two uniformed guards sprang to attention as they passed. The delegation was then led up a wide red-carpeted staircase to the second floor, where they were ushered into a huge, ornately decorated room that was dominated by a long oak table surrounded by high-backed red leather chairs that would have graced a palace, and probably once had. They were invited to take their places along one side of the table, where Sasha found his name card three from the far end. Once the British delegation were seated, they were kept waiting for some time before the Russians made their entrance, taking their places on the opposite side of the table.

Their host made a long and predictable speech, which didn't need translating. Sasha felt that Fiona's reply was not up to her usual standard. Not that it mattered much. The final communiqués had already been drafted by the mandarins, and would be released on the last afternoon of the conference, whatever anyone said during the next couple of days.

For the morning session they broke up into smaller groups to discuss student exchanges, visa restrictions, and the loan of the Walpole Collection from the Hermitage that was to be exhibited at Houghton Hall. The Russians only seemed to be worried about whether they'd get their paintings back.

It was during the lunch break that Sasha spotted him standing alone on the other side of the room. He was dressed in a bottle-green uniform that boasted a row of campaign medals, while his gold epaulets suggested that he had risen swiftly through the ranks. Sasha would have known those calculating cold blue eyes anywhere. Vladimir smiled and walked purposefully across to join him. When he was a couple of feet away he came to a halt, not unlike a boxer facing his opponent in the middle of the ring, waiting to see which one of them would throw the first punch.

Sasha had already prepared his opening gambit, although he suspected Vladimir had been working on his for some time, as the meeting clearly wasn't taking place by chance.

"I must say, Vladimir," he said in Russian, "I'm surprised you found the time to attend such an unimportant gathering."

"I wouldn't normally bother," said Vladimir, "but I've been looking forward to seeing you for some time, Sasha."

"I'm touched that Ares found time to come down from Olympus."

"First, allow me to congratulate you on your success since you fled our country," said Vladimir, ignoring the allusion. "However, I must advise you not to visit Leningrad. Your old friend Colonel Polyakov just might be waiting for you. Not a man who believes in forgiving and forgetting."

"So what dizzy heights have you reached, Vladimir?" asked Sasha, trying to land a blow of his own.

"I'm a lowly colonel with the KGB, stationed in Dresden."

"A staging post no doubt on the way to higher things."

"Which is why I wanted to see you. Some of my men were at your meeting last night. It seems that if you were to return and stand for president, you could be a serious contender, which is, after all, what you've always wanted."

"But Mr. Gorbachev has already beaten me to the punch, so there's no reason to return. In any case, I'm an Englishman now."

Vladimir laughed. "You're Russian, Alexander, and you always will be. Just as you told your adoring public last night. And in any case, Gorbachev won't last forever. In fact he may be going far sooner than he realizes."

"What are you suggesting?"

"That we should keep in touch. No one knows better than you that timing is everything in politics. All I ask in return is to be appointed head of the KGB. Which is no more than you promised me all those years ago."

"I made no such promise, Vladimir, as you well know. And in any case, my views on nepotism haven't changed since the last time we discussed the subject," said Sasha. "And that was when we were still friends."

"We may no longer be friends, Alexander, but that doesn't stop us having mutual interests."

"I'll take you at your word," said Sasha, "and even give you a chance to prove it."

"What do you have in mind?"

"Your boys taped my minister last night."

"Yes, the stupid bitch was very indiscreet."

"She's only a junior minister, and she might be much more useful at a later date."

"But she's not even a member of your party."

"I realize, Vladimir, that's a concept you must find difficult to come to terms with."

Vladimir didn't reply immediately, then shrugged his shoulders. "The tape will be in your hotel room within the hour."

"Thank you. And do tell your operatives to get their files up to date. I've never cared for redheads."

"I told them they were wasting their time with you. You're incorruptible, which will make my job so much easier when you appoint me as head of the KGB." Vladimir walked away without the suggestion of a good-bye, and Sasha would have returned to his little group, if someone else hadn't walked across to join him.

"You don't know me, Mr. Karpenko," said a man who must have been about his own age, and was wearing a suit that hadn't been tailored in Moscow, "but I've been following your career with some considerable interest."

In England, Sasha would have smiled and taken the man at his word, but in Russia . . . he remained silent, and suspicious.

"My name is Boris Nemtsov, and I think you'll find we have several things in common." Sasha still didn't respond. "I am a member of the Duma, and I believe we both share the same high opinion of one particular man," said Nemtsov, glancing in the direction of Vladimir.

"My enemy's enemy is my friend," said Sasha, shaking Nemtsov by the hand.

"I hope in time we will be friends. After all, there will be other conferences and official meetings where we can casually meet and exchange confidences, without someone opening a file."

"I think you will find that someone's already opened a file," said Sasha.

"So let's give him the first entry. I don't agree with you," he shouted, loudly enough to ensure that all those around him turned to listen to the exchange.

"Then there's nothing more to discuss," said Nemtsov, who stormed off without another word.

Sasha would have liked to smile as Nemtsov marched away, but resisted the temptation.

Vladimir was staring at both of them, but Sasha doubted that he had been fooled.

38

ALEX

Boston, 1988

When Alex entered the bank on Monday morning, he didn't notice the man sitting in the corner of the lobby. On Tuesday, he registered the lone figure for a moment, but as he had a meeting with Alan Greenspan, the chairman of the Federal Reserve, to discuss OPEC's latest demands on oil prices and the strengthening of the dollar against the pound, the lone figure didn't remain uppermost in his mind. On Wednesday, he looked more closely at the man before stepping into the elevator. Could it be possible he'd been sitting there for three days? Pamela would know.

"Who's my first appointment, Pamela?" he asked, even before he'd taken off his overcoat.

"Sheldon Woods, the new chairman of the local Democratic Party."

"How much did we give them last year?"

"Fifty thousand dollars, chairman, but it's an election year."

"Election time always brings back memories of Lawrence. So let's make it a hundred thousand this year."

"Of course, chairman."

"Anyone else this morning?"

"No, but you're having lunch with Bob Underwood at the Algonquin, and don't forget, he's always on time."

Alex nodded. "Do you know what he wants?"

"To resign. 'Time to hang up my boots,' if I remember his exact words."

"Never. He remains on board until he drops dead."

"I think that's what he's afraid of, chairman."

"And this afternoon?"

"You're clear until your session at the gym at five. Your coach tells me you've missed the last two workouts."

"But he still charges me even if I don't turn up."

"That's not the point, chairman."

"Anything else?"

"Just to remind you it's your wedding anniversary, and you're taking your wife to dinner tonight."

"Of course it is. I'd better go downtown after lunch and get her a present."

"Anna's already chosen the present she wants," said Miss Robbins.

"Am I allowed to know what it is?"

"A Chloé bag, from Bonwit Teller."

"OK, I'll pick one up this afternoon. What color?"

"Gray. It's already been gift-wrapped and was delivered to my office yesterday. All you need to do is sign this." She placed an anniversary card on his desk.

"I sometimes think, Pamela, that you'd make a far better chairman than me."

"If you say so, chairman. But in the meantime, can you make sure you sign all the letters in your correspondence file before Mr. Woods arrives?"

Getting Pamela to return to her old job was the wisest decision he'd ever made, thought Alex as he opened his correspondence file. He read each letter carefully, making the occasional emendation and sometimes adding a handwritten postscript. He was considering a letter from the president of the Harvard Business School inviting him to address the final-year students in the fall, when there was a tap on the door.

"Mr. Woods," said Miss Robbins.

"Sheldon," said Alex, jumping up from behind his desk. "Has it really been a year already? Can I offer you some coffee?"

"No, thank you," said Woods.

"Now, before you say anything, yes, I am aware it's an election year, and I've already decided to double our contribution to the party, in Lawrence's memory."

"That's very generous of you, Alex. He would have made a fine congressman."

"He would indeed," said Alex. "In fact not a day goes by when I don't mourn his death. That man quite literally changed my life, and I never had a real chance to thank him."

"If Lawrence were alive, it would be him who was thanking you," said

Woods. "Everyone in Boston knew the bank was in serious trouble before you took over. What a turnaround. I hear you're to be named as banker of the year."

"A lot of credit for that must go to Jake Coleman, who couldn't be more different from his predecessor."

"Yes, that was quite a coup. I assume you've heard that Ackroyd was released from prison last week?"

"I did, and I wouldn't have given it a second thought if he hadn't been seen boarding a plane to Nice the following day."

"I'm lost," said Woods.

"And it's better you stay that way," said Alex, as he signed a check for one hundred thousand dollars and handed it to Woods.

"I'm most grateful," he said. "But that wasn't the reason I came to see you."

"Isn't a hundred thousand enough?"

"More than enough. It's just that we, that is to say my committee, hoped you would allow your name to go forward as the next Democratic candidate for junior senator here in Massachusetts."

Alex couldn't hide his surprise. "When you asked me to stand for Congress after Lawrence's death," he eventually managed, "I reluctantly turned the offer down so I could take on the chairmanship of Lowell's. However, I confess I've often wondered if it was the right decision and whether politics was my real calling."

"Then perhaps it's time for you to take on an even bigger challenge."

"Sadly not," said Alex. "Although the bank is finally back on its feet, I now want to take it to the next level and join the major leagues. How much do you expect the Bank of America to contribute to the Democratic cause?"

"They've already given a quarter of a million toward the campaign."

"Then I'll know we've arrived when you ask me for the same amount, and more important, when I don't give it a second thought."

"I'd rather have a hundred thousand, and you as the candidate."

"I'm flattered, Sheldon, but the answer is still no. However, thank you for asking." Alex touched a button under his desk.

"Pity. You'd have made an outstanding senator."

"That's a great compliment, Sheldon. Perhaps in another life." They shook hands as Miss Robbins entered the room to escort Mr. Woods to the elevator.

Alex sat back down and thought about how different life might have been if Lawrence hadn't died—or even if he and his mother had climbed into the other crate. But he soon snapped out of "what might have been" and returned to the real world, putting a tick on the top of the letter from the president of the Harvard Business School.

Miss Robbins had just closed the door behind her when the phone rang. Alex picked it up and immediately recognized the voice on the other end of the line.

"Hi, Dimitri," he said. "It's been too long. How are you?"

"Well, thank you, Alex," said Dimitri. "And you?"

"Never better."

"I'm glad to hear that, Alex, but I thought you ought to know that Ivan Donokov has been released from prison and is on his way back to Moscow."

"How can that be possible?" asked Alex, turning ice cold. "I thought he was sentenced to ninety-nine years without parole."

"The CIA exchanged him for two of our agents who'd been languishing in a Moscow hellhole for over a decade."

"Let's hope they don't come to regret it. But thank you for letting me know."

"I only hope you don't live to regret it," said Dimitri, but not until after he'd put the phone down.

Alex tried to get Donokov out of his mind while he continued signing letters. His thoughts were interrupted when Miss Robbins reentered the room to pick up the correspondence file. "Before I forget, Pamela, there's a man who's been sitting in reception for the past three days. Do you have any idea who he is?"

"A Mr. Pushkin. He's flown over from Leningrad in the hope that you would agree to see him. Claims he was at school with you."

"Pushkin," he repeated. "A great writer, but I don't recall anyone from my school by that name. But as he's so determined to see me, perhaps I ought to give him a few minutes."

"He says he needs a couple of hours. I tried to explain that you don't have a couple of hours before Christmas, but it didn't deter him, which made me wonder if he worked for the KGB."

"The KGB don't sit around cooling their heels in reception for three days, especially when everyone can see them. So let's see the rabbit before we shoot it. But make sure you rescue me after fifteen minutes—tell him I have another meeting."

"Yes, chairman," said Miss Robbins, not looking at all convinced.

Alex was still signing letters when there was a gentle knock on the door. Miss Robbins entered the room followed by a man he thought looked familiar, and then he remembered.

"How nice to see you again, Misha, after all this time," said Alex, as Miss Robbins left the room.

"It's good to see you too, Alexander. I'm only surprised you remember me."

"Captain of the junior chess team. Do you still play?"

"Occasionally, but I never reached your dizzy heights, so don't bother to challenge me."

"I can't remember the last time I played," admitted Alex, which only brought back memories of Donokov. "Before you tell me what brings you to Boston, how is the city of my birth?"

"Leningrad is always beautiful at this time of year, as you will remember," said Pushkin, in Alex's native tongue. "There are even rumors that it won't be too long before its name will be changed back to Saint Petersburg. Another symbol to perpetuate the myth that the old regime has been replaced."

Hearing Pushkin speaking Russian made Alex suddenly feel sad, even a little guilty, that he'd lost his accent, and now sounded like any other Boston WASP. He looked at his visitor more closely. Pushkin was around five foot eight, with a thick brown mustache that reminded Alex of his father. He wore a heavy tweed suit with wide lapels, which suggested either that he had no interest in fashion, or this was the first time he'd traveled outside of the Soviet Union.

"My father worked in the docks when your father was chief supervisor," said Pushkin. "Many of the lads still remember him with respect and affection."

"And my uncle Kolya?"

"He's now the docks' supervisor. He asked to be remembered to you and your mother."

I owe him my life, Alex was about to say, but stopped himself when he remembered that if Major Polyakov was still alive, that wasn't a risk worth taking.

"Please give him my best wishes, and tell him I hope it won't be too long before we meet again."

"I'm hoping it will be sooner than you think," said Pushkin. "I see him from time to time, usually at the football every other Saturday."

"The two of you standing on the terraces cheering on Zenit F.C., no doubt."

"There are no terraces nowadays. Everyone has a seat."

"Can I assume my old friend Vladimir has found his way into the chairman's box?"

"I haven't seen him for years," said Pushkin. "When I last heard, he was a KGB colonel stationed somewhere in East Germany."

"I can't imagine that's part of his long-term plan," said Alex. "However, I'm sure you didn't travel all the way to Boston to reminisce. What did you mean when you said you hoped I might see my uncle sooner than I thought?"

"You will be well aware that the new Soviet regime is very different from the old. The hammer and sickle have been run down the flagpole to be replaced with a dollar sign. The only problem is that after so many centuries of oppression, first by the tsars and then the communists, we Russians have no tradition of free enterprise." Alex nodded, but didn't interrupt. "So nothing has really changed on that front. When the government decided to sell off some of the state's more profitable companies, it shouldn't have come as a surprise that no one was qualified to handle such a dramatic upheaval. And dramatic is what it turned out to be, which I found out when my own company was put up for sale," said Pushkin as he handed over his card.

"The Leningrad Petroleum and Gas Company," said Alex.

"Whoever the new owners of LGP turn out to be, they're going to become billionaires overnight."

"And you'd like to be one of them?"

"No. Like your father, I believe that wealth should be shared among those who have made the company a success, not just handed to someone who happens to be a friend of a friend of the president."

"What's the asking price?" asked Alex, trying to find out if the meeting would be lasting more than fifteen minutes.

"Twenty-five million dollars."

"And what was LGP's turnover last year?"

Pushkin unzipped an old plastic bag, took out some papers, and placed them on the desk. "Just over four hundred million dollars," he said, without needing to refer to them.

"And the profit?"

"Thirty-eight million six hundred forty thousand dollars."

"Am I missing something here?" said Alex. "With that profit margin, the company must be worth over four or five hundred million."

"You're not missing a thing, chairman. It's just that you can't expect to replace Communism with capitalism overnight simply by exchanging a boiler suit for a Brooks Brothers tuxedo. The Soviet Union may have some of the finest universities in the world if you want to study philosophy, even Sanskrit, but very few offer a serious business course."

"Surely any major Russian bank would lend you the money if you can guarantee those sort of returns," said Alex, looking intently at his fellow countryman.

"The truth is," said Pushkin, "the banks are just as much out of their depth as everyone else. But they're still not going to lend twenty-five million dollars to someone who earns the equivalent of five thousand dollars a year, and has less than a thousand dollars in his savings account."

"How long have you got before I need to make a decision?" asked Alex.

"The deadline for the deal is October thirty-first. After that, it's open to anyone who can put up the money."

"But that's only a month away," said Alex as Miss Robbins entered the room prepared to escort Mr. Pushkin to the elevator.

"Which suits the KGB, who I know already have their eyes on it."

"Cancel my lunch, Pamela, and then contact every senior member of the management and investment team and tell them to drop everything and report to my office immediately."

"Certainly, chairman," said Miss Robbins, as if there was nothing unusual about the request.

"I'll also need half a dozen pizzas for delivery at one o'clock. And before you ask, that's a decision my mother can make."

Miss Robbins didn't enter the chairman's office again until the meeting had finally broken up some five hours later.

"You missed your afternoon gym session again, chairman."

"I know. The meeting overran."

"Will you still be taking your wife to dinner?" asked Miss Robbins, placing the anniversary gift on his desk.

"Damn," said Alex. "Tell Jake that I won't be able to join him and Mr. Pushkin for dinner after all. Explain to them that something even more important has come up."

39

ALEX

Boston

Evelyn picked up the phone to hear a familiar voice, which she hadn't spoken to for some time.

"I need to see you."

"Why would I want to see you?" she asked.

"Because you know damn well I didn't steal the Warhol," said Ackroyd.

"Is this conversation being taped?"

"No, because I certainly wouldn't want anyone else to hear what I'm about to tell you."

"I'm listening."

"I didn't waste my time when I was in prison, and I've come up with a way for you to make half a billion dollars, and embarrass Karpenko at the same time."

There was a brief pause before Evelyn said, "What would I have to do?"

"Just confirm that I'll get ten percent of the deal if we pull it off."

"I'm still listening."

"I'm not saying another word, Evelyn, until I have your signature on the bottom line. I haven't forgotten that the last time we made a deal, I ended up in jail."

"In which case, Douglas, you'll have to fly down to the south of France, and bring the contract with you."

⊸o⊷

Alex arrived at Marliave ten minutes early, and was making some calculations on the back of his menu when Anna arrived.

"Happy anniversary, darling," he said as he rose to kiss her.

"Thank you. And here's your trick question," said Anna, sitting down at their favorite corner table. "How many years have we been married, or was that what you were trying to work out on the back of your menu?" Fortunately Miss Robbins had reminded him just before he left.

"Thirteen, but it would have been fourteen if Lawrence hadn't left me his fifty percent of the bank."

"You live to fight another year. What's this?" Anna asked coyly.

"Open it and you'll find out."

"I suspect it will be more of a surprise for you than me."

Alex laughed. "I'll pretend I've seen it before."

Anna slowly removed the red ribbon, unwrapped the parcel, and lifted the lid to reveal a small, elegant light gray Chloé bag that was both practical and stylish.

"It's so you, I thought, the moment I saw it," said Alex.

"Which was just now," said Anna, leaning across and kissing him again. "Perhaps you could remember to thank Pamela for me," she added as the maître d' appeared by their side.

"I know exactly what I want, François," she said. "Salade niçoise and the Dover sole."

"I'll have the same," said Alex. "I've made quite enough decisions for one day."

"Dare I ask?"

"I can't say too much at the moment, because it could turn out to be either a complete waste of time or the biggest deal that's ever crossed my desk."

"When will you know which?"

"By this time next week, would be my bet. By which time I should be back from Leningrad."

"But haven't you always said you'd never go back to Russia in any circumstances, and Leningrad in particular?"

"It's a calculated risk," said Alex. "However, I think it's safe to assume that after all these years, Polyakov will have retired."

"Your mother once told me that KGB officers never retire, so what does she think?"

"She won't relax until she's attended his funeral. But when I promised to see her brother, Kolya, find out how the rest of the family are, and visit my father's grave, she reluctantly came around."

"I don't want you to go," said Anna quietly. "Let Jake Coleman take your place. He's just as good a dealmaker as you are."

"Maybe, but the Russians always expect to deal with the chairman. By the way, there's a spare seat on the plane if you'd like to come."

"No, thank you. Not least because I've got an opening on Wednesday."

"Anyone I know?" asked Alex, pleased to change the subject.

"Robert Indiana."

"Oh yes, I like his work. I'll be sorry to miss the opening."

"The show will still be on when you get back. If you get back."

"It's not that bad, my darling. So am I allowed to know what my anniversary gift is?" asked Alex, hoping to lighten the mood. "Because I don't see a package."

"It was too big to bring with me," said Anna. "It's a six-foot-square bronze by Indiana called LOVE." She drew an image on the back of the menu.

L *O*
V E

"How much is that going to cost me?"

"With the usual discount, around sixty thousand. And if you were to gift it to Konstantin, he can avoid estate tax."

"So let me try and understand this, one I love," said Alex. "My anniversary present is going to cost me sixty thousand dollars, but it's Konstantin who will actually own it?"

"Yes, my darling. I think you've grasped the idea. But the good news is, there's now an outside chance you'll go to heaven." Anna paused. "Not that you'll enjoy it."

"Why not?" demanded Alex.

"Because you won't know anyone," she said as the waiter returned with their first course.

"So what do I get?"

"To look at it for the rest of your life."

"Thanks," said Alex. "And can I ask where the beneficiary is?"

"He's staying overnight with his grandmother."

"Does that mean my mother has taken a night off?" Alex asked in mock disbelief.

"Half a night. Konstantin likes Elena's margheritas better than anything I ever cook for him," Anna said as she finished her salad. "And don't give me that *me too* look. So what else have you been up to today?"

"Sheldon Woods came to see me this morning to ask if I'd be interested in standing for the Senate."

"How long did it take you to turn down that attractive offer?" asked Anna as the waiter whisked away their empty plates.

"I thought long and hard about it for twenty seconds."

"I can remember the time, not so long ago, when you were fascinated by politics," said Anna. "The only thing you ever wanted to be was the first elected president of an independent Russia."

"And I confess that would be far more tempting than the Senate," said Alex. "But that all changed the day Lawrence died," he added as the waiter reappeared and presented them with two Dover soles.

"On or off the bone, madam?"

"Off please, François, for both of us. My husband isn't making any important decisions tonight."

"And the management hoped that you would enjoy a bottle of Chablis Beauregard to mark this special occasion, with our compliments."

"I should have married you, François, as it's clear you would never have forgotten our wedding anniversary, and would have known exactly what gift to give me."

François bowed and left them.

"But when Lawrence left you his fifty percent of the bank's shares, they were worthless," said Anna, "and now they must be worth a fortune."

"Possibly, but I can't afford to offload any of my stock while Evelyn still owns the other fifty percent, because then she'd have overall control."

"Perhaps she might consider selling her shares? After all, she always seems to be short of cash."

"Quite possibly, but I don't have that sort of capital available," said Alex.

"But if I remember correctly," said Anna, "on the day our son was born Evelyn offered you her shares for a million dollars and I suggested you might live to regret not buying them."

"Mea culpa," said Alex. "And at the time I even considered selling off Elena's so I could buy the shares myself, but that would have been one hell of a risk, because if the bank had gone under, we'd have ended up with nothing."

"Hindsight," said Anna. "But dare I ask what those shares are worth now?"

"About three hundred million dollars."

Anna gasped. "Will the bank end up having to pay her the full amount?"

"Possibly, because we can't afford to let another bank get hold of fifty percent of our stock, otherwise we'd be looking over our shoulders for the rest of our lives, especially if Doug Ackroyd turned out to be advising them."

"Perhaps you should have agreed to run for the Senate. Far less hassle, and a guaranteed salary," said Anna.

"While having to listen to the views of millions of voters, rather than a dozen board members."

"It would be even more, if you fulfilled your lifelong dream and ran for president."

"Of America?"

"No, Russia."

Alex didn't reply immediately.

"Ah," said Anna, "so you do still think about the possibility."

"Aware that like any dream, I'll wake up," said Alex, as François reappeared by their side.

"Can I tempt you with dessert, madam?" he asked.

"Certainly not," said Anna. "We've both had quite enough. Anniversaries should not be an excuse to put on weight. And he," she said, pointing to her husband, "missed his gym session again today. So definitely nothing for him."

François filled their glasses and took away the empty bottle.

"To another memorable year together, Mrs. Karpenko," said Alex, raising his glass.

"I wish you weren't going to Russia."

⊸o⟜

"I wish you weren't going to Russia," said Elena, as she placed two pizzas in front of them.

"You and Anna," said Alex as a waiter rushed across and said, "I'm sorry to bother you, Mr. Karpenko, but your secretary has just called to let you know there's been a problem with the visas, and asked if you could return to your office as soon as possible."

"I'd better go and find out what the trouble is," said Alex. "I'll be as quick as I can."

He left his mother and an anxious-looking Pushkin to finish their pizzas, while he quickly made his way back to the office, where Miss Robbins was waiting for him.

"Is it all going to plan?" she asked.

"Yes, Misha and my mother were sharing a pizza when I left them. She may not know a great deal about banking or business, but when you've been in the catering trade for as long as she has, there's not much you don't know about people. Anything important before I head back?"

"Ted Kennedy's assistant called to confirm that all five visas will be on your desk by four o'clock this afternoon, and she also reminded me that the senator will be running for reelection next year."

"That's going to cost me another hundred thousand."

"I've also got you a thousand dollars in cash and the equivalent in rubles, as checks and credit cards still don't seem to cut much ice in the Soviet Union. The team are booked into the Hotel Europa for five nights."

"One night might turn out to be enough."

"And Captain Fullerton is expecting you at Logan around eleven this evening. He has a slot booked for eleven thirty. You'll refuel in London, before flying on to Leningrad. So now you can go back and find out what your mother makes of Mr. Pushkin."

Alex took his time returning to Elena's, and when he arrived, he could see his mother listening attentively to every word Misha was saying. The anxious look returned to the Russian's face when Alex joined them.

"A problem with the visas?" he asked.

"No, it's all been sorted out. I hope you enjoyed the pizza."

"I've never had one before," admitted Pushkin, "and I have already told your mother I know the ideal spot to open the first Elena's in Leningrad. If you'll excuse me for a moment, I have to go and do what you Americans call 'freshen up.'"

The moment he disappeared downstairs, Alex asked, "What's your verdict, Mama?"

"He's pure gold," said Elena. "Not even gold plated. I know nothing about gas except how to turn it on and off, and I accept I've only just met Misha, but I'd happily leave him standing next to an open register."

"Family?" asked Alex, not wanting to waste a moment before Misha returned.

"He has a wife, Olga, and two children, Yuri and Tatiana, who are both hoping to go to university, but he thinks their daughter's chances are better than his son's, whose sole interest seems to be motorbikes. Frankly, Alex, I don't think Misha could pull the wool over your eyes, even if you were fast asleep."

Pushkin reappeared at the top of the stairs.

"Thank you, Mama. Then it looks as if I'm on my way to Leningrad."

"Please remember to visit your father's grave, and do try to catch up with your uncle Kolya. I can't wait to hear all his news."

40

ALEX

Boston and Leningrad

Alex had assembled a team of four heads of department, led by Jake Coleman, to accompany him to Russia. All were experts in their fields: banking, energy, contract law, and accounting. Dick Barrett, head of the bank's energy department, had already spent several hours with Pushkin and admitted that he'd come away mightily impressed.

"That man knows more about the industry than many so-called expert consultants, yet he's never earned more than a few thousand dollars a year. So for him, this is quite literally the opportunity of a lifetime. He reminded me that Russia has twenty-four percent of the world's natural gas reserves, as well as twelve percent of its oil. I'll need to sit next to him on the plane so that by the time we touch down in Leningrad, I just might be able to hold my own."

It was Andy Harbottle, the company's new in-house lawyer, known as "Mr. Downside," who would have to draw up the final contract. But not before his father had given the document his stamp of approval.

Jake had been able to confirm that Pushkin didn't have a great grasp of finance, and warned Alex that they wouldn't know if the figures stacked up until they got to LGP's headquarters and were able to study the books.

"How could he be expected to grasp something this complex?" said Alex. "No one has ever been offered deals where you can make a profit of a thousand percent virtually overnight. What's happening in Russia today is like the gold rush in California in the 1850s, and we must take advantage of it before our competitors do."

"I agree," said Harbottle. "And although I'm a cautious individual by nature—"

"The son of your father," suggested Alex.

"I've never known anyone to seize an opportunity the way you do, and this might even turn out to be that breakthrough you so often talk about that will allow us to join the major leagues."

"Or bankrupt us."

"Unlikely," said Harbottle. "Don't forget, we have one big advantage over our rivals. Our chairman is Russian, and was born in Leningrad."

Alex didn't add, *and escaped after nearly killing a senior KGB officer.*

⤙○⤚

The six passengers boarded the Gulfstream jet bound for Leningrad, chasing what Jake now called "the gas rush." None of them had any idea what to expect. The plane refueled at Heathrow, where the team disembarked to stretch their legs and grab a meal in the terminal. Alex would like to have gone into town and visited the Tate, the National Theatre, and even the House of Commons, but not this time.

Alex woke with a start when the captain announced that they were beginning their descent to Pulkovo airport, and asked his passengers to fasten their seatbelts. He thought about the city he'd left all those years ago, also in midair, about his father, his uncle, and even Vladimir, who was more likely to be in Moscow than in Leningrad by now. He tried to push Major Polyakov into the recesses of his mind and concentrate on a deal that could put the bank into another league. Or would he be arrested even before they'd cleared customs?

He looked out of the cabin window, but could see little other than the terminal lights, and a sky full of stars he hadn't seen since he was a boy.

His emotions were torn. He wasn't sure if he was glad to be back, but the moment he disembarked, he was reminded of the pace things moved at in Russia. There was slow, slower, and if you were stupid enough to complain, even slower. They waited for over two hours to have their passports checked, and he realized how many things he took for granted living in the States. Had he imagined it, or did the inspector take even longer when he saw the name Karpenko? They then had to wait around for another hour before their bags were released and they were finally allowed to escape.

Pushkin led them out of the terminal and onto the pavement. He raised a hand in the air and five cars immediately swerved across the road, coming to a halt in front of them. Alex and his team looked on in disbelief as

Pushkin selected three of them. Everything on four wheels in Leningrad was a taxi, he explained.

"The Astoria," he instructed each of the chosen drivers. "Make sure you don't charge more than a ruble," he added as his new associates piled into the waiting cars.

"But that's only about a dollar," said Alex, when Misha joined him in the back seat.

"More than enough," he replied as the car shot off toward the city center. Another long journey.

By the time they'd all checked into the hotel, they were exhausted.

"Get a good night's sleep," said Jake, "because I need you all at your best tomorrow."

They met up in the dining room for breakfast the following morning, and although one or two of them looked as if they were still struggling with jet lag, after a couple of black coffees had been drained, and caffeine had entered their bloodstreams, they were all ready for their first assignments.

Jake and Alex set off for the Commercial Bank to try and discover if they could wire transfer twenty-five million dollars to Leningrad at a moment's notice. After last night's airport experience Alex couldn't help feeling a little pessimistic. Dick Barrett accompanied Misha to the LGP factory on the outskirts of the city, while Andy Harbottle went off to meet the company's lawyers to discuss the contract for the biggest and most complicated deal he'd ever come across. His father would have considered there were altogether too many naughts involved for it to be credible.

Andy had already prepared the first draft of a contract, but he warned Alex, "Even if the Russians sign it, what guarantees do we have that any payments will ever be forthcoming? This may be the new gold rush, but with it went cowboys and this lot aren't even our cowboys."

The one statistic he was able to confirm was that when an American sued a Russian in the Soviet courts, he had a four percent chance of winning the case.

The team reassembled in Jake's room at the hotel at six o'clock that evening. Jake and Alex reported that although Russian banks had been overwhelmed by the government's recent 180-degree policy U-turns, it had been made clear to them that foreign investors should be welcomed and, unlike Oliver, encouraged to come back for a second helping.

Barrett confirmed that everything Pushkin had claimed about the operation on the ground had proved accurate, although he did feel the company's safety record left a little to be desired. Alex didn't stop making notes.

"And the balance sheet?" asked Jake, turning to their number cruncher.

"They don't seem to understand the basic tenets of modern accounting practice," said Mitch Blake. "Which isn't surprising, as their economy's been run by party hacks for decades. But it's still the best goddamn bottom line I've ever seen."

"So let's play devil's advocate for a moment," said Alex. "What's the downside?"

"They could steal our twenty-five million," said Andy Harbottle. "But I don't think we should pack our bags just yet."

Over dinner that night, Alex was pleased to see the team relaxing for the first time.

"Are you still seeing your uncle for lunch tomorrow?" asked Jake.

"Sure am. I'm hoping he might be able to give me some inside knowledge on how to handle the current regime."

"Do you know what this country needs?" said Jake as he cut into a tough steak.

"For my mother to open a pizza parlor on Nevsky Prospect—Elena's Thirty-seven."

"That first, and then you should run for president. An honest Russian who understands free enterprise is exactly what this country needs at the moment."

"That was always my boyhood dream," said Alex. "If my father hadn't been killed, then perhaps . . ."

"Perhaps what?" said Jake, but Alex didn't reply as he stared directly ahead. He'd just noticed the three men seated at a table on the other side of the restaurant. The one fear he'd pushed to the back of his mind was suddenly facing him. He wasn't in any doubt who the older man was, or why the two thugs seated on either side of him were there.

The vicious scar that stretched down the left side of the man's face and neck was an instant reminder of where he and Alex had last met. Polyakov's chilling words, "You'll hang for this," reverberated in his ears. Anna was right, he should never have made the trip. Jake and his team were more than capable of handling the deal without him. But he'd allowed the thrill of the chase to overrule common sense.

The man continued to stare at Alex, his eyes fixed on him. Alex wasn't in any doubt of his intentions. While the rest of the team discussed tactics for the next day, Alex sat on the edge of his seat, tense and alert as he waited for the major to make the first move in a game of chess, which wasn't likely to end in stalemate.

Alex touched Jake's elbow. "Listen carefully," he whispered. "The man I nearly killed the day I escaped from Leningrad is sitting directly opposite us, and I don't believe in coincidences."

Jake glanced across at the three men, and said, "But, Alex, that was over twenty years ago."

"Look at that scar, Jake. Would you forget?"

"And the two men with him?"

"KGB, so they're above the law. They'll have no interest in how I die, only when."

"We must get you to the American Consulate as quickly as possible."

"I wouldn't make it to the front gate," said Alex. "What's important is for all of you to carry on as if nothing has happened. If anybody asks, tell them I've been held up at a meeting, or I'm visiting my uncle Kolya. Just keep stalling. I'll let you know when I'm safe."

"Shouldn't we at least call the consulate and ask their advice?"

"Take another look at the three of them, Jake, and ask yourself if they're the sort of men you'd invite to a lunch. This isn't the time for diplomatic exchanges."

"So what are you going to do?"

"Go native. Don't forget I was born and raised in this city. You concentrate on closing the deal. I'll take care of myself."

As Alex was speaking, a party of six was being shown across the restaurant to their table. The moment they passed between him and Polyakov, like a cloud blocking the sun, Alex slipped away. Jake turned and said, "Did you notice—" but he was no longer there.

Alex didn't waste time waiting for the elevator, but headed straight for the stairs. He charged up them three at a time, constantly looking back over his shoulder. When he reached the sixth floor, he quickly unlocked the door of his room, then locked himself inside, not bothering to put out the DO NOT DISTURB sign. He tapped six numbers into the pad of the little safe in the wardrobe, opened it, and grabbed his passport and some loose change. He touched his jacket pocket to make sure his wallet, containing the rubles Miss Robbins had supplied, was still there.

When he heard voices outside in the corridor he rushed across to the window and pushed it open. As he stepped out onto the fire escape, someone began banging on his door. He climbed down the ladder, checking up and down, unsure where the danger was more likely to come from. When he reached the bottom rung, he looked up to see one of the thugs staring down at him from the window of his room.

"There he is!" the man shouted, as he dropped onto the pavement.

Three other men were standing in the hotel's entrance staring all around them, so he quickly headed off in the opposite direction. He looked over his shoulder to see one of the men pointing, and then he started running down the hotel steps toward him.

Alex turned into a side street and broke into a run, aware that his pursuer couldn't be far behind. He could see a main road looming up in front of him but didn't stop running, narrowly missing being knocked over by a tram. He ran after the moving vehicle, praying it would stop. It squealed to a halt about a hundred yards ahead of him, sparks flying into the air. He wished he hadn't missed so many training sessions.

Looking back, Alex saw his pursuers rounding the corner. He leaped through the tram doors moments before they closed, flung a kopek at the driver, remembering how much he paid the airport taxi, before slumping down into an empty seat near the back. He stared out of the window to see his pursuer, head down, hands on knees, trying to catch his breath. Alex knew only too well that within minutes the spider's web of KGB operatives would be fanning out across the city in search of an American wearing a Brooks Brothers suit, white shirt, blue tie, and penny loafers. So much for going native.

He slumped down in his seat, aware of the occasional surreptitious glance from the other passengers—in Russia everyone's a spy—as a succession of familiar landmarks from his youth passed by. And then he remembered that in a couple more stops they would be outside the main railway terminal—the end of the line.

When the tram pulled up outside Moskovsky station, he joined the trickle of passengers getting off. He walked cautiously toward the entrance, wary of anyone dressed in a uniform, or even standing still. Just as he reached a large archway, he ducked into the shadows, hoping for a few uninterrupted moments to form some sort of plan.

"Are you looking for someone?"

Alex turned in panic to see a slim young boy smiling at him.

"How much?" asked Alex.

"Ten dollars."

"Where?"

"I've got a place just around the corner. If you're interested, follow me."

Alex nodded, but was careful to remain a few paces behind the youth as they walked down a dimly lit alley. And then, without warning, he ducked into a dilapidated prewar tenement block, not unlike the one Alex had grown up in. Alex climbed three flights of littered steps, before the boy opened a door and beckoned him inside.

The boy held out his hand and Alex gave him ten dollars.

"Are you looking for any particular service?" the boy asked, like a waiter offering him a menu.

"No. Just get undressed."

The boy looked surprised, but carried out the request, until he stood there in his underwear. Alex took off his jacket, trousers, and tie, and pulled on the boy's jeans, but found he couldn't do up the top button.

"Do you have a jacket of any kind?"

The boy looked puzzled, but took him through to his bedroom, opened the wardrobe, and stood aside. Alex selected a loose tracksuit top that stank of marijuana, and rejected a New York Yankees baseball cap. There was no mirror to check how he looked, but it had to be better than a Brooks Brothers suit.

"Now listen carefully," said Alex, taking a hundred-dollar bill from his wallet. The boy couldn't take his eyes off the money. "No more jobs tonight. Once I've gone, you lock your door and wait here until I come back, when you'll get another of these." He waved the bill in front of him. "Do you understand?"

"Yes, sir."

"Just be sure you're here when I get back."

"I will be, I will be."

Alex handed over the money and without another word left the boy standing in his underpants, looking as if he'd won the lottery. He waited until he heard the key turn in the lock before making his way cautiously back down the steps and out onto the street, mingling with the locals entering the crowded station. But when he was only yards away from the entrance, Alex spotted a policeman, eyes searching in every direction. It wasn't difficult for Alex to work out who he was looking for. He turned back and walked slowly toward the main road. The policeman wasn't interested in anyone leaving the station.

He spotted a taxi in the distance heading toward him, and raised a hand, quite forgetting what had happened at the airport when he'd first arrived in Leningrad. The taxi, three other cars, and an ambulance immediately pulled over, all wanting to give him a lift. Alex decided the ambulance would be his safest bet. He opened the passenger door and joined the driver on the front seat.

"Where are you heading?" asked the young man in Russian.

"The airport."

"That's going to cost you."

Alex produced another hundred-dollar bill.

"That should do it," said the driver, who pushed the gear lever into first, swept around in a semicircle, ignoring the cacophony of protesting horns, and sped off in the opposite direction.

Alex considered his next problem. Surely the airport would be just as risky as the station, but his thoughts were interrupted when he spotted a police car parked at a roadblock up ahead, and two officers checking licenses.

"Stop!" shouted Alex.

"What's the problem?" said the young man, drawing into the curb.

"You don't want to know. Better I just disappear."

The driver didn't comment, but when Alex jumped out, he found the back door of the ambulance open and an outstretched arm beckoning him. He climbed inside and joined a second man who was wearing a green paramedic's uniform, his left hand held out. Alex knew that look, and produced another hundred-dollar bill.

"Who's after you?"

"The KGB," said Alex, knowing that there was a fifty-fifty chance the man either detested them or worked for them.

"Lie down," said the paramedic, pointing to a stretcher. Alex obeyed him and was quickly covered with a blanket. The man turned to the driver and said, "Put the siren on, Leonid, and don't slow down. Just go for it."

The driver obeyed his colleague's command and was relieved when one of the police officers not only removed the barrier but waved them through. Had they stopped the ambulance, they would have found the patient lying on a stretcher, his head wrapped in bandages, only one eye staring up at them.

"When we reach the airport," said the paramedic, "where are you hoping to go?"

Alex hadn't thought about that, but the man answered his own question. "Helsinki will be your best bet," he said. "They're more likely to be checking flights heading west. Your Russian is good, but my guess is it's a long time since you were last in Leningrad."

"Then Helsinki it is," said Alex as the ambulance sped on toward the airport. "But how will I get a ticket?"

"Leave that to me," said the paramedic. The open palm appeared once again, as did another hundred dollars. "Do you have any rubles?" he asked. "Wouldn't want to draw attention to myself."

Alex smiled and emptied his wallet of all the rubles Miss Robbins had supplied, which elicited an even wider smile. Not another word was said until they reached the airport, when the ambulance drew into the curb, but the driver left the engine running.

"I'll be as quick as I can," said the paramedic, before opening the back door and leaping out. It felt like an hour to Alex, although it was no more than a few minutes before the door was opened again. "I've got you on a flight to Helsinki," he said, waving the ticket in triumph. "I even know which gate the plane's departing from." He turned to Leonid and said, "Head for the emergency entrance, and keep your lights flashing."

The ambulance shot off again, but Alex had no way of knowing where they were going. It was only a couple of minutes before they stopped when the back door was opened by a guard in a shiny gray uniform. He peered inside, nodded, then closed the door. Another guard raised the barrier, allowing the ambulance to proceed.

"Head for the Aeroflot plane parked at gate forty-two," the paramedic instructed his colleague.

Alex didn't like the sound of the word "Aeroflot," and wondered if he was being led into a trap, but didn't move until the back door opened once again. He sat up, fearful, anxious, alert, but the paramedic just grinned and handed him a pair of crutches.

"I'll have to replace them," he said, and only released the crutches after he received another hundred-dollar bill, almost as if he knew how much Alex had left.

The paramedic accompanied his patient up the steps and onto the aircraft. He handed over the ticket and a wad of cash to a steward, who counted the folded rubles before he even looked at the ticket. The steward pointed to a seat in the front row.

The paramedic helped Alex into his seat, bent down, and offered one final piece of advice, and then left the aircraft before Alex had a chance to thank him. He watched from the cabin window as the ambulance headed slowly back toward the private entrance, no flashing lights, no siren. He stared at the plane's open door, willing it to be closed. But it wasn't until the aircraft took off that Alex finally breathed a sigh of relief.

By the time the plane landed in Helsinki, Alex's heartbeat was almost back to normal, and he even had a plan.

He had taken the paramedic's advice, so that when he reached the front of the queue and handed over his passport there was a hundred-dollar bill enclosed where a visa should have been. The officer remained poker-faced as he removed Benjamin Franklin and stamped the empty page.

Once Alex was through customs he headed for the nearest washroom, where he removed his bandages and disposed of them in a bin. He shaved, washed as best he could, and once he was dry, reluctantly put the young man's clothes back on and went in search of a shop that would solve that particular problem. He emerged from a clothes store thirty minutes later wearing slacks, a white shirt, and a blazer. His loafers were the only thing that had survived.

An hour later Alex boarded an American Airlines flight to New York, and he was enjoying a vodka and tonic by the time the shop assistant came across an old pair of jeans, a T-shirt, and some crutches that had been left in the changing room.

When the plane took off, the steward didn't ask the first-class passenger what he would like for dinner, or which movie he would be watching, because Alex was already fast asleep. The steward gently lowered the passenger's seat and covered him with a blanket.

⊸o⊷

When Alex landed at JFK the following morning, he called Miss Robbins and asked her to have his car and driver ready to pick him up the moment he arrived at Logan.

During the short flight to Boston, he decided he would go straight home and explain to Anna and Konstantin why he would never be going back to the Soviet Union again.

After he'd disembarked, he was pleased to see Miss Robbins standing outside the arrivals gate waiting for him, a perplexed look on her face.

"It's wonderful to be home," he said as he sank down into the back seat of his limousine. "You'll never believe what I've been through, Pamela, and how lucky I was to escape."

"I've heard part of the story, chairman, but I can't wait to hear your version."

"So you've been told about Major Polyakov and his KGB thugs waiting for me in the hotel restaurant?"

"Would that be the same Colonel Polyakov who died a year ago?" asked Miss Robbins innocently.

"Polyakov is dead?" said Alex in disbelief. "Then who was the man in the restaurant with the two KGB minders?"

"A blind man, his brother, and a friend. They were attending a conference in Leningrad. Jake was just about to tell you he'd spotted his white stick, but by then you were already on the run."

"But the scar? It was unmistakable."

"A birthmark."

"But they broke into my room . . . I heard him shouting 'There he is!'"

"That was the night porter. And he didn't break into your room, because he had a passkey. Jake was standing just behind him and was able to identify you."

“But someone was chasing me, and I only just managed to jump onto the tram in time.”

“Dick Barrett said he had no idea you could run that fast . . .”

“And the ambulance, the road block, not to mention—”

“I can’t wait to hear all about the ambulance, the roadblock, and why you didn’t get on your own plane, chairman, where you would have found a message from Jake explaining everything,” said Miss Robbins as the limousine swung off the road and drove through a gate marked PRIVATE. “But that will have to wait until you get back.”

“Where are we going?”

“Not we, chairman, just you. Jake called earlier this morning to say he’s closed the deal with Mr. Pushkin, but a problem has arisen because you told the chairman of the Commercial Bank in Leningrad that the contract wouldn’t be valid without your signature.”

The limousine drew up next to the steps of the bank’s private jet awaiting its only passenger.

“Have a good flight, chairman,” said Miss Robbins.

BOOK FIVE

41

SASHA

London, 1994

"Order! Order!" said the Speaker. "Questions to the Foreign Secretary. Mr. Sasha Karpenko."

Sasha rose slowly from his place on the opposition front bench, and asked, "Can the Foreign Secretary confirm that Britain will finally be signing the Fifth Protocol of the Geneva Convention, as we are the only European country that has so far failed to do so?"

Mr. Douglas Hurd rose to answer the question, as a badge messenger appeared by the Speaker's chair, and handed a slip of paper to the Labour whip on duty. He read the name before passing it down the front bench to the shadow minister. Sasha unfolded it, read the message, and immediately stood and walked uneasily along the opposition front bench, stepping over and sometimes on his colleagues' toes, not unlike someone who has to leave a crowded theater in the middle of a performance. He stopped to have a word with the Speaker to explain his actions. The Speaker smiled.

"On a point of order, Mr. Speaker," said the Foreign Secretary, leaping up, "shouldn't the honorable member at least have the courtesy to stay and hear the answer to his own question?"

"Hear, hear," shouted several members from the government benches.

"Not on this occasion," said Mr. Speaker without explanation. Members on both sides began to chatter among themselves, wondering why Sasha had left the chamber so abruptly.

"Question number two," said the Speaker, smiling to himself.

Robin Cook was on his feet by the time Sasha had reached the members' entrance.

"Taxi, sir?" asked the doorman.

"No, thank you," said Sasha, who'd already decided to run all the way to St. Thomas's Hospital rather than wait for a taxi that would have to drive around Parliament Square and contend with half a dozen sets of traffic lights before reaching the hospital. He was out of breath by the time he was halfway across Westminster Bridge, having had to dodge in and out of camera-laden tourists. With each step he was made painfully aware just how unfit he had allowed himself to become over the years.

Charlie had suffered two miscarriages since the birth of their daughter, and Dr. Radley had advised them that this could well be their last chance of having another child.

When Sasha reached the southern end of the bridge, he ran down the steps and along the Thames until he reached the hospital entrance. He didn't ask the woman on reception which floor his wife was on, because they had both visited Dr. Radley the previous week. Avoiding the overcrowded lift, he continued on up the stairs to the maternity wing. This time he did stop at the desk to give the nurse his name. She checked the computer while he caught his breath.

"Mrs. Karpenko is already in the delivery room. If you take a seat, it shouldn't be long now."

Sasha didn't even look for a seat, but began pacing up and down the corridor, while offering a silent prayer for his unborn son. Elena hadn't approved of them wanting to know the child's sex before it was born. He could only wonder why a situation like this always caused him to pray, when he didn't at any other time. Well, perhaps at Christmas. He certainly neglected to thank the Almighty when things were going well. And they couldn't have been going much better at the moment. Natasha, whom he adored, had had him obeying her every command for the past fifteen years.

"Otherwise what's the point of fathers?" Charlie had overheard her telling a friend.

Although they'd tightened their belts—another of his mother's expressions—after the closure of Elena's 3, it had taken another four years before the company was back in profit and the taxman had been paid in full. Elena's 1 and 2 were now making a comfortable profit, although Sasha was aware that he could have made a lot more money if he hadn't chosen to follow a political career. The prospect of a second child made him wonder about his future. A minister of the Crown? Or would his constituents dismiss him? After all, Merrifield was still a marginal seat, and only a fool took the electorate for granted. Perhaps they were never going to be rich, but they led a civilized and comfortable life, and had little to complain about. Sasha had long ago accepted that if you decide to pursue a political career, you can't always expect to travel first-class.

He had been delighted by his promotion to Shadow Minister of State at the Foreign Office when Tony Blair took over as leader of the opposition. A man who seemed to have an unusual failing for a Labour leader: he actually wanted to govern.

Robin Cook, the Shadow Foreign Secretary, was calling for an ethical foreign policy, and told Sasha that he expected him to keep reminding his Russian counterparts that their country's newfound wealth should be distributed among the people, and not handed out to a group of undeserving oligarchs, many of whom had not only taken up residence in Mayfair, but weren't paying any tax.

Sasha told Cook privately that not only did he agree with those sentiments, but he had even given some thought to returning to his homeland and contesting the next presidential election if things didn't improve. Although he had been delighted to see the end of Communism, he didn't much care for what had replaced it.

Getting any reliable information out of Russia was never easy at the best of times, but Sasha had become a close friend of Boris Nemtsov, who was now a junior minister in the Duma, as well as developing a close circle of friends among the younger diplomats at the embassy. They met regularly at official gatherings, conferences, and parties at other embassies, and Sasha quickly discovered that one young second secretary, Ilya Resinev, was even willing to pass on information from his uncle.

When President Gorbachev was replaced by Yeltsin, Ilya let Sasha know that his old school friend Vladimir was among the new president's inner circle, and was expecting to be promoted. Vladimir had recently resigned as a colonel when the KGB was dissolved, and thrown in his lot with his old university professor Anatoly Sobchak, who had become the first democratically elected mayor of Saint Petersburg. Vladimir was among his early appointments as head of the city's foreign and economic relations committee. Ilya told Sasha that no oil or gas deal in the province could be closed without Vladimir's approval, although he rarely put his signature to the final document, and no one seemed surprised when he moved house three times in three years, always into an ever grander establishment, despite being on a government salary.

Ilya warned Sasha that if Sobchak was reelected, there would be no prizes for guessing who would be his successor as the next mayor of Saint Petersburg. "And after that, who knows where Vladimir would end up?"

Sasha stopped pacing and looked in the direction of the delivery room, but the doors remained stubbornly closed. His mind drifted back to Russia, and his upcoming meeting with Boris Nemtsov, who, as a rising minister was planning to visit London in the autumn, when he would bring Sasha up to date as to whether it was at all credible for him to consider standing as president. Yeltsin had disappointed even his most ardent supporters, who felt he lacked the reforming zeal they had been looking for. And too many world leaders were complaining in private that they couldn't hold a meeting with the Russian president after four o'clock in the afternoon. By then, he was no longer coherent in any language. During a recent stopover in Dublin, Yeltsin hadn't even been able to get off the plane, leaving the Irish Taoiseach standing on the runway waiting in vain to greet him.

Sasha checked his watch for the umpteenth time, and could only wonder what was going on behind those closed doors, when suddenly they swung open, and Dr. Radley, still in his scrubs, stepped out into the corridor. Sasha walked eagerly toward him, but when the doctor removed his mask, he didn't need to be told that he would never have a son.

Sasha wondered if he would ever come to terms with Konstantin's death. He had held the baby in his arms for a few moments before they took him away.

His colleagues in the Commons couldn't have been more understanding and sympathetic. But even they began to wonder if Sasha had lost his appetite for politics after he missed several three-line whips, and on a couple of occasions failed to turn up for his front-bench duties.

The leader of the opposition had a word with the Shadow Foreign Secretary, and they agreed to say nothing until the House returned in the autumn following the long summer recess.

Elena suggested that what they both needed was a holiday, and as far away from Westminster as possible.

"Why not visit Rome, Florence, and Milan," suggested Gino, "where you can indulge yourself in the finest opera houses, art galleries, and restaurants on earth. Pavarotti and Bernini, accompanied by endless pasta and Sicilian red. What more could anyone ask for?"

"New York, New York," suggested another Italian from their car radio. Charlie and Sasha decided to take Sinatra's advice.

"But what shall we do about Natasha?"

"She can't wait to get rid of you," Elena assured them. "In any case, she was hoping to join her school friends on a trip to Edinburgh to see Kiki Dee."

"Then that's settled."

⤙o⤚

Sasha set about planning a holiday Charlie would never forget. They would spend five days on the *QE2*, and on arrival in New York, take a suite at the Plaza. They would visit the Metropolitan, MoMA, and the Frick, and he even managed to get tickets for Liza Minnelli, who was performing at Carnegie Hall.

"And then we'll fly home on Concorde."

"You'll bankrupt us," said Charlie.

"Don't worry, the Conservatives haven't yet brought back debtors' prisons."

"It will probably be in their next party manifesto," suggested Charlie.

The five-day voyage on the *QE2* was idyllic, and they made several new friends, one or two who thought the Labour Party might even win the next election. Every morning began with a session in the gym, but they still both managed to put on a pound a day. On the final morning they rose before the sun and stood out on deck to be welcomed by the Statue of Liberty, while the skyscrapers of the Manhattan skyline grew taller by the minute.

Once they'd checked into their hotel—Charlie had talked him out of the presidential suite in favor of a double room several floors below—they didn't waste a minute.

The Metropolitan Museum entranced Charlie with its breadth of works from so many cultures. From Byzantine Greece, to Italy's Caravaggio, to the Dutch masters, Rembrandt and Vermeer, while the French Impressionists demanded a second visit. The Museum of Modern Art also delighted her and surprised Sasha, who couldn't always tell the difference between Picasso and Braque during their cubist period. But it was the Frick that became their second home, with Bellini, Holbein, and Mary Cassatt to draw them back again and again. And Liza Minnelli had them standing on their feet crying "Encore!" after she sang "Maybe This Time."

"What shall we do on our last day?" asked Sasha as they enjoyed a late breakfast in the garden room.

"Let's go window-shopping."

"Why don't we stroll into Tiffany's and buy everything in sight?"

"Because we've already gone over our budget."

"I feel sure we've still got enough to buy something for both grandmothers and Natasha."

"Then we'll window-shop on Fifth Avenue, but buy everything from Macy's."

"Compromise," said Sasha, folding his newspaper. "Bloomingdale's."

Charlie selected a pair of leather gloves for her mother, while Sasha chose a Swatch for Elena that she'd hinted about more than once. *And such a reasonable price,* she'd reminded him.

"And Natasha?" asked Sasha.

"A pair of these Levi's. They'll be the envy of her friends."

"But they're faded and ripped before you even buy them," said Sasha when he first saw them in a shop window.

"And you claim to be a man of the people."

They were on their way back to the Plaza laden down with bags when Charlie stopped to admire a painting in a gallery window on Lexington Avenue. "That's what I want," she said, admiring the mesmerizing colors and brushwork.

"Then you married the wrong man."

"Oh, I'm not so sure about that," said Charlie. "But I still intend to find out how much it's going to cost you," she added before going in.

The walls of the gallery were crowded with abstract works, and Charlie was admiring a Jackson Pollock when an elderly gentleman approached her.

"A magnificent painting, madam."

"Yes, but so sad."

"Sad, madam?"

"That he died at such a young age, when he still hadn't fulfilled his promise."

"Indeed. We had the privilege of representing him when he was alive, and this painting has been through my hands three times in the past thirty years."

"Death, divorce, and taxes?"

The old man smiled. "You're not in the art world, by any chance?"

"I work as a conservator for the Turner Collection."

"Ah, then please give my regards to Nicholas Serota," he said, handing her his card.

Sasha walked across to join them. "Dare I ask the price of the painting in the window?"

"The Rothko?" said Mr. Rosenthal, turning to face his customer. "Alex, I had no idea you were in town. But you must know that your wife has already purchased the painting for the collection."

"My wife has already bought it?"

"A couple of weeks ago."

"Not on a Member of Parliament's salary, she didn't."

Rosenthal adjusted his glasses, took a closer look at the customer, and said, "I do apologize. I should have realized my mistake the moment you spoke."

"You said 'the collection,'" said Charlie.

"Yes, the Lowell Collection in Boston."

"Now that's a collection I've always wanted to see," said Charlie, "but I understood that it was locked up in a bank vault."

"Not any longer," said Rosenthal. "The paintings were all returned to their original home in Boston some time ago. I'd be happy to arrange a private view for you, madam. The curator of the collection used to work here, and I know she'd enjoy meeting you."

"I'm afraid we're booked on a flight back to London later this evening," said Charlie.

"What a pity. Next time, perhaps," said Rosenthal, giving them both a slight bow.

"Strange," said Charlie once they were back on Lexington. "He obviously mistook you for someone else."

"And someone who could afford a Rothko."

"Come on, we'd better get moving if we're going to make it to JFK by five," said Charlie. She took one last look at the painting in the window. "Can you imagine what it must be like to own a Rothko?"

⊸o⊷

"I know, I know," said Sasha. "If God had meant us to fly, he would have given us wings."

"Don't mock," said Charlie. "This plane is going far too fast."

"It was built to travel at this speed. So just sit back, relax, and enjoy your champagne."

"But the whole plane is shuddering. Can't you feel it?"

"That will stop the moment we break the sound barrier, and then it will feel just like any other aircraft, except you'll be traveling at over a thousand miles per hour."

"I don't want to think about it," said Charlie, closing her eyes.

"And don't go to sleep."

"Why not?"

"Because this will be the first and last time you'll ever travel on Concorde."

"Unless you become Prime Minister."

"That's not going to happen, but—"

Charlie gripped his hand. "Thank you, darling, for the most wonderful holiday I've ever had. Though I must confess, I can't wait to get back home."

"Me too," admitted Sasha. "Did you read the leader in *The New York Times* this morning? It seems that even the Americans are beginning to believe we're going to win the next election." Sasha glanced down to see that Charlie had fallen asleep. How he wished he could do that. He turned and looked across the aisle, to see someone he recognized immediately. He would have liked to introduce himself, but didn't want to disturb him. The man turned and looked in his direction.

"This is most fortuitous, Mr. Karpenko," said David Frost. "I was only saying to my producer this morning, we ought to get you on our breakfast show as soon as possible. I'm particularly interested in your views on Russia, and how long you think Yeltsin will last."

For the first time, Sasha really did believe it might be only a matter of time before he was a minister.

⟜○⟝

Sasha enjoyed the party conference in Blackpool for the first time in years. No longer was there speech after speech from the platform demanding changes the government ought to make, because this time the shadow ministers were spelling out the changes they would be making once the Tories had the guts to call an election.

Whenever he left his hotel to stroll down to the conference center, passersby waved and shouted, "Good luck, Sasha!" Several journalists who in the past didn't have time for a drink in Annie's Bar were now inviting him to lunch or dinner that he couldn't always fit into his diary. The stark message of the leader's closing speech couldn't have been clearer. Prepare for government with New Labour. Like everyone else in the packed hall, Sasha couldn't wait for John Major to call a general election.

⟜○⟝

Sasha felt guilty that he hadn't visited the countess for some time. His mother had tea with her once a week, and over the years they had become close friends. Elena regularly reminded him that it was the countess's Fabergé egg that had changed all their fortunes. However, it was months since the old lady had attended a board meeting, despite still owning fifty percent of the company.

When Sasha knocked on the door of her flat in Lowndes Square, the same faithful retainer answered, and for the first time, led him through to her mistress's bedroom. Sasha was shocked to see how much the countess had aged since he'd last seen her. Her thinning white hair and deeply lined face suggested to him the harbingers of death. She gave him a weak smile.

"Come and sit by me, Sasha," she said, tapping the edge of the bed. "There's something I need to discuss with you. I know how busy you must be, so I'll try not to waste too much of your time."

"I'm in no hurry," said Sasha as he sat down beside her, "so please take your time. I'm only sorry it's been so long since I last saw you."

"That doesn't matter. Your mother keeps me up to date on everything you've been up to. The company's back making a handsome profit, and I just hope I'll live long enough to see you become a minister of the Crown."

"Of course you will."

"Dearest Sasha, I've reached the age when death is my next-door neighbor, which is the reason I asked to see you. You and I have so many things in common, not least a devotion to and love for the country of our birth. We owe a great deal to our British hosts for being so civilized and tolerant, but it's still Russian blood that runs in our veins. When I die—"

"Which let us hope will not be for some time," said Sasha, taking her hand.

"My only wish," she said, ignoring the interruption, "is to be buried next to my father and grandfather in the church of Saint Nicholas in Saint Petersburg."

"Then your wish will be granted. So please don't give it another thought."

"That's so kind of you, and I will be forever grateful. Now, on a lighter note, dear boy, a little piece of history that I thought might amuse you. When I was a child, Tsar Nicholas the Second visited me in my nursery and just like you sat on the edge of my bed." Sasha smiled as he continued to hold her hand. "I suspect that I will be the only person in the history of our country who's had both a Tsar and a future president of Russia sit on her bed."

42

SASHA

Westminster, 1997

John Major held out until the last moment, finally going to the country on the last day of the fifth year of the Parliament. But by then, no one was discussing whether Labour would win the general election, only how large their majority would be.

Sasha's seat of Merrifield was no longer considered marginal, so he was deployed across the country to address gatherings in constituencies which up until then had seldom seen anyone wearing a red rosette. Even Fiona Hunter, with her 11,328 majority in the next-door constituency, was knocking on doors and holding public meetings as if she were defending a key marginal.

Sasha spent the final week of the campaign among friends and supporters in Merrifield as they waited to learn the nation's verdict. In the early hours of the morning of Friday, May 2, the returning officer for the Merrifield constituency declared that Mr. Sasha Karpenko had won the seat with a 9,741 majority. Alf reminded him of the days when it had been in double figures, and then only after three recounts.

That morning he read the same one-word headline on the front page of almost every national newspaper: LANDSLIDE.

When the final seat was declared in Northern Ireland, the Labour Party had won an overall majority of 179 seats. Sasha was disappointed that Ben Cohen had lost his seat, but had to admit, if only to himself, that he was pleased Fiona had survived by a couple of thousand votes. He would call Ben later that day to commiserate.

He switched on the television while Charlie boiled a couple of eggs.

"No television until you've finished your prep," scolded Natasha, wagging her finger.

"This is my prep, young lady," said her father, as they watched a black Jaguar being driven slowly along the Mall toward Buckingham Palace, carrying a passenger who had an appointment with the monarch. Everyone knew that Her Majesty would ask Mr. Blair if he could form a government, and he would assure her that he could.

When the car reemerged through the Palace gates some forty minutes later, it traveled straight to number 10 Downing Street, where the passenger would take up residence for the next five years, along with the titles of Prime Minister and First Lord of the Treasury.

"So what happens next?" asked Charlie.

"Like so many of my colleagues, I'll be sitting by the phone, hoping to receive a call from the PM."

"And if he doesn't call?" said Natasha.

"I'll be sitting on the back benches for the next five years."

"I don't think so," said Charlie. "Meanwhile, some of us have to do a day's work. Be sure to call me the moment you hear anything. And don't forget you're taking Natasha to school this morning," she added before leaving to catch the Underground to Victoria.

Sasha topped his egg to find it had already gone hard. When Natasha left the room to collect her bag, he tried to read the morning papers. History. How he wanted to read tomorrow's papers and discover if he'd been offered a job.

Natasha stuck her head around the door. "Come on, Dad, it's time to go. I can't afford to be late."

Sasha abandoned his half-finished egg, grabbed the car keys from the sideboard, and quickly followed his daughter out onto the street.

"Did I tell you I'll be playing Portia in the school play this year, Papa?" said Natasha as she fastened her seatbelt.

"Which Portia?" asked Sasha as he drove off.

"*Julius Caesar.*"

"*You are a true and honorable wife, as dear to me as are the ruddy drops that visit my sad heart.*"

Natasha paused, before she delivered the next line. "*If this were true, then should I know this secret. I grant I am a woman; but withal a woman that Lord Brutus took to wife.*"

"Not bad," said Sasha.

"We're still looking for a Brutus, Papa, just in case you've got nothing better to do," Natasha said as they drew up outside the school gates.

"Not a bad offer. I'll let you know this evening if I get a better one."

"By the way," Natasha said as she got out of the car, "you made a one-word mistake."

"Which word?"

"Haven't you always told me, don't be lazy, child, look it up? Have a good day, Papa, and the best of luck!"

⊸o⊷

Sasha let the phone ring three times before he picked it up.

"Sasha, it's Ben. Just calling to wish you luck."

"I'm sorry you lost your seat, old friend. But I'm sure you'll be back."

"I doubt it. I have a feeling your party will be sitting on the government benches for some time."

"Perhaps they'll send you to the Lords?"

"Too young. And in any case, there's likely to be a fairly long queue in front of me."

"Let's keep in touch," said Sasha, aware that that was no longer going to be quite as easy.

"I'll get off the line," said Ben. "I know you must be waiting for a call from Number 10. Good luck."

Sasha hadn't even sat back down before the phone rang again. He grabbed it before it could ring a second time.

"This is Number 10," said a switchboard voice. "The Prime Minister wondered if you could see him at three twenty this afternoon."

I'll check my diary and see if that's convenient, Sasha was tempted to say. "Of course," he replied.

For the next hour he pretended to watch the news, read the papers, and even eat lunch. He took calls from several colleagues who had already received the summons, or were still anxiously waiting, and from many others, including Alf Rycroft, to wish him luck. In between, he fed the cat, who was fast asleep, and read the second act of *Julius Caesar* to discover his one-word mistake.

He drove to the Commons just after 2:30 p.m., and parked in the members' car park. The policeman on the gate saluted the moment he saw him. Did he know something Sasha didn't? He left the Palace of Westminster just after three, and walked slowly across Parliament Square and up Whitehall past the Foreign Office. Were the mandarins inside waiting for him? The policeman on duty at Downing Street didn't need to check his clipboard.

"Good afternoon, Mr. Karpenko," he said, and opened the gate to let him through.

"Good afternoon," Sasha replied, as he began the long gallows walk up Downing Street to discover his fate.

He was surprised when the door to number 10 opened while he was still a few paces away. He stepped inside for the first time, to find a young woman waiting for him.

"Good afternoon, Mr. Karpenko. Would you be kind enough to follow me?" She led him up a flight of stairs, past the portraits of former Prime Ministers. John Major was already in place.

When they reached the first floor, she stopped outside a door and knocked quietly, opened it, and stood aside. Sasha walked in to find the Prime Minister sitting opposite an empty chair in which it looked as if several people had already sat. A secretary, pen poised, was seated behind him.

"I'm sure this won't come as much of a surprise," said the Prime Minister once Sasha had sat down, "but I'd like you to join Robin at the Foreign Office as his Minister of State. I hope you'll feel able to accept the post."

"I'd be honored," said Sasha. "And delighted to serve in your first administration."

"I'd also like you to keep me briefed on what's happening in Russia," said the Prime Minister, "particularly if your personal situation should change."

"My personal situation, Prime Minister?"

"Our ambassador in Moscow tells me that if you were to return to Russia and stand against Yeltsin, you'd end up with an even bigger majority than I have. In which case it will be me trying to get an appointment with you."

"But Yeltsin doesn't come up for election for another three years."

"Yes, but the polls currently show his approval rating is in single figures, and still falling."

"The polls are irrelevant, Prime Minister. What matters in Russia is how many voting slips end up in the ballot box, who put them there, and even more important, who counts them."

"So much for glasnost," said Blair. "But I have a feeling your time may well come, Sasha, so please keep me informed, and in the meantime, good luck in your new job."

The secretary leaned forward and whispered in the Prime Minister's ear. Sasha didn't need to be told the meeting was over, and was about to leave when the PM added, "Your name is also on the list of ministers who will be invited to join the Privy Council."

"Thank you, Prime Minister," said Sasha as he rose, and the two men shook hands.

When Sasha left the PM's office, he found the same young woman still standing in the corridor. "If you come with me, minister, you'll find a car outside waiting to take you to the Foreign Office."

Denis Healey had once told Sasha that you never forget the first person who calls you minister. But within a week, you'll think it's your Christian name.

As Sasha left number 10 he passed Chris Smith on his way in, and wondered what job he was about to be offered. He stepped out onto the pavement, and a burly man who looked as if he might play in the front row of his local rugby team introduced himself. "Good afternoon, minister, my name is Arthur, and I'm your driver," he said, holding open the back door of the waiting car.

"I'd prefer to sit in the front," said Sasha.

"I'm afraid not, sir. Security reasons."

Sasha climbed into the back. He couldn't help wondering why he even needed a car, as the Foreign Office was only a few hundred yards away. "Security reasons," he could hear Arthur assuring him.

"Can I make a phone call?"

"It's in the armrest, minister. Just pick it up and you'll be straight through to the FO's switchboard. Tell them who you want and they'll connect you immediately."

"Presumably I'll need to give them the number?"

"That won't be necessary, sir."

Sasha lifted the armrest and picked up the phone. "Good afternoon, minister," said a voice, "how can I help?"

"I'd like to speak to my wife."

"Of course, sir, I'll put you through."

Fiona had once told him it takes a little time to get used to the sudden change of lifestyle from opposition to government.

"Hello?" said the voice on the other end of the line.

"Good afternoon, this is the Right Honorable Sasha Karpenko, Her Majesty's Minister of State at the Foreign and Commonwealth Office."

He waited for Charlie to burst out laughing. "I'm so sorry, minister," said the voice, "but your wife is away from her desk at the moment. I'll let her know that you called."

"I do apologize—" began Sasha, but the phone had already gone dead.

"I've just made my first gaffe, Arthur."

"And I feel sure it won't be your last. But I must admit, you're the first of my ministers who managed it even before he'd reached the Foreign Office."

43

ALEX

Boston and Davos, 1999

The board meeting had gone smoothly enough until Jake raised the final item on the agenda, "Any other business."

"Evelyn wants what?" asked the chairman, staring in disbelief at his chief executive.

"To sell her fifty percent stake in the bank. She's offering us first refusal."

"How much would her shares fetch on the open market?" asked Bob Underwood.

"Four, possibly five hundred million."

"And how much is she asking for?" asked Mitch Blake.

"A billion."

A group of men who were capable of playing poker for hours without moving a facial muscle gasped in disbelief.

"Evelyn's well aware that while she owns fifty percent of the company's stock, she can put a gun to our head."

"Then she may as well pull the trigger," said Alex, "because we don't have that sort of money available."

"As George Soros once said, if you own fifty-one percent of a company you are its master, if you own forty-nine or less, you are its servant."

"Anyone got any ideas?" asked Alex, looking around the boardroom table.

"Kill her," said Bob Underwood.

"That wouldn't solve the problem," said Jake matter-of-factly, "because her husband, Todd Halliday, would inherit her estate, and then we'd have to deal with him."

"We could call her bluff," said Underwood. "She'd soon find out that no one else is willing to pay her such a ridiculous sum."

"I wouldn't be so sure of that," said Jake. "The Bank of Boston would love to get their hands on our Russian portfolio, which is now outperforming all our rivals, and I suspect they'd be willing to pay well above the asking price."

"Why don't we just ignore the damned woman," suggested Blake, "and perhaps she'll go away."

"She's already anticipated that," said Jake, "and decided to park her tanks on our front lawn."

"And what does she plan to use as ammunition?" asked Alex.

"The company statutes."

"Which one in particular?" asked Andy Harbottle, who thought he knew them all off by heart.

"Number 92."

The rest of the board waited while Harbottle thumbed through a well-worn leather-bound book. When he came to the relevant statute, he read it out loud. "Should one shareholder or group of shareholders own fifty percent or more of the company stock, they would be entitled to hold up any board decision for six months."

"She's listed eleven decisions we've made during the past year that she intends to challenge," said Jake. "That would bring the bank to a standstill for six months, and she says that if we don't pay up, she'll come to the AGM next month and carry out her threat in person."

"Who put her up to this?" said Underwood.

"Ackroyd would be my bet," said Jake. "But as he's got a criminal record, he can't risk putting his head above the parapet. So we're going to have to deal with Evelyn personally."

"But in view of her past relationship with Ackroyd," said Underwood, "why don't we offer her four hundred million and see how she responds?"

"We could try," said Jake. "But have I got any room to maneuver?"

"Six hundred, and even that's extortionate," said Alex.

"I think, as a board, we'll have to assume that she'll carry out her threat," said Jake. "In which case Ackroyd will advise her to offer her shares to the Bank of Boston for seven hundred million."

"She should be hanged from the nearest gibbet, as many of her English ancestors were," said Underwood.

"It's me who should be hanged," said Alex. "Don't forget, she once offered me her fifty percent for a million dollars, and I turned her down."

"Drawn and quartered," said Underwood.

"Not quite yet," said Jake. "We still have one ace up our sleeve."

⤚o⤙

"Congratulations," said Anna. "It's always a bit special to be recognized by your peers."

"Thank you," said Alex. "Especially as Davos is attended by all the players who really matter in the financial world."

"What do they want you to speak about?"

"Russia's role in the new world order. The only problem is, it couldn't have come at a worse time for the bank."

"Evelyn causing trouble again?"

"She's threatening to hijack the AGM if we don't agree to her outrageous demands."

"Perhaps we should cancel our weekend in London and fly straight to Davos?"

"No, we both need a break, and you've been looking forward to the trip for months."

"Years," said Anna, "ever since Mr. Rosenthal told me I'd never really understand the significance of the English watercolor until I'd seen the Turners at the Tate."

⤚o⤙

After paying a discreet visit to Boston's most exclusive wigmaker he booked a return flight to Nice, and paid with cash. The travel agent also reserved him a room at the Hôtel de Paris, open-ended, as he couldn't be sure how long it would take him to carry out his plan.

By training he was a micromanager, obsessed with detail. His hero, General Eisenhower, had written in his memoirs that all things being equal, planning and preparation are what will decide who wins the battle. By the time he boarded the plane for Nice, he was more than ready to confront her on any battlefield she chose.

Miss Robbins had booked them into the Connaught, Lawrence's favorite hotel in London. As they only had a long weekend before flying on to Davos, every minute of their stay had to be accounted for.

The National Gallery, the Wallace Collection, and the Royal Academy were compulsory viewing, and didn't disappoint. Henry Goodman's haunting Shylock made them want to extend their visit and see every other production at the National Theatre. And how did one decide between the Natural History Museum, the V&A, and the Science Museum, unless you did all three of them on the run?

Anna saved the Turner Collection at the Tate for their last morning, and both of them were standing outside the entrance even before the gallery had opened its doors. *A View of the Archbishop's Palace*, painted when the artist was only fifteen, could not have left anyone in any doubt of Turner's genius. But after seeing *The Shipwreck* and *Venice*, Anna wanted to say to Alex, *Why don't you go on to Davos without me?*

She turned to see him chatting to a woman who didn't look like a tourist, and her lapel badge suggested she might work at the Tate. Anna had for some time wanted to ask someone about Turner's fractious relationship with Constable, his great contemporary and rival, so she strolled across to join them.

"I'm so sorry," the woman was saying. "I thought for a moment you were my . . . How stupid of me." She hurried away, looking embarrassed.

"What was that all about?" asked Anna.

"I'm not sure, but I think she mistook me for someone else."

"Leading a double life are you, my darling?" she teased. "Because she's just your type, dark eyes, dark hair, and she looked highly intelligent."

"I found one of those some time ago," said Alex, putting his arm around his wife, "and frankly, one is quite enough."

"Do I sense that you're beginning to feel a little nervous about your speech?"

"You could be right."

"Then let's go back to the hotel and we can go over it one more time."

Neither of them noticed the gallery's head conservator watching them from her office window as they made their way out onto Millbank and hailed a black cab. If it hadn't been for the Brooks Brothers suit and his

American accent, Charlie could have sworn . . . and then she remembered. Could it possibly be the woman who'd worked at the Rosenthal gallery, and was now the curator of the Lowell Collection?

⤙o⤚

He took his seat in first class, and was relieved to find he didn't recognize any of the other passengers. He used the long flight across the Atlantic to go over his strategy again and again, although he knew he would need to look surprised when they first met. As with any seasoned orator, even the ad libs had to be rehearsed.

He turned to her personal file, suspecting that by now he knew more about her than even her closest friends. By the time the plane touched down, he was wondering what could go wrong. Because there would always be something you hadn't anticipated. Eisenhower.

Once he'd passed through passport control and retrieved his two large leather cases, he took a taxi to the Hôtel de Paris, checked in, and was accompanied to his suite. He gave the porter a large tip, all part of the plan. He needed to be remembered. He could never sleep on planes, so he went straight to bed and didn't wake until eight the following morning.

He spent the day acquainting himself with the layout of the hotel as well as the casino on the other side of the square, not that he ever gambled. It was important for him to look and sound like a regular before they bumped into each other. And most important of all, it was the evenings that needed to be rehearsed to a split second.

On Monday night, he dined alone in the hotel restaurant, and took his time gaining the confidence of Jacques, the maître d', helped by leaving another extravagant tip before he returned to his room. By Tuesday, Jacques had confirmed that she and her husband dined at the hotel restaurant every Friday, before walking across the square where they would remain at the gaming tables until the early hours.

On Wednesday, Jacques moved him to the table next to the one they always sat at, and he selected a seat that would place him with his back to her. By Thursday, Jacques was well aware of the part he was expected to play. But then, monsieur had left him several large incentives, and he anticipated that if he played his part, there was still more where that came from.

On Friday evening he was seated in his place thirty minutes before the curtain was due to rise. He placed his order, but told Jacques he wasn't in a hurry.

The two of them entered the dining room just after eight o'clock, and Jacques didn't even look in his direction as he accompanied his guests to their usual table. He continued to read the international *Wall Street Journal,* as he needed her to be aware that he was alone.

Jacques waited until their main courses had been cleared before the curtain rose for the second act, when Jacques walked back on stage to play his cameo role. He bent down and whispered in her ear.

"Did you notice who's sitting at the next table, madam?"

"If you mean the elderly gentleman with his back to me, I can't say I did."

"It's George Soros. He always gives me a share tip whenever he stays, and it usually doubles in value by the time he returns."

"He's a regular then?"

"He stays with us once a year, madam, just for the week. A chance to relax, somewhere no one will recognize him."

"I won't have a dessert tonight, Jacques," she said. "And neither will my husband."

Todd looked disappointed, because he always enjoyed the bitter chocolate roulade, but he knew that look.

"As you wish, madam," said Jacques. As he passed the next table, he filled the guest's glass with water, the sign that he had performed his role and was leaving the stage.

A few moments later, Todd got up and discreetly left the dining room. The diner at the next table turned a page of his paper, and continued reading. Evelyn stood up, pushing her chair back until it bumped into his.

"I'm so sorry," she said as he turned around.

"Not at all," he said, rising from his place and giving her a slight bow.

"Good heavens, are you who I think you are?"

"That would depend on who you want me to be," he said, smiling warmly.

"Mr. Soros?"

"Then my cover is blown, madam."

"Evelyn Lowell," she said, returning his smile.

He bowed again. "I had the privilege of knowing your father," he said. "A fine man, from whom I learned a great deal."

"Yes, dear Papa. I wish he was still alive so I could seek his advice on a problem I have."

"Perhaps I might be of assistance?"

"Oh no, I wouldn't want to impose . . ."

"My dear lady, it would be an honor to advise the daughter of James Lowell, and perhaps in some small way repay his kindness over the years. Please, join me," he said, pulling back the chair next to his.

"How kind of you," said Evelyn as she sat down.

"Jacques, a glass of champagne for the lady, and I'll have my usual." The maître d' hurried away. "Now, how can I help, Ms. Lowell?"

"Evelyn, please."

"George," he said, as he sat back and allowed Evelyn to take her time telling him everything he already knew between sips of champagne, while he enjoyed a brandy.

"Not an uncommon problem when it comes to inheritance," he said once she'd come to the end of her tale. "Especially when rival siblings are involved. It's known as the fifty-fifty dilemma."

"How interesting," she said, hanging on his every word.

"There is a simple solution, of course."

"And what might that be?"

"First, I must ask you, Evelyn, can you keep a secret?"

"Most certainly I can," she said, placing a hand on his thigh.

"Because we'll need to work closely together over the next few days, and I wouldn't want anyone, and I mean anyone, to know the source of what I'm about to divulge, even your husband."

"Then perhaps it might be wiser to go up to your room where we won't be disturbed," she said, moving her hand a little farther up his thigh.

This certainly wasn't something Bob had anticipated, but if that's what it took . . .

⤙o⤚

The last time Alex had been this nervous was on the battlefield in Vietnam. And just as then, the waiting was the worst part.

His first anxiety was that no one would turn up to hear him speak. When Nelson Mandela, George Soros, and Henry Kissinger are also on the menu, you have to accept that at best you're the dessert. However, the organizers assured him that "Russia's Role in the New World Order" was the dish of the day, and that most of the delegates had been ordering it.

When an attendant knocked on the door of the speakers' room and told him it was time to make his way backstage, Alex didn't even have the nerve to ask how the house was looking. When he could finally bear it no longer, he peeked through a gap in the curtain, to find that the organizers hadn't exaggerated. The hall was so packed that some of the delegates were sitting in the aisles.

Klaus Schwab rose to introduce him, and opened his remarks by telling the delegates that Alex Karpenko had been among the leading investment bankers in the burgeoning Russian republic for the past decade, closing deals that had stunned his more cautious rivals who'd been left in his wake. Lowell's had brought a new meaning to the words "risk reward ratio," having secured at least one deal that had made a thousand percent profit in its first year, while at the same time raising the wages of every one of the company's workers.

"In the days of the gold rush," said Schwab, "you needed to climb on the bandwagon and head west. In today's Russia, it's a private jet, and you have to head east."

Alex was relieved that Schwab didn't also mention that he had once escaped from Saint Petersburg in an ambulance, but not before his wallet had been emptied by a rent boy and an off-duty paramedic.

The applause was friendly when he emerged from behind the curtain to take Schwab's place at the podium. The kind of reception that hints, we'll wait and see how the speech goes before we pass judgment.

Alex looked down at row upon row of expectant faces and made them wait for a moment before delivering his opening line.

"Whenever I address my local Lions club, a student forum, or even a business conference, I'm usually fairly confident that I'll be better informed than anyone else in the room. I accepted this invitation without realizing that everyone else in the room would be far better informed than me."

The laughter that followed allowed him to relax a little.

"Lowell's Bank has been working in Russia with the local people for the past ten years, and Mr. Schwab kindly described us as one of the leaders in the field. The same bank has been doing business in Boston for over a century, and we are still thought of as upstarts. However, in the context of Russian investment banking, we are regarded as part of the establishment after only a decade. How can that be possible?

"Less than fifty years ago, Stalin ruled over one of the largest empires on earth. When he died in 1953, he was mourned as a national hero and statues of him were erected in even the smallest of towns. The people referred to him affectionately as Uncle Joe, and around the world his name was mentioned in the same breath as those of Roosevelt and Churchill. But today you will be hard-pressed to find a statue of Stalin anywhere in the former Soviet Union, other than in his hometown.

"After Stalin, there followed a series of unelected despots who had sheltered in his shadow for years: Khrushchev, Kosygin, Brezhnev, Andropov, and Chernenko, all of whom clung on to power until they died or were forcibly removed from office. And then suddenly, almost without warning, that all changed overnight when Mikhail Gorbachev appeared on the scene and announced the birth of glasnost. A simple translation being, the policy or practice of more open consultative government and a wider dissemination of information.

"From March 1990, when Gorbachev became the first elected president of the Soviet Union, the country began to change rapidly, and for the first time entrepreneurs were able to operate without the restrictions of a centralized command economy.

"However, the people who oversaw this transformation were the same gang of thugs who'd run the old regime. How would you feel if the leader of the Communist Party in America was handed the keys to Fort Knox? And this despite the fact that the Soviet Union had one of the finest educational systems in the world, that is, if you wanted to be a philosopher, or a poet, but not if you wanted to be a businessman. In those days you had a better chance of studying Sanskrit at Moscow University than of finding your way around a balance sheet.

"Russia has twenty-four percent of the world's gas reserves, twelve percent of its oil, and more timber than any other nation on earth. But while the average worker may no longer consider himself a comrade, he is still earning less than the equivalent of fifteen dollars a week, and few people are paid more than fifty thousand a year. Less than my secretary. So the transition from Communism to capitalism was never going to be easy.

"We are all aware that first impressions tend to linger, so I should not have been surprised when, after I had been back in my homeland for only a few hours, some of Russia's problems were brought home to me. I was standing on a street corner trying to get a taxi, and I couldn't help noticing that while there was no shortage of BMWs, Mercedes, and Jaguars, there was almost no sign of a Ford Fiesta or a VW Polo. The disparity between rich and poor is starker in Russia than in any other nation on earth. Two percent of Russians own ninety-eight percent of the national wealth, so who can blame ordinary citizens for rejecting capitalism and wanting to return to what they now regard as the good old days of Communism? If Western values are to prevail, what Russia most needs is a middle class who, through hard work and diligence, can benefit from their country's staggering wealth and natural resources.

"This doesn't mean that there aren't great opportunities to do business in Russia. Of course there are. However, if you're thinking of going east, young man, be warned—it's not for the faint-hearted.

"Mr. Schwab told you that Lowell's had closed a deal that made my bank a thousand percent profit in a year. But what he didn't tell you was that we also signed three other contracts where we lost every penny of our investment, and in one case even before the ink was dry on the paper. So the golden rule for any company considering opening a branch in Russia is to choose your partner wisely. When there's the potential for a thousand percent profit in a year, the stupid, the greedy, and the downright dishonest will appear like cockroaches from under the floorboards. And should your partner breach a contract, don't bother to sue, because the judge will almost certainly be on their payroll.

"Could this all change for the better? Yes. In the year 2000, the Russian people will go to the polls to choose a new president. We can safely assume they won't reelect Boris Yeltsin, who by now would have been impeached in Washington and banished to the Tower in London."

Laughter followed, humor often emphasizing the truth. Alex turned a page.

"The Communist Party, which appeared to be dead and buried a decade ago, has once again raised its head, and is now comfortably ahead in the polls. But if a candidate were to run for president whose first interest was in democracy, and not in lining their own pockets, who knows what could be achieved?

"You see before you a Russian who escaped to America some thirty years ago, but who in recent years has regularly returned to his homeland, because Lowell's Bank takes the long view. I hope that in a hundred years' time, America will still be Russia's greatest rival. Not on the battlefield, but in the boardroom. Not in the nuclear arms race, but in the race to cure disease. Not on the streets, but in the classrooms. But that can only be achieved if every Russian vote is of equal weight."

A long round of applause followed, as Alex turned another page.

"Two hundred years ago, America was at war with Britain. In the past century, the two nations have twice united to fight a common enemy. Why shouldn't America and Russia have a similar aim?" Alex lowered his voice almost to a whisper. "I hope there are those among you who will join me, and try to make that ideal possible by building bridges and not destroying them, and by believing, as any civilized society should, that all men and women are born equal, whatever country they are born in. I can only hope that the next generation of Russians will, like the next generation of Americans, take that for granted."

An audience that had decided to wait and hear Alex's words before they passed judgment rose as one, and caused him to wonder, not for the first time, if he should have taken Lawrence's place not in the boardroom, but in the political arena.

"You were magnificent, my darling," said Anna when he walked off the stage. "But I don't remember those last couple of paragraphs when you were rehearsing your speech in the bathroom this morning."

Alex didn't comment. And it didn't help, during the next couple of days that whenever he was stopped in the conference hall, in his hotel, in the street, and even at the airport, that delegates suggested, "Perhaps you are the man who should be standing for president in your country?" And they didn't mean America.

"You did what?" said Doug Ackroyd.

"I sold one percent of my shares in Lowell's for twenty million dollars," said Evelyn proudly.

"Why would you do something as stupid as that?"

"Because by letting go of one percent for twenty million, I established that the true value of my fifty percent was a billion dollars."

"While at the same time you handed over control of the bank to Karpenko," said Ackroyd, spitting out the words. "They now have fifty-one percent of the company, while you only have forty-nine."

"No," protested Evelyn, "I didn't sell my one percent to the bank."

"Then to whom, dare I ask?"

"To George Soros, who I'm sure you'll agree knows a damn sight more about banking and investments than either of us."

"Indeed he does," said Ackroyd. "But how, may I ask, did you happen to bump into the great man?"

"I met him two weeks ago in Monte Carlo. A happy coincidence, don't you think?"

"No, I do not think it was a happy coincidence, Evelyn. It was a well-planned set-up, and you fell for it."

"How can you say that?"

"Because two weeks ago George Soros was in Davos, giving a lecture on the Exchange Rate Mechanism. I know, because I was sitting in the audience."

Evelyn's legs gave way and she collapsed into the nearest chair. She was silent for some time before saying, "So what do I do now?"

"Accept the bank's offer of six hundred million dollars before they change their mind."

"Mrs. Lowell-Halliday has accepted the bank's offer of six hundred million dollars for her shares," said the company secretary. "But I'll need the board's approval before I can sign off on it."

"But that was when she owned fifty percent of the bank's stock," said Jake. "Thanks to Bob's brilliant coup, she now only has forty-nine percent, and we're in control."

"Offer her three hundred million," said Alex, "and settle for four."

"Do you think she'll agree to that?" asked Mitch Blake.

"Without a doubt," said Alex. "Ackroyd will advise her that she won't get a better offer anywhere else, and if she agrees, the good news is that the bank will end up not having to pay her a penny."

"How come?" said Alan Gates.

"Simple really, but perhaps the time has come for Jake to tell the board a little more about the ace that we've always had up our sleeve."

Jake opened a file and turned several pages before he came to the signed agreement. "Mrs. Lowell-Halliday took out several loans over the years when her brother, Lawrence, was chairman of the bank. Ackroyd, as CEO, approved the transactions, and in order to give the deal some legitimacy, Evelyn agreed to pay an interest rate of five percent per annum until the loans were repaid. Unfortunately for her, but fortunately for the bank, she hasn't returned one red cent, but then, she never intended to." Jake turned a page before he continued. "The result is that after more than twenty years of debt and accumulated interest, she currently owes the bank just over four hundred and fifty-one million dollars." Jake closed the file. A long silence was followed by a round of applause.

"But she will still owe the bank over fifty million," said Bob, "even if she accepts the offer."

"Which we will agree to write off in exchange for her forty-nine percent shareholding in the bank," said Jake.

"Bravo," said Alex, before looking around the boardroom table. "However, I still can't wait to hear the details of how Bob managed to make it all possible?"

The rest of the directors turned their attention to the longest-serving member of the board, who no longer had a shock of white hair.

"A gentleman should never be indiscreet where a lady is concerned," said Bob, "but I can report to the board that Mrs. Evelyn Lowell-Halliday doesn't know the difference between being laid and being screwed. By the way, chairman, can I now resign?"

44

SASHA

London, 1999

"Does the right honorable gentleman plan to visit his other constituency in the near future?"

Sasha smiled, while some laughed at the gibe, but then he had his answer well prepared.

"I can tell the right honorable member that I have no plans to visit Russia in the near future. But I am looking forward to seeing the opening night of *Swan Lake* at the Royal Opera House, danced by the Bolshoi Ballet." He was about to add, the greatest ballet company on earth, but thought better of it.

"Mr. Kenneth Clarke," said the Speaker.

"When the right honorable gentleman does next visit Moscow, could he point out to President Yeltsin that for a nation now posturing as a democracy, his country's human rights record leaves much to be desired."

This time the hear, hears were loud, and not in jest.

Sasha rose again. "If the right honorable gentleman would be kind enough to bring to my attention any particular examples he has in mind, be assured I will look into them. However, members of the House may be interested to know that Mr. Boris Nemtsov, a former vice premier of Russia, is sitting in the Distinguished Strangers' Gallery, and I'm sure he will have heard the honorable gentleman's question."

Sasha glanced up at the gallery and smiled at his friend, who seemed amused by his moment of notoriety.

When questions to the Foreign Secretary came to an end and the Speaker called for the business of the day, Sasha quickly left the chamber and made his way to the Central Lobby, where he had arranged to meet up with Nemtsov.

"Welcome to Westminster, Boris," he said as he shook his guest warmly by the hand.

"Thank you," said Nemtsov. "I was delighted to see you more than holding your own against the rabble. Although I have to agree that our record on human rights does not bear close scrutiny, and it will give me a great deal of pleasure to tell my colleagues back home that I heard the subject raised in the British House of Commons."

"Do you have time to join me for tea on the terrace?" asked Sasha, reverting to his native tongue.

"I've been looking forward to it all day," said Nemtsov. Sasha led his guest down the green-carpeted staircase and out onto the terrace, where they sat at a table overlooking the Thames.

"So what brings you to London," asked Sasha as a waiter appeared by their side. "Just tea for two, thank you."

"Officially I'm here to visit the Lord Mayor of London to discuss environmental issues affecting overpopulated cities, but my main purpose is to see you, and bring you up to date on what's happening on the political front back home."

Sasha sat back and listened attentively.

"As you know, the presidential election is due to be held in a year's time."

"Not long before the next general election in Britain," said Sasha.

The waiter returned and placed a tray of tea and biscuits on the table.

"Yeltsin has already announced that he won't be fighting the next election, possibly influenced by his current approval rating, which, according to the opinion polls, is languishing around four percent."

"That's quite difficult to achieve," said Sasha, pouring them both a cup of tea.

"Not if you wake up every morning with a hangover, and are drunk again before lunchtime."

"Does Yeltsin have an anointed successor?"

"Not that I'm aware of. But even if he did, it would be the kiss of death. No, the only name in the field at the moment is Gennady Zyuganov, the Communist Party leader, and most people accept that it would be a disaster if we were to return to the past, although the possibility can't be dismissed. Frankly, Sasha, you may never get a better chance to become our next president."

"But perhaps my approval ratings would also be around four percent."

"I'm glad you raised that," said Nemtsov, taking a slip of paper from an inside pocket, "because we've conducted some private polling, which showed you are currently on fourteen percent. However, twenty-six percent didn't even recognize your name, and thirty-one percent haven't made up their minds yet. So we were encouraged. If you were to come to Saint Petersburg and officially announce your intention to stand, I have no doubt those figures would change overnight."

"I admit I'm torn," said Sasha. "Only last week *The Times* said in a leader that if Labour were to win the next election, which looks highly likely, I could well be the next Foreign Secretary."

"And after hearing your performance in the House this afternoon, and your grasp of so many subjects, frankly I'm not surprised. However, I would suggest that president of Russia is a far bigger prize for someone who was born and raised in Saint Petersburg."

"I agree with you," whispered Sasha, "but I can't afford to let my colleagues know that. Besides, I'd need to be convinced that I have a realistic chance of success before I'd be willing to give up everything I've worked so hard for."

"That's understandable," said Nemtsov, "but we won't really be able to evaluate your chances until we know who your main rival is."

"But you were the vice premier," said Sasha, "why don't you stand?"

"Because my poll ratings aren't much better than Yeltsin's. However, with my backing, I'm convinced you can win."

"It's good of you to say so. But Vladimir could still prove a problem. After all, he was deputy mayor of Saint Petersburg, and won't like the idea of me standing for president."

"You needn't worry about Vladimir. He left Saint Petersburg only minutes before he would have been arrested for embezzlement of public funds. He disappeared off to Moscow and was last sighted in the Kremlin."

"Doing what?"

"Rumor has it that he's working closely with Yeltsin, but no one's quite sure in what capacity."

"Vladimir's only interested in one thing, and that's becoming director of the FSB."

"Who did they think they were kidding when they abolished the KGB and it reemerged later as the Federal Security Service? The same bunch of thugs doing the same job, even in the same building," Nemtsov mused. "But if Vladimir was to pull that off, you would be wise not to make an enemy of him. In fact if he was on your side, it might even help your cause."

"But if he was on my side," said Sasha, "it could only harm my cause. I couldn't hope to achieve anything worthwhile with him continually looking over my shoulder. In fact the very changes I would want to make as president, he would be vehemently opposed to."

"But in politics," said Nemtsov, "you occasionally have to compromise—"

"Compromise is for those who have no courage, no morals, and no principles."

"You don't have to convince me, Sasha, that you're the right man for the job, but first we have to get you elected."

"I'm sorry to be so negative, but I wouldn't want to become president only to find that someone else was pulling the strings."

"I understand. But once you get the job you can cut those strings. Remember, there is no power without office."

"Of course you're right," said Sasha. "And I'll let you know as soon as I've made my decision."

"Do you have any idea when that might be?"

"It won't be much longer, Boris. But there are one or two people I still have to consult before I can make a final decision."

"Surely your mother must be pressing you to stand? After all, your father certainly would have wanted you to be president."

"She's the only one in the family who's one hundred percent against the idea," said Sasha. "She's a great believer in a 'bird in the hand' . . ."

"I don't know the expression," said Nemtsov. "And what about your wife?"

"Charlie's sitting on the fence."

"Now that's an expression every politician in the world is familiar with."

Sasha laughed. "But she would back me if she felt I really wanted the job, and believed I could win."

"What about your daughter?"

"Natasha's only interest at the moment is someone called Brad Pitt."

"An aspiring politician?"

"No, an American actor who Natasha is convinced would fall in love with her, if only they could meet. And she doesn't understand why a foreign office minister can't arrange it. *Just how important are you, Dad?* she keeps asking."

Nemtsov laughed. "It's no different in our home. My son wants to be a drummer in a local jazz band, and has absolutely no interest in going to university."

Big Ben struck four times in the background.

"I'd better get back and join my colleagues," said Nemtsov, "before they work out why I really came to London."

"Thank you for giving me so much of your time, Boris, and your continued support," said Sasha, as they walked back up to the Central Lobby together.

"Every time I see you, Sasha, I become more convinced that you're the right man to be our next president."

"I'm grateful for your backing, and I'll let you know the moment I've made up my mind."

"If you were to return to Saint Petersburg," said Boris, "you might be surprised by the welcome you would receive."

"I'm glad I don't have to make the decision," said Charlie.

"But you do, my darling," said Sasha. "Because I wouldn't even consider taking on such a risky enterprise without your blessing."

"Have you taken into consideration how much you have to lose?"

"Of course I have. And as Labour look almost certain to win the next election, it would be easy for me to just sit back and hope I become Foreign Secretary. The far bigger risk would be to resign from the Commons, return to Russia, and spend a year campaigning to become president, only to see someone else snatch the prize."

"Especially if that someone else turned out to be your old friend Vladimir."

"As long as he's Yeltsin's bag carrier, he's more likely to end up in prison than the Kremlin."

"Then let me ask you a simple question," said Charlie. "If I were to offer you both of those positions on a plate, president of Russia or British Foreign Secretary, which one would you choose?"

"President of Russia," said Sasha without hesitation.

"Then you have your answer," said Charlie, "and mine. Otherwise you'll spend the rest of your life wondering, 'What if?'"

"Do you think there's anyone else I should consult before making such an irrevocable decision?"

Charlie thought long and hard before she said, "No point in asking your mother, because we both know exactly where she stands. Or your daughter, who is otherwise preoccupied. But I'd be fascinated to hear Alf Rycroft's opinion. He's a shrewd old buzzard, who's known you for over twenty years, and he has that rare ability to think outside the box. And probably even more important, he'll only have your best interests at heart."

⊸o⊷

"And to what do I owe this great honor, minister?" asked Alf, as he accompanied Sasha through to the sitting room.

"I need your advice, Alf."

"Then have a seat. We're unlikely to be disturbed, as my wife, Millicent, is out doing good works. I think it's her day at the hospital as library monitor."

"She's a saint."

"As is Charlie. Truth is, we both got lucky in the lottery of marriage. So how can I help you, young man?"

"I'm forty-six," said Sasha. "You used to call me young man when I first came to the constituency over twenty years ago. Now, nobody does."

"Wait till you reach my age," said Alf, "you'll be only too grateful if anyone calls you young man. Now, when you called to say you wanted to discuss a private matter, it wasn't difficult to work out what was troubling you."

"And what conclusion did you come to?"

"Naturally I'd like you to become Foreign Secretary, then I could spend the rest of my days telling the lads at the bowls club that I was the first to spot your potential."

"No more than the truth," said Sasha.

"I knew you were a bit special the day we interviewed you for Merrifield. So what I'm about to say, Sasha, may come as a bit of a surprise. I think you should resign from the Commons, return to Russia, and, if it's not too dramatic a statement, fulfill your destiny."

"But that would mean risking everything, when there's an easy option still open to me."

"Agreed, but then it's never been your style to take the easy option. When you had the opportunity to represent a safe London seat, you chose instead to return to Merrifield and fight a marginal."

"There's a lot more at stake this time," said Sasha.

"As there was for Winston Churchill, when he crossed the floor of the House to join the Conservatives, because he certainly would never have become Prime Minister if he'd remained on the Liberal benches."

"But I've spent the last thirty years in this country," said Sasha. "So compared to crossing the floor of the House, it would be some walk to Moscow."

"Lenin didn't think so, and don't forget he was stuck in Switzerland when the Revolution began."

"Can't you think of a better example?" said Sasha, laughing.

"Gandhi was a practicing lawyer in South Africa when he sensed revolution in the air and returned to India to become its spiritual leader. So my advice, Sasha, is to go back home, because your people will see in you what I spotted over twenty years ago, a decent, honest man, with unwavering convictions. And they will embrace those convictions with relief and enthusiasm. But my opinion is no more than the ramblings of an old man."

"Made all the more powerful," said Sasha, "because it wasn't what I expected."

⤙○⤚

Sasha always enjoyed his visits to the Russian Embassy, not least because no one threw a better party than their ambassador, Yuri Fokin. Gone were the days when the building was surrounded by impenetrable barriers, and few people knew what went on behind its closed doors.

Sasha could remember when, if you asked a Russian diplomat what the time was, he would tell you the time in Moscow. Now, the ambassador would happily answer any question you put to him. All you had to decide was when he was telling the truth.

On this occasion, however, Sasha wasn't visiting the embassy to enjoy a relaxed and convivial evening. This would be his last opportunity to gauge his chances should he decide to stand for the presidency. Among the guests would be half a dozen Russians who could influence his decision one way or the other, and he needed to make sure he spoke to every one of them. The other guests would be the usual mixture of politicians, businessmen, and hangers-on, who would attend any party as long as the drinks were flowing and there were enough canapés to ensure they didn't need to go to dinner afterward.

Sasha's driver took a right off Kensington High Street, and came to a halt in front of a barrier that led into Kensington Palace Gardens, more commonly known as Embassy Row. A long straight road lined with elegant town houses that rarely came on the market.

A guard saluted, and the barrier was raised the moment he saw the minister's car. They passed India, Nepal, and France before they reached Russia. A valet rushed forward to open the back door of the limousine. The minister stepped out, thanked him, and made his way into the embassy.

The embassy could have been an English country house at the turn of the century, with its oak-paneled entrance hall, grandfather clock, and portraits of historical figures. It always amused Sasha that there was no sign of a tsar, or even Lenin or Stalin. History seemed to have begun, for one of the oldest empires on earth, in 1991.

When Sasha walked into the drawing room, he noticed that some of the guests broke off their conversations, and turned to look at him; something he still hadn't got used to and wondered if he ever would.

He looked around the packed room, and soon identified four of his targets. One of them, Anatoly Savnikov—diplomatic attaché his official title, head of the Russian secret services in London his real job—was chatting to Fiona. If this hadn't been the Russian Embassy, Sasha might have thought he was chatting her up. No doubt there were a dozen other spies in the room who would be far more difficult to identify. The Foreign Office rule was simple enough: assume everyone is a spy.

As Sasha turned, he noticed the ambassador was deep in conversation with Charles Moore, editor of the *Daily Telegraph*. Sasha would have to bide his time before he had a few words with Yuri, words that had already been carefully scripted.

He made his way across to Leonid Bubka, the trade minister, hoping he might show his hand, but Bubka changed the subject every time the word "election" came up in conversation. Sasha didn't give up easily, but

Bubka continued to block every attempt to score with the skill of Lev Yashin. When his old friend Ilya Resinev, the second secretary at the embassy, touched his elbow, Sasha moved discreetly to one side and listened intently to what he had to say.

"Have you heard who's been appointed director of the FSB?" whispered Ilya.

"Don't tell me Vladimir finally made it?"

"I'm afraid so," said Ilya.

"The old KGB by any other name," said Sasha, "being run by the same bunch of thugs, dressed in suits instead of uniforms. Who did he have to blackmail this time?"

"Yeltsin, it seems," said Ilya. "Vladimir promised him that no matter who succeeded him as president after the next election, he would make sure that he and his family wouldn't face any charges of corruption or fraud."

"Then the first thing I'd do as president," said Sasha, "would be to sack Vladimir and make it clear that no one who's committed a serious crime against the state will be granted immunity."

"If you do that, Sasha, you're going to have to build a lot more prisons."

"So be it."

"But be careful who you say that to, because his deputy is here tonight."

"Which one?"

"The tall, heavyset man talking to Fiona Hunter."

Sasha glanced over Ilya's shoulder to see a man handing Fiona his card. Someone he would be avoiding. As he turned back, he noticed the ambassador was standing alone by the mantelpiece, lighting a cigar.

"Forgive me, Ilya. I need to have a private word with your boss. But thank you for the information, most valuable." Sasha moved swiftly across the room.

"Good evening, Yuri," he said. "Another memorable party." Sasha positioned himself with his back to the wall to make sure the ambassador had to turn away from his guests, so that only the most determined, or tactless, would consider interrupting them.

"I spotted you at the Bolshoi last week," said the ambassador. "Still one of our finest exports."

"Gudanov was magnificent," said Sasha.

"We've got a problem with him that I may need to discuss with you, but now is not the time. What I would like to know, Sasha, is have you made a decision yet?"

"Before I answer that question, Yuri, I'd be fascinated to hear what you think of my chances."

"As you well know, minister, I am not allowed to express an opinion. I'm but a humble mouthpiece for the government I serve. But," said Yuri, switching languages, "if I were a betting man, which of course I'm not, I would place a small wager on you being my boss by this time next year."

"Only a small wager?"

"Ambassadors always have to hedge their bets," said Yuri, without even the suggestion of a smile.

Sasha laughed, and wondered how many other politicians he'd delivered those same words to in the past six months.

"And could I make a small request," said Yuri. "It would be helpful if I could be briefed before you make any official announcement."

"If I do decide to stand, I'll make sure you see any statement long before I release it to the press."

"Thank you," said Yuri. "There's one more thing I need to ask you before—"

"Ambassador, what a fantastic party," said a man who seemed not to have noticed they were deep in conversation and might not have wanted to be interrupted.

"Thank you, Piers," said the ambassador. "It was good of you to come." The moment had passed, and Sasha slipped away, as the editor of the *Daily Mirror* wasn't one of the four people he needed to speak to. He began to make his way slowly toward the exit, stopping to exchange a few words with several other guests, paying particular attention to those who spoke to him in Russian, as his constituency boundaries might be about to change. As he glanced back into the drawing room, he saw the man he had avoided staring at him.

The clock in the hall chimed once, reminding Sasha he had a vote in the Commons in thirty minutes' time. Within moments the party would be denuded of politicians of every color as they made their way back to the House for a three-line whip, not that Sasha had any idea which bill they would be voting on.

As he stepped out of the front entrance of the embassy, his car appeared from nowhere, and Arthur leaped out to open the back door.

Sasha was just about to get in, when a voice he recognized called out his name.

"Sasha!" He turned to see Fiona running down the steps. "Can I cadge a lift?"

"Of course," said Sasha, standing aside to allow his old nemesis to join him in the back seat.

"Good evening, Arthur."

"Good evening, Miss Hunter."

"I would have liked to stay a bit longer," Fiona said as the car moved off, "but the chief wouldn't appreciate it if I missed a three-liner. But more important, Sasha, when are you going to answer the only question that was on everybody's lips at the party?"

"And what were they saying about my chances?" asked Sasha, falling back on the old political trick of answering a question with a question, although he knew Fiona wouldn't be fooled.

"Everyone who spoke English was in favor of your standing, as were half of the Russians, although one of them," she said, taking a card out of her bag, "Ivan Donokov, is certainly no friend of yours. He asked me the strangest question: Had you ever lived in America?" Sasha looked puzzled. "I told him not that I was aware of. I then pressed him on what he thought of your chances should you throw your hat in the ring."

"And how did he respond?"

"He acknowledged you were probably the front-runner, but said there was a dark horse coming up on the rails."

"Did he name the horse?" asked Sasha, trying not to sound anxious.

"He thought that an old friend of yours called Vladimir—"

"He's no friend of mine," said Sasha. "In any case, that man's only interest was becoming head of the FSB, and now he's achieved that, he won't be looking further afield, just making sure he clings on to his job."

"That wasn't Donokov's opinion. In fact he was fairly sure Vladimir was also gazing across Red Square, his eyes now fixed on the Kremlin."

"But that's not realistic."

"Why not, if he's got Yeltsin backing him?"

"But why would Yeltsin even consider backing such a flawed individual?"

"It seems Yeltsin's daughter and son-in-law were about to be arrested and charged with fraud, and Vladimir somehow managed to make the problem disappear. I'm told the video of a call girl caught performing her particular special services on the desk of the prosecutor general's office is well worth watching."

"But that's no reason to back someone for president who's totally unsuitable for the job."

"How would you feel, Sasha, if you were president and your daughter was likely to end up in prison for several years?"

"I'd allow the law to take its course."

"I do believe you would," said Fiona, "which only proves how lucky they'd be to get you. But are you also willing to sacrifice the Foreign Office, when you could end up with nothing?"

"Did Donokov let you know where he stood?" asked Sasha, once again not answering her question.

"No. But surely if he's the deputy director of the FSB, he'll be backing his boss."

"It doesn't always work that way in Russia. So did he offer an opinion on my chances?" repeated Sasha, still gnawing at the same bone.

"No, but he did say that if you don't stand, he wasn't in any doubt who would be the next president."

"I can't think of a better reason to stand," said Sasha, lowering his guard. He'd never thought for one moment that Vladimir could be a serious candidate, but accepted that if he did stand, it would be a no-holds-barred contest, because wrestling was the one sport Vladimir had excelled in.

"If you do decide to stand," said Fiona, interrupting his reverie, "I can only hope you win. You'd be sorely missed in the House, and would have made a damned good Foreign Secretary. But Russia is a far greater challenge. And if you were to become president, relations with the West would improve overnight, which can only be good for everyone concerned, including the Russian people."

"That's kind of you to say so, Fiona. And now that I know who I'm likely to be up against, I could do with one or two of your particular political skills."

"I'll take that as a compliment," said Fiona, as the car swept through the members' entrance and into Old Palace Yard. As Sasha climbed out of the car, the division bell began to ring, so they parted and went their separate ways.

Ironic, thought Sasha as he entered the "Ayes" lobby, that it wasn't what he'd gleaned at the embassy party that had helped him to finally make up his mind, but a piece of information picked up in the back of a car from the most unlikely source.

⊸o⊷

When Sasha told Elena that he would be returning to their homeland to run for president, it was as if she hadn't heard a word he'd said.

"Of course, Mama, I'd understand if you felt you didn't want to come with me."

"I will be going with you," she said quietly.

Sasha was at first surprised, then delighted, and finally sad when she told him the reason for her change of heart. "I'm so sorry," he said, embracing his mother. "Uncle Kolya was such a fine man, and we both owe him so much."

"The family have asked me if you would be kind enough to deliver one of the tributes at his funeral."

"Of course I will. Please tell them I'd be honored."

"His wife told me Kolya's last words," said Elena. "'Tell Sasha, if he's the son of his father, he'll make a great president.'"

⊸o⊷

Sasha issued a brief press statement to the lobby journalists at ten o'clock the following morning.

> The Rt Hon. Sasha Karpenko resigned this morning as Minister of State at the Foreign Office. He will also step down as the Member of Parliament for Merrifield with immediate effect, as he intends to return to his homeland of Russia and stand for president in the forthcoming election.

The Prime Minister, speaking from Downing Street, responded. "The government has lost a quite outstanding minister and a formidable parliamentarian. I hope and believe that those same skills will be put to good use when he returns to the country of his birth. And should he be elected to the high office to which he aspires, we can all look forward to a positive new era of Anglo-Russian relations."

Lord Cohen was among the first to call. "If you're looking for a campaign manager, Sasha, I'm still available."

"I won't get a better one, Ben, that's for sure."

The former Deputy Prime Minister of Russia called the following morning while he was shaving.

"I couldn't be more delighted by the news," said Nemtsov. "The media have gone into meltdown, and the first poll published in the morning papers has you on twenty-nine percent."

"And how's Vladimir faring?" asked Sasha.

"Two percent, and he was on four percent only a week ago."

Perhaps the biggest shock for Sasha was how many heads of state and Prime Ministers called from all around the world during the next forty-eight hours to say, in less than coded language, *I only wish I had a vote.*

The night before Sasha was due to fly to Saint Petersburg, the Russian ambassador called.

"Sasha, I've been trying to get in touch with you for the past couple of days, but your phone's constantly engaged. Have I missed something?" Sasha laughed. "My masters have instructed me to make sure that your journey back to Saint Petersburg is as smooth as possible. We'll lay on a car to take you and your family to the airport, and I've instructed Aeroflot that the first-class cabin should be cordoned off from the rest of the passengers so you won't be disturbed."

"Thank you, Yuri, that's most considerate, as I'll have two important speeches to work on."

"So do you want to hear the good news first, or the bad news?"

"The good news," said Sasha, playing along.

"Over fifty percent of Russian women think you're better-looking than George Clooney."

Sasha laughed. "And the bad news?"

"You're not going to be pleased to learn who Yeltsin has appointed as his new Prime Minister."

BOOK SIX

45

ALEX AND SASHA

En route to Amsterdam, 1999

Alex picked up the phone on his desk.

"There's someone on the line called Dimitri," said Miss Robbins. "He says he's an old friend, and that he wouldn't bother you if it wasn't urgent."

"He goes back even further than you, Pamela, and is indeed an old friend. Put him through."

"Is that you, Alex?"

"Dimitri, it's good to hear from you after all this time. Are you calling from New York?"

"No, Saint Petersburg. I thought you'd want to know the sad news that your uncle Kolya has died." Alex was speechless. He felt guilty that he hadn't been able to see his uncle when he'd last visited Saint Petersburg. "I would have called Elena, and not bothered you," continued Dimitri, "but I didn't know how to get in touch with her at work."

"You can bother me whenever you want to, Dimitri. I'll let my mother know, because she'll want to go to the funeral. Do you know when it is?"

"Next Friday, at the Church of the Apostle Andrew. I know it's short notice, but if you were able to come, the family are hoping that you might deliver one of the tributes."

"It isn't short notice for someone who saved my life," said Alex. "Tell them I'll be honored."

"The family will be so pleased. You're a bit of a hero in this city, so be prepared for quite a homecoming."

"Thank you, Dimitri. I look forward to seeing you."

Alex put the phone down and pressed the button under his desk. Miss ɔbbins appeared moments later, pad in hand, biro poised. "Clear the diary. I'm going to Saint Petersburg."

⊸o⊷

"It's at times like this," said Charlie with an exaggerated sigh, "that I wish you had a private jet, so we didn't have to bother with endless queues and hold-ups."

"Would you please open your bag, madam?"

"Were you put through all this hassle when you were a minister, Dad?" asked Natasha as she unzipped her bag.

"No, but then it's always in the back of your mind that you'll only be in government for a limited period. Margaret Thatcher once said, only the Queen can afford to get used to it."

"But if you became president . . ."

"Even that has a statutory limit of eight years," said Sasha as he retrieved his bag. "The Duma recently decreed that a president can only serve two consecutive four-year terms, and who can blame the Russians after suffering centuries of dictatorship. Besides, frankly, eight years is more than enough for any sane person."

"Grandma's looking a bit down," whispered Natasha, as they strolled through duty-free. "I didn't realize she's never been on a plane before."

Sasha turned around and his mother gave him a weak smile. "I don't think that's the real reason she's so nervous," he said. "Don't forget, she hasn't been back to Russia for more than thirty years, and it was her brother who made it possible for us to escape and begin a new life in England."

"Do you sometimes wish you'd got into the other crate, Dad," asked Natasha, "and ended up living in America?"

"Certainly not," said Sasha, placing an arm around her shoulders. "If that had happened, I wouldn't have had you to brighten up my life. Although I have to admit, it has crossed my mind from time to time."

"You might have been a congressman by now. Even a senator."

"Or perhaps my life would have gone in a totally different direction and I wouldn't even have been involved in politics. Who knows?"

"You might have ended up with that private jet Mum so yearns for."

"I'm not complaining," said Charlie, linking her arm in Sasha's. "By selecting that crate he also changed my whole life."

"Will all passengers traveling on BA flight 017 to Amsterdam please make their way to gate number fourteen, where boarding is about to commence."

⤙o⤚

Anna looked out of the little cabin window to see Alex striding across the tarmac, the inevitable phone nestled on his shoulder as if it were a third arm.

"Sorry, sorry," he said as he entered the cabin. "I sometimes wish the cell phone had never been invented."

"But not that often," said Anna as he took his seat next to her. No sooner had he fastened his seatbelt than the heavy door was closed and a few moments later the plane began to taxi toward the south runway, exclusively reserved for private aircraft.

"Your mother's hardly spoken since she got on the plane," whispered Anna.

Alex looked back to see Elena sitting next to Konstantin, who was holding her hand. She gave him a weak smile as the Gulfstream jet began to accelerate down the runway.

"Don't forget my uncle was her only sibling, and she would have gone back to see him a long time ago if it hadn't been for the thought of Major Polyakov standing on the tarmac waiting to welcome her."

"But she must be excited about returning to Russia after so many years?"

"And apprehensive at the same time, I expect. She's probably torn between fear and excitement, a toxic combination."

"How different your life would have been if Polyakov had gone to the football match that afternoon," said Anna, "and you'd decided to stay in Saint Petersburg."

"All of us can point to a moment in our lives when something happens that causes us to go in a totally different direction. It can be as simple as that time you stepped onto a train and decided to sit next to me."

"Actually, it was you who stepped onto the train and decided to sit next to me," said Anna as the plane took off.

"Or choosing which crate to get into," said Alex. "I often wonder—"

"Dad, where will we stop to refuel?" asked Konstantin.

Alex looked over his shoulder and said to his son, “Amsterdam. We’ll have a short break there before flying on to Saint Petersburg.”

⊸o⊷

“How long will we be in Amsterdam?” asked Natasha as they strolled into the transit lounge.

“A couple of hours before we have to make the connection with our Aeroflot flight.”

“Will there be enough time for us to take a taxi to the Rijksmuseum?” asked Charlie. “I’ve always wanted to see *The Night Watch*.”

“I’d rather not risk it,” said Sasha. “The mayor of Saint Petersburg told me he’s expecting a large turnout at the airport, and if we were to miss the plane . . .”

“Of course,” said Charlie, once again reminded just how nervous her husband was. “In any case, I can always visit the Hermitage while you’re electioneering, and we can do the Rijks another time.”

“On the way home, perhaps,” said Natasha, grinning.

“In eight years’ time, you mean,” said Charlie.

“I’ll tell you what I’ll do,” said Sasha. “If I become president, we’ll all go on holiday to Amsterdam, when we can do the Van Gogh museum as well as the Rijks.”

“Russian presidents don’t go on holiday,” said Elena. “Because if they did, when they returned, they’d find that someone else was sitting behind their desk, and they’d been left in the out-tray.”

Sasha laughed. “I think you’ll find that’s all changed, Mama.”

“I wouldn’t count on that, while your old friend Vladimir is still around.”

⊸o⊷

“How’s Elena feeling?” asked Anna when Alex returned to his seat.

“She wishes she’d gone back to Saint Petersburg years ago, and thanked Kolya properly for risking his life to help us escape.”

“She invited him to visit Boston several times,” Anna reminded him, “but he never took up the offer.”

“I suspect Polyakov made sure he couldn’t get a visa,” said Alex. “Elena’s always said she would happily have gone home to attend that man’s funeral.”

"After all these years, she still thinks of Saint Petersburg as home," said Anna. "Do you feel the same way?"

Alex didn't reply.

"Please fasten your seatbelts," said the captain, "we'll be landing in Amsterdam in about twenty minutes."

"What a pity we don't have enough time to visit the Rijksmuseum," said Anna as the plane began its descent through the clouds.

"The last time we did something like that," said Alex, "was after we flew back from Davos and visited the Tate."

"That was before Davos, not after," Anna reminded him. "My abiding memory of that visit is you lying in the hotel bath rehearsing your speech."

"When I dropped the script in the water and you had to retype it."

"And you fell asleep," teased Anna, "while I carried on typing."

"Seems a fair division of labor to me," said Alex.

"So what are we expected to do now, O master," said Anna as the plane touched down. "Check out the airport pizzeria and see what our competitors have to offer?"

"No, I've already discovered there's nothing to rival Elena's in Amsterdam. However, when we get off the plane there'll be a car waiting to take us to the Rijks and then on to the Van Gogh museum. But we can only spend an hour in each as we can't risk missing our take-off slot."

Anna threw her arms around him. "Thank you, darling, two of Mr. Rosenthal's must-see-before-you-die galleries."

"I wasn't planning on dying for some time," said Alex, as the plane taxied to a halt beside a waiting limousine.

⊸o⊷

Sasha and his family boarded Aeroflot flight 109 to Saint Petersburg just after midday. The captain came out of the cockpit to welcome them.

"I just wanted to say what an honor it is to have you on board, Mr. Karpenko, and I, along with my crew, would like to wish you luck at the election. I will certainly be voting for you."

"Thank you," said Sasha, as an attentive stewardess showed them to their seats and offered them all a drink. Even Elena was impressed.

The aircraft took off at 12:21, and while the rest of the family dozed, Sasha went over the speech he would deliver on arrival at the airport.

He also needed to prepare a eulogy for his uncle's funeral, but that would have to wait until they checked into their hotel.

"Let me begin by thanking you all for this overwhelming welcome . . ." Sasha leaned back in his seat and wondered what Nemtsov had meant by a large turnout. He looked back down at his notes.

"I may have been away for some time, but my heart has always . . ."

⟜○⊸

Alex and his family were driven back to the airport just after 11:30 in the morning, having visited both the Rijks and the Van Gogh museums.

"*The Night Watch* and the *Sunflowers* in under two hours," said Anna, as she began looking through all the postcards she'd bought.

Captain Fullerton had secured a take-off slot that would allow them to land in Saint Petersburg around five thirty that afternoon local time. He was relieved to see Mr. Karpenko's limousine driving through the security gate with a few minutes to spare.

Once the family were safely on board, the captain taxied slowly out to the east runway, where he came to a halt and waited for an Aeroflot flight ahead of him to depart, before air traffic control gave him clearance for take-off.

BOOK SEVEN

46

ALEXANDER

En route to Saint Petersburg

They were about a hundred kilometers from their destination when the plane began to shudder. Only a little to begin with, and then more violently. At first Alexander assumed it was no more than heavy turbulence, but when he looked out of the cabin window he could see they were losing altitude fairly rapidly. He turned to check on how the rest of his family were coping, to find they were all fast asleep, seemingly oblivious to any problem. He would have gone up front to speak to the captain, but just clung on to his armrest and prayed.

"Mayday, mayday, mayday. Alpha Foxtrot four zero nine. Number two engine failure, unable to maintain altitude, descending to three thousand meters, request radar vectors to Pulkovo."

"Roger, Alpha Foxtrot four zero nine. Make your heading three three zero degrees, the airfield is six zero kilometers ahead, runway ten left is being cleared for landing, three thousand meters available. Will you require emergency services?"

"Stand by. I am unable to maintain heading or altitude. I can see a range of hills ahead of me."

"You're just about forty-two kilometers away. You are cleared to land runway ten left. Surface wind easterly at five meters per second."

"Four zero nine, number one engine failure," said the captain, trying not to sound desperate. "Unable to reignite either engine. I am now gliding."

"You're now thirty kilometers from the field. Once you've cleared those hills, there's nothing but flat grassland ahead of you. Emergency services are on standby."

"Roger. I can see a gap in the hills. If I can't reach the runway, I'll make an emergency landing." He pressed a button to lower the landing gear, but the wheels didn't respond. He hit the button again, but they remained stubbornly in place. He flicked another switch as the plane continued to descend.

"Attention, this is the captain speaking. We are about to make an emergency landing. Fasten your seatbelts and assume the brace position now."

Alexander turned to look at his family, and felt guilty that he'd allowed his ambition to override their safety. But even he hadn't realized just how far Vladimir would go to ensure he had no serious rivals for the presidency.

The plane was now spinning out of control, down, down, down, in ever decreasing circles, until it finally smashed into the side of the hill, and burst into flames, killing the crew and all its passengers.

An elite team of Russian paratroopers were on the scene within minutes, but then they'd been on standby for several hours. Once they had located the black box, they disappeared back into the forest.

Another aircraft continued on its flight to Saint Petersburg, unaware of the tragedy.

⊸o⊷

When the plane touched down at Pulkovo airport, Alexander peered out of the cabin window to see acres of flat grassland. In the distance, tall gray concrete blocks dominated the skyline.

The plane swung around and came to a halt in front of the terminal, but it wasn't until the engines had been turned off that he heard the chanting, "Kar-pen-ko! Kar-pen-ko! Kar-pen-ko!"

He looked back at his family, and gave them a reassuring smile which Elena didn't return. The cabin door was opened, and the steps lowered into place. Alexander emerged into the pale fading sunlight. Nothing could have prepared him for what was about to happen.

He was greeted by a mass of people, stretching as far as the eye could see, all chanting, "Kar-pen-ko! Kar-pen-ko!" He instinctively raised an arm in acknowledgment, and a sea of hands waved back.

At the bottom of the steps stood a reception party, led by the mayor and his senior staff. As Alexander began to walk down the steps, the noise reached a crescendo, and he wasn't sure how to react to such unbridled enthusiasm. He looked back to see his family following him down the steps, his mother apprehensive, his wife bemused, while his only child seemed to be enjoying every moment.

As he set foot on the tarmac, a roar went up that no Russian president had ever experienced. The mayor stepped forward and shook hands warmly with the prodigal son.

"Welcome back to Saint Petersburg, Alexander. Even in our wildest dreams, we didn't anticipate this. The chief of police estimates that over a hundred thousand of your fellow countrymen have come out to welcome you back to your homeland. This show of support should leave you in no doubt how many people want you to be our next president."

"Thank you," said Alexander, unable to find the words to express how he felt at that moment.

"Perhaps you would like to say a few words to your loyal supporters," suggested the mayor. "Most of whom have been waiting for several hours."

"I wasn't prepared for such a welcome," admitted Alexander, but his words couldn't be heard above the chants of "Kar-pen-ko! Kar-pen-ko!"

The mayor led him toward a small rostrum that had been erected on the edge of the runway. Although he was surrounded by a hundred thousand people all chanting his name, Alexander had never felt more alone in his life. He had to wait several minutes before the crowd had settled enough to make it possible for him to address them, which at least allowed him a little time to gather his thoughts.

"My fellow countrymen," he began, "how do I begin to thank you for such an overwhelming welcome? A welcome that has inspired me to dream on your behalf. But for that dream to become a reality, I will need every one of you to also work on my behalf."

Once again, the chanting and cries erupted, confirming their willingness to do so. He made no attempt to continue until the crowd had fallen silent again.

"I have long believed that Russia is capable of taking its rightful place among the leading nations of the world, but to achieve this, we must finally remove the shackles of dictatorship, and ensure that the nation's great wealth is shared among the many, rather than being allowed to line the pockets of the few. Let us at last release our latent genius so the world is no longer fearful of our military might, but instead is in awe of our peacetime achievements. Why are the British described as world leaders when they are smaller than our smallest state? Because they box above their weight. Why is America always described as the leader of the free world? Because we are not free. That freedom is now within our grasp, so let us embrace it together." He raised his arms high in the air, and once again it was several minutes before he was able to continue.

As he looked down at the expectant faces gazing up at him, he tried not to let their adulation sway his judgment, although he knew that an opportunity like this might never happen again, and that he needed to take advantage of it. He leaned forward until his lips were almost touching the microphone, and there followed a stillness he realized could only last for a few moments before the spell would be broken.

"It is my father, not I, who should be standing here receiving your acclamation. He risked his life defending this city against our common enemy, for which a grateful nation awarded him the Defence of Leningrad. But now we face a more insidious enemy, who has no morals, no scruples, and whose only interest is self-interest. These were the men who murdered my father because he wanted to set up a union to protect the rights of his fellow workers. Greedy, selfish men who represent no one other than themselves."

The hush that had fallen over the crowd was almost palpable.

"My fellow countrymen, I have not returned to the land of my birth to seek revenge, but to follow in my father's footsteps. Inspired by your belief in me, my only wish is to serve you. I will therefore allow my name to go forward for the highest office in the land, and seek to become your president."

The storm of applause and cheering that followed must have been heard in the center of Saint Petersburg. But like Mark Antony, Alexander knew there was nothing more he could say, as the time had come for him to march onto the battlefield. He had sown the seeds of revolution, and would now have to wait for them to take root. As he quietly left the stage his followers continued to chant, "Kar-pen-ko! Kar-pen-ko!"

Standing alone at the back of the crowd was a smartly dressed, heavily built man who didn't join in the applause. The recently appointed head of the secret service dialed a number on his mobile phone, but had to wait for some time before he heard a voice on the other end of the line.

Donokov held his phone high in the air so his boss could better hear the acclamation of the crowd.

"I was about to issue a press release," said the Prime Minister, "expressing my deep sorrow on learning of the tragic deaths of Alexander Karpenko and his family. A heroic figure, who would surely have become our next president, and played a major role in the building of a new Russia, if I recall my exact words."

"A little premature, I would suggest," said Donokov. "But be assured, Prime Minister, it is under control. I shall not make the same mistake a second time."

"Let's hope so for your sake," said the Prime Minister as he continued to listen to the exuberant crowd in the background.

"I am confident," said Donokov, "that it shouldn't be too long before you are able to issue a more up-to-date press statement."

"That's good to hear. But I shall still wait until after I've delivered the eulogy at the funeral of my old school friend, before I announce I will be standing for president," said Vladimir Putin.

Turn the page for a sneak peek at
Jeffrey Archer's next novel

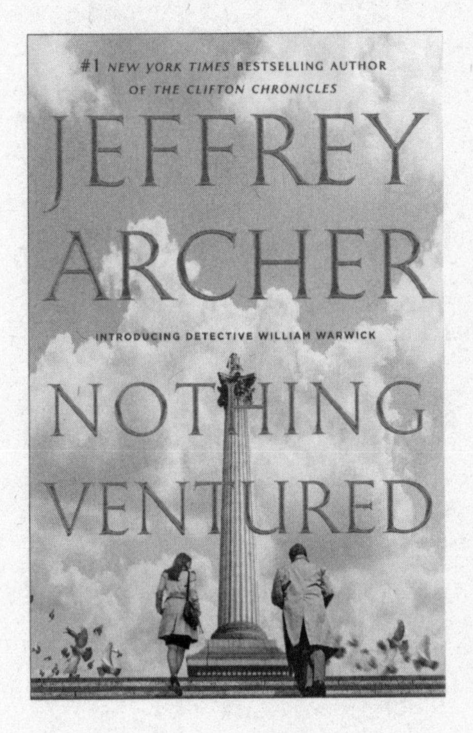

Available September 2019

Dear Reader,

After I finished writing the last of the Clifton Chronicles, several readers wrote to tell me they'd like to know more about William Warwick, the eponymous hero of Harry Clifton's novels.

I confess that I had already given the idea some thought before I began working on *Nothing Ventured,* the first in the William Warwick series.

Nothing Ventured opens when William leaves school and, much to his father's dismay, decides he wants to join the Metropolitan Police, rather than become a pupil in his father's chambers. William perseveres, and in this opening novel we follow his life on the beat with a cast of characters, some good, some not so good, who cross his path as he tries to become a detective and transfers to Scotland Yard.

During the series, you will follow William's fortunes as he progresses from detective constable to the commissioner of the Metropolitan Police.

I'm currently working on the second novel in the series, which will focus on William's time as a young detective sergeant in the elite drugs unit.

Should he ever make it to commissioner will depend as much on William Warwick's determination and ability as my hopes for longevity—mine, not yours.

Jeffrey Archer
September 2019

1

July 14, 1979

"You can't be serious."

"I couldn't be more serious, Father, as you'd realize if you'd ever listened to anything I've been saying for the past ten years."

"But you've been offered a place at my old college at Oxford to read law, and after you graduate, you'll be able to join me in chambers. What more could a young man ask for?"

"To be allowed to pursue a career of his own choosing, and not just be expected to follow in his father's footsteps."

"Would that be such a bad thing? After all, I've enjoyed a fascinating and worthwhile career, and, dare I suggest, been moderately successful."

"Brilliantly successful, Father, but it isn't your career we're discussing, it's mine. And perhaps I don't want to be a leading criminal barrister who spends his whole life defending a bunch of villains he'd never consider inviting to lunch at his club."

"You seem to have forgotten that those same villains paid for your education, and the lifestyle you presently enjoy."

"I'm never allowed to forget it, Father, which is the reason I intend to spend my life making sure those same villains are locked up for long periods of time, and not allowed to go free and continue a life of crime thanks to your skillful advocacy."

William thought he'd finally silenced his father, but he was wrong.

"Perhaps we could agree on a compromise, dear boy?"

"Not a chance, Father," said William firmly. "You're sounding like a barrister who's pleading for a reduced sentence, when he knows he's defending a weak case. But for once, your eloquent words are falling on deaf ears."

"Won't you even allow me to put my case before you dismiss it out of hand?" responded his father.

"No, because I'm not guilty, and I don't have to prove to a jury that I'm innocent, just to please you."

"But would you be willing to do something to please me, my dear?"

In the heat of battle William had quite forgotten that his mother had been sitting silently at the other end of the table, closely following the jousting between her husband and son. William was well prepared to take on his father but knew he was no match for his mother. He fell silent once again. A silence that his father took advantage of.

"What do you have in mind, m'lud?" said Sir Julian, tugging at the lapels of his jacket, and addressing his wife as if she were a high court judge.

"William will be allowed to go to the university of his choice," said Marjorie, "select the subject he wishes to study, and once he's graduated, follow the career he wants to pursue. And more important, when he does, you will give in gracefully and never raise the subject again."

"I confess," said Sir Julian, "that while accepting your wise judgment, I might find the last part difficult."

Mother and son burst out laughing.

"Am I allowed a plea in mitigation?" asked Sir Julian innocently.

"No," said William, "because I will only agree to Mother's terms if in three years' time you unreservedly support my decision to join the Metropolitan Police Force."

Sir Julian Warwick QC rose from his place at the head of the table, gave his wife a slight bow, and reluctantly said, "If it so please Your Lordship."

⊰o⊱

William Warwick had wanted to be a detective from the age of eight, when he'd solved "the case of the missing Mars bars." It was a simple paper trail, he explained to his housemaster, that didn't require a magnifying glass.

The evidence—sweet papers—had been found in the waste-paper basket of the guilty party's study, and the culprit wasn't able to prove he'd spent any of his pocket money in the tuck shop that term. And what made it worse for William was that Adrian Heath was one of his closest pals, and he'd assumed it would be a lifelong friendship. When he discussed it with his father at half term, the old man said, "We must hope that Adrian has learned from the experience, otherwise who knows what will became of the boy."

Despite William being mocked by his fellow pupils, who dreamed of becoming doctors, lawyers, teachers, even accountants, the careers master showed no surprise when William informed him that he was going to be a detective. After all, the other boys had nicknamed him Sherlock before the end of his first term.

William's father, Sir Julian Warwick Bt, had wanted his son to go up to Oxford and read law, just as he'd done thirty years before. But despite his father's best efforts, William had remained determined to join the police force the day he left school. The two stubborn men finally reached a compromise approved of by his mother. William would go to London University and read art history—a subject his father refused to take seriously—and if, after three years, his son still wanted to be a policeman, Sir Julian agreed to give in gracefully. William knew that would never happen.

William enjoyed every moment of his three years at King's College London, where he fell in love several times. First with Hannah and Rembrandt, followed by Judy and Turner, and finally Rachel and Hockney, before settling down with Caravaggio: an affair that would last a lifetime, even though his father had pointed out that the great Italian artist had been a murderer and should have been hanged. A good enough reason to abolish the death penalty, William suggested. Once again, father and son didn't agree.

During the summer holidays after he'd left school, William backpacked his way across Europe to Rome, Paris, Berlin, and on to St. Petersburg, to join long queues of other devotees who wished to worship the past masters. When he finally graduated, his professor suggested that he should consider a PhD on the darker side of Caravaggio. The darker side, replied William, was exactly what he intended to research, but he wanted to learn more about criminals in the twentieth century, rather than the sixteenth.

⊸o⊷

At five minutes to three on the afternoon of Sunday, September 5, 1982, William reported to Hendon Police College in north London. He enjoyed almost every minute of the training course from the moment he swore allegiance to the Queen to his passing-out parade sixteen weeks later.

The following day, he was issued with a navy-blue serge uniform, helmet, and truncheon, and couldn't resist glancing at his reflection whenever he passed a window. A police uniform, he was warned by the commander on his first day on parade, could change a person's personality, and not always for the better.

Lessons at Hendon had begun on the second day and were divided between the classroom and the gym. William learned whole sections of the law until he could repeat them verbatim. He reveled in forensic and crime scene analysis, even though he quickly discovered when he was introduced to the skid pad that his driving skills were fairly rudimentary.

Having endured years of cut and thrust with his father across the breakfast table, William felt at ease in the mock courtroom, where instructing officers cross-examined him in the witness box, and he even held his own during self-defense classes, where he learned how to disarm, handcuff, and restrain someone who was far bigger than him. He was also taught about a constable's powers of arrest, search and entry, the use of reasonable force, and, most important of all, discretion. "Don't always stick to the rule book," his instructor advised him. "Sometimes you have to use common sense, which, when you're dealing with the public, you'll find isn't that common."

Exams were as regular as clockwork, compared to his days at university, and he wasn't surprised that several candidates fell by the wayside long before the course had ended.

After what felt like an interminable two-week break following his passing-out parade, William finally received a letter instructing him to report to Lambeth police station at 8 a.m. the following Monday. An area of London he had never visited before.

Police Constable 565LD had joined the Metropolitan Police Force as a graduate but decided not to take advantage of the accelerated promotion scheme that would have allowed him to progress more quickly up the ladder, as he wanted to line up on his first day with every other new recruit on equal terms. He accepted that, as a probationer, he would have to spend at least two years on the beat before he could hope to become a detective, and in truth, he couldn't wait to be thrown in at the deep end.

From his first day as a probationer William was guided by his mentor, Constable Fred Yates, who had twenty-eight years of police service under his belt, and had been told by the nick's chief inspector to "look after the boy." The two men had little in common other than that they'd both wanted to be coppers from an early age, and their fathers had done everything in their power to prevent them pursuing their chosen career.

"ABC," was the first thing Fred said when he was introduced to the wet-behind-the-ears young sprog. He didn't wait for William to ask.

"Accept nothing, Believe no one, Challenge everything. It's the only law I live by."

During the next few months, Fred introduced William to the world of burglars, drug dealers, and pimps, as well as his first dead body. With the zeal of Sir Galahad, William wanted to lock up every offender and make the world a better place; Fred was more realistic, but he never once attempted to douse the flames of William's youthful enthusiasm. The young probationer quickly found out that the public don't know if a policeman has been in uniform for a couple of days or a couple of years on William's second day on the beat.

"Time to stop your first car," said Fred, coming to a halt by a set of traffic lights. "We'll hang about until someone runs a red, and then you can step out into the road and flag them down." William looked apprehensive. "Leave the rest to me. See that tree about a hundred yards away? Go and hide behind it, and wait until I give you the signal."

William could hear his heart pounding as he stood behind the tree. He didn't have long to wait before Fred raised a hand and shouted, "The blue Hillman! Grab him!"

William stepped out into the road, put his arm up, and directed the car to pull over to the curb.

"Say nothing," said Fred as he joined the raw recruit. "Watch carefully and take note." They both walked up to the car as the driver wound down his window.

"Good morning, sir," said Fred. "Are you aware that you drove through a red light?"

The driver nodded but didn't speak.

"Could I see your driving license?"

The driver opened his glove box, extracted his license, and handed it to Fred. After studying the document for a few moments, Fred said, "It's particularly dangerous at this time in the morning, sir, as there are two schools nearby."

"I'm sorry," said the driver. "It won't happen again."

Fred handed him back his license. "It will just be a warning this time," he said, while William wrote down the car's number plate in his notebook. "But perhaps you could be a little more careful in future, sir."

"Thank you, officer," said the driver.

"Why just a caution," asked William as the car drove slowly away, "when you could have booked him?"

"Attitude," said Fred. "The gentleman was polite, acknowledged his mistake, and apologized. Why piss off a normally law-abiding member of the public?"

"So what would have made you book him?"

"If he'd said, 'Haven't you got anything better to do, officer?' Or worse, 'Shouldn't you be chasing some real criminals?' Or my favorite, 'Don't you realize I pay your wages?' Any of those and I would have booked him without hesitation. Mind you, there was one blighter I had to cart off to the station and lock up for a couple of hours."

"Did he get violent?"

"No, far worse. Told me he was a close friend of the commissioner, and I'd be hearing from him. So I told him he could phone him from the station." William burst out laughing. "Right," said Fred, "get back behind the tree. Next time you can conduct the interview and I'll observe."

-o-

Sir Julian Warwick QC sat at one end of the table, his head buried in *The Daily Telegraph*. He muttered the occasional tut-tut, while his wife, seated at the other end, continued her daily battle with *The Times* crossword. On a good day, Marjorie would have filled in the final clue before her husband rose from the table to leave for Lincoln's Inn. On a bad day, she would have to seek his advice, a service for which he usually charged a hundred pounds an hour. He regularly reminded her that to date, she owed him over twenty thousand pounds. Ten across and four down were holding her up.

Sir Julian had reached the leaders by the time his wife was

wrestling with the final clue. He still wasn't convinced that the death penalty should have been abolished, particularly when a police officer or a public servant was the victim, but then neither was the *Telegraph.* He turned to the back page to find out how Blackheath rugby club had fared against Richmond in their annual derby. After reading the match report he abandoned the sports pages, as he considered the paper gave far too much coverage to soccer. Yet another sign that the nation was going to the dogs.

"Delightful picture of Charles and Diana in *The Times*," said Marjorie.

"It will never last," said Julian as he rose from his place and walked to the other end of the table and, as he did every morning, kissed his wife on the forehead. They exchanged newspapers, so he could study the law reports on the train journey to London.

"Don't forget the children are coming down for lunch on Sunday," Marjorie reminded him.

"Has William passed his detective's exam yet?" he asked.

"As you well know, my dear, he isn't allowed to take the exam until he's completed two years on the beat, which won't be for at least another six months."

"If he'd listened to me, he would have been a qualified barrister by now."

"And if you'd listened to him, you'd know he's far more interested in locking up criminals than finding ways of getting them off."

"I haven't given up yet," said Sir Julian.

"Just be thankful that at least our daughter has followed in your footsteps."

"Grace has done nothing of the sort," snorted Sir Julian. "That girl will defend any penniless no-hoper she comes across."

"She has a heart of gold."

"Then she takes after you," said Sir Julian, studying the one clue his wife had failed to fill in: *Slender private man who ended up with a baton*. Five, seven, and four.

"Field Marshal Slim," said Sir Julian triumphantly. "The only man to join the army as a private soldier and end up as a field marshal."

"Sounds like William," said Marjorie. But not until the door had closed.

Jeffrey Archer was educated at Oxford University. He served five years as a member of Parliament in the House of Commons and has served twenty-seven years as a member of the House of Lords. Now published in ninety-seven countries and more than thirty-seven languages, all of his novels and short story collections—including *Kane & Abel, Only Time Will Tell,* and *Heads You Win*—have been international bestsellers. Jeffrey is married with two sons and three grandchildren, and lives in London, Cambridge, and Majorca.